HOCKEYVERSE

Finding the FORWARD

PART TWO

JANE HANDLER

A WHY CHOOSE OMEGAVERSE HOCKEY ROMANCE

Finding the Forward Part Two

A Why Choose Omegaverse Hockey Romance

Jane Handler

Edition 1.0

Cover design by Marie Mackay

Art by Teddy.r, Laba Design, Viola Pilipenko, and Samira Ribeiro.

You are enough.

About This Story

Welcome back to the HockeyVerse! *Finding the Forward, Part Two,* is the *conclusion* of a why-choose non-shifting omegaverse hockey romance *duet.* If you haven't read part one, you're going to want to do that so you don't get confused.

Finding the Forward takes place in 'the parallel omegaverse.' It's a *parallel universe* that's similar to ours. However, this world has evolved a bit differently, which affects everything from physical places to technology to laws. For example, the drinking age and driving age are both eighteen. The biggest difference is that alphas, betas, omegas, and many other designations exist. Each designation has specific characteristics.

In this world all love is legal and accepted, with same-sex and polyamorous relationships being common. Sometimes an alpha and omega will be a scent-match, soulmates, however this is rare and plenty of people mate happily without it. Many people live in packs, and registered packs have all the legal rights of families, no matter what designation comprises them. There are also plenty of couples and throuples. Gender and racial equality are widespread. Birth control is freely available for all genders and designations.

While this story and world aren't particularly dark, this book contains things that may be upsetting, such as gun violence, hospitalization, medical issues, harassment, characters struggling with their designations, and someone getting their designation outed. There's also references to past events such as parentification, emotional and physical abuse, having a stroke, a career-ending injury, incarcerated parents, death of loved ones, having their designation outed, a previous (non-fatal) overdose, sexual harassment, and bullying.

This is a 'why choose' romance, so the female main character gets her happy ending with multiple people. Verity's story is m/m/m/m/f. Some of the guys in the pack have established relationships with each other. There's crossing of swords and group scenes. There are graphic spice scenes, meant for adult readers, and contains acts such as bonding, biting, knotting, locking, spanking, hand necklaces, light bondage, DVP, and heats.

With two sports teams, there are a lot of characters in this book. There are full team rosters and a list of Verity's family in the back. Also, since I have some elements that you may not be familiar with, there's a limited glossary as well.

I hope you enjoy the conclusion of Verity's story.

About the Sports in This Story

The HockeyVerse is *not our world.* While many things are the same, there are plenty of differences. Even familiar sports may have different rules, terminology, leagues, and teams–both because it is a parallel world and how having a/b/o designations and gender equality can change things. If you're looking for a hyper-realistic sports romance, this might not be for you.

For example, in this world, WAGs (wives and girlfriends) are MASOs (mates and significant others) which encompasses mates, packmates, spouses, girlfriend, boyfriends, partners, and significant others.

Soccer (Football) is extremely popular and is referred to as ***fútbol*** worldwide. It's a co-ed, mixed-designation sport, and beta-heavy. Most beta kids play fútbol in their youth. They don't have a draft system.

Ice Hockey is a co-ed, mixed-designation sport. It is alpha and male heavy, with very few omegas, especially at the professional level. The Professional Hockey League (PHL) has thirty-two teams in four countries. They have a minor-league and draft system. The hockey season runs October-March, with pre-season in late September and playoffs in April and May. The PHL falls under the International Association of Team Sports (IATS), like fútbol.

Skate Smash is like roller derby on ice held at a rave. It's a high-energy contact sport with lots of dance breaks. It's co-ed, mixed-designation, but tends to be alpha and female heavy. There are no professional omega skate smash players, but there is a very popular all-omega semi-pro league. The Professional Skate Smash League (PSSL) falls under the International Coalition of Ice Sports (ICIS) like figure skating, speed skating, and curling. They have a draft system, a minor league, and a team-sponsored junior system (Discovery League). Skate smash players also have more control over the team roster than in many other sports.

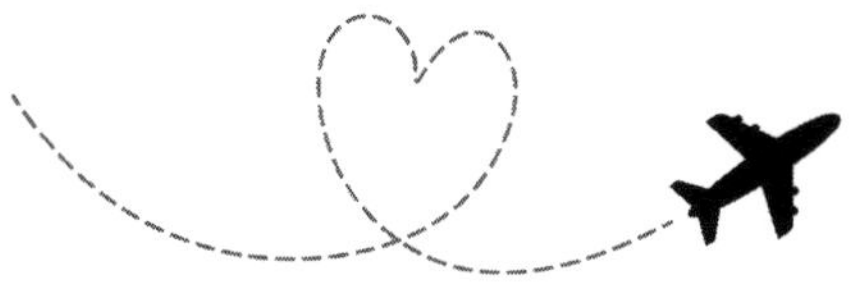

Chapter One

AJ

The stench of horny omega smacked me in the face as I slipped into the Knights' locker room at the training center. As an omega player's alpha packmate, I now had access to some of the restricted places here–including the locker room code.

Hopefully, Verity's panicked recount of what happened between her and Grif on the bleachers was overstated. Maybe I'd find him at practice as usual, asking his teammates how to patch up their fight.

Deep down, I knew I wouldn't.

My belly sank as the door closed behind me. Rotten and sour scents entwined with lust, arousal, cozy sweaters, and rain. For a moment, I flashed back to when I'd gone to Grif's and found his apartment awash in these same scents–minus the sweaters. Back when I'd discovered him passed out on his bed with a bottle of bourbon and an empty container of heavy-duty omega blockers.

"Fuck." I punched one of the metal lockers. Pain coursed through my hand and I shook it, hoping no one noticed the small dent.

No. Not again. Never again.

I stalked through the locker room. Where the fuck were they? Urgency tugged at me. It was only a matter of time before a trainer, equipment manager, or someone came in.

Grif had Dean pushed against the wall of the training room, his teeth sinking into Dean's pale pectoral right by his tattoo. Dean moaned, still in his skates and gear. His green eyes were wild with desire, his strawberry blond hair falling into his freckled face.

My belly dropped further. While this was infinitely better than what I'd found back then, it still posed a problem. This wasn't the day for Grif to come out as an omega, especially without the pack contracted.

Hopefully, Jonas noticed something was wrong and came looking for them. If I was to contain this, I had no time to spare to get him. Since he was currently on the ice, I couldn't text him, either.

Leaving them for the moment, I threw open the door to the storage area. Relief shot through me as I found plenty of scent-removing cleaning products. Giant container of de-scenter sanitizer in hand, I walked back into there, where Grif held Dean to him.

"What the fuck did you two just do?" I growled, more worried than annoyed. If those two had bonded each other, we'd have a whole other set of problems to deal with.

"Dean loves me." Panic filled Grif's voice as he turned to look at me, his taller, huskier frame protecting Dean, angst in his green eyes.

Shit. I was in over my head here.

"I know. He loves you so much. I love you, too," I soothed. No, now wasn't the time for scolding. It was time for patience and understanding.

That's what this was ultimately about. The hidden omega part of Grif wasn't feeling loved, secure, or understood. We let practicality get ahead of his needs because we often forgot he was an omega, too.

My heart squeezed. I'd been a bad alpha to him. Fuck. Because what Grif *wanted* and what he *needed* were two different things. I'd gotten so tangled up in his wants I hadn't tended to his needs like I should.

"AJ, why are you here?" Dean's expression went sheepish. The two of them reeked of sex and each other.

"To save your asses." I turned and kissed Grif, his red beard soft as I ran my hand through his hair. "I love you and was worried about you. Right now, I need you and Dean to hit the showers. Now."

As they left, I sprayed down the training room with de-scenter. Then I got the de-scenting soap from Dean's locker and brought it to them as they kissed each other in the shower. A bite marked Dean's chest–as did one on Grif's cock.

Shit. They'd bonded.

Right now the bigger problem was how the locker room smelled. I sprayed down the locker room and showers, and then I hit the training room again. My eyes stung from the industrial strength cleaner.

Where the fuck was Jonas? He should have felt them bond through his bond with Dean.

I put their clothes and Dean's skates in a garbage bag, doused them in cleaner, and tied it off. If it ruined anything, well, it was only money.

The door opened as I shoved it awkwardly in Dean's duffle.

Silas, a slim, middle-aged beta who was one of the equipment managers, looked at me. His nose scrunched. "Are you supposed to be in here?"

Shit.

"I'm AJ, I'm Dean's other alpha. He's sick. Can you get Jonas–now? Please?" I asked, trying to keep calm, as I zipped up the duffle and put it on the bench.

"Oh, of course." He darted out.

I found the backup blocker Grif kept in his wallet. While I had so many questions, right now this was pure damage control.

"For fuck's sake. Stop kissing, please," I growled as I returned to the showers to find their bodies still entwined under the water. We didn't have time for this.

I shoved the pill in Grif's mouth, again more worried than angry. "Take this. Wake the fuck out of whatever stupor you two are in. Use the soap, get out, and dress. We need to get out of here."

It was just shy of a bark. If I had any hope of containing this, we needed to leave before the team got out of practice.

And if we didn't...

No. There was no time for such thoughts.

Back in the main part of the locker room, I sprayed everything one more time as I tried to piece things together. When Verity had sobbed to me on the phone, I knew exactly what happened. Somehow, Grif's omega had come out with a vengeance, and her insistence on not biting him in that moment had struck a chord with him.

Grif leaving her in anger instead of him just shutting down baffled me a little. Not to mention, I worried about her falling. Obviously, no one was at fault. Though she had every right to be pissed. Grif would need to let Verity in on his secret if he wanted to salvage their relationship.

It was time.

I might not show it like they did, but I wasn't certain my heart could take it if she left us.

"What happened? I felt something through the bond, and now Silas says Dean's sick?" Jonas, dressed for practice, skates on, and urgency in his amber eyes, burst into the locker room.

Finally.

"Dean and Grif are in the shower. We need to get them out of here," I told him, continuing my cleaning efforts.

"Why does it reek of cleaner? Also, is Grif here? Dimitri said something about him and Verity getting into a fight, and he's not in practice. What happened? Why are you here?" Jonas looked both puzzled and frantic as he looked around.

My voice went low as I kept working. "I'm here because Verity called me. Let's take them home and figure this out. There's a shit-ton more to this than whatever you're getting through the bond."

"Oh, fuck." Jonas raked his hand through his blue hair. "That's why you're spraying this place down. This has to do with *Grif.* I thought Dean had a breakthrough heat or something."

Oh, we didn't need that either.

"Verity inadvertently triggered something and he started to spiral. Dean found him and attempted to make it all better." I put the cleaner away in the closet.

He sunk down onto the bench and tore off his skates. "Let's get them home and you can fill me in. I wasn't expecting to feel them *bond* while I was in the middle of practice."

Getting my phone from my suit pocket, I rescheduled my next meeting. Verity had texted, but I'd read those later.

The guys came into the locker room from the showers as Jonas was changing. Dean still looked sheepish, but Grif seemed dazed.

I wrapped my arms around Grif's muscular, damp body, getting notes of the de-scenting soap covering all the other scents, especially the troubling ones. "Are you okay, Boo-Boo?"

"I... I don't know what happened. Okay, I know some of what happened." Grif glanced at Dean, his look smoldering. "But I don't know how we got there. One moment, I was sitting with Verity on the bleachers, the next moment I had Dean up against the wall..." A frown tugged at his lips.

"You spiraled, but we can talk about it at home." Dean squeezed Grif's large hand. "Though for the record, I don't regret what we did one bit."

"Oh shit," Jonas muttered as he rubbed his scarred jaw.

Spirals were bad news for omegas. It was a spiral that had caused Grif to overdose on blockers.

"I don't either. But I don't exactly know what happened. Did something happen?" Grif's brow furrowed.

"We'll talk about it at home." I put an arm around him in reassurance.

The door opened, and the team doctor came in. Shit. Did he smell it? Would he care? I didn't know him well.

"Hey, Dean, you're still not feeling great after last night? I can send you in for some scans. At least there's no game tonight and you have tomorrow off." Dr. Moser had a worried look on his face.

"If I go home and rest, I should be fine. We can meet the day after tomorrow to see if I still need anything?" Dean offered as he pulled a shirt over his head.

While lies had smells, Dean's statement wasn't totally false. Rest made a lot of things better.

"Great. I'll set up a time. I'll let Coach know you're going home. Jonas, are you going with him?" The older alpha doctor looked at Jonas.

If the doctor noticed anything amiss, he had the good sense to not say anything.

Jonas sat on the bench and put on his shoes. "Yes. I already told Coach I'd probably take him home."

"Grif, you're going back to practice?" The doctor's eyebrows rose as Grif continued to dress.

"Um, I feel weird. I'm going home, too," Grif sputtered, clutching his stomach.

"Okay, I'll let Coach know." Dr. Moser shot him a skeptical look. He shrugged and left the locker room.

"While I understand waiting, maybe you should go to the doctor to get those tests *today*," I whispered to Grif, worry coursing through me. Not only could his omega coming out to play impact his career, but it could affect *him*. He'd been hiding as a beta for years and that came at a price.

"What does that have to do with what happened?" Grif murmured back, frowning.

"Everything," I told him.

I'd tried to be supportive of him hiding, but had I crossed the line into complacent?

"What tests?" Jonas shoved his phone in his pocket without looking at it and then closed his locker.

Grif grimaced, grabbing his stuff. "The kind I should get every year and never have."

"Let's do that. We're also going to talk about this. *All* this. You two, whatever happened with Verity, and how we'll contain everything." Jonas frowned as he looked at everyone. "AJ, can you come back with us? Or are you going to fill us in as we drop you off at the office? How did you know what's going on, anyway?"

"I told you, Verity called me." I glanced at my phone and realized I'd missed several calls from her.

The door to the locker room slammed open hard. "Grif, you better fucking be in here you fucking ding-dong."

Mercy, Verity's teenage sister, marched in with a bossy-pants expression on her face, even though she was about six inches shorter than the shortest of us. Like always, her light brown hair was in two neat Dutch braids, secured with scrunchies. She wore a Maimers hoodie, some leggings, and fuzzy boots.

She turned to Grif, scowling, spicy plumy anger wafting off her. "I know you had a fight, and I'm fucking pissed at you. But I need you to walk me off the property right fucking now, because I need to leave and you're on the fucking list."

"Mercy, we have a lot going on right now. Where's your sister?" Jonas slung his bag over his shoulder. "How did you even get in here?"

"You think we don't know your codes? Cute. Look, you're clearly leaving. It's not that hard to walk me out. I can get to her myself." Her brown eyes narrowed as Dean closed his locker.

"Something's wrong," I breathed, recalling the missed calls from Verity, and realizing that Mercy had her bag.

"Ya think? If you fuckers checked your phones, you'd know. I thought she meant something to you. Especially you, Grif." The young alpha's hands fisted like she was itching to throw a punch.

Shit.

"I'll take you. Verity put me on the list. I was supposed to meet her, anyway. Where is she? What happened?" I asked, hoping she hadn't collapsed or something.

"If something happened to Verity, I'll go with you." Grif's rain scent went sour.

"Not sure she wants to see you after what you did. Do you know how fucking scary that was to watch? She could have gotten hurt." Mercy glanced at her phone then scowled again. "Come *on*. I need to go. Jonas, you *should* fucking care, since all this is because of you fucknuggets."

Grif strode toward the locker room door, phone in hand, look frantic. "What happened? All I have is an apology text."

"Seriously? You don't remember?" Mercy followed in a cloud of anger, skepticism in her voice.

"He doesn't. It's complicated. Please go easy on him. Grif, go to the doctors," I ordered. "I'll take care of Verity. You can grovel later." I walked out the locker room doors with Mercy, Grif, and the others trailing.

"What happened to Verity?" Hurt rang through Dean's voice as we strode through the halls of the training complex.

"AJ, you should come with us," Jonas said through gritted teeth. "Grif needs you. You can go to Verity after."

"Are you shitting my dick right now? I don't have time for your alpha bullshit, Jonas." Mercy stood toe-to-toe with our head alpha, not afraid that he was taller or larger than her.

Not that she was that small.

"Mercy, I don't know what's going on here. We're having a bit of a medical emergency." Jonas scowled at her.

I shook my head. "If one of us doesn't go with Mercy, we're going to lose Verity after what happened this morning."

"Whatever happened this morning was that bad?" Jonas looked puzzled.

"Uh, duh." Mercy rolled her eyes.

Grif shook his head. "Go with her, AJ. I'm fine."

No, Grif wasn't fine, but Jonas and Dean could handle it for the time being.

Mercy waved at Rusty, who'd joined us in the hall. The alpha captain of the Manhattan Maimers looked fucking pissed. A pissed-off Rusty was never a good thing.

"Do you need me to walk you out? No one will fucking care," Rusty told her, red hair back for practice revealing her undercut.

"AJ's got it. I should still make it to the game tonight," Mercy replied, shifting her weight impatiently.

"If not, call me. Also, if she's still tied up with the police and can't bring you to the arena, I'll get you." Rusty glared at Grif and stalked off.

"Police? What happened this morning that made you so pissed? We could *lose* her?" Grif's voice broke, and his scent went salty.

"You had a fight and left the stands. She chased after you, slipped, and fell. *You didn't stop.* She called for you, *and you didn't stop and help her.*" Mercy's voice rose. "You seriously don't fucking remember? Because we do."

Grif's face fell. "I… I don't. Honest. One minute, we were making jokes about Spencer buying a hockey team, and then I'm in the locker room."

"It's not your fault. It's not her fault. We'll fix this." I squeezed his shoulder, wishing I had time to soothe him, but we had to triage the situation.

I glanced at my phone and read through Verity's texts. My heart plummeted at the photos, and I texted her immediately. Guilt at not answering earlier ate at me.

Me

I have your sister. We're on our way.

"Why is she with the police? What happened?" Grif checked his phone and frowned. "I have nothing."

I showed Grif a picture. "Someone vandalized her greenhouse."

"Mercy, I care about Verity, but I need AJ right now," Jonas told her. "We'll call her later."

"She needs one of you to actually give a fuck. Someone didn't simply *deface* her greenhouse. They destroyed *everything* in it. I'm not sure you ding-dongs understand." Mercy's voice broke. "This isn't her research not working out. *Every single plant is dead.* Some asshole put gasoline and salt on them. They even ruined the roses she was making for Grif. She's lost her *life's* work. Because she's dating *you* assholes. Do you know how long this will set her back? Sure, a medical emergency is important, but one of you can be there for her. Unless she really is just some power-up." Mercy's hands were on her hips, voice carrying.

"Someone destroyed her plants. Because of us?" Grif took out his phone and he put a knuckle to his mouth. "Fuck."

Oh fuck indeed. While I knew there were people unhappy that she was dating Grif, never did I think it would come to this.

"Jonas, stop being a knothead. Is she one of you or not? Grif, go get checked out, but be prepared to grovel because you hurt her." Mercy's voice filled with authority.

Grif flinched and bowed his head the way an omega chastised by an alpha might. Dean clung to Jonas. Even Jonas looked surprised at her ferocity.

He shouldn't.

There was no fury like a pissed-off sister. It wouldn't be long before her alpha came in fully, and she was going to be fucking dominant.

Like a force-to-be-reckoned-with dominant.

Mercy took my arm. "Let's go see my sister."

"Sorry, Mercy. There's a lot going on today. We'll check up on her later," Jonas told her.

"Good. I'm not above making your life miserable." She shot him a hard look and continued to head toward the lobby, only her tight grip on my arm revealing her worry.

Verity, we're coming. It was only mid-morning and today was already a fuckfest.

Chapter Two

Verity

"You have *no idea* who'd do something like this?" the police officer asked me, eyeing me critically as she took my statement inside the lab. *Again.*

"It could be any of the people sending me threatening texts," I replied, leaning on my crutch, fatigue pressing down on me. "I told you, I'm dating a hockey player. People don't like that."

"Why would someone care if you're dating a hockey player?" She looked completely baffled.

"You're shitting me, right? Why do *you* think people would care?" Saphira shoved a cup into my hand while putting an arm around me. "We have cameras, we'll find them, Ver." Her brown eyes narrowed at the officer.

Already I'd texted my older brother Creed, who was getting big sister Grace's hacker packmates to pull video footage from all around campus. Thanks to my plant monitor programs, I knew when everything happened so we could narrow the search.

Because campus police didn't seem to care.

"I can't believe someone would do this." I sniffed, wiping my eyes with my hand. There was nothing salvageable in my greenhouse.

At least they hadn't been able to get into the lab and ruin everything in there, too.

Losing all my flowers was still a giant blow to my PhD research. Some people might consider genetically engineering flowers to make people happier to be silly, but it was important to *me*. My phone beeped.

Grace

I'm sorry about your plants. I'll pack up what you gave me and get them to you.

Me:

Thank you.

Grace had some of my omega lilies that were of a decent enough evolution that I wouldn't have to start over completely.

Also, I could dig up the ones I'd planted in the public gardens at Briar University. That would help.

"I'm here." Saphira squeezed my hand. She'd gotten her hair redone over break, and it was now in goddess braids.

"Thank you." I gulped, grateful, as I took a sip of chai latte. While the police didn't comprehend what a loss this was for me, she understood.

If it had been her research, heads would have been rolling. Saphira might be beta, but she took a lot less shit than I did.

We finished with the police and campus security, but they wouldn't let us clean up yet, so I sat in our break room, obsessively checking to see if Dr. Winters had texted me back. How mad would NYIT be about this? Hopefully, they wouldn't yank my funding.

Ugh. The very thought made me sick to my stomach.

Dr. Winters hadn't replied, but Grif texted.

Grif

I'm so fucking sorry for what happened in the stands. It wasn't you. I'll explain when I can. I love you.

Me

I love you too. Confused. Hurt. But I still love you.

As puzzled as I was about our strange fight and everything that had happened at the training center, I wished he was here with me. Grif gave excellent hugs, and I needed one right now.

"Verity, are you okay?" Mercy rushed into the room and embraced me, spiced plum scent tinged with worry.

"You didn't have to leave for me. I would've been done in time to get you." I hugged her tightly.

"Of course I'm here, you ding-dong." Her eyes rolled.

"Princess." AJ wrapped me in a hug of his own, pulling me to his chest, his vetiver, and something else, enveloping me as he put out soothing pheromones.

Like nearly always, he was in a fancy suit, with designer sunglasses nestled in his dark hair.

"AJ." I buried my head in his shoulder, the fabric of his expensive suit soft against my face, noting he was alone. "They're still in practice?"

Not that I expected the others to come. I hadn't even told Grif or Dean. Just Jonas.

My nose wrinkled. "You smell weird."

"This morning has been a shit show. But I'm here. What happened back at the training center wasn't anyone's fault. Grif loves you, and you're overdue for a talk. Trust me, since it might take a moment. The pack has to get its shit together first." He held me tight.

"Okay, I trust you." I leaned into him.

"What happened at the training center?" Saphira asked.

"Let's just say today's already going fucktangular and it isn't even lunch," I sighed.

My mind spun. Grif had a secret. One that could affect a lot of people–at least that's what *the pack has to get its shit together* sounded like to me.

Grif being a gamma fit with that. Gammas had a lot of omega traits. Also, every gamma was a little different because they were made by circumstance and not born like the other designations.

My big sister Grace was *very* omega-like sometimes–especially after more than a year of living with an omega.

Oh. Grif now lived full-time with Dean. Omegas drew out omega traits in gammas, and their pheromones could balance out gamma hormones. At least that's what I learned spending a summer with my big sister's pack.

Also, if Grif was a gamma, he was on blockers and stuff. After a while they might stop working or cause health problems.

I could still be a good alpha to a gamma, right? They weren't that different from omegas, though they didn't react to barks and pheromones the same way. The biggest difference was their danger response. It was as if their bodies completely overrode *fight or flight* and went straight to *random*.

Glancing at my phone, I itched to ask Grace about gammas, but she'd want to know why. Already, I'd mentioned my theory inadvertently to Creed. I'd search the internet later.

There was also *me*.

Alphas awakened things in omegas. Given how intense things were between us after just a couple of months, *I* could have caused this.

Yes, this was why I felt so connected to him. It explained why Grif grew impatient with me wanting to wait to bond until Mercy was eighteen and signed a new contract with the Maimers.

It was a primal, biological instinct that went beyond want and impatience. I may have caused a chain reaction. Given his hiding was intentional, because of his career, who knew what the fallout would be?

My belly clenched. Shit.

"I'm sorry someone fucked up your research. We'll get you new plants," AJ whispered, stroking my hair with a golden hand a bit darker than mine, bringing me to the here and now.

My flowers were easy. It would take time, but my research could be replicated. What I really wanted was for everything between us to be okay.

Mercy had helped for a bit but returned home to eat lunch and nap before her game. Saphira and AJ stayed and helped throw away pot shards, sweep up dirt and glass, right all my tables and shelves, and pick up what remained of years of my flower project.

My poor flowers. They weren't so happy anymore.

Everyone insisted I didn't need to do this now. But I was about to leave with the Maimers for over a week. I should clean up so repairs on the greenhouse could be made in my absence.

Every dead plant, every shattered pot, broke my heart. Sure, with my notes and samples, I could reconstruct everything.

With all my setbacks, was it even worth it? NYIT wanted me to stretch my research. I could do something else.

But what? I loved my happy plants. Not to mention, I *had* been making good progress.

I cradled the poor dead roses I'd started grafting for Grif. It wasn't like I'd spent years on it, like my lilies. It still cut hard, especially after today.

They even had to wreck this. Why? Who could be so mean?

"Are you okay? What kind of plant is that?" Dean crouched down next to me among the ruins, his cozy scent full of worry and his pale red brows furrowing.

When did they get here? Who'd told them? Mercy, probably. Did Grif come with him? I didn't smell him, but I got a hint of moss and worry.

"I planned on breeding a rose for Grif. They even killed that. Why would they do such a vile thing? The flowers have done nothing to deserve this." Anger welled up inside me.

"People can be fuckers." Jonas joined him, wearing sweats. "You're making him a flower? Amazing. How can we help?"

"Is Grif here?" I looked around, needing a hug from him so badly. AJ's had been nice, but nothing would beat one from Grif right now.

"Grif's at the doctor's. We brought lunch." Dean held up a paper sack.

"Grif's at the doctor's *alone*?" Something inside me did *not* like that. My belly rumbled at the thought of food.

"I know. I don't like being away from him. But he made us come to you. He'll be okay." Dean's muscular arms wrapped around me, his cozy scent reassuring.

"Will he?" My head buried in Dean's pale neck. He smelled like Grif today. The rain and coziness did it for me. *Mmmm.*

It made me miss him all the more. *I'll fix this.*

I'd fight for him. *Us.*

"He put off some tests he shouldn't have, but he will," Dean replied, planting a kiss on my temple.

Sitting on the ground with us, Jonas pulled me into his lap. I loved how I fit in his tattooed arms.

"I'm sorry that happened. Also, I'm sorry that Grif's past bit you both in the ass today." Jonas' lips brushed my ear. "Go with the Maimers. Have a wonderful time. Then you'll come back and you two can have that big talk. Don't run. Please?"

"By then we'll hopefully have our pack contract, which will make things so much better." Dean rubbed my back.

Big talk. My belly dipped.

"I don't want to run. I want this to work. But I didn't mean to hurt him. Wanting to wait to bond felt like the practical choice. Though I don't have to if it's harming people. I simply wanted to talk to everyone first." I looked at Jonas, willing him to understand.

Jonas stroked my hair. "I love that flexibility. It makes me happy that you didn't do anything rash. We'll talk about all that when you get back, okay?"

"Maybe I shouldn't go. I need to fix my plants. If Grif's not okay, I should be here with him." My chest heaved as everything inside me fragmented.

AJ crouched in front of me, my big boys boxing me in. He took my face in his hands. "Trust us to take care of Grif for you? It'll take time for the repairs to be made to your greenhouse. For you to get your replacement things. It makes sense to go with the Maimers on your West Coast adventure as planned."

I tipped my forehead to his, believing him, as he gently wiped the tears away with his thumbs. "I trust you."

While the Maimers would understand if I stayed, and Mercy would be fine traveling with the team alone, I'd feel bad backing out on my commitment.

"Good. If something happens and Grif needs you, I'll call. I promise," AJ told me, wiping another stray tear away with his thumb. "I'll even buy your ticket back from wherever you are."

That offer made me feel much better, especially since we'd be across the country.

"Whatever shitty thoughts you're thinking about yourself *are not true.* You're enough, Verity. I apologize for every time I ever made you think you weren't." Jonas squeezed my manicured hand. Mercy had painted my nails sky-blue with little palm trees on them.

I leaned up and kissed him, needing to hear that.

"Grif said you make happy flowers?" Dean looked around at the mess.

"Did anyone give you an omega lily in a pot when you either mated Jonas or married Grif?" I asked, not recalling seeing one at their place, but I'd hardly seen all of it. It was a pretty traditional gift.

Dean nodded. "A couple people did, to bring happiness to my new home. They're in the laundry room. My mom grows them in her garden for the same reason."

"There's some scientific truth to it. I'm trying to harness it. So yes, I am making happy flowers," I explained.

Jonas beamed at me. "I love it. I could've used a shit-ton of those around the house growing up."

"Me, too. All I want to do is make people happy. I'm glad you came." It wasn't necessary for them to leave hockey practice, but it meant everything.

"Why don't we have the food we brought, then we'll help you finish up." Jonas assisted me off the ground.

"I'd like that, thanks. I have a lot to do before I have to take Mercy to the arena." It was nice of them.

Though, what I wanted was Grif.

"I need to get back to work." AJ snagged me by the waist, pulling me away from my sweeping inside the chilly greenhouse. Dirt smudged his suit and a leaf rested in his wavy hair. Smart suit aside, he hadn't shied away from helping put things right.

"Okay, I'll probably work until I finish cleaning, or it's time to get dressed to take Mercy." I leaned into him, inhaling his vetiver scent, which had intensified with the work he'd been doing. "Thanks for helping."

It hadn't taken us long to clean up after eating. It was only early afternoon.

His arms tightened around me, and he buried his face in my hair. "Anytime, Princess. Since you've done your inventory, I think you should go with Dean and Jonas and let them take care of you for a bit before you have to get to the arena."

The words to fight him were on my tongue, but we'd done as much as we could for now.

"Will you come, too?" I looked up into his brown eyes. AJ had *really* been there for me today, and I didn't want to let him go.

"I'm not like that with those two and I'm not about to fight Dean for you today. Another time, I promise." His thumb stroked my cheekbone, sending shivers through me.

Oh. Being taken care of like that? Yes, I could use that sort of reassurance. The idea that they still cared for me despite whatever had happened today with Grif made me feel good.

They could easily be angry at *me* for waking up whatever I did. After all, I was the alpha.

"Be good for Jonas." AJ leaned in and kissed me sweetly. "Have a pleasant trip with the Maimers."

AJ kissed me. *May I have another?*

"Come on, Little Alpha." Jonas had my backpack.

Dean put an arm around me and kissed my temple. "We're going to make you feel so much better."

I needed to get out of my head. "Could I be the filling in a hockey sandwich?"

"I think that can be arranged." Jonas snagged a kiss.

Dean got my crutch for me and we left the greenhouse.

I bit my lower lip. "Can we let Grif know that he can join us if he comes home? I...I..."

"You want Grif." Dean leaned into me. "Me too."

We got in Jonas' SUV and drove back to their place. I texted Mercy to let her know I'd be back in time to go to the arena with her. At least I'd already packed since we were leaving for their away game stint from tonight's home game.

As we walked into their place, Dean took my coat, hung it in the closet. Jonas put my backpack and crutch on the sectional couch, which looked like it had gotten even more throw pillows since the last time I'd been here. All the holiday decor was gone except a single string of lights by Grif's gorgeous, full-sized piano.

I took off my shoes and Jonas put them on the little rack by the door, along with his and Dean's.

"You deserve to be with us. You *belong* with us. None of this was your fault." Jonas picked me up and carried me down the hall to his room. The room, which was done in grays and dark blues, smelled of him, Dean, and lavender oil.

Gently, Jonas removed my clothes, his moss scent flaring with desire.

I gulped as he unhooked my pink lace bra. “I still triggered something with Grif.”

And angered whoever didn’t think I should be with Grif enough to *deface my greenhouse.*

“Not your fault, Sweet Girl. Grif’s a good man and he loves you.” Jonas’ hands stroked my naked torso as he unbuttoned my slacks and peeled them off my body.

“I love all of you, too,” I admitted as Jonas took off my pink panties.

“You do?” Dean came in, stark naked, and closed the door but left it open a crack. I loved the little trail of strawberry blond hair on his lower stomach.

I nodded. There was a *bite* on his pec. A fresh-looking one right next to the infinity heart tattoo he had that matched Grif. Huh. While not all bites were bond marks, this made me wonder. Grif had been waiting for Dean to bite him until they got the pack contract, too.

Gammas *could* bond people the way omegas did.

“Dean?” I didn’t touch it, but I looked at it.

“Grif was upset, and we got a little carried away in the locker room.” He shrugged.

From the undertones in his scent, I knew there was more. But I wouldn’t push.

I had a feeling I knew exactly what happened.

“I’m happy you were able to comfort him.” I gave Dean a kiss.

Jonas picked me up and tossed me on the bed. The comforter was softer this time as I sank into it. Like last time, it was neat and orderly, yet inviting.

Like last time, the spanking bench sat in the corner and parts of me grew wet remembering what had happened.

"Dean, eat her pussy," Jonas directed as he took off his shirt, revealing all his delicious muscles and tattoos.

"I've never actually eaten a pussy. What do I do? Lick it?" A naked Dean climbed on the bed and got between my legs, his omega perfume coming out.

Aww, I was his first? Adorable.

Jonas shucked off his sweats and boxer briefs and joined him. "Lick it. Suck it. Write how much you love her with your tongue on it." His pierced tongue flickered out as he pushed down Dean's head. "There."

Dean's mouth caressed my clit and my body bucked.

"Right there," I gasped. "Yes!"

"Putting fingers in there is good, too." Jonas grabbed Dean's hand and showed him what to do.

"Oh, this I understand. It's like what you do to me, but a different hole," Dean said between licks of my clit as his fingers slid in and out of me.

"Exactly. I'm going to get that hole ready." Jonas scooted over to the nightstand and got out the lube. "I think our little alpha needs a nice thick knot in her ass while you take her pussy, so she feels all better after her shitty day. Would my sweet girl like that?"

"Oh, yes, please." My back arched as his fingers slipped past the muscles, as he worked my other hole, going around Dean's head.

While I hadn't taken a knot at all, I think I'd like that right now.

"Jonas' knot is an excellent cure for a shitty day, as is my cock. You can take everything out on it anytime," Dean mumbled into my pussy. "I like how you taste."

"More licking, less talking," Jonas play-growled. "We need her to come."

One of Jonas' hands toyed with my nipple as he slipped another finger in my ass, which made my pussy flutter around Dean's fingers as I gasped in delight.

"Ooh, I like that," Dean murmured.

Another wave of pleasure crested over me as Jonas hit a delightful spot.

"Come for us, Little Alpha. Come for us so we can fuck our sweet alpha and let her know how much she belongs here between us." Leaning over, Jonas bit my nipple lightly.

I screamed as an orgasm took me hard and fast and I came all over their hands.

"Mmmm, that's our girl," Jonas encouraged.

Dean continued licking my pussy, teasing, and nibbling, making aftershocks course through me.

"Omega, you lick our little alpha's pussy so good. Now, lie on the bed," Jonas directed. "Sweetheart, are you up for riding him while I fuck your ass?"

I frowned because I ached from my fall. "I don't think I am. I'm sorry."

"Don't be." Dean kissed me.

"Lie down next to your omega and face him," Jonas told me.

I adjusted my position as directed. Looking Dean in the eyes, I played with his hair. "Hi."

"Hi." His beautiful cock stood erect and ready, dripping with pre-cum and slick. It wasn't as long as Jonas', but it was nice and fat, designed to fit right into my pussy and give me all the pleasure.

"Can you take him that way? Maybe move your leg so it's on top of him a bit to give some leverage, if that doesn't hurt you?" Jonas asked, his long, thick, pierced cock also ready and willing.

Hello there. Come inside, please.

"I think I can do that." I wrapped my leg around Dean while he entered me. "That feels so good, Hot Stuff."

"You know what to say if it's too much." Jonas cupped my ass.

Dean put a hand on my hip as he began to thrust. A moan escaped my lips. I ran my fingers through his soft hair, then pushed his face to mine, kissing him deeply. His omega perfume surrounded us in a thick cloud, making everything hazy.

"I enjoy watching you two fuck." Jonas stroked his double-pierced cock, as his pierced tongue flickered out and licked his lips.

And I enjoyed fucking them.

If only Grif were here. I could suck his cock while Dean and Jonas had their ways with me.

Jonas patted my ass. "I'd like to take your cute ass now, Little Alpha. Can I have you bare? Someone needs to be stuffed with alpha cum, so you feel better. I got on birth control, too."

Oh? While alpha cum had serotonin and oxytocin production capabilities, I didn't realize it worked on *alphas.*

Jonas got behind and slowly worked his cock in, stretching me.

I gasped. "I feel so full."

Like I'd burst at the seams in the best way.

"That's what you need. When you come, I'll knot you. Then we'll cuddle you and take care of you until you have to leave," he murmured as he withdrew his cock and thrust hard, one of his legs over mine and Dean's.

We got into a rhythm. Ooh, being sandwiched between them felt nice. It was like spooning... but *sexy.*

"I love your boobies," Dean sighed, as his hand cupped one. "I'm going to come soon."

Pleasure at being between two guys I cared for lapped over me.

"Come for us," Jonas said. "Make sure you lock him."

My pussy clenched at the motion and Dean groaned.

"Strangle my cock, I'm coming," Dean cried, his hot cum shooting into me as my pussy continued to spasm and flutter, getting ready to lock him down.

"Come for me, Sweet Girl." Jonas swatted my ass.

I came, my pussy locking down Dean hard. Jonas thrust into my ass and seated himself fully inside me.

"Alpha," I cried as his knot stretched me even further, stinging a little. But in a good way.

"That's it, you're doing so good," Jonas soothed, kissing my temple.

"Fuck, I feel you, Jonas. Fuck." Dean rested his forehead on mine. "Doesn't it feel so good."

"Yes," I gasped. Sensation and pleasure overwhelmed me as I was knotted while locking someone–something I'd never done, considering I'd yet to take a knot.

"Dean, you take her lock so good. That's it. See you took it so good. You feel so much better with my knot, don't you?" He pulled the soft blue blanket over us.

"Oh, I do." I rested my head on Dean's sweaty shoulder, Jonas at my back. I felt so secure. So loved and cared for.

So full.

The fact that they not only helped me clean up the mess at the greenhouse but took me home and fucked me meant everything.

"You both took care of me so well." Fatigue at the emotional toll of the day washed over me. Closing my eyes, I took Jonas' hand and squeezed it as I purred.

This was precisely what I wanted on a shitty day. Or a good day.

Or a Tuesday.

Hopefully next time, Grif would be here, too.

Chapter Three

Grif

I glanced at my phone as I sat in the exam room of the doctor's office, wearing nothing but a thin gown. The room was comfortable, with a picture of blue butterflies on the wall.

It was still a doctor's office and all those years of fearing doctors because of my secret didn't lessen my anxiety.

Dr. Arya had asked a lot of questions and then ran a bunch of tests. Including the tests I hadn't wanted to do until the off-season because I feared I'd need to go off blockers.

Not only had I been here all afternoon, but I hadn't heard much from Verity. Hopefully, she was busy getting fucked and not mad at me.

The idea of my kitten being angry made my skin itch.

While Jonas and Dean had wanted to accompany me to the doctor, I'd sent them away. This clinic saw *secret* omegas and didn't like alphas being around.

Though I regretted it. With the bond between Dean and me being so fresh, I just wanted to hold him. Especially because I could feel through the bond that he was fucking *someone.*

Fucking someone sounded great right now.

However, it made more sense for them to be with her than me. She needed to know that she was important to us. Losing her research because of us must have shattered her.

Of course, in hindsight, I should've kept Dean and sent Jonas. Being alone with my thoughts was *not* good for me right now. Verity had fallen down the stairs and I'd been so in my head that *I hadn't noticed.* I had no recollection of asking her to bite me. All this had come via AJ's texts.

The fact she thought that *she'd* fucked up cut me.

So, my omega had pitched a bitch fit because Verity wouldn't bite him this moment. I understood that. Still, why *now?* Why did I react so badly that I *spiraled?* I'd always known she couldn't commit to me until Mercy turned eighteen. It made sense.

Though, the idea of waiting six more months made something in me squirm. Hopefully, it would get better once I bonded with AJ.

One thing I didn't regret was finally bonding with Dean. I could feel him in my heart, sending love, reassurance, and lust. This had been a long time coming.

Someone figuring out I was an omega based on this morning's locker room encounter with Dean was only one of many worries. Verity had fallen in front of the Maimers, and they were livid. I should make up with her before they trashed our locker room.

Obviously, I'd have to tell Verity what actually happened at some point. I owed her that.

Where did I even go from here?

Did I ask my agent for help? Chet didn't know I was an omega.

No. I should talk to the pack before telling him my secret. Not to mention, his text about leaving Verity last night still bothered me. He'd never responded.

I texted the group chat I had with the guys.

Me

What's a good big romantic gesture I can pull off before Verity leaves?

The doctor came back in. I gave the small, older, omega doctor a hopeful look. "Am I done? I need to do some groveling before my alpha leaves on her trip."

A lot of groveling.

Maybe we couldn't have that conversation yet, but I needed to let her know how much I loved her before she left with the Maimers.

"I'd like to give you a shot to stabilize your hormones. It will make you feel less shaky, though I'd recommend staying close to your alphas–and your bonded omega," she told me, holding up a syringe. Dr. Arya had graying hair and kind eyes.

"Okay. What's wrong with me that I suddenly did that? Today surprised–and scared–the shit out of me," I admitted as she rubbed my arm with an alcohol wipe.

"Nothing's *wrong* with you. These are natural things that happen." She got the syringe ready.

"But I'm on blockers and suppressants. I need to keep everything locked down." I winced as she gave me the shot. My career was on the line.

"You've been on them non-stop for what, seven years? You live with an omega full-time. Also, you have two alpha partners that you want to bond with. It's perfectly natural for your instincts to pop out in situations like this." She tossed the used syringe in the biohazard box.

Oh. Jonas *had* warned me.

I also knew it could happen. And I'd ignored it.

Still, I didn't regret finding Verity and starting a relationship with her.

"Maybe I need to go back to a higher dosage of blockers?" I offered as she put a pink bandage over the injection site.

"How about if we wait until all the labs come in, and we can go over everything and discuss your options? I know you have a demanding schedule, but can you come in tomorrow?" she asked, consulting her tablet.

"I can do that. I'll set up an appointment." Worry balled in my chest–not just that I'd have to go off blockers completely, but of the toll they'd taken on my body.

I was finally with my pack. Hopefully, I hadn't destroyed myself to the point where I wouldn't get to enjoy them as long as I wanted.

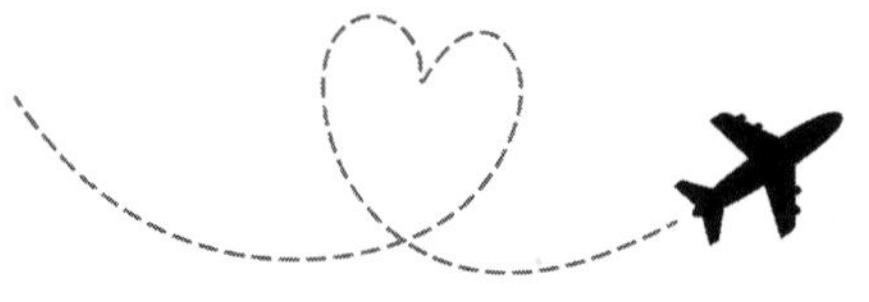

Chapter Four

Grif

Nerves shot through me as I entered the arena full of skate smash fans wearing both Manhattan Maimers and Boston Blockingjays jerseys.

Dean had outsourced my big romantic gesture to the Knights group chat. Apparently, the Maimers had glitter-bombed our locker room. They'd also hidden a bunch of our equipment after defacing it with Maimers stickers.

The team consensus was that something needed to be done in front of the Maimers before our equipment managers quit. Sure, the Maimers were going on the road, but if anyone could wreak havoc from afar, it would be them.

Now, here I was. Alone. Wearing an unofficial *Team Mom* jersey that Carlos' brother-in-law's print shop made me while carrying a handmade sign and a teddy bear.

Skate smash was all about the nicknames. There were lots of signs for *Have No Mercy, Grievous Bodily Charm, Rusty Nails,* and the like. The fact that Verity had a nickname all her own only cemented that she wasn't simply their underage rookie's chaperone, she was one of them.

In skate smash, if you fucked with one of them, you fucked with the whole team. Considering it was even rougher than hockey, that was quite a threat.

I squeezed past an empty seat and two teenage girls, one wearing Mercy's jersey, the other Kaiko's. They both had long, colorful nails, big hoop earrings, lots of glow necklaces and smelled of fake strawberries.

Beside the girls was an empty seat, then mine. The seats were directly behind the Maimers' bench, only the glass separating us. It felt odd to be here but not playing. The same family owned both our team and the Maimers', so we shared not only the training facility but also the ice, benches, and stands.

On the other side of me sat a bunch of women a little older than me, who sounded like they'd started drinking a few hours ago.

One of the teenagers I'd passed to get to my seat eyed my sign and jersey. Her eyelashes were done in Manhattan Maimers colors–red and black. She made a face. "Gross. You know she's taken, right?"

"Um, I do. She's mine. I'm surprising her tonight." I grinned at them even though my belly twisted a little, hoping those words still held true.

"Um, *no.* She's dating some sports dude. What does he play?" The other one snapped her gum. Her ponytail had Maimers colors and *blinking lights.*

"Ice Rugby, maybe?" The first one shrugged.

Two more teenagers, one with their cat-eared hoodie up, the other wearing a beanie, entered the row heading towards the ones sitting next to me. One carried hot-chip nachos, popcorn, and a lime whirl with a bendy straw. The other had dinosaur-shaped pizza nuggets and ice cream.

"We're sitting here? You're shitting my dick," the one with the hoodie up said as she handed the first girl the ice cream. She, too, had glow necklaces.

The girl with the red and black eyelashes took the ice cream and gave her a kiss on the cheek. "Told you my pops got us good seats."

"This is better than a blowjob from a dinosaur. I've never sat this close before." The guy in the beanie handed the second girl the nachos and sat on the far empty seat.

Wow, they made me feel old. I didn't understand half of what they'd said.

The hoodied one sat next to me, bumping my leg. "Sorry, dude." She looked over and sucked in a breath. "Fuck me dead and bury me preggers. You're Grif Graf."

"Shit." The guy leaned over and waved. "Hey, Grif Graf."

"Who?" The girl with the eyelashes blinked.

"The chief whacker of haters for the New York Hits People with Sticks," the guy added.

"We saw him last night on TV. He scored *three* goals and gave Team Mom the jersey," the girl next to me with the blinking ponytail added. "Wow, dude. What are you doing here?"

"I'm here for her." I gestured to the sign. "She made me a sign the first time she came to one of my games."

"Oh." The one with the ponytail snapped her gum. "You're her actual sports dude. Huh."

That's all I got? A *huh?* I did like being referred to as the *chief whacker of haters*. Maybe I should add that to my social media profile. Along with *sports dude.*

"Can we get a selfie?" The beanie guy held up his phone.

The lights blinked, and an announcer's voice boomed, "Welcome to tonight's game featuring the Manhattan Maimers and the Boston Blockingjays. It's blanket toss night, with all blankets going to the crisis units for the Manhattan Omega Center and the New York City Police. Tonight's special guests are the Brooklyn Blankets, our local all-omega skate smash team."

"After," the girl with the eyelashes hissed. "The blanket toss is going to start."

The arena darkened and spotlights lit up the ice as music played. First, the mascot came out. Dizzy was a red fuzzy monster with an ax.

A bunch of people skated out in a chain, one of them looking a little awkward. As they got into the light, my grin spread. I knew she was helping, hence my plan, but I didn't know they got her on skates. I pulled the sign closer to me.

"Aww, Team Mom's on the ice," the one with the eyelashes gushed. "She doesn't skate, does she?"

"I don't think so," the one with the ponytail said. "I've only seen one picture of her on skates, and that was with Grif Graf."

"Hi everyone. I'm Team Mom. Rusty, Liv, Dizzy, the rookies, and I welcome you." Verity beamed, her voice a bit shaky, as the big screens of the arena broadcast her. She was holding Mercy's hand. "Your help today means everything."

"I'm Rusty Nails, and thanks for joining us. I'd also like to thank the Brooklyn Blankets for helping us out today." Rusty said into the mic and got everyone riled up.

Dizzy and the rookies skated around the rink, encouraging everyone to hold up their blankets.

Someone tossed a blanket onto the ice.

"Uh uh uh." Verity made a fake scoldy mom face. "Not until we say."

"Let's count down from ten. I want to hear you *scream!*" Rusty shouted.

Colorful lights flashed around the arena as numbers counted down on the screen, and the crowd joined in. This differed from how we did it in hockey, where everyone tossed them on the ice after the home team scored their first goal.

On *one,* thousands of blankets rained down from all corners of the arena. I didn't have a blanket, but the teens next to me launched theirs over the glass and bench and onto the ice.

The lights continued to pulse as the DJ played thumping music, and the overhead bubble machines went off. Because of the angles of the arena, many blankets landed in the lower seats instead of the ice.

"I don't know any of these songs, but this mix is *fire,*" the girl with the blinking ponytail said as she tossed armfuls of the blankets over the glass, where Maimers staff stuffed them in bags.

"Have No Mercy might have done it? She always has the best songs no one knows on her Musify," the one with the eyelashes added, tossing another blanket over.

The Maimers' DJ texted me that it was almost time. Carlos knew her and had convinced her to help me tonight.

The person operating the crowd cams that put fans on the big screens in the arena was the same for our games. So that had been an easy ask.

The announcer warned everyone to finish throwing their blankets as people wearing uniforms for the Brooklyn Blankets and people in Omega Center polos and police uniforms helped the rookies put the blankets in sacks. Dizzy kept pushing people into the piles.

The music changed to what I'd been told was Verity's favorite upbeat song. I shot up out of my seat, the sign high over my head.

"Team Mom, Team Mom!" the teens shouted and pointed to me.

"Hey, you're Grif Graf," one of the drunk ladies beside me slurred. She turned to her friends. "Help him get Team Mom's attention. This is *so* romantic."

There I was, up on *every* screen in the arena, wearing my Team Mom jersey and holding my handmade sign that says *Grif Graf Loves Team Mom* in the center of a big heart. Everyone started yelling *Team Mom,* and saying *look, it's Grif Graf.*

Verity's face as she saw the screen was everything.

My heart melted. In that moment, I knew everything would be okay.

The screens split, showing me on one side and her reaction on the other. She scanned the arena, looking for me in the stands.

"Here, right here!" the teens yelled, pointing to me.

Verity waved. She skated toward me and wavered a little. Rusty put an arm around her, and they skated until they were right in front of the bench.

Beaming, she made a heart with her hands, and scrambled onto the bench with Rusty's help, nearly stumbling.

"Grif." She faced me, looking like she was *happy* to see me, the glass between us.

My heart burst with love.

I put down the sign, well aware that we were still on the giant screens. "Love you, Team Mom."

"Love you, too, Grif Graf." Verity placed a manicured hand on the glass. Her long, near black hair was back in a French braid. Like nearly always, she had that shiny pink gloss on her lips. She wore knee pads over her leggings, and had on wrist guards.

I put my large hand to her smaller, golden one, wishing there was no glass.

The teens next to me took pictures and waved frantically.

"Hi there." Verity smiled and waved, taking some beaded bracelets off her wrist and throwing them over the glass.

One girl jumped up and down and threw one back, which Verity caught and put on her other wrist.

Verity's blue-green eyes turned on me. "Hi."

"Hi. I wanted to see my favorite girl before she left." I put my forehead on the glass.

Rusty came up beside her, dressed in her red and black Maimers jersey and black shorts, with colorful socks. Like always, she had a rusty nail temporary tattoo on her cheek.

"That was sweet, Grif. But Team Mom and I have to go," Rusty told me.

"I'll be right here the whole game." I blew her a kiss. "Oh, this is for you. If you get lonely, hug him and know I'm with you." Taking the fluffy little bear, I tossed it to her over the glass.

She held it to her, a giddy look crossing her face. Verity blew me a kiss back and waved as she and Rusty left. People continued to clean up all the blankets on the ice so the game could start, though the rookies had left.

Well, all but one. Mercy stood in front of me. Like Rusty, she was in full gear and uniform except for her helmet. Her makeup was a lot more dramatic than she wore day-to-day, and she had fishnets over tan leggings, which were probably the cut-proof kind.

Mercy's big brown eyes focused on me. "That was good."

Someone yelled her name, and with a wave, Mercy left the bench.

"Do you think that went well?" I asked the teens next to me. Anxiousness sizzled through me as I wished I could talk to Verity, hold her.

"That was so romantic," the one with the eyelashes said. "She gave me a bracelet. Hers are so fancy." She held out her wrist, the bracelet filled with round crackly beads and letters spelling out *Smash It.* Bracelet trading was a thing in skate smash.

"Oh, I thought you were going to propose," the drunk woman on my other side sighed.

"Another time." I'd absolutely marry that woman. Mate her. Live with her.

Love her always.

"Can we get that selfie now before the game starts?" The guy on the end held out his phone.

My phone buzzed.

Verity

That was sweet and unexpected. I'll visit you at intermission.

I looked over at the expectant faces of the teenagers, which were lit by their glow necklaces. "Absolutely."

Chapter Five

Verity

My heart thudded in my ears as I awkwardly made my way back to the locker room, one of the equipment managers handing me my crutch. Being out there on the ice with them had been *fun,* though my leg and ass still ached from my fall.

When the song shifted to my favorite, I hadn't expected to see Grif on the screen holding a sign. Very romantic.

"Did you know he was going to do that?" I asked Mercy and Rusty, cradling my teddy bear with my free hand.

I still wanted an explanation, but his gesture meant a lot, especially given he'd missed his date night with Dean to be there.

And pulled strings. The song and getting on the screens–all of this had been planned.

"Nope. I told him to grovel. They *all* should grovel. Well, I think AJ's exempt since he showed up." Mercy held the door to the locker room open, where everyone was making last-minute preparations.

"True. But Jonas and Dean brought me food and helped clean up," I pointed out. And fucked me well.

Mercy scowled as she went to her stall to grab her red helmet. "After I yelled at Jonas. Fucking alphas."

"Still make Grif grovel." Rusty bent down to adjust her knee-high socks, which had nails on them.

"Absolutely. A public display is nice, but it doesn't fix everything," Liv added, fixing her makeup.

Ash adjusted his helmet. "He needs to work for it."

"Are you wearing pants, Ash?" My eyebrows rose.

"If you want to see my ass, just ask." Lifting his jersey, Ash turned and waggled his ass, which was covered in black bootie shorts instead of bike shorts or cut-proof tights.

I sat down and took off my skates, wiggling my toes. Mercy had yelled at Jonas? Then again, she didn't have the same issues standing up for herself as I did.

"Team Mom, you did so good out there," Kaiko told me as she fixed her fake freckles, her dark hair with pink streaks in their usual puffs.

I checked my phone and snorted as I saw Mama's text and showed it to Mercy.

Mama

What did he do?

Mercy laughed. "It would serve him right if she smacked him with her cooking spoon."

The image made me giggle.

"I'd pay money to see that," Rusty guffawed as she tightened the strap on her helmet.

Me

We had a fight, but everything's fine now.

Well, maybe? I wasn't sure. I hoped so. But I wasn't going to tell Mama all that.

"What happened anyway?" Mercy added as she fixed her make-up in the mirror.

"Not sure, other than I triggered something, and it was no one's fault." I put my shoes on and put the skates in my bag.

"Love Grif Graf, but he's got abandonment issues from being away from everyone for so long. He's got the shittiest agent ever." Rusty grimaced as she fixed the laces on her skates.

Skate smash skates differed from both hockey skates and figure skates. The blades gave them speed as they raced around the rink, the capacity to handle curves at high speeds, and the agility to do the team dance-offs that the public enjoyed so much.

Ash thought for a moment. "Does this mean we need to call off the pranks we planned for while we're gone?"

"You were going to prank them for me?" My hand went to my heart. Awww.

"We already did. No one messes with one of ours." Rusty gave me a hug. "We should call off all but one. Just to keep them on their toes."

"You'll be okay? I'm going to go visit Grif," I told Mercy during the first intermission. They were down after the first period, but not by much. "Can I put my bear with your things for safekeeping?" It even smelled like him.

"Sure. You can sit with Grif for the rest of the game." Mercy took a long gulp from her water bottle.

"Where, on his lap?" Because that row was full of giggly teenagers and drunk ladies.

"I don't think he'll mind." Mercy grinned. "Remember, there should be groveling."

"Lots of groveling," Rusty called as she grabbed a handful of hydrogels from the bowl on the snack table.

"Sure." With a wave, I left the locker room, leaning heavily on my crutch, feeling my fall from earlier today. I didn't need groveling. I needed answers.

But I wasn't sure I'd get them yet.

"Hi." I used my arena credentials to get into Grif's section. Standing at the end of the row, I gave him a wave. The teenagers weren't in their seats. I reached out my hand. "Come with me."

I led him back into the underbelly of the stadium, flashing my credentials and waving at security. We went into the small room I often studied in while the team was in their pre-game meetings and locked the door. No one would bother us here. It served as a green room or VIP area when they had events or concerts and had a couch, some chairs, a small table in the corner, and a small bar area.

Slipping into his arms, I inhaled his rainy scent, which still held the same sweeter notes it had this morning. Like his cum had tasted last night.

"I'm so sorry. I... I don't even remember what happened. You know I never meant to hurt you, right?" he murmured in my ear, red beard tickling me softly.

"I know. But I need to understand." It was nice leaning into his arms. Today emotionally exhausted me.

"I know. While I can't give you all the answers tonight, I want you to know how much I love you. You know, my family saw me give you my jersey last night and now want to meet. Especially Sissy," he told me.

"I'd love to meet Sissy. Also, I'm pretty sure that Grace is planning our wedding. But her wedding was lovely. Do you want a wedding or some sort of fancy mating party?" I asked. Not everyone did anything. Sometimes, it was a house party or lunch at a restaurant.

Or nothing at all.

Despite everything today, I still wanted to mate and marry him. Probably in a beautiful garden, with a stunning gold designer dress, fun music, and lots of tasty food.

"Marry you? Absolutely. I promise I'll explain everything when you get back." He kissed me, and I wondered if we had time for other things.

"Okay. I did trigger something, didn't I?" My breath caught in my chest.

He caught my face in his hands. "You did. But it's not your fault, Kitten."

"It still hurt me." I squeezed my eyes shut, recalling the panic I'd felt. Not to mention being bruised from the fall.

"I'm so fucking sorry." His voice shook. "I have baggage. We'll work through it together. Promise."

"Okay. Did everything go well with the doctor?" I added, shutting down other questions I wanted to ask.

He sighed. "I hope so. They did a shit-ton of tests."

I squeezed his hand, not missing the hints of anguish in his voice. Was he faced with the prospect of going off blockers? Or maybe having health problems that long-term usage could cause?

"We're not breaking up, are we? No third-act breakups, remember?" I bit my lower lip anxiously.

"Never. It's just a minor setback. Everyone has them. We'll talk it out when you get back. Would you like me to show you how much I love you? This is so much more comfortable than the room we were in last night. I didn't even know it was here." His lips met mine as he walked me back toward the couch. Every step backward made my core liquify.

"Please. When I found my plants destroyed, all I wanted was you. Even when Dean and Jonas took me home and made me the filling in a hot hockey sandwich, I wanted you." We fell onto the couch, my crutch on the floor beside us.

"Fuck." He bundled me to him, so we were on our sides, me between him and the back of the couch. His eyes met mine. "I'm sorry I wasn't there for you. I'm sorry my job made you a target."

My legs wrapped around his, like entwining myself in his body could soothe the raw edges of my soul. "It... it comes with the territory. You date someone famous and it happens."

"Please tell me they caught them?" His hands caressed the length of me, making it ache for him as if everything could be fixed by him burying his cock inside me.

"Sadly, no. No prints. They were wearing a hoodie and a mask. The footprints were on the smaller side, so it could be a woman, but who knows? Campus police want to brush it off as a harmless prank. Even though the destruction is hardly *harmless*." My voice grew bitter.

The cost of fixing the damage would be high, and I hoped my university would cover some of it.

"That's shitty. I hope they catch them. This won't cause you problems with the university, right?" His strokes focused on my ass as his hard-on jutted into me.

"Dr. Winters assured me that everything is fine, and I can have the time I need. Which is a relief. Still, are all these setbacks trying to tell me something? Should I stop this research? There's most likely a good reason why no one's done this before." Despair filled me.

"What? Kitten, no." He touched his forehead to mine. "If you love your research, if you believe in it, then keep on with it. We don't let the assholes win, remember?"

"I know." That, too, went a long way in soothing my soul. "It'll be a lot of work to set everything up again. I'm so tired."

The idea of starting over daunted me. Also, part of me, once again, wished for a blizzard, trapping us here in New York so I could have some rest.

He stroked my hair in a hypnotic rhythm. "I know. You work so hard. Hey, you get to go to Bayside to see your little brother. And to Hawai'i. I'm sure you'll do some fun things with the Maimers."

"I do. But all I want is you." I sighed, kissing him.

"You have me. How do you want me? Soft and slow? Hard and fast? Here on the couch? Against the wall? I'm all yours." He kissed me again as heat ignited between us.

Intermission was about over. This couch probably had seen more ass than backstage at fashion week. I should say *no*.

I didn't care. The need to unite with him overwhelmed me to the point where I could think of nothing but locking him deep inside me.

"Kiss me like you missed me." I unzipped his pants as our lips crashed together. His tongue probed mine as he worked my pants and panties off.

"You're so wet for me," he gasped as his hand worked my wanting slit.

"I need you." I palmed his hard cock, beading with pre-cum, and... sticky? Putting my hand to my mouth, I made a show of licking it.

Yes, it was sticky–and sweet like last night. Sweeter even. It reminded me a little of Dean's slick, though it wasn't quite the same consistency. I said nothing as he kicked off his pants.

Pinning my hands over my head on the oversized couch, he impaled me with one smooth, hard stroke, filling me to my very soul.

"How's that, Kitten? Is that what you need?" His green eyes never left mine as he pulled almost all the way out and slammed back in. "Because you're what I need. Always."

Jolts of pleasure shot through me as his ruthless and unrelenting thrusts pounded my pussy. His eyes stayed on me as he told me how much he needed me. How much he loved me.

An orgasm shuddered through me, making me gasp. "I love you, too, Grif."

One hand kept my arms over my head, as his free hand worked my clit, bringing me toward another rise of pleasure.

"I'm going to come, Kitten. I'm going to pour my cum into your sweet pussy the way I hope us fucking fills your heart with all my love." He pulled out all the way this time and slammed in, giving two hard strokes.

His fingers flicked my clit, sending me into another orgasm as hot cum rushed into my pussy. Grif's mouth fell on mine as he kissed me over, our bodies entangled as my cunt locked down on his cock, keeping him inside me.

He fell on top of me, hand letting my wrists go. We rolled back onto our sides as he held me tight. Yep, it was well into the second period.

But I didn't mind because I had him. Finally.

In the arena parking garage, I leaned into Grif. The two of us stank of sweat and sex. Something the Maimers had teased me about unrelentingly as I slipped back onto the bench for the third period.

Between the bits he'd told me and his smell and taste, I was pretty sure my hypothesis was correct. I had some homework to do.

"Tiger, I'm going to miss you." I cupped his face with my hand. Everything was loaded onto the bus that would take the Maimers to the airport.

Grif planted another kiss on my lips. "Be safe on your trip."

"Thanks for my stuffie. It'll be nice to have something to cuddle at night." I leaned my head on his shoulder.

"Do you want to take Lucky?" he asked in earnest.

I laughed, still amazed that the imaginary cat I made up that day we met on the airplane was a thing. "Please don't tell me he's been here the whole time?"

"Noooo. He appeared during the third period." Grif continued to hold me tight.

"It's not that long, you ding-dongs." Mercy joined us. "There are also these things called phones. Come on, Ver, we're the last on the bus."

"Coming," I told her. Turning back to Grif, I hugged him tight. "I love you so much, Tiger." Leaning up, I whispered in his ear. "I'll always love you. No matter what. Even if you're a gamma."

Before he could answer me, I gave him one last kiss and went to the bus, not looking back. I didn't want him to feel like he had to reply.

Why *had* I said that?

My heart thudded so hard in my chest that I was afraid it would thump right out of my body. At the same time, I wanted him to know I'd support him. I didn't want to come back from my trip only to get broken up with because he got so in his head while I was gone that he thought it was for the best.

I got on the bus and sat next to Mercy.

"We're moving in with them, aren't we?" Mercy waved as Grif stood there in the parking garage. He waved back, looking forlorn.

I blew him a kiss. "Would that be so bad?"

"Probably. We could make it work. Maybe." She shrugged. "Despite me being pissed about today, they're not bad dudes. Jonas even texted me and told me he was sorry for being an asshole. I just don't enjoy living under other people's rules."

Something I completely understood.

"Wait, Jonas was an asshole?" I frowned, not liking that.

"I don't think he meant to be." She shrugged again, scrolling on her phone as the bus pulled away.

"True. We haven't gotten there yet. I have a feeling it might get a little hard to wait six months. But I won't do anything without your input," I reassured, because it was important for her to feel like she had a say in major changes in our household.

Grabbing my phone, I texted Grif.

Me

I love you.

"And I appreciate that." She leaned her head on my shoulder.

"I'll still have time for you if I take a mate or two. Promise that I won't disappear." I played with her light brown braids as the bus headed into the dark and busy streets to take us to the airport.

"I know. But I like it when you say it. Only two?" Her eyebrows rose in disbelief. "You're not going to be like Grace, and *catch them all* as she puts it?"

Grif

Love you, too. We'll talk when you get back.

Promise. Have fun and travel safe.

"Maybe." My head ducked as a smile twitched on my lips. I could see myself ending up with all four of them. "Just maybe."

Chapter Six

Jonas

"Grif was an absolute beast in practice today. Something I always love to see. But is he okay? He and his girl didn't actually break up, right?" Coach Atkins stopped me in the upstairs hall of the training center as I went to go get my cardio in.

"No, they didn't. They're fine," I assured, leaning against the wall. At least, I thought they were.

I'd understand if she wasn't. She had a right to be hurt and confused. The fact that she trusted us enough to wait for an explanation until she got back astounded me. Personally, I wasn't sure I would.

"Oh, good." Coach Atkins didn't leave. He stroked his chin, which meant he had more to say.

Grif wasn't fine. It had nothing to do with Verity and everything to do with what happened on the bleachers, along with whatever tests the doctor was supposed to discuss with him yesterday, but postponed.

Not that I could tell Coach that.

"Um, Grif's happy here, right? With you all and his girl." His voice grew low as he leaned in, raking a hand through his graying hair.

"Of course he's happy being a Knight. Is there a reason for him not to be?" My voice quieted. "Is that why it's taking so long for the pack contract to be negotiated? Management's still not happy with the way he's playing?"

Given the silence, I'd wondered if they still wanted to get rid of Grif. We still had a couple of months until the trade deadline.

"I'm happy with how he's playing, and as far as I know, everyone else is. Sure, it was a little rocky at the beginning, but he rose to the challenge." Coach Atkin's frown deepened. "I'm not part of pack contracts other than being asked if I recommend it–which I did. All I know is that I was asked who we might look at to fill Grif's place."

"Shit. I'll be honest, Coach, I don't know if Dean can take being away from Grif again." Not only because they'd bonded with each other.

But the Knights never wanted Grif, anyway. He'd taken a *pay cut* to be a Knight. This entire season had been a race to get the pack contract in place so we could sleep at night.

"I know." Coach's look grew grim. "Dean's looking to have a record season. I'm guessing that has a lot to do with having his pack together. I'd hate to lose you three. As would the team. And not simply because we have a real chance of going all the way this year."

Was he trying to tell me something? Or just being heartfelt?

"We like being Knights, Coach. Grif included. Like Dean, the only team he'd want to leave for would be the Royals and that's simply because of childhood nostalgia," I told Coach, though it wasn't like he hadn't heard this before.

"Okay. I wanted to check. Boston. Not say... Rockland?" His look went sly.

Oh. Relief sluiced over me. Someone must have heard Grif and Verity talking on the bleachers. Grif had mentioned them joking about Spencer buying teams.

"If this has to do with Verity's sister's pack buying the Daredevils and trading us to them so Verity will work for Compass BioTek, I'm pretty sure it's a joke. Not to mention she's several years from finishing her PhD." By then, we might be looking to retire. Though the Daredevils were a decent team, and Rockland was a nice place. I'd live there for a while if it made everyone happy.

"A joke, okay." He nodded. "Got it. That was making people a little nervous."

"We like being Knights, Coach. We just want to get our pack contract and be happy. A lot of things are waiting on that," I admitted honestly.

"Like I said, I'd hate to lose you three." He patted my shoulder and walked down the hall.

I got my phone, and I went upstairs into a small conference room that was often used by the goalies and called my agent. I'd also gotten a text to call him.

"Stu, what's up?" I asked, sitting in one of the rolling chairs, belly clenching.

"That's what I wanted to ask you. Most specifically, why am I trying to get a pack contract when one of your pack members clearly doesn't want it?" Stu Thomas of Venture Management asked, sounding genuinely puzzled, not pissed.

Stu had been my agent since the very beginning. He knew my high school coach back in Toronto. He'd been Dean's agent for several years.

"You're the second person to ask me this today, the first being our coach. This is news to me because at breakfast this morning, Grif asked when he should bug his agent again about the pack contract." I frowned at my phone as I texted Grif.

Me

You want a pack contract, right?

"Huh. Chet's made it nearly impossible to schedule a meeting. He misses most of them, and when he attends, he makes it seem like Grif's unhappy and *wants* out," Stu replied.

"*Chet's* holding up the contract?" I rubbed my forehead. Why would he do that? Not that it actually surprised me.

Grif

Yeah. Does someone think I don't?

Where are you? I'm going to hit the small rink and practice some more.

Me

I've got some things to handle. Go for it.

Though I worried that all the extra practice time would burn him out.

"Chet dislikes that woman Grif's seeing immensely," Stu added. "She's a model?"

I sighed. "She does some modeling. Chet's been giving Grif shit about her. Which is weird."

"Eh. Depends on who she is and if she'll impact his image negatively," Stu replied. "If you *do* want the contract, I'll try to salvage it. But if Grif doesn't reign Chet in, you might not only be out of a pack contract, Grif might find his ass traded. Possibly to a shitty team, because Bunty's not happy."

"Fuck." That's the last thing we needed. Bunty Longfellow was the general manager for the Knights. He just might be getting a bit weird in his old age.

Not that I'd ever say that.

"We have to lock down this pack contract. Dean needs the security of knowing his husband won't get traded away from him.

Fucking Chet. I can't get Grif to leave him." Frustration raged through me.

"Something's not right about Chet." He sighed.

I rested my face in my hand. "If I can convince Grif to fire Chet, will you take him?"

"You know I will. Honestly, it's for the best if Grif leaves him. The past couple of years have given Chet a reputation where reputable people don't want to work with him *or* the people he reps," Stu replied.

The depth and breadth of his words hit me. Grif's lack of sponsors even though he'd won a title. His difficulty getting to us. Taking a pay cut. This could all be because of *Chet?*

"If Chet has something on Grif that's forcing him to stay, we can help manage it by getting ahead of it," he added.

"Is that something Chet does?" I frowned. I mean, he was a slimeball, but...

"Unfortunately."

"I'll check with Grif." Huh. That was something to consider.

"You might want to check out the model. I've got someone if you need them," Stu added.

"Already have. And thanks." I wasn't ready to tell Stu Grif's secret, but given how he'd saved Dean's career after he was outed, I trusted him to help us.

"One more thing. I've had three players call me and ask me if they can get traded to the Rockland Daredevils after that biotech guy Spencer Thanukos buys it. Which is strange because I didn't know it was for sale. Or that he was interested in owning a team. Or that you three are apparently part of this dream team he's building? You know how this business is, but considering it's got people spooked, I'm curious." Amusement tinged his voice.

"As far as I know, it's a *joke.* Grif's girlfriend's related to the Thanukos pack. Why are people threatened by him buying a team? He wouldn't be the first eccentric billionaire to do so." I shrugged, finding all this a little silly.

"I'm not sure. It's sort of fun to see owners and GMs shaken up, though. I just wanted to check. I've got to go, but Grif needs to deal with Chet *now* or it could undermine everything you've been working toward," he warned.

"Thanks, Stu." I ended the call. Ugh. While I hated to exert my power as head alpha, I couldn't let Chet impact the pack.

"Everything okay, Jonas?" Coach Kirov, the goalie coach, opened the door.

Both goalies, and all three EBUGs were with her. Everyone had plates of food.

"Yeah, I'm fine. Sorry for taking your space." I got up. They were probably going to watch films and talk strategy.

Dean gave me a concerned look and squeezed my hand. "I felt that. What's wrong, Babes?"

I squeezed his hand back. "I'll tell you later, Love."

First, I needed to talk to Grif.

"Chet has shit on people so they stay with him?" Grif frowned over his salmon burger as we ate in the back of our black SUV in the training center garage.

While it wasn't that comfortable, it was private. Sure, people might assume we were having sex, but they did that anyway. The other people with packmates on the team were all *with* each other. It wasn't uncommon to catch Nakey and Pauly in the showers.

"I guess." I shrugged as I took a bite of my chicken burger.

Grif's brows furrowed. "I was one of his first clients, and I stayed with him out of loyalty because he believed in me. If he has something on me, I don't know what it is. Fuck, what if he knows?"

"Then we'll deal with it. I can't let him wreck the pack or our careers." I sipped on my vitamin water.

"What about *mine?* If he knows, and tells, it's over." He looked stricken, his scent going sour.

I put my arm around him. "After you talk to the doctor, we need to come up with an actual plan. Depending on what your body is going through, your days of hiding might be numbered, anyway. Though I'm confident Stu can fix things for you like he did with Dean."

"I'm not Dean." He sighed and took another bite.

"We'll still love you if you don't play hockey. People *want* you to conduct. People *want* your songs. Worst case, we get you a music agent, set you up with a studio, and you make music and join AJ's recreational league. Spend more time fucking our little alpha in her greenhouse. Maybe coach some kids." I gave him another squeeze.

Grif was so sure his life would be over if he had to come out as omega. I didn't think his career would end there. Even if he did, there was so much he still could do and had to live for.

But then hockey had always been how he proved his value. It made my heart ache that after all these years he didn't see how he was so much more.

Though I did worry about his health.

Grif's eyes met mine, wary. "You'd be okay if I didn't play hockey? Don't get me wrong, I'd much rather play hockey, but my biggest hesitation about pursuing music is that I wouldn't be able to contribute what everyone else does to the pack."

"Grif." I pulled him tighter, careful of our food. "Our pack isn't hurting for money–and one of the great things about packs is that they allow for everyone to have a job they like. Not to mention, you'll still make more than our little alpha."

"Until she works for Spencer and changes the world with her happy flowers." He snorted, head resting on my shoulder. "You know I've been getting texts asking me about his dream team. The Daredevils are an established team. It's not like he'd fire everyone and start over."

"I've been asked, too. Look, I know the idea of coming out as omega is scary. We'll be behind you–always. Verity will still love you. Do I want you to stay with the Knights? Yes. Will we go after the Knights legally if they fire you for being an omega? Yes. Will we figure something out if you have to go to another team? Of course. We love you and we're here." I toyed with his red hair.

"That... that means a lot." His voice choked up. "I don't want to be an omega. Never have. If I come out, I'm afraid that's all people will see me as. It's hard to only be seen for something you don't even want to be."

"We've always seen you as you, Grif, you know that–and Verity will, too." I hoped that she'd forgive him for this.

"She will. I'm sure of it. All of this is terrifying, and you're right, I've been feeling everything so much more since I found her. Oddly enough, I *like* some of it. Which then makes me feel like shit for putting AJ off for so long because I didn't want to deal with my feelings." He sighed again.

"AJ loves you." I squeezed his hand. AJ was a good guy and brought a lot to the pack, even if he was a stubborn fuck sometimes.

"I'm not ready for my career to be over." He pinched the bridge of his nose with his thumb and forefinger. "Not to mention, we can't just pick up and leave. There are no professional omega forwards. Not even in the minors. There's a couple at the collegiate level." Defeat crossed his face. "But..."

"*Public* omegas in the *PHL*. We know of what? Five secret omegas? Three of which are forwards. That's not including Ellie." Who we were pretty sure was a gamma, but told everyone she was a kappa. She was a forward and *enforcer* for the Sasquatches.

The other two were a goalie and defender who masqueraded as a beta couple and were part of an omega pod–an all-omega pack. Dean had a secret omega support network going on.

"True." His shoulder slumped.

"I'm not afraid of moving elsewhere. We can make things work. Or Verity can have Spencer buy the Royals instead of the Daredevils, and we can move into the house you bought Dean for Christmas. Problem solved." I grinned.

He laughed. "Absolutely. It can be our wedding present. You know she wants a fancy wedding. In a garden."

"Of course she does. With a string quartet, fairy lights, and tiny food. And it will be beautiful." I could see it now, and I hoped to the very depths of my soul that it happened one day.

"Can we really make this work if I have to come out? I'm terrified of what the doctor will tell me. I'm a nervous wreck over this." His head bowed.

Burnt sugar fear tinged Grif's rain scent, and I pulled him to me, holding him tight and comforting him the best I could. I'd text AJ later to let him know to give Grif some extra care tonight. Maybe he could bring home those empanadas from that place Grif liked.

"We'll make this work. We're a pack and that's what we do. Don't worry about Verity, I'm sure she'll love you no matter what." I rubbed his back as I put out soothing pheromones to help calm him down.

He got an odd look in his eyes. "I know."

Huh.

"Sorry, I didn't mean to have this big conversation here in the car. It's supposed to be about you firing Chet. You don't need to hire Stu, but it would make things easier." I continued to rub his back, to calm him down before we had a team strategy meeting.

"I… I've been thinking about it ever since Chet sent that text the night I gave Verity the jersey. It seemed so out of line. Honestly, do you think it's his reputation hurting my career? I sort of thought the big sponsors didn't like me because, as Kylee once put it, I'm *an emotionless tank that only melts for Dean.*"

"I think there is a distinct possibility Chet gave you a reputation. That he's spun you a certain way."

"But *why?* Why is Chet doing this? He makes money when I do." Grif frowned.

"Maybe he doesn't care about the money? Maybe he steers you to sponsors he can control? I have no idea," I told him. Perhaps Chet just enjoyed being a dick.

Why would Chet have such an issue with Verity? She was one of the nicest people I'd ever met.

"Okay." Defeat crossed Grif's face. "While I'm grateful for everything he's done, you're right. It's time to end it with Chet before it hurts us even further."

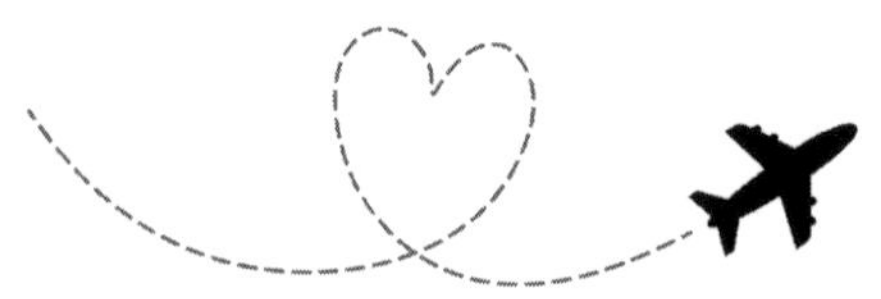

Chapter Seven

Verity

"Hey, that tickles." I laughed as Mercy, Kaiko, and Jack buried me in the sand. It was day three of our West Coast trip. After playing the Pacific Pummelers, we had today off. Tomorrow, we played the Bayside Bludgediers.

So here I was, on the beach, as they made me into a human sandcastle. It wasn't exactly swimming weather, but it was a beautiful day for January.

My phone beeped. Unfortunately, my arms were both buried. "Who is it?"

Mercy shrugged. "Probably someone commenting on the pictures I posted to your group chats. The guys are fans. So are the siblings." She looked over to where it sat on a towel and fake winced, dramatically throwing her hand over her face. "Oh, my eyes. Just kidding. Grif didn't send you sexts. Dean did."

He would.

I missed my guys. Grif and I talked every day. This morning, he'd had a chai latte and lemon muffin sent to the hotel for me.

It wasn't quite the same.

"What I'd like to know is why Riley keeps sending you logos for the *Rockland Theorems?*" Mercy scrolled through my phone and made a puzzled face. "What sport is that supposed to be?"

"Boredom. Grace told them how people think Spencer's actually going to buy the Daredevils. So, the pack has been designing shit and trolling the internet," I laughed. It was funny that people latched on to that since literally Grif joked about Spencer buying the Royals right after.

My phone rang. I froze. Was I getting mean phone calls now? I craned my neck, sending sand cascading down the side of their creation.

"Don't move," Kaiko scolded, as she patted the sand back.

"Verity's phone. How can I help you?" Mercy answered before I could stop her. Her expression changed from playful to serious. "Of course, Dr. Winters, she's right here."

My belly tightened. Was this where they kicked me out because I had no research?

"Sorry." My hands were all sandy, so I wiped them on the towel and took the call, heart pounding. "Dr. Winters, is everything okay?"

"I was calling to see if *you* were okay. I know what your research means to you, and that was a devastating blow," Dr. Winters told me.

"Oh, thank you, I appreciate that." Though, my body didn't relax. "Please tell me they caught them?"

"Not yet. Do you have an inventory list? Or better yet, a list of how much it's going to cost you to replace everything? I'd like to add it to the repair costs so that we're ready when we catch this person. I'm livid for you–as is everyone else in the department. What a horrible thing to do to someone," he added.

"The replacement list isn't finished because I'm trying to figure out the best options. But I have one," I said tentatively. While I'd ordered a few things, it would cost a lot, and I wasn't sure if I should ask Creed or Grace for help.

However, I'd asked my brother Hale to dig up my flowers in the public gardens at Marquess and Briar. I gave him money for regular lily bulbs to replace them with.

"Send over what you have. Our department head thinks we can get you a little from the emergency fund because you shouldn't have to wait for us to catch them," he told me.

"Thank you, Dr. Winters. This means a lot. I was a little worried that the university would be unhappy that I lost my research." Or working hard enough.

It felt odd that here at NYIT they wanted me to *enjoy* my break and not use it to get twice the work done.

"I believe in you, though..." His sigh made me freeze. "There's someone overly concerned about your position in the program because your research was destroyed. Someone who has no business being concerned but is. Can you write me something stating how you'll get back on track?"

Oh. A chill rushed through me because I knew how universities worked.

"I already created an action plan. I was going to read over it one more time and send it to you tonight," I told him, apprehension rising inside me.

"That would be fantastic. Also, our department head wanted me to reassure you that you don't worry about your place here–or your funding. She's impressed that Compass BioTek is interested in you, and has mentioned being able to expedite things given your circumstances, if you choose to go that route," he added.

Those words made me relax. The university was happy.

"Oh. Huh. I still haven't decided." Though Spencer had talked to me about it when I was there at Christmas.

"It might not be a bad idea," Dr. Winters told me. "You know how this game is played."

"I know." Being backed by Compass BioTek offered more than funding. It also gave me credibility.

"Think about it. Though like I said, everyone is happy with you. Now, enjoy the rest of your break." Dr. Winters ended the call.

Mercy looked at me expectantly. "Is everything okay?"

"NYIT is happy with me." That was such a relief because I knew people gossiped.

"That's great. I mean, who wouldn't be?" Mercy dumped a bucket of sand over me. "Now, let's finish."

After we finished–and they took the requisite pictures–we found some food. While we were eating burritos, my phone buzzed.

Riley

Found her. Know who she is?

Picture after picture came through on my phone. Not just grainy camera shots, but also social media posts. How had Riley found these? If anyone could do it, it would be Riley, the teenage super hacker.

My hands shook as I looked at the photos. That was absolutely not who I expected. I scrolled through everything. Her social media marked her as a biology major and a rabid Knights fan with much appreciation for Grif.

Me

Yes.

Thank you so much.

I looked over at Mercy. "Riley found who trashed my greenhouse."

"I knew she would. Who did it?" Mercy made a face.

"Her name's Samantha. I've seen her around, but I don't actually know her. She's an undergrad." I showed them what Riley found. Especially her open distaste for him dating *some plant ho.*

It seemed like a shitty reason to vandalize university property and ruin my life's work. It's not like I stole him from her.

"There we have it then–motive and everything," Mercy replied, grabbing more chips and guacamole.

"*Plant ho* is so uninspired, though." Jack rolled his eyes and shook his head. He'd dyed his hair blue in honor of our West Coast adventure. "*Botanical slut* is much better."

"*Plant ho* is what they call the botanists and plant biology people at NYIT." I sent the screenshot of her social media to Saphira.

Me

She might be the culprit.

Also, Jack says Botanical Slut is better than Plant Ho.

In some ways, I felt bad for this girl. She was Hale's age. Obviously passionate. I didn't want to see her expelled for one bad choice. But I wanted her to be punished because of all the damage she caused.

A weight lifted off my shoulders. We found her. Now, to pass this information on to the authorities.

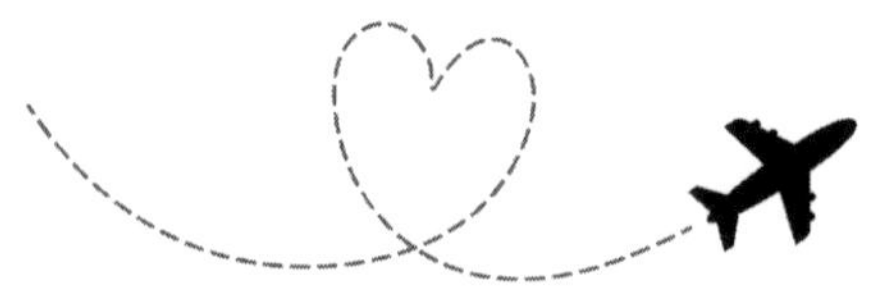

Chapter Eight

Grif

Nerves collided in my belly as I sat in an exam room at the doctor's office. With the game tonight, I should be napping. However, the need to know whatever it was the doctor had to tell me burned me from the inside out. I wasn't sure I could go another day living with that uncertainty.

So here I was.

As I waited, I scrolled through pictures of Verity being buried in the sand by Maimer rookies. Her absence left a gaping hole in my soul. Sure, we talked, we texted, but it wasn't the same.

One thing we hadn't spoken about was what she'd whispered in my ear as she got on the bus. *I'll always love you. No matter what. Even if you're a gamma.*

While I loved the sentiment, it baffled me. What gave her the idea that I was a *gamma*?

Still, she'd figured *something* out. On her own.

If she'd done that, who else had?

My phone lit up and I silenced it. Chet was *not* taking me firing him well. Stu had smoothed things over with the Knights GM. Hopefully, we'd have that contract before Verity returned from her trip.

Again, my phone lit up, but it wasn't Chet.

"Hey, Stu." Anxiousness filled me. Hopefully, it was good news.

"Hi, Grif. Did you see that they've announced the fan picks for the All-Star game?" Stu asked me.

"No. Dean got it, didn't he?" While as nice as a rest during the All-Star break sounded, it was always fun to attend. Dean had gotten to play a couple of times. I'd only been once for the rookie games with AJ, back when we'd been Hurricanes.

This year, Elias Royce, our team captain, was captaining one of the four All-Star teams–a huge honor. But Elias had been at this a long time and was getting ready to retire.

"Sadly, Dean didn't make it this year. Goalies are tough considering how few of them are on a team compared to other positions," Stu said. "However, *you* made the popular vote cut. By quite a bit."

I pulled it up on my phone to check. "Did I? Wow, I didn't even know I was up for consideration."

This year I'd been too busy to follow it. Especially when I hadn't gotten it last year, from either the Hurricanes or the fan vote.

"Congratulations. It's in Boston this year, so that should be fun for you," he told me.

"I can't believe it. Wow. Thanks for letting me know." My mind reeled. I'd gotten picked *by the fans* for the All-Star team, and it was in Boston. Perfect. We could stay in the house I'd bought Dean and I could see what all needed to be fixed.

"There's a few tickets available for sale for your family, so let me know and I'll handle it," he added.

"I'll buy every ticket they'll let me have," I told him. The pack would want to come, as would my family and Dean's. "Thanks again."

I ended the call and took a screenshot of me being chosen and I sent it to the group chat–and to Verity.

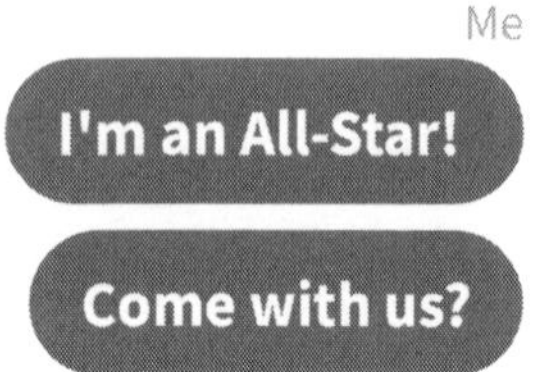

It would be great fun. There weren't only the games, there were contests for the mascots, rookies, and goalies. There were also fun skill competitions and other mayhem.

Verity

If I can, I will! Congratulations.

Jonas, AJ, and Dean all bombarded me with well wishes.

Griffin McGraff, All-Star. Fuck me.

Dr. Arya, in her lab coat, came into the tiny exam room and sat down in the chair adjacent to the exam bed where I sat.

"Griffin, my apologies for making you wait. People kept having emergencies." She consulted her tablet.

"Okay, so what's wrong with me?" *And how do we fix it?* My knee jiggled with nerves, that high of being chosen for the team evaporating.

"Let's start with the good news. Your hormone levels are fantastic, which is probably *why* all these things are happening to you." Dr. Arya looked up at me.

"That makes sense." How they could read my hormones with all the crap in my system, I didn't know. While for an ordinary omega, fantastic hormones were a good thing, I was *trying* to keep mine under wraps.

I hadn't even considered that finally getting my pack together might put my omega in the ideal position to burst out. Not only did I not want that, I didn't need my body deciding to override my suppressants and go into heat or any other omega biological bullshit.

My belly dipped as I went to my real question. "What about my kidneys?"

"They're not as good as I hoped, but not as bad as I feared." Her look grew pensive.

"Well, that's good, right?" Because that kept me up at night. I wanted to ruin my omega parts, not the rest of me.

She showed me a graph on her tablet. "You're going to have to make some choices if you don't want to have serious health problems very soon."

The graph made little sense and I frowned at it.

"I should be able to go off the blockers and suppressants for the summer. But I'm afraid of what will happen if someone finds out that I'm hiding my designation. My career is important to me." I winced because this was a lot all at once.

"I know," she soothed. "People are going to find out eventually. Right now, it's a tossup over what outs you first–you collapsing because of kidney or heart problems during a game or your nature bursting out for all to see. One of those will happen before the season is over and after that, all the blockers and suppressants in the world won't help you."

Bile rose in my throat because I didn't like either of those scenarios. They were both incredibly possible, especially after what happened in the locker room with Dean.

"I'm surprised, given what you told me in your last visit about your blocker overdose, that major health setbacks haven't happened sooner," she told me, checking her tablet again.

I sighed. "We all were. What am I going to do, Doc? We're finally together."

"I changed your blockers and give you a nutrition plan to follow. It will buy you time to talk to your pack and make a plan. This is a *when* not *if* situation," she warned.

That was a lot to swallow in itself.

No, I didn't want that to happen to me. If it did, my hockey career really would be over. It could also change my quality of life and the time I had with my pack.

I'd hidden for so long, had so much fear...

"What about suppressants?" I worried about going into heat. I'd only had a couple, and none had been very good experiences.

"For now, those should be fine–as long as you don't push yourself too hard. A light scent blocker for work should be okay, too. I know this is hard. You don't have to do this alone," she added.

Not sure a light scent blocker, the type omegas might take before going out or to their average job, would be good enough for the PHL. Dean took something heavier than that before games, so it wouldn't tamper with gameplay. Not that he took anything close to what I did now that he no longer had to hide.

I gulped, feeling sick. "My pack will support me."

But could I get through it myself?

"Not only do you have your pack, but once you have a gamma or omega designation in your file, you can go to the Omega Center and have full access to all their services. Including medical services, counseling, and an advocate to help you through this," she assured.

Oh. I hadn't even thought of that. Dean had gotten legal help from them after he'd been outed. He also had an advocate, who was basically a personal counselor and caseworker.

"One thing to think about–quickly–because your hormone levels are rising, is what would you rather have your official designation listed as–gamma or omega? It looks like you're going to push back over to omega pretty soon, which is rare but happens.

I don't understand enough about hockey to know which would be better. At this moment, it is an option," she said. "Obviously, if you pushed over to omega, you could get retested and have the new designation put in your file if you wished."

Once a designation was in your file, it stayed there, unless you got retested and had it changed, which was part of how I could hide as a beta. Though, if you had enough money, you could pay someone to change it for you.

Dr. Arya turned her tablet so I could see some tables I didn't understand, showing genetics and hormones.

If Verity were here would she be able to help me understand it?

I stared at the chart as her words soaked into my brain.

"Wait, I actually did something to my omega after I overdosed and made myself a gamma?" I hadn't even realized one could become a gamma *after* awakening as an omega. I'd never gone back for a follow-up after I overdosed, out of fear.

"You didn't know? Yes. When you're fully tested, you register as a gamma. Though barely." She rubbed her forehead.

Oh. Wow. The basic prick test only registered the three main designations. A full test was required for other designations, such as gammas, kappas, and iotas. Though it didn't pick up illegal designations. That was a separate and highly regulated test.

Dr. Arya continued, "Every gamma is different, but generally the closer you are to awakening as an omega when you become a gamma, the more omega-like you are. Given you were already omega when it happened, it makes sense it would push back into place when your situation changed."

"That's something to think about," I told her, slowly. Not that I knew which would be better.

I'll always love you. No matter what. Even if you're a gamma.

Verity was right. How did she even know? I yearned to ask. But it wasn't a text message conversation. I'd wait until she returned.

"Thank you, Doc." Tonight, I'd have to talk to the guys about all this. Hopefully, they'd have some good ideas.

First, I had to get ready for the game.

"Are you okay, Grif Graf? While you played great, there was something off." Coach Atkins came up to me in the locker room after the game with a worried look on his face.

It had everything to do with how heavily everything weighed on me. Though the team *had* won, 2-1, and I'd scored a goal.

"I'm not feeling good," I told him. It was all nerves. I was still reeling from the information I'd gotten from Dr. Arya.

"Well, rest up. We've got another game tomorrow." He patted me on the shoulder. "Congrats on making it to the All-Star team. While it's a thrill to be selected, I always thought it was extra special when the fans chose you."

"Good game." Carlos smacked me on the ass with a towel.

Everyone was in a good mood as we listened to the coaches give their rundown, hit the bikes and ice baths, showered, and got dressed. A lot of them were making plans to head to Tito's.

Finding a quiet place in the corner, I called Verity. She'd texted me while I was playing.

"Please tell me they caught whoever wrecked your greenhouse?" I blurted. The idea of them out there still made me nervous. Also, I felt terrible. They went after her because of us.

"We identified her. I haven't heard if she's officially been caught yet. The university is going to give me funding to help cover the costs of the damage, which is nice. They said I can go after external funding–and I'm considering it. It's short term. Don't worry, I won't sign a long-term contract without talking to you, since well, it could affect our future," Verity told me.

Our future. That settled my nerves a little.

"How so?" I wasn't sure what she was talking about.

"It would be with Spencer. If I did anything with him long-term, I'd need to make sure I can stay with you," she told me.

She wanted to stay with me after everything that happened? Relief sluiced over me.

"Thank you. Though, Rockland doesn't seem that bad. You know that rumor hasn't died down at all," I laughed. "Someone said he's renaming the team the *Theorems.*"

"That's his packmates being trolls," she giggled.

"If it's best for you, then do it. We will figure it out and I know you always have all our interests at heart." This seemed like a wonderful opportunity for her.

"Though..." Her voice went tight. "I think someone at the university is unhappy with me."

"Some uptight trustee hates happiness?" Having met some of the BosTec trustees back when I went there, I could see that happening.

"Or a rival of my parents. They had a shit-ton of professional and academic rivals. And of course, the people who think that my omega dad should be at home making pork chops instead of teaching." She snorted. "There's a good reason Mama and I did most of the cooking. Hey, how did the doctor's visit go?"

"I have a lot to think about. Kitten, did... did you mean what you whispered in my ear when you got on the bus?" My heart skipped a beat as I waited for an answer.

"I did. I'll love you no matter what," she assured. "Promise."

A voice spoke in the background.

"Do you need to go?" I asked. Her words made me feel better.

"I don't want to," she sniffed. "I'm hiding."

"What happened? Weren't you visiting your aunts' so you could see your cousins and little brother?" I closed my eyes, wishing she was here so I could hold her.

The two parents that lived in Bayside were out of town. It wouldn't surprise me if it were on purpose.

"Auntie invited my grandmother." She sighed. "My relationship with the family of my Baba, my alpha dad, is complicated. Especially with me being a female alpha. My omega grandmother has decided I need a pack, and she's the person to find me one."

I tried hard not to laugh, because AJ's omega mother used to be like that too, before Jonas and Dean moved in with him. "So, she's trying to set you up with eligible packs all over the West Coast?"

"Worse. While Baba wants me to marry an investment banker, she thinks I need a pack full of doctors and an omega who is an accomplished cook. She's been scouring New York for prospects. Don't worry, I won't let her set me up. But she's relentless and doesn't understand what hockey is. Even then, nothing's better than a pack of doctors." She snorted.

"You're an excellent cook. Is that a slight to you?" I frowned. An entire pack of doctors? That sounded like a lot.

"Actually, no. That's her way of acknowledging that I'm a breadwinner. While it's good for an alpha to be able to cook, especially for their omega, it's nice to come home to a hot meal and a tidy house." She laughed again. "Designation norms, am I right?"

"We love you, and even though we're not doctors, we're the pack for you," I assured, glad that the prospect didn't sway her.

"You are, and I miss you. Anyhow, my aunt is calling for me. I should go downstairs and *stop being dramatic.*" She sighed heavily.

"I vote for being twice as dramatic. Love you, talk to you tomorrow." I ended the call. Closing my eyes, I leaned against the wall, heart full. She still loved me.

"Hey, want to go to Tito's?" Dean asked me as I rejoined him and Jonas.

I got out of the way as Clark chased Dimitri around the locker room with a pickle. I snorted. Clark looked like if he took off his black glasses he'd be a superhero and Dimitri looked like the villain in an international spy movie.

Shaking my head, I put my arms around Dean. "Can we go home? All of us? Please, Jellybean."

"Sure." Dean planted a kiss on my forehead.

Verity said she loved me no matter what. Hopefully, everyone else would, too.

Chapter Nine

Dean

"You're a *gamma*? I didn't see that one coming. I knew your omega was muted, but I didn't think it was to that level," Jonas said to Grif as I leaned into him, curled on the sectional, his scent going salty with worry.

"That's what the tests say." Grif's shoulders slumped as he paced, our drinks forgotten on the coffee table in our living room.

We were all still in our suits, though AJ had on the jersey with Grif's number that he always wore to our games.

"Grif, you know we don't care, right?" My chest tightened at his anxiousness. I worried, too. It wasn't him being a gamma that concerned me. It was his test results. Because I knew how to read these.

Part of me wanted Grif to go off everything *now.* Things could go sideways so quickly. We could find him a new career, but we couldn't get a new him.

Who knew what other damage he'd done to his body?

"I'm so glad to hear that." Grif exhaled sharply but didn't stop pacing, hands behind his back. "She also said that with my hormone levels, I might be back to omega soon. Something about living with omegas can cause that to happen." He shot me a fond look. "And I should consider if I wanted to be a gamma or an omega in my file."

AJ's head cocked as he rubbed his dark goatee. "Would it make a difference? Aren't gammas under omega law?"

I put up a hand. "Hear me out. People rarely ask gammas questions, since most have haunting pasts. Gammas vary so much, so a lot of things can be brushed off as *gammas, right?* It could be your best chance of keeping your job, playing up gamma unpredictability and their oddball danger response."

"I don't have any unpredictable behaviors or reactions, though." Grif leaned against his piano, running a hand through his hair, anxiety lacing his rainy scent.

Jonas snorted. "Because giving Verity your jersey at the game was so omega-like?"

"It could be. Omegas being possessive of their alphas and all that. You know we have a game on my birthday." I smirked. If she was free, I wanted her there. Maybe she could sleep over.

"Your playing changed after the overdose. You've always been a brawler, but you became fiercer, quicker to act," Jonas told him.

"We need a plan. A quick one," AJ added from the ottoman. "What do *you* want?"

"For everything to stay the same? Actually, I'd rather come out on my own terms than collapse during a game or have it become a scandal. I didn't think this would be the year we'd do this. I was sort of hoping it would never happen." He looked away, and sadness came through our bond, his scent going salty.

"I know, Boo-Boo," AJ soothed. "After we get the pack contract, can we bond, release a statement that we've mated, and then announce it? Get ahead of things so we can start taking care of you? I worry about your health." He stood and wrapped his arms around Grif.

"I guess? Though I'd like to talk to Coach before we go public with it," Grif admitted, leaning into AJ. "I worry about getting fired."

"They can't legally fire you because of your designation. If they do, that's what lawyers are for." AJ stroked his hair.

"That's a good idea–talking to Coach. Part of what made staying with the Aces so hostile, well, besides Beau, was how the coaches and staff felt betrayed," I told them.

My goalie coach especially. The Aces hadn't fired me, but playing with my bully, and the hostility, motivated me to bond with Jonas so I could move to the Knights.

"We'll need to tell Stu, too. He might even have ideas on how to do this," Jonas added.

"Okay, so we'll tell Stu first, then finalize our plan. Next, you can talk to Coach. Probably after you have the pack contract. Then you can come out however Stu thinks is best. Maybe loop in Knights PR and HR at some point." AJ nodded as if making a mental list–which he might be.

"Or however you want. Maybe you want a press conference. Or do an interview," I interjected.

AJ grinned at Grif. "You could do an exclusive interview with the Creative Collective omegas in my building. They can do a photoshoot of you with alpacas in hockey jerseys. Have you seen the picture of Verity in the bathtub with the goldfish? It's up now, and it's *art.*"

I was thinking about a major news outlet, or the SportsBeat reporter that was always around, but that could be fun, too.

Oh, I'd seen the bathtub photo. It would be better without clothes.

"I did, and I love that idea." Grif's brows furrowed. "Are you okay with this? Because it could cause backlash for all of us, not just me."

"We're a pack." Jonas stood and put his arms around Grif. "We got through Dean being outed. And you know, we'll get through this, too. We stand together."

"Absolutely. It'll be better to come out on your own terms." I joined them using our bond to send as much love to him as I could.

"There is one thing we haven't talked about," Jonas said slowly. "How does Verity fit in? She should know *before* you go public, Grif. Especially if you think it might affect anything."

A whimper escaped my throat. "She won't leave us. She wants an omega. And kids. And a dog."

"She can walk the dog, because I'm not," AJ mock-grumbled. "You can't honestly think she won't be okay with it. Verity and Grif were talking about a wedding in a garden. While she might need a moment, she won't leave."

Verity and Grif talked about a *wedding?* Happiness filled my heart. Maybe I could be a flour boy and hand out tiny heart-shaped loaves of sourdough bread to everyone as they waited.

"Hey, it's okay, Jellybean. She'll be fine with it. Also, she, um, she sort of knows." Grif ran his fingers through my hair.

"You told her before us?" Jonas frowned and rubbed his bare chin.

Grif shook his head, letting go of me and plopping down on the couch. "She guessed. At that point, *I* didn't know I was a gamma. I have no idea how she knew."

"Well, she was with you when you reacted the way you did." I joined him on the couch and put my head on his shoulder.

"She *is* fucking smart. Isn't her sister a gamma? Has anyone given any thought to how fucked we're going to be when there are little genius baby omega Veritys running around?" Jonas sandwiched me between him and Grif.

Be still my heart. If only I could be so lucky one day.

I looked over to AJ. "We should be afraid of the super alphas she and AJ could make."

AJ's eyebrows rose. "We're making babies now?"

"She's attracted to you. Or did your dick down her throat not tell you that?" Grif smirked at AJ.

"She sucked your dick? It was the night Grif gave her his jersey, right? I knew it." I grinned at AJ.

AJ shrugged as he sat on the arm of the sectional and put an arm around Grif. "I don't kiss and tell."

Those two *would* have super alphas. She and Jonas would make adorable troublemakers. We were vastly underestimating the kids Verity and Grif would have. The very *tall* kids. All our kids would be amazingly athletic, too.

"While I can't wait to bond with AJ, I want Verity, too. I want to add her to the pack. Bond with her. Raise kids with her. And I *won't* be able to wait until June," Grif told us earnestly. "How can we make that work given she's raising Mercy? Do we move them both in? Though we only have one guest bedroom. While I'm sure Verity won't sleep much in her bed, she should have her own space. Do we keep two households and I alternate where I sleep until Mercy turns eighteen?"

I tried to smooth away the worry in his face with my hand.

"We could give Verity the upstairs guest room and turn the upstairs office into a room for Mercy, even though it doesn't have a bathroom," Jonas offered.

"That would work," Grif added, rubbing his red beard. "Though we'll need some house rules to accommodate a teenager."

Jonas nodded. "Like a *clothes in public* spaces rule."

Ugh. Not that. But if we were housing a teenager, there needed to be boundaries.

"I… I could give up my office for Verity, given it's next to Grif's room, and has a bathroom," AJ said slowly, squeezing Grif's hand.

Oh. That would work.

"You'd give up your office?" Grif gave him a kiss.

"I never use it. I'd rather work out here." AJ shrugged. "I'm okay with her moving in sooner rather than later. Though she does *not* get to redecorate the common spaces in pastels and twinkle lights."

We should do that next time he went on a business trip. We could get lots of throw pillows in cute shapes, whimsical blankets, and a variegated fuzzy rug.

Oooh, and cutesy tea towels and kitchen decor. Maybe a fancy teapot?

The possibilities were endless. Like a pretty stand for her cupcakes and cake pops.

"She needs an enormous bathtub," I added, remembering her lamenting not having a bathtub at her place to drink wine and read books.

"With grips or bars so she can get in and out easily," AJ added.

"What about making her pack?" Jonas eyed AJ.

I raised my hand. "Fuck, yeah."

"Sure. I want Grif to be happy. Also, she's not terrible. I'd have a kid and spend a lifetime with her." AJ shrugged again.

Not terrible? It was difficult not to snort. Those two texted *a lot.* Was AJ in love with her? I mean, he did just say he'd have her babies. I loved how he'd gone from hating Verity to wanting a life with her.

We talked for a while longer, trying to work out as much as we could at this time of night.

"You want to go to bed, Boo-Boo?" AJ murmured, stroking the back of his neck.

I could smell the anxiousness in Grif's scent, feel it in our bond. My dearest husband desperately needed to go to bed–but not with AJ.

Not yet.

"Firstsies." I grinned and tugged on his hand as I stood. "You're mine, Gumdrop. The alphas can wait." Not only did I want my husband, for once, I was the one who knew exactly what he needed.

"If you insist, Jellybean." Grabbing me by the collar of my shirt, Grif pulled me to him and gave me a searing kiss. Wisps of my perfume came out as my blockers wore off.

"Oh, I do." I met his eyes with mine, and tugged on his hand again, sending sheer unbridled lust through the bond.

"Well, then." With a lusty gleam in his eyes, Grif stood.

AJ waved him off. "You know where I am. Jonas and I should go over some stuff, anyway."

"AJ, you should call Verity. Her matchmaking grandma wants her to mate with a pack of doctors. She was hiding from her earlier because obviously, that's not what Verity wants," Grif told him.

Verity mating with people not us? No. I didn't like that idea at all, and I growled a little.

"Same, Dean. A pack entirely of doctors? No." AJ chuckled. "I'll call her."

"We're going to my room tonight." I pushed Grif into my room. Closing the door behind me, I flipped on the switch that lit my room, which was done mostly in red and orange fairy lights. "Shirt off."

I stripped mine off and threw it onto the floor. Then I drew the heavy curtains, closing off the magnificent view of the city my corner room offered me.

"You're in charge tonight, Jellybean?" Grif smirked as he took off his shirt. My bite mark on his pec had faded. Omega bond marks didn't leave a silvery scar like alpha ones, but the bond itself was still there.

"Yes. Well, for now." I grinned as I climbed the ladder that led to my loft nest.

"You want me up here with you?" Grif's voice wavered as he looked up at me.

"Come on." I waved him up. While he sometimes joined me in my nest, it was mostly up at the cabin. Here, we usually fucked–and snuggled–in his room.

This was my safe spot, my cozy, quiet place. I'd decorated my loft nest in the same reds and oranges as my room, but it wasn't tall enough to stand in. Pillows, stuffies, blankets, and things stolen from my packmates filled the loft.

As he climbed up the ladder, I pushed the button on the wall that turned off all the lights but the ones up here. I closed the curtain that blocked it off from the rest of the room. Tugging his hand, I pulled him into the nest with me.

We laid down together, nestling under the soft and cozy blankets. Putting my head on his chest, I ran my fingers through his hair and said nothing. No, as I purred, I let the scents of all my favorite people comfort him, along with the cozy glow of the lights.

I watched as the tension drained out of his face, smelled as his scent changed back to normal, and heard his heart rate slow.

For a long while, we laid there, quiet, bodies entwined. It reminded me of all the times we'd done this as kids–or at university–usually in a blanket fort.

At some point, we stopped making blanket forts. I didn't drag him into a nest with me just for cuddles. We snuggled on the couch or in bed–but that wasn't the same.

This was exactly what he needed tonight. No matter what he called himself, how often we forgot, deep down, he was an omega, and liked snuggly, safe places. Just like I did.

He sighed deeply and looked over at me with his big green eyes. The ones that tugged at my heart that first day we'd played hockey when he almost cried because he didn't know he needed his own gear, unlike the league he'd been playing in. Since his parents hadn't stayed, I'd done what any other small child would do. I took him by the hand, brought him to my mom, and demanded she fix it.

Those eyes that grew wide the first time he came over to my house after practice. His parents were happy that he'd made friends. There was never any jealousy or anger, only a little wistfulness that they couldn't do it themselves. If anything, they were happy my parents could give him so many opportunities.

I'd share *everything* with him.

Those eyes were full of anxiety on the first day of our exclusive prep school, when he'd gotten a 'scholarship' so he could attend with me. I'd later learn that most of the scholarships Grif got to attend school and camps with me or to cover his hockey fees were actually my parents, knowing we needed to stay together.

Those eyes that gleamed when we'd made a top collegiate hockey team together.

Those eyes became misty when we realized that for us both to achieve our PHL dreams, we'd have to be apart for the first time in years.

Those eyes teared up in that private clinic when he'd torn my heart out balefully admitting why he'd taken an entire bottle of heavy-duty blockers in an attempt to get rid of his omega out of fear of being outed like I'd been.

Those eyes lit up as he proposed to me in front of an *entire fucking stadium* after winning the PHL championship for the Hurricanes.

Those eyes melted my soul when we married in front of all our family and friends back in Boston.

My hand cupped his face. His beard softly scratched against my hand. "Feeling better, Gumdrop?"

"Much." He scrunched his nose, face pressing into my hand. "I miss our epic blanket forts."

"Me, too. We *can* still build them. You know, when I awakened my mom said she wasn't surprised, considering how many blanket forts we'd built." My thumb stroked his cheekbone.

We'd build them all the time–to eat an after-practice snack, study for that test, watch movies, make out, or simply try not to be overwhelmed. It was our special place where we could block everyone out.

Grif laughed, his deep chuckle filling the nest. "I don't think you ever told me that."

"We can make a space for you. I know you've always said you didn't need your own nest, but I also know why."

I'd never forget his expression when he awakened. There'd been so much fear. His identity, his future, had been so wrapped up in hockey. He fought against his nature, hard, because he was afraid of what would be left of him if that were stripped away.

He winced, and I pressed my forehead to his as if I could quiet his thoughts.

"It's a good idea. It just makes it all real." He sighed, eyes closing.

"I know. Think about it. We should tell my mom before it goes public. She's always been Team Grif." Also, she had a lot of contacts, and we'd need all the help we could get. That joke about omegas knowing the strangest people was completely true.

"She doesn't know? I mean, we'd never talked about it, but I thought you told her. Especially considering the gifts she gets me." His green eyes blinked as his nose wrinkled in confusion.

"I never told her, but I'm sure she guessed." I planted a kiss on his nose to unwrinkle it.

He turned on his side to face me better, but our legs were still tangled. "True, and you're right. I should tell a parent or two."

"Oh, you should–and Sissy." Because we'd never hear the end of it if he didn't.

"Very true." His arms wrapped around me as he dragged me so I laid on top of him.

"I love you so much. I've been where you are and I'm here for you every step of the way. We all are." Like they'd been there for me.

"Thank you. Because I... I'm so out of sorts, Dean." His voice grew ragged. "I wasn't expecting any of this. What if I come out as an omega but still have health problems? Or if my career ends at its peak? What if–"

My lips met his, trying to both silence him and quell his fears as I poured love through our bond. "One thing at a time, Gumdrop."

He stilled under my kisses, his scent losing its bitter saltiness and once again just being rain with a hint of sweetness.

"Can you purr for me some more?" he asked, snuggling into me. Grif never got his purr.

I gave him a kiss. "Anything for you. Gumdrop. Anything."

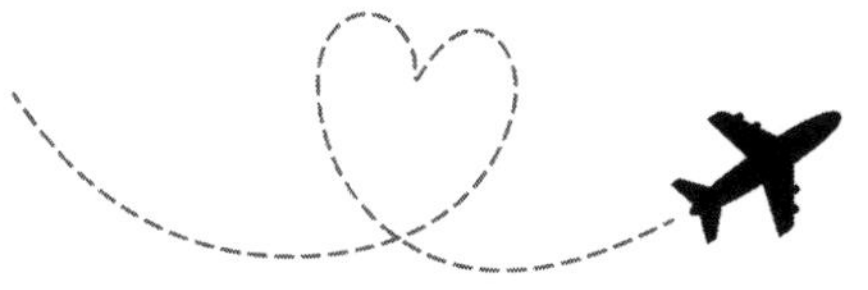

Chapter Ten

Verity

"Go, Grif!" I cheered as I watched Grif score a goal on my tablet. "He's on fire tonight," I told AJ, who I was video chatting with as I sat in a green room at the arena in Portland.

"He's close to breaking some records. Someone's probably going to get a boner tonight. He'll save that for you." AJ grinned at me from the corner of the tablet screen.

"I'm sure he will." I still thought it was a little silly that getting three goals in one game was called a *boner.*

The other team took the puck and raced across the ice, fueled by the need to retaliate. Their forward powered through. Jonas confronted her, and she passed it to someone who smacked it at Dean. Dean dropped into full butterfly, blocking the goal.

"Dean might get a shutout, too." AJ took a lazy sip of beer.

I grew a little wet at the idea of rewarding my guys for playing well when I returned. Perhaps more than once.

My phone buzzed, followed by a picture of Grace and Riley.

Grace

Got snacks? We're at the food court.

Me

Why are you in Portland? I'll meet you when they go warm up.

What a delightful surprise. My attention turned back to my tablet as Dean did a little dance in the goal.

"What do defensemen get? It seems unfair to Jonas," I asked as Jonas came over to Dean and knocked helmets, in what was basically their in-game version of a kiss.

"You want some of that, Princess?" AJ smirked as he took another pull of beer.

"Don't you? How can you limit yourself to Grif when there is so much yumminess in your pack?" After five days, I was beyond horny for my boys. My vibrators didn't compare. Not even the green tentacle one.

He nearly spit out his beer. "I'll leave you to think of something. They'll be away when you get in, but you know where I am if you need me."

"What are you offering, Cow Boy?" My eyebrows waggled.

We'd never addressed him and Grif spit-roasting me in a storeroom. Or him saying that it would be nice to get naked with us.

And him telling me at the greenhouse that he'd take care of me another time.

"Aw, you miss me?" AJ put a hand to his heart.

Mercy

Done with the meeting. Where r u?

"I miss you so, so much, AJ. Hey, I'm being summoned by my sister. Talk to you later." I blew him a kiss and ended the call. Gathering my stuff, I made my way to the locker room.

"Where have you been?" Mercy asked as she applied lipstick in a mirror.

"Watching the Knights game while video chatting with AJ." I hung up my blazer and swapped out my blouse for my *Team Mom* jersey. "Grace and Riley are here."

"I know. There's a seat for you if you want to be with them during some periods." She added sparkles to her eyelashes.

"That's nice. Thank you." I checked my hair in the mirror.

They finished getting ready and went to warm up on the ice. I found Grace, Spencer, her giant omega, Evan, and his teenage sister, Riley, in the food court sitting at a table.

Grace's pretty face lit up when she saw me. She pushed her fries over. "Nacho fries. Oh my god."

"What are you doing in Portland?" Plopping down in a free chair, I leaned my crutch against the table. I took a fry, covered in cheesy goodness.

"Harassing my omega's sister. I mean touring the school for geniuses that my sister-in-law is dean of and visiting our foundation's very first science scholar," Grace told me, her blue-gray eyes dancing.

The Thanukos pack's foundation gave scholarships to talented betas in the sciences. I was pretty sure one of Compass BioTek's secret projects was being housed at said genius academy.

"I had the most interesting conversation with the owner of the Rockland Daredevils." A smile twitched on Spencer's lips. Today, the Greek billionaire wore Mercy's jersey with his wool slacks and expensive shoes.

While Grace had other alphas, most were antisocial, including her scent match, so Spencer was the one who tended to travel with her.

Sometime, I should introduce Spencer and AJ. Certainly, they'd get along.

"Making fake logos and putting them on the internet wasn't my idea." I put my hands up in surrender.

"Naw, it was mine, and they're fire." Riley grinned as she bit the head off of a dinosaur-shaped pizza nugget. Heaps of beaded bracelets lined her wrists.

"I assured him that I wasn't looking to buy his team. Yet." Spencer grinned back. "For some reason, powerful people fear me buying a hockey team, and I have no idea why. It makes me want to do it. Maybe buy more than one."

"Spence. We don't buy things just to piss people off." Grace fake slugged her alpha, who was *much* larger than she was.

"Apparently, people are afraid you'll build a dream team and circumvent the salary budget by also hiring their spouses. Apparently, a lot of MASOs have degrees you'd find useful," I told him, repeating what someone had told me.

"Hmmm. To change the subject, I signed the papers for your funding, but..." Spencer leaned in, and I could detect the notes of concern in his leather scent. "Is this what you want? If you're worried about replacing everything, please don't. We'll help you regardless of whether or not you work for me."

"It's mostly to give me credibility, if that makes sense. You being interested in my flowers means something to people. I talked to Grif about it. He highly suggests you buy the team in Boston. And a place for me to work." I popped another cheesy fry in my mouth.

"Boston? Is that where you all want to settle down after you finish your degree?" Evan asked, taking a sip of his lime whirl. Grace's omega was part of the giant-omega club, and bigger than Dean, but not as big as Grif. Like Riley, he had light brown skin and dark hair.

"I think so." I nodded. "Thanks for catching the person who wrecked my greenhouse. She'll be facing the disciplinary committee," I told Riley.

All I could think of was that it was a drunken dare. Because online passion for hockey aside, Samantha was an excellent student, who other people described as being kind and compassionate.

"Let me at those assholes who talk shit about you online, like those exes of yours that are dating each other." Riley took another slurp of lime soda. Tonight, she wore a Maimers shirt, which had been cropped, shredded, and studded, worn over a fishnet bodysuit, with a studded mini and tall boots.

I grimaced, imagining the trash they were talking about me. "Never dated Derva. We just worked together sometimes. She wasn't the most... conscientious co-worker."

Back when I was in undergrad, I sometimes saw her in Research Circle, which was weird. She must have known people there, though her sister lived here in New York. Derva was always like *it's none of your business.*

"Is everything okay with you and Grif?" Grace asked quietly, her peach and ice cream scent taking on notes of concern.

I took another fry. "We made up, but we still have a lot to talk about when I get back."

"Is there anything you want to talk about with me? Given you're not flying out tonight, we can go to the pizza arcade after the game, and the girls can play games while we have a beer in the corner." Grace offered, as her small hand smoothed back her short blonde hair.

"I'd like nothing better than to get advice from you and Evan on this, but I can't yet." I sighed in defeat. Sure, I'd done a lot of research online. The Omega Center had some great information in its online public archives. Still, Evan worked for the Omega Center as an advocate and Grace was a gamma, they'd be a great resource—but it wasn't my secret to tell.

"Why not?" My brother Creed appeared, wearing a Maimers jersey. He and Grace looked a lot alike. However, my alpha brother towered over her.

"Is this about trying to balance Grif *and* Dean, or is something amiss with the other alphas? I can send you a video. Dean should involve the Center's integration team if this is going where I think it is. They can help," Evan offered, stealing one of Riley's pizza nuggets.

"Maybe?" I stood, leaning on my crutch as I hugged Creed, inhaling his nectarine scent. "What are you doing here?"

"I thought you'd need a hug, so I tagged along. Also, I miss you." His arms stayed tight around me. We were about the same height and build, though he'd bulked up a bit since moving to Rockland to work for Spencer.

"I miss you, too. I'm sorry if I've been quiet." While we texted daily, we didn't talk as much, as I turned more to my guys than to him.

Creed shook his head. "I know you're slammed between Mercy, your PhD, your boys, and modeling. Why were you in a bathtub of fish?"

"It was such a beautiful photo. I love that website," Grace told me.

Ooh, they'd love her. I should introduce them.

"Because they paid me?" I shrugged.

"Am I planning a wedding?" Grace looked smug. My phone buzzed, and I saw she sent me a link to a pin board titled *Verity Wedding Inspo.*

I couldn't help but smile. "Grif said he likes weddings. You basically had my dream wedding, so I trust you to help me execute my wedding vision."

"It'll be so much fun. If you're getting married in the hockey off-season, let me know as soon as you can. It doesn't give me much time. Where were you thinking? Greece, in a field of your lilies?" Grace took a pull from her bottle of beer as she leaned into Spencer.

"Oooh. That's a great idea. I've always wanted a garden wedding. A field of my lilies would be lovely," I agreed, imagining it.

"Considering your research, Greece would be quite fitting. There are many lovely places." Spencer nodded as he had a sip of red wine.

"Absolutely. Were you thinking of a formal reception, or more of a summer picnic, where we could bring in tulle tents and big cushions?" Grace started typing things into her phone.

"I'm up for whatever, as long as there's dancing and good music." I nodded.

"Grace, don't push them. Isn't that fast?" Creed frowned at her.

I shrugged, enjoying the wedding planning conversation. "Part of our fight was we're not moving fast enough."

"I know to you it's practical and makes sense to wait, but as an omega, Dean's going to have quite the time waiting until after Grif. Especially since you don't want to mate Grif until summer." Evan nodded as he took one of Grace's fries.

"I know." I sighed. "Mercy likes them, but she's enjoying it being just the two of us instead of a houseful." What else did we do other than wait or move in?

"That's why the integration team would be useful," Evan pushed, his brown eyes glowing with concern.

Not sure we needed an integration team, which helped out when new members joined a pack.

Creed looked at me and held out his hand. "Come with me to get food?"

I looked up at the giant TVs in the food court and saw that the Maimers were still warming up. "Sure, I have time."

He draped an arm around me as we got in the burger line. "You're really going to stay with Grif? Mate him? Marry him? You talked it out? What happened?"

"We haven't had the big talk, because we wanted it to be in-person. But..." I lowered my voice. "Based on our non-conversation, my earlier hypothesis might be correct. If so, that explains everything."

"Fuck." His look stayed pensive. "It would."

I sighed as I leaned on my crutch. "I was trying not to rush things. But I don't want to take things so slow that they hurt people. Mercy could be amenable to moving in with them. There's a lot to work out."

"That there is. I'm here if you need to talk." He squeezed my shoulder.

Creed placed his order and got his food. Then we started walking back toward everyone else.

"I'm proud of you for getting on the ice with the team the other day," he told me.

"The entire time I worried about falling and getting more injured." I grimaced. "I never used to worry about stuff like that," I replied.

"We're adults. We no longer believe we're invincible," Creed replied as we rejoined the group. "But you can't let it stop you."

"I know. One of these days I might join the mascot on the ice with my snack cannon. I miss skating." Even after I stopped taking lessons and competing with Creed, I'd still skated for fun–and had taught most of my younger siblings how to skate.

Riley's eyes lit up. "Ooh. I want to shoot snacks at people. Is the cannon yours? Can I have it?"

"It's the teams', and not unlike the potato guns Creed and I used to make," I told her. Usually, I shot it from the bench. It had been Sonny the social media manager's idea to shoot pre-packaged snacks instead of T-shirts to go with my *Team Mom* theme.

"What's a potato gun?" Riley asked.

Grace sucked in a breath. "I remember those. We'd shoot them off in the back field. Yes, let's make one."

Evan rubbed his temples, probably imagining the calls he'd get from Riley's school about the aforementioned snack cannon. On the TV screens, I saw the teams skating off as warmups ended.

"Duty calls, but I'll see you all second period?" I gave everyone hugs.

"Perfect," Creed told me.

"You can talk to me, promise," Grace whispered as she hugged me tight.

"I know." I was grateful that even though we hadn't grown up together, that Grace and I had easily slipped into sisterly roles.

Soon enough, we'd have a *lot* to talk about.

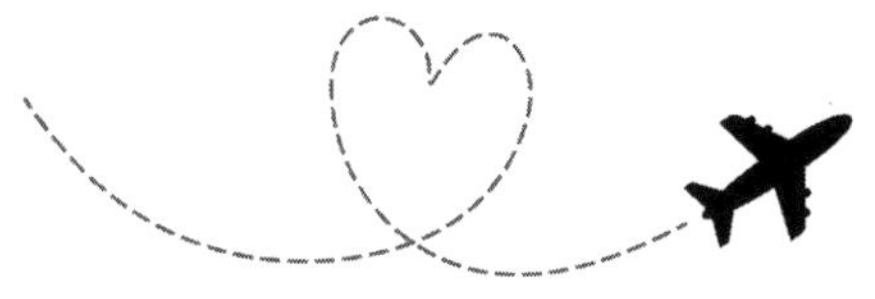

Chapter Eleven

Grif

"Thank you for telling me, Grif," Stu said as I sat across from him in a stiff chair in his office at Venture Management, in-between Jonas and Dean.

My heart didn't unclench. I'd done it. I'd told Stu my secret in hopes he could keep my career from being completely fucked.

Stu was an older alpha and no-nonsense, his suit well-made but understated. The walls hung with pictures of his high-profile clients, awards, and signed memorabilia.

"Can you spin it like you did with Dean? Omega goalies make sense. The team protects the goalie. Grif plays a position even betas are wary of." Jonas rubbed his bare chin.

"I'll draw up a plan." Stu nodded and made a note of it on his laptop. "Meanwhile, you might want to familiarize yourself with what to do if you're outed."

"Do you think it's a possibility?" I frowned. The Omega Center had a list, which had really helped Dean after fucking Beau Bachman outed him.

"For all we know, Chet is aware. Being prepared won't hurt. Grif, I'd also love to see what we can do to rehab your image." He took the tablet back.

"*Chet* tarnished my image?" My nose wrinkled. Why would he even do that? My success meant his success.

"I'm sorry to say that he did. Though everyone loves all this with you and your girl–and your and Dean's playoff win story. And you making All-Stars as a fan vote? Yes, they all adore you. However, I have questions about your girl. Especially since Chet used to be her agent," Stu replied, eyebrows rising.

"She was repped by Dave over at Star for sports. She has a different agent for modeling." I'd learned that when I tried to find her.

"Before that."

I frowned, recalling what she'd said in Boston. "Oh, you're right. She was with someone else. She fired him because he was fucking with her career."

That made sense. She probably signed with him five or six years ago, maybe longer, when he was approaching a lot of young collegiate players, hoping some of them would make it big.

What time was it in Hawai'i? They'd arrived yesterday.

Me

Were you ever represented by Chet Chesterton?

Verity

He was my first agent. My old coach introduced me. The one who told people I didn't model. He was a huge mistake and helped fuel the haters.

That's not Dean and Jonas' agent, right?

I read them the text.

Me

No. He was my old agent.

"Well, that solves the mystery as to why Chet didn't want you with her. Why doesn't it surprise me that Chet is friends with her douchey ex-coach?" Jonas scrolled through his phone.

"Shit." My heart clenched. I didn't like that I caused my kitten problems.

Stu continued, "Chet keeps trying to convince Bunty you're still his client. He's trying to fuck things up with your sponsors. You might need a restraining order."

"Given the threatening texts he's sent me, maybe. What if we can't do this with the Knights? I mean, they didn't want me, anyway. Why give me a pack contract?" My shoulders slumped as feelings of worthlessness coursed through me.

Dean squeezed my hand, sending love through the bond.

"According to Bunty, they wanted you. But the demands were ridiculous, so he turned them down. The second, third, and fourth, too." Stu leaned forward on his desk, entwining his fingers.

My mind reeled as I took this in. "What? They never said they'd only take me if I won the Hurricanes the title?"

"He said it, sort of. It was a joke in the sense that it would be much easier to justify your salary demands if you won the championship. In actuality, he was trying to get you to go down in your asking," Stu told me.

"I don't remember what I was asking, but I'm pretty sure it was standard. Shouldn't Chet have told me if it was too much?" My eyebrows knitted.

"Chet's been lying to you." Stu's look grew grim. "He was the one that told you that the Knights never meant it seriously and only signed you because it made the news?"

"Yeah, and why I'm being paid less than I was on the Hurricanes." My chest clenched.

"Are you saying Grif could have been a Knight years earlier, but Chet was making extreme salary demands Grif never asked for?" Jonas squeezed my shoulder.

Stu nodded. "Precisely. That's also why you don't have many sponsors. He asks too much or for strange things, giving you a reputation of being hard to work with."

"Fuck. I could have what?" My heart split in half. Those last two years had been so hard.

Dean sent more love through the bond. "You're a Knight now. And you have a championship ring."

But I couldn't get that time *back.*

"So, the team wanted me. And there was no hesitation. They didn't take me only because I went public with why I was winning?" It grew hard to breathe. Chet *robbed* me of time I could have been with my pack.

Jonas took my hand. "We're right here."

"It surprised the shit out of Bunty when you did that because he'd forgotten he said it. He loved the PR spin on it. You're a solid player. It came down to cost," he explained. Teams had player budgets and got fined if they went over.

"Then why was there so much pressure on him at the beginning of the season, to be *Finals Grif* every game?" Dean frowned at Stu.

"Hockey is a business." Stu shrugged. "They want a return on their investment. There's always been some hesitation because you're a beta enforcer. That's pure designation bias, considering you get the job done. Everything's fine now. Bunty's happy with you."

"I'm glad. But why would Chet do that?" I raked my hair with my hand. "I don't understand." It seemed counterproductive.

Stu exhaled heavily. "That boy's not right. Like when he fucked up a trade for a client, and the client dropped him, then sued for damages. When asked, Chet said *I felt like it.* It's no secret that his dad does a lot of cleaning up for him. Chet started his own agency because he got kicked out of the one he worked for and the other big firms didn't want him. Not that it worked out. It's now just himself. He doesn't even have an office anymore. He works out of the home his wife owns."

Chet had a *wife?* Also, he'd told me he was branching out on his own because it was best for his clients. Not because he'd gotten fired.

"That's insane," Dean breathed. "I'm glad you got out."

"Me, too." This sounded wild.

Stu pushed a tablet across the desk to me. "This is the contract that you signed with the Knights that *Bunty* sent me. Which differs from the one you gave me."

"Oh fuck," Dean breathed, as we looked at it. Especially the amount I was supposed to be paid.

"I don't understand. The team is paying me one amount, but I think I'm getting another? Wouldn't I notice?" I frowned as I looked at the very generous figure.

"How are you getting paid?" Stu asked.

"The same way as always, through the account Chet had me set up years ago. I got a good account because of his family's connection... oh shit. He must have done something." All I could do was stare at the figure.

They were paying me how much? Now, the pressure at the beginning of the season made a lot more sense.

"Notice there's a clause in the contract saying they can't publish your salary. I'd recommend opening a new bank account today. Preferably at one not owned by the Chestertons. Go into HR and get your payment information changed. Make sure whatever automatic payments you have for Chet, and anyone else, are shut off. I've already reached out to the Hurricanes and the sponsors and compared things." Stu's brow furrowed. "I'm so sorry, but you're being robbed."

The realization punched me in the gut. Chet *stole* from me.

"Why? Why would he tell me they didn't really want me? What could he hope to gain if I left the Knights? Why would he steal?" I couldn't wrap my head around it. How could he even get away with this?

He shouldn't be able to fake contracts and steal my money, even if his family-owned banks.

"I mean, why was he pressuring you to go to Mexico City when you wanted to be near *us*? Nothing he does ever makes sense." Dean leaned into me.

"The Tigres like their players giant. If I didn't want to get closer to you, it could have been a good career move for me," I replied. That was when I'd started second-guessing my career, and my desirability as a player.

"What does he gain from you losing contracts? He makes money when you do. Though someone from a family like him might not need the money. Chet has a giant sense of entitlement and little sense of reality." Stu shook his balding head.

This was all too much. My eyes closed and my chest shuddered. Dean pulled me close.

"When did it start?" My voice shook as my eyes opened.

"After you signed back on with the Hurricanes after your rookie contract was up. It was when it started happening with sponsors, too." Stu's look grew intense. "You need to hire a lawyer and go after him. I know a good one that you can meet with today."

"Ok. That seems good." I'd trusted Chet. Defended him. Stayed with him.

For what?

"Shit, I wonder if that's why those trades fell through. I really thought the Jersey one would work," Jonas muttered.

That was one of the many times I'd been so close to getting near them only for it to not work last minute.

"It wouldn't surprise me. It felt like what he did with that fútbol player, Freddie something-or-other, when his trade fell through. That's only because I know the agent negotiating for the other player. Though he's still with Chet and didn't take him to court like that other player he repped," Stu added as he took his tablet back.

"Freddie is one of Chet's." I remembered the hurt, the animosity, between Freddie and Verity. She'd probably brought him on. Chet used to pressure me to refer my friends.

"Are you okay with this? Taking legal action against Chet?" Jonas asked, brows furrowing with worry.

"I... I guess. More to stop him from doing it to others than anything." It wasn't about the money. He deserved punishment for his wrongdoings.

Chet had also robbed me of my self-worth. Did he keep it low so that I'd stay?

"Great. People like him give agents a bad name." Stu picked up the phone.

"Wait, what was the other reason you called us in here?" I asked. Hopefully, it was good news, unlike this mess.

Stu beamed. "Congratulations, boys, you have a pack contract. Now, let's see if we can get this asshole out of agenting for good so he doesn't hurt anyone else."

Chapter Twelve

AJ

Taking my rolling suitcase out of the overhead compartment, I walked off the airplane. I'd cultivated a lot of clients in other places so that I'd have reasons to see Grif.

I hadn't heard much from the pack today, other than they were meeting with Stu, and that tonight's game was canceled because of a storm. This was shaping up to be a stormy winter.

Everything was fine, I was sure. I trusted Jonas. While sometimes he was a little pushy, he knew what he was doing regarding the pack, which was why he was head alpha.

Sure, I could do it. But he liked it, and I wasn't about to fight him for it.

I had gotten a picture of Verity at a beautiful waterfall in Hawai'i. Yeah, no snow storms there.

Grif

Text me when you get in, I'm in the car lot.

Aww. How sweet. I'd planned on ordering a car.

Me

Thank you. On my way. Hungry?

Grif

Absolutely. See you soon.

I found my way to the pickup spot, wrapping my jacket around me against the January cold. Though the storm affecting the game wasn't anywhere near New York.

Grif's sports car stopped in front of me and the window rolled down. "Hey, good looking, need a ride?"

"Hey, Boo-Boo." I tossed my suitcase, briefcase, and jacket in the tiny trunk and then climbed into the front seat. "Thanks for getting me. Sorry, the game was canceled." Kissing him, I put on my seatbelt.

Soft music played in the background. Oooh, he'd turned the seat warmer on.

"It happens. Jonas and Dean are on a date, so I thought maybe we could spend some time together. We, um..." A wide grin broke out across Grif's face, and his scent grew syrupy with happiness. "We got the pack contract."

Elation flooded me. "You did! I... I'm so happy for you."

Finally. I'd been afraid the team wouldn't grant it. They weren't obligated to.

His expression went bashful. "We don't have to bond tonight, but… but we can. Dean and Jonas even offered to stay in a hotel if we wanted some privacy."

"I'd love to. Though I haven't courted you the way I'd wanted. Also, you're going away for a couple of days." Sure, I'd given him some gifts, but there'd been no fancy dates or lavish trips. Time had gotten away from us.

He whimpered. "I… I don't need that. Only you."

Inwardly, I flinched. *Good going, dumbass.* No, if he wanted me to bond with him tonight, I would. We'd make everything work.

I could give him gifts and take him on dates and trips after we bonded, too.

"You have me. Why don't I take you out for a nice dinner, then we'll go home, and I'll show you exactly how much I love you," I crooned, putting my hand on his thigh.

I didn't have to work tomorrow, and he had the day off. So, I could fuck him all night, all day, then take him on a date.

Grif's eyes blew out with desire as we drove away from the airport. "Perfect."

"Would you like to change and go someplace fancy for dinner or as we are?" I asked, thinking of all the places we could go.

"Surprise me." He grinned, eyes on the road.

While Grif navigated New York traffic, he told me all about Chet stealing his money and trying to wreck his career.

My heart dropped. "You're going to sue Chet Chesterton? Be careful."

Our families ran in similar circles. I disliked Chet intensely. He always told his dad on us, saying we didn't like him because he wasn't an alpha.

We didn't like him because he was an asshole and a user who let his dad clean up his messes.

"He should be punished," Grif snapped.

"Yes, he should. It does need to be handled carefully. His family's even more concerned about appearances than mine. Chet's dad always knows people's secrets and how to exploit them." Like who had gambling debts or was cheating.

I scrolled through an app that helped you find last-minute reservations at hotspot restaurants. Oh, there was a reservation *there*? Perfect. We'd go fancy tonight.

"Do you understand what he did to me? I was convinced the Knights didn't want me. That I wasn't a worthwhile player." Grif's voice broke as salty sadness flooded the car.

"I know." Squeezing his knee again, I shot off texts to my dad to warn him, since he did business with the Chestertons. Also, I'd text a few of my friends in case we needed help.

"Stu, the lawyers, and the police have it under control." Grif shot me a confident smile. "Where are we going?"

Police? No. We might need the feds for this. I sent off another text.

"Let's stop at our place to change. I hope you had a nice suit ready for the game that never happened." Because I planned on giving Grif a night he wouldn't forget.

"Dinner was amazing, thank you." Grif sipped his wine as he stared out the window at the city below. Even though it was late, the restaurant was full of well-dressed couples, throuples, and packs, having a nice dinner out.

Skyline was on the top floor of the Stonefeld Manhattan Hotel, with lush place settings and cozy lighting. They specialized in multi-course tasting menus with beverage pairings.

Right now, it was a crème brûlée served with a sweet muscat. We'd had a great evening talking about sports, movies, puzzles–even the podcast I'd listened to on the plane.

"Did you want to do that puzzle house tomorrow? Or would you rather see a movie? I just want to spend time with you." I'd guiltily enjoyed having more of him to myself with Verity away. If she moved in, I'd have him even less.

No. Not if. *When*. The past few days had been a whirlwind of moving my stuff out of my office and painting and decorating it. They'd also started renovating the bathroom and fixing up the guest room upstairs.

Well, hiring people to do it.

I didn't know why they wanted to do everything so quickly. It wasn't as if she'd move in as soon as she returned. After all, she and Grif still needed to talk about a lot of things.

Still, it made them happy. So, why not? It was only money.

"The puzzle house sounds fun." He beamed at me as he took another sip of wine.

This. This was all I'd ever wanted. Tonight, I'd finally bond Grif. My love. My mate.

Our dishes were cleared and they served the last course, a plate of four beautifully presented truffles.

"The mignardise, paired with a vintage port." Brandishing fresh glasses, the server filled them with the dark, sweet liquid. "Enjoy."

Grif took a sugar-coated truffle, biting it in half and closing his eyes, his expression making me hard. "This is delicious. Cranberry."

I tried a cocoa-dusted one. "Cognac. Try?"

As I fed him the remainder of my chocolate, my insides lit on fire when his lips nipped at my fingers.

"Delectable." Grif's gaze smoldered as his eyes met mine.

My cock strained against my pants. *Soon.*

I checked my phone.

Verity

Grif told me about the pack contract. While you don't need my permission, I think you should go for it tonight.

She'd added a few suggestive emojis and a rather graphic meme. Well then.

Me

Oh, I will, Princess. Be jealous.

Verity

I am, Cow Boy. I am.

We finished our truffles, port, and my coffee, then I paid the bill. Taking his arm, we took the elevator downstairs, walked outside, and waited for the valet. He pressed me up against the wall, mouth smashing against mine.

Grif's lips tasted of chocolate and port, the kiss itself laced with a cocktail of desire and passion. My arms wrapped around him as I kissed him back, letting him know my plans for tonight with my tongue.

"Take me home, Alpha," he breathed, breaking it off. He gestured toward the driver's seat when the valet brought our car.

He was letting me drive his precious car? That was his one extravagance and had come with him from Florida. While I had a license, I didn't have my own car. If I needed one, I took our pack's SUV.

When we got home, we went upstairs to our place, which glowed with the fairy lights near the piano that Dean refused to take down.

Pushing him toward my room, my mouth pressed against his. Our clothes came off, leaving a trail to my bedroom at the far end of the hall, and I kicked the door closed.

With a few pushes, I had him naked on my bed. There was no light on, just the city lights streaming in from the windows, which were the entire length of the wall with the balcony.

I grabbed the lube and wipes out of my nightstand. Other instruments of pleasure greeted me. Did I restrain him? Blindfold him? Maybe use some toys.

Later.

"Mine," I growled, straddling him, my cock aching to fill him, my knot swollen and ready. "Mine." I lubed up his ass and worked his hole as my kisses continued. "Mine." My kisses trailed down his jaw to his collarbone, where I nibbled lightly as his hands ran up and down my back. "Mine."

I bit down gently where I planned on marking him. My teeth ached with the need to claim him. Mark him.

Mine.

"I'm all yours, Alpha." Grif melted under me, his sweet arousal permeating the room with his usual rain.

Those words went straight to my cock as I continued to prepare him for me. I lubed up my hard and aching cock. Straddling him, my eyes meeting his, I entered him.

"I love it when you're inside me." His voice grew low and needy, eyes closing.

"Open your eyes when I take you," I ordered as I seated myself all the way inside him.

Grif's eyes opened, and I stared at his face. That handsome face that snared me from across the rink all those years ago. Back when I left my team in Bucharest, where I'd been happy in hopes of actually achieving my PHL dreams and showing my parents I wasn't wasting my time with my *hockey nonsense*.

He hadn't had a beard then. I liked his beard. We'd grown them together one season, but I preferred my goatee.

"Will you be mine? Will you let me bond you right here?" I kissed the spot I'd chosen. "Mark you? Claim you? I love you more than anything."

Even myself.

"I can't imagine spending one more moment without you." Years. I'd been waiting for years for this moment—the moment I made Grif mine.

"Please, Alpha. Make me yours." Grif bent his neck, exposing his throat in beautiful submission.

How did I get to be so lucky?

I bit down on that juncture at his neck and collarbone. A needy whine echoed through the room. My teeth continued to ache and as I bit down all the way, the metallic taste of his blood filled my mouth.

"AJ," he moaned in pleasure, his body writhing under me.

One of my hands held him down. He stilled under my touch. *Good boy.*

Warmth filled me as I continued to bite down, the proteins in my saliva entering his bloodstream through the bite mark, bonding us. That hit me square in the chest, hooking my heart to his, joining our very souls.

A happy growl burst from my throat as I released his flesh.

"You took my bite so good, Boo-Boo." I started lapping at the mark to help heal it, so a silvery mark would be left behind.

Marked and bonded. I'd marked and bonded Grif. Finally.

Sparks of his pleasure, his happiness filled me. *There you are.*

And there he'd stay.

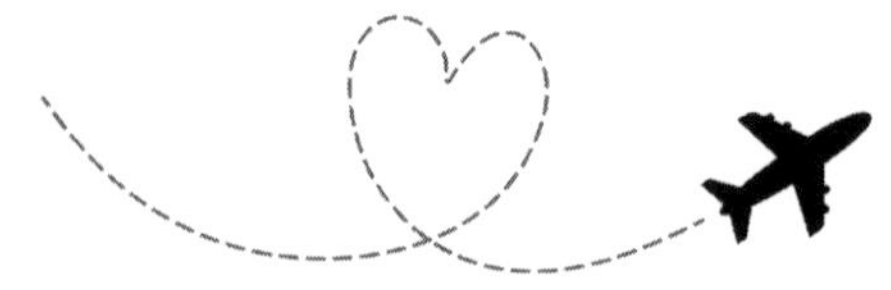

Chapter Thirteen

Grif

His teeth clamped down on my neck. I whimpered, my body aching for him to complete the bite.

He bit down, the bite warm and burning as it rushed through me, setting every cell of my body on fire with pleasure.

"AJ," I moaned, my body writhing with need.

His hand pressed down on me, and I stilled. When I was with him, he was in control. I gave him that because a tiny part of me occasionally needed that dominance, that care.

Sparks of him filled my heart, right next to Dean.

"You took my bite so good, Boo-Boo." He licked the bite as he continued to thrust in and out of me.

The uneasiness brewing inside me for days settled, not unlike when I'd bonded with Dean.

One more thing had been made right with my world.

"You're mine." He stopped licking the bite, eyes on me as his hand wrapped around my throat.

"I was already yours, Pepperjack. And you're mine. My alpha. *Mine.*" My pleasure rose as he continued to fuck me, ride me, and kiss me with his hand still around my throat as the other stroked my chest, my cock.

I gasped.

The need to claim him back consumed me. "Where can I mark you?"

"Right here." AJ pushed my head down to his throat, hard, holding it there as the motion sent another jolt of need and desire right to my cock. "Don't you dare come before I knot you. Claim me. Mark me back."

Oh, I would.

While no harm would come to either of us from a one-sided bond, like when alphas claimed betas, that long-dormant part of me rose up in vengeance, needing to mark him back.

"Mine." I bit down on his neck, my body aching for him. His blood filled my mouth as my desire built.

Knot, my body screamed. *Knot now.*

"Oooh, I felt that. Someone needs to be knotted?" he moaned, my teeth still clamped down on his neck as his pace increased. "Good. Because I'm going to knot you hard. When it deflates, I'm going to have you again and again."

"Yes, please, Alpha," I groaned as his balls slapped against my ass as I licked the bite mark.

AJ withdrew and slammed into me, hard, pushing his knot past the ring of muscles as my pleasure, my world, exploded in a burst of stars. His desire pulsed through the bond as I came all over myself and him.

He pulled me to him, locked in me as he filled my ass with his cum.

For a moment we laid there, curled in each other's arms, breathless. Warmth, reassurance, and possession came through our connection.

Our lips collided, and I put everything into that kiss. How happy I was that things were right between us. How amazed I was to finally be here in this moment with him after everything we'd been through.

Everything *I'd* been through.

"I'm yours," he whispered to me, as we cuddled in the darkness, locked together. "No matter what happens, I'm yours forever."

Chapter Fourteen

Jonas

A buzzing sound wormed its way into the edges of my consciousness. With a grunt, I rolled over into the warmth Dean offered and drifted off to sleep.

The buzzing sound didn't stop. My eyes cracked open. The green glow of the clock told me that it was 3:32 am. Ugh. Fatigue pressed down on me. Dean and I had gotten back from our date late in order to give AJ and Grif space.

With everything Dean was getting through his bond with Grif, he'd also wanted attention. Lots of attention. So really, I'd just gotten to sleep.

I worked up the energy to roll over to see who it was, because if they didn't stop calling, it must be important.

Shit. Was it my sister?

Little Alpha flashed up on the screen along with how many times she'd called and texted.

Verity

I know it's late, but I need you.

Please.

That wrenched my heart. Fuck.

Grabbing my phone, I tossed on a pair of shorts and crept out to the dark living room so I wouldn't disturb Dean, who'd passed out on the bed like a starfish. From the sounds–and smells–in the hallway, Grif, and AJ were still at it and had moved to Grif's room.

Maybe now that they'd bonded, AJ would feel like he was truly part of the pack. Sometimes, I wondered if he was only here for Grif, which was fine. Dean and I valued him, too. We just didn't show it the way Grif did.

Slumping on the couch, leaving the room dark, I pressed redial.

"Jonas." Her voice broke.

"What's wrong, Sweetheart?" My eyes closed as I rested on one of the many cushions littering the sectional. We'd put away the Christmas cushions, but plenty remained. I think they multiplied when no one was looking.

"I'm so scared for Grif, and I can't help but feel like all this with Chet is partially my fault. After all, he hates me. Still, I'm not sure

I can do this again. It's been riding me all afternoon and evening." Her voice shook. "I need you."

"I'm right here." My brain had trouble processing her rapid and panicked words.

One thing was evident–my little alpha had come to me. *Me.*

Peeling myself up off the couch, I let myself onto the patio, so the snow and cold could wake my ass up and I could be of use to her.

"It'll be okay," I soothed, leaning against the freezing cold railing. The snow wasn't coming down hard. It was more refreshing than shocking and reminded me of my youth.

"But will it?" Her voice cracked.

My heart shattered. "It will. You did the right thing by calling me. Sorry it took so long for my ass to wake up. We're *not* better off without you. You leaving won't make anything better. In this pack we don't run from our problems, we talk them out like fucking grownups."

Did I forget anything?

Her breathing went ragged. "Okay."

"Breathe, Sweetheart. Breathe with me." Closing my eyes, I lead her through some breathing to calm her ass down. She couldn't tell me what was wrong if she was sobbing too hard to speak. "Better?"

"Thank you." Her voice shook a little. "I... I'm scared. How do we protect them?"

"It's okay to be scared. Now, walk me through everything again. Please?" I returned inside and got some water from the fridge.

"I don't want Grif to go through what I did when I fired my coach—or Chet. It was awful. Chet harassed me so much. Not to mention, he riled up a lot of people when I got Coach fired. He came after me again when I didn't go pro. Said I was ruining my life and if I came back to him, he'd fix my career." Her words got a bit garbled as she sniffed.

"Chet harassed you, too? Though it makes sense, given they were friends." I took a drink of water as I stood barefoot in the dark kitchen. Fuck, he was such an asshole.

"Everyone harassed me. Now it's happening again. The texts don't stop. Now, the friends of the girl who wrecked my greenhouse are all over the internet accusing me of ruining her life. It's going to happen to Grif, too. Chet's rich, so nothing will happen to him. I hate that people get away with awful things because of their money and power." Her voice grew angry.

"Me, too. I get it now. I'm sorry I haven't done more about your phone haters. We'll protect Grif, okay? None of this is your fault. I wish I were there to hold you." Regret shot through me. I hadn't even thought about all that. How this might be for her.

I should have fucking done something sooner. She'd been getting these texts for weeks and all I did was have her document and block them.

"We'll win against Chet. We'll protect everyone. It won't be like it was. Promise. We're stronger together. Three alphas can protect better than two, right?" I tried appealing to her alpha instincts as I leaned against the counter and had another sip of water.

"Yes."

"That's my girl," I praised. If she were here, I'd fuck her good. Though I'd probably need to put her over my knee first to get her out of her head so she could relax. "We're stronger together."

"Yes. We're stronger together, Alpha Jonas," she assured. "And we don't let the assholes win."

I couldn't help but smile. *Alpha Jonas.* She was feeling better.

"I'm proud of you." We talked a while longer, and she seemed to relax with every word. "Do you need me to stay on the phone while you fall asleep?" I suppressed a yawn.

"I'm supposed to be getting ready to go dancing. Mercy and Kaiko became friends with one of the Hawai'i rookies at all-rookie camp over the summer. He's been taking them to all the best spots today. I think he likes Kaiko. They want me to go out with them," she told me.

"That sounds good. Put on a cute dress, have a drink, dance. Everything will be okay," I assured her as I finished my water.

"I hope so. But I won't drink at the club since I need to keep an eye on them. Maybe Rusty or some others will still be awake when we get back," she replied.

"That sounds like a good plan. Rusty's safe to drink with."

"Thank you. I feel better now. I... I miss you." Her voice went soft.

"I miss you, too. Only a few more days until you come back." Once again, I wished she was here so I could hold her.

"Can't wait. I... I love you."

She did? Those three words hit me in the heart.

"Sweet Girl, I love you, too. I'll talk to you tomorrow." I put my glass in the sink. Really, I should put it in the dishwasher, but it needed to be emptied, and I didn't want to do that right now. Instead, I filled it back up and brought it into my room.

"Talk to you tomorrow." She ended the call.

I returned to bed. Putting the glass of water on the nightstand, I snuggled into Dean, who didn't even move–and took up most of the bed.

Fuck. I needed to take care of my little alpha better. Because while I knew Grif and Dean wanted to bond with her, I think I did, too.

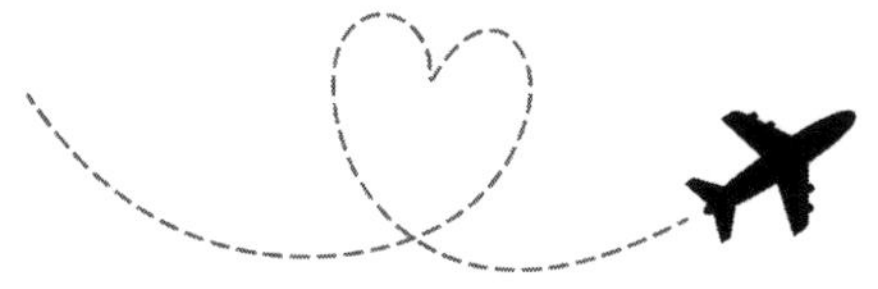

Chapter Fifteen

Grif

"Hey, Sleepy-Boo, going to stay in bed all day?" A playful voice teased me into wakefulness.

"Mmmm, come back to bed, Pepperjack." Eyes still closed, my hand tapped the empty and cold spot beside me.

"I have coffee." The bed shifted as AJ sat down next to me, his vetiver scent teasing my nose.

Eyes opening, I focused on the steaming mug in his hands. My gaze lingered on his bare, muscular chest and how low he wore his cotton shorts. "Thanks for the coffee, but I'll take some of that."

AJ grinned, joy and lust coming through our bond. He set the mug on the nightstand. Right, we were in my room.

"Later. I'm making you food." His look smoldered in promise.

"Two meals made by you in one day? Lucky me." I propped myself up on one elbow, eyeing him. Pretty sure he was bare under those shorts. His body was just as fit as when he'd played professionally.

"A sandwich at five am doesn't count as a meal. But we had quite the night." More lust came through the bond as his eyes glimmered.

"That we did." So much that we'd come to my room in the middle of the night. Lust hung in the air. Scents were getting more pronounced, but only a little. I hadn't been lying when I'd told Verity I'd had one too many pucks to the face.

He leaned in and gave me a kiss, his lips tasting of coffee. "Make sure you put pants on. There are contractors renovating the bathroom, and deliveries and shit going on."

"Oh, right." The world's fastest bathroom renovations were in full swing. I'd let Dean take charge of that because he enjoyed decorating.

AJ left, and for a moment, I lounged in bed, sipping my coffee. It had been a long time since anyone brought me coffee in bed.

I pulled on some sweats and came out to the kitchen. AJ had a hockey-themed apron on as he cooked bacon.

Kissing him, I poured myself some more coffee. "This is where I like my alphas, in the kitchen."

He swatted my ass with a potholder. "Go get Dean and Jonas, please? They're upstairs."

Coffee in hand, I walked up the staircase in the corner of the living room. Bags, boxes, furniture, and pails of paint filled the landing, the small, open, sunken living area, and the hall.

I walked into the upstairs guest room, which had been transformed. The walls were dark green, though the built-in bookshelves on both sides of the glass door that led to the terrace were white. A little bistro table that hadn't been there before sat outside. The chairs had green pillows with mountains on them. The room had green and brown accents, including the furry rug on the hardwood floor. Jonas was on the rug, putting a bed together.

One wall was now a giant black and white forest scene, which Dean currently highlighted with different colors.

"These are Mercy's favorite colors. At least according to all the *shop with me* and *decorate my room* videos she has on social media," Dean told me as he continued to dab color onto the wall with his paintbrush.

"You stalked a teenager on social media to make her room? Isn't that creepy?" I took another sip. It did look nice.

Dean snorted as he dipped his brush in more green paint. "It's her public social media. Also, you've been over to their place tons of times and all you could tell me was that she doesn't like pastels, enjoys pizza, and is fond of nail polish and crafting."

"I'm dating Verity, not her." I shrugged. Those were all important details.

"Did you paint that?" I wasn't sure where that forest was, but it was spectacular.

"That's one of Mercy's photos. She's quite good, isn't she?" Dean didn't turn, continuing to dab a color on the wall.

Jonas grinned at me as he screwed the headboard into the frame. "Tough night?"

"It was amazing. Thanks for giving us space." I wasn't sure what time they'd gotten in, but it was pretty late.

"I'm so happy for you two." Jonas continued to work.

Dean looked over from painting. "Me too."

"Thanks. Oh. AJ says food is almost ready." I took another sip of my coffee.

"Can you help me get this done? The delivery people will bring the mattresses later today," Jonas asked.

Putting down my coffee, I helped him put together the bed while Dean cleaned up his paints.

We joined AJ at the glass dining room table, which was laden with delicious-smelling food. Someone had opened the curtains to reveal our incredible view.

"Oh, you made shakshuka." I grabbed a plate and dug into the egg dish.

"I know how much you like it. There's more coffee if anyone wants any." Giving me a kiss, AJ sat beside me, his foot snagging mine under the table.

"Thanks, AJ," Jonas told him. "Again, so happy for you two."

AJ pulled me to him with one arm. "Me, too. We'll have to wait to register the bond, but I have a mate agreement drafted for you to review."

We had to wait because registering was for alpha-omega pairs.

"I'd like that." It was pretty common to have some sort of mate agreement, especially among designations beyond alpha and omega. It added an extra level of legal protection.

AJ squeezed my hand.

"There's been so much waiting," I told them. "Now I feel like we can finally move forward." Even though yesterday had sent my mind reeling, some of it was freeing, too.

"Me, too. Anyone talk to Verity recently? I got yelled at by Rusty this morning." Dean drank his matcha latte.

"Isn't it barely morning in Hawai'i?" AJ took a sip of espresso, eyebrows raising.

"It was like four am there when she called me. Wanted to know what we did to Verity. They were playing drinking games last night." Dean frowned over his oversized mug shaped like a croissant.

"It's *us* who did something? She's not mad that Grif and I mated, is she? I mean, she texted me and told me to go for it." AJ took a bite of buttered toast.

"What, no?" I gave him a reassuring kiss.

"Has anyone given any thought to how all this might impact her, given everything she's been through in the past?" Jonas replied slowly. "How crazy fans trashing her greenhouse and months of hateful texts might be affecting her? That maybe hugs and promises to get her a new number aren't enough? Chet was her first agent and was an asshole to her. Now we're going after him legally–and some of his actions could be because of your relationship with *her*."

"Oh." My heart dropped. I'd been so into my own feelings about Chet that I didn't consider that hers were just as valid.

Me

I love you with all my heart. It'll be okay.

"Well, if she needs to stay over to make sure we're safe at night, I'm okay with that. I volunteer my bed since her room isn't done." Dean grinned as he finished his eggs.

"Might be a good idea. Any plans for the day?" Jonas took a drink of coffee.

"Grif and I are going on a date tonight. I got us reservations at the puzzle house." AJ squeezed my hand, and I squeezed it back.

I'd been wanting to go to a puzzle house for a while. Each room had a mystery to solve. At the end, there was food and drinks, sometimes dancing or a show, depending on the theme.

"After the mattresses come and the contractors leave, Jonas and I are going back to Blankets and Beyond. Want to come?" Dean asked me.

"If I have time, yes. Some flannel sheets and an extra cozy comforter would be nice. I've been living with mild winters for way too long," I admitted. New pillows and a soft blanket might be on my list, too.

"Sounds like a good idea. We're in for a big snowstorm. I'll make sure the main supplies are topped off in case we get snowed in," AJ added. "Jonas, do we need anything?"

Ugh, snowstorms. Something I hadn't missed. As kids, they were great. Adults, not so much.

"I think we're good. We have flashlights, batteries, generator fuel, and candles," Jonas replied.

"If anyone needs their tux cleaned for the fundraising gala for the Squire Foundation, please leave them in the coat closet so I can take them in the weekly run," AJ told us. "Grif, do you need help with necklace shopping for Verity? I already got shoes for her dress."

"I've got it." Why did he keep getting her shoes? That wasn't a bad thing. I just didn't understand it. Like why they were going to such lengths to fix the ruined dress.

But I'm sure it would be well worth it when I saw her at the gala.

Chapter Sixteen

Verity

I sat in the back of the chartered bus in the hotel parking lot. My head throbbed, and exhaustion pressed down on me.

Getting only a couple hours of sleep after a night of drinking would do that.

I sipped my chai latte from my travel mug, which was pink, and said *what the fucculent* on it. It had been a Christmas gift. While I didn't get drunk, I'd been feeling super good when I'd finally gone to my room around four am.

Mercy sat with Kaiko and Jack, all looking chipper in matching Maimers tracksuits. We'd gotten back from the club around two.

I was the one who decided to afterparty in Rusty's room after getting a bad text about how I should die like my plants.

How much more of this could I take?

Rusty took a seat next to me on the bus, in her matching sweats, holding a Maimers travel mug.

She eyed me. "How the fuck do you look so awake?"

"It's my makeup. A trick I learned in modeling," I replied, taking another sip. "I can send you a link to what I use and give you a tutorial. It's industrial strength and waterproof."

Rusty toasted me with her mug. "I'd love that. I'm *not* playing drinking games with you anymore. When I woke up, I was still drunk."

Putting my travel mug between my knees, I rummaged through my backpack. "I feel like shit."

"Has Mercy ever seen you drunk?" She laughed, lowering her voice.

"No. She hasn't even seen me tipsy, well, until last night. While she's seen me hungover a couple times, I'm not sure she knew it." I was always careful about that. I was about as inexperienced at drinking as I was with sex.

What the parents didn't know didn't piss them off.

I pulled out my first aid bag. "Let's see, I have hydrogels, vitamin shots, hangover helper, and headache powder–which works better than pills for hangovers." I leaned in. "I have Sobrex if you need it. But don't tell. I don't want to become the team supplier."

It was the same thing Jonas had given me after Dean and I had gone to Margarita Manis. I had them because one of these days,

Mercy was going to get shit-faced drunk and not know what to do about it.

"Hangover helper? I haven't used that in ages. I'll take that and a vitamin shot. I've got hydrogels." She patted her bag.

I doled them out. "I have more if you need them. The campus clinic has baskets of them. Thank you for letting me hang out with you. I appreciate it."

"Anytime," she told me.

Ash caught my eye and asked for a vitamin shot. I tossed him one of the little bottles and then stuffed the bag in my backpack. He'd had a great time at the club and hadn't come back with the rest of us.

"What *did* your guys do to you?" She used the shot to take the pills.

"Them? Nothing. Shit's going down with Grif's old agent. He was my first agent, and it's terrifying." The very thought of Grif going through the vitriol I did made me want to vomit. I closed my eyes and took a breath.

She patted my knee. "It'll be okay. Jonas and AJ can handle it until you get back. I know that doesn't make it easier, but they will. It's nice that you've found such a great pack."

I opened my eyes. "Me, too. It's difficult being far away for so long."

"I miss my pack, too." Rusty took another sip of coffee. "Maybe Grif will share his location with you? That helps me when I'm away. So does getting pictures."

"Oh, I like that idea." I scrolled to text Grif and realized that Jonas had already invited me to join their group on Location Finder. I accepted. Perfect.

The bus took off. We were going to be separated into groups, doing clinics all over the island and then organizing the fan event with the trading cards.

Creed

Everything okay?

I filled him in on what happened. Back in undergrad, Creed had held me when I cried so many times because of the haters.

Jonas picking up the phone last night despite the late hour, had made me so happy. Because I'd been beside myself–and trying to keep it from Mercy and the others.

With Jonas, I could let go. I knew he'd believe me. Help me.

For that, I was grateful.

I had never been somewhere as picturesque as this university. I stood on the outdoor deck of the ice rink where Mercy's group was running their clinics. The ocean stared back at me, the blue waves lapping against the sandy shore. Mercy and company were doing three clinics today: one for the university team, one for a bunch of high schoolers, and an open choreography workshop. Then we'd head back for the fan event.

Because it was so far, a lot of teams did clinics and extra things when they were in Hawai'i.

My phone rang.

"Hey, Jonas." I leaned against the deck railing, letting the breeze kiss my face. "I'm literally staring at the beach right now."

The ocean beckoned. It was *January,* but here, people were wearing bikinis and surfing.

"Hawai'i sure is pretty, isn't it?" he commented.

"Why didn't anyone tell me I could have gone to undergrad here? The university on the big island has a tropical flower program." I took a sip of coffee. Usually, I wasn't a coffee girl, but the snack bar had no chai lattes and I needed caffeine desperately.

"I never would've gone to class," he laughed.

"Me, neither. Thanks for inviting me to your location group." It *had* helped.

"I should've added you last week. I didn't consider how being away from them might affect you and I should have. I'm sorry," Jonas told me.

"Thank you, and it does. Honestly, I never thought about how being away from you would affect me other than missing you." Well, that and being horny. But there are people on the deck and I wanted to keep my end of the convo family-friendly.

"I miss you, too, Sweet Girl."

There he went with his nicknames. It made me want to sit on his pierced dick and stuff his knot into me.

"This is all so new to me. I wasn't expecting to be so torn up inside. It's like something is clawing in my chest." I shuddered a little as I leaned forward more on the railing.

"Because you love them. Also, like I told you in Glitter City, they're yours."

"I haven't gotten that ass tattoo." I laughed.

"You're still ours, right?" There was a tentativeness to his voice I wasn't used to hearing.

"Of course I am," I assured him.

"That's my girl. I'm so fucking proud of you for calling me last night when you needed me," he breathed.

"Are you going to reward me for that?" My voice grew husky as his praise warmed me all the way to my clit.

"Oh, yes. They're going to want your attention so badly when you get back. Don't worry, I'll make time to give you everything you need—then reward you for being so good and brave," he cooed, making me gush.

"What do I need, Sexypants?" Other than his pierced cock and that magic tongue.

"Mmmm, that depends. What you needed last night was very different from what you need right now." His voice became liquid sex.

I walked to the far end of the deck so we wouldn't be overheard—and my arousal wouldn't be smelled. "Oh, yeah?"

"Last night you needed to be put over my knee so badly. I'd spank you to get you out of your head. Then I'd make you come over and over until you passed out. Probably have to gag you so you didn't wake everyone up with your screams," he growled. "After you passed out, I'd hold you all night to keep away the nightmares, then I'd tongue you awake in the morning and knot you in the shower."

Could I have some of that *now?*

I gushed again as arousal flooded me, and I wished I was alone in the hotel so I could play with myself as we talked. "Oh, yes, please."

"Today I'd put our fluffiest feather bed on top of the mattress, then cover it with our softest sheets. I'd light a bunch of candles and put something nice and relaxing in the diffuser. I'd strip you naked and tie you to the bed with silk ties—just tight enough that you feel safe. I wouldn't blindfold you so you can see me. You'd sink right into the softness, and I'd spread you wide and feast on you. If you couldn't take my knot in your pussy, I'd knot your ass. Then I'd hold you close and tell you how amazing you are," he breathed.

"Oh, I want all of that, Alpha Jonas, sir. Please." I closed my eyes on the brink, voice breathless, clit throbbing.

Was it possible to come with only dirty talk?

"Oh, you'd take me so good. Because you're my sweet girl," he breathed. "After we'd take a bubble bath, and I'd rub you down with that warm oil you like."

"Mmmm, and then I'd take care of you with my mouth." I kept my voice low. No one needed to know we were having phone sex.

He groaned. "Oh, yes, take me all in that delicious mouth of yours and swallow me down so you feel better."

Voices interrupted us. It sounded more like an announcement than conversation—and it wasn't from the rink.

"Where are you?" I asked, shifting positions, rubbing my legs together, trying to ease some of my need.

"I'm watching Dean and Grif, who are taking *forever.* Grif needed some flannel sheets and a warmer blanket," he replied. "Also, a shit-ton of new pillows."

"You're in public?" My cheeks burned. Sure, so was I, but I barely said anything. I'd thought he was alone in his bedroom.

Jonas chuckled. "I'm at a *home store.* Everyone here either hopes to go home and be fucked senseless or can't wait to leave so they can fuck someone senseless."

"*Jonas.*" Embarrassment filled me.

"There's a couple of snowstorms coming. Like the kind where the power goes out and you can get snowed in, so make sure you have supplies. What do you need?" he asked.

That was quite the subject change, but that could be why Grif wanted warm blankets.

"That's a good idea. I could use some flannel sheets. Oh, and Grace had this down comforter with a flannel cover on my bed when I was there at Christmas. It was like a cloud. I should get one of those." I hummed. Grace's place had a lot of comforts, like towel warmers and zillion thread count sheets.

"Do you want me to pick some up for you?" he offered.

"Yes, I'd like that, thanks. Let me know what it comes to, and I'll send it over. Can you get a green waffle blanket for Mercy, too? She doesn't like flannel." That would be helpful.

I texted Creed. They had snowstorms in Rockland, right? We'd gotten snow in Research Circle but it wasn't very much—and certainly no one got snowed it.

Me

How do I prepare for a snowstorm?

Hopefully, the heat would be back on by then. Campus housing had texted that the heat was out in our building. We could always get some little heaters.

"Oh, Sweet Girl, you won't be paying me back with money. Mmmm, I could think of so many ways." He spoke in a honeyed voice.

That got me right in my already hot and bothered pussy.

"Tell me more," I practically panted into the phone.

"You could wrap that sweet mouth of yours around my—"

"Are you having phone sex with Verity?" Dean's voice interjected and there were some muffled sounds. "Hi, Little Alpha. What are you wearing?"

Nothing like a little cockblocking from my favorite overzealous omega.

"My very own Maimers tracksuit. I match everyone else." Though, I'd taken off my jacket. "Jonas was going to get some things for me."

"If I get some things for you, can I have a blowjob, too?" He laughed.

There was a scuffle.

"It's me," Jonas replied, taking over. "I was calling because it looks like Chet will be arrested soon. AJ and I will keep them safe. Promise. I wanted to update you myself. It must be difficult for you to face everything like this."

"Thank you. I like being updated. I... I need a picture of them," I blurted, remembering what Rusty had said to me.

"Absolutely. If you need to be around them extra when you get back, we'll make that happen," he told me.

"I think I'd like that, too." I'd figure something out with Mercy.

A moment later, a picture of Grif hitting Dean with a pillow came through and something deep within me settled.

"Thank you," I breathed, a weight lifting off me.

"AJ and I have this until you come back. Trust us, Sweet Girl."

"I trust you." Why did I turn into a pile of goo every time he called me that?

"I love you, and we can talk over everything you need when we get back," he told me.

"Oh, I hope we can do more than talk." I smirked.

"Believe me, we will. See you in a few days."

"Love you." I couldn't wait.

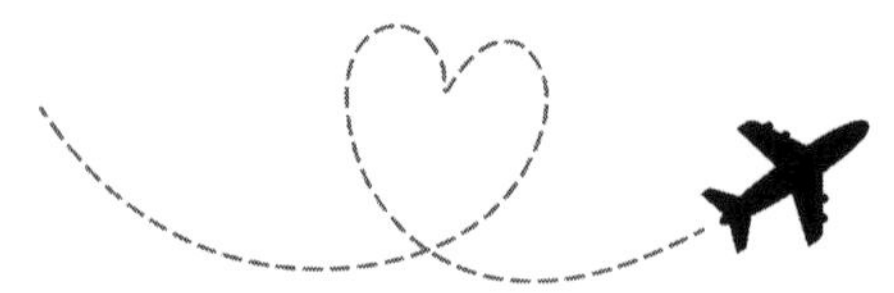

Chapter Seventeen

VERITY

Mercy and I got off the airplane in New York City, the weather clear, and crisp, though the sun was fading with the day. No sign of the impending snowstorm that made my brother send me preparedness videos.

I couldn't wait to sleep in my own bed.

Unfortunately, Grif, Dean, and Jonas were on the road. Worry balled in the pit of my belly because it was just Jonas to protect both of them. Not to mention, Grif and AJ recently bonded.

AJ stood there, waiting for us on the tarmac of the private wing of the airport where the Maimers' jet landed along with some of the Maimer's family members. He was wearing a suit and sunglasses, like always, which *did* things to me.

"Hey." AJ flashed me a big smile, like he was genuinely happy to see me.

"Hey." I bit my lower lip as want for him flared in my core. *So yummy.*

"Oh." Mercy deflated as we grabbed our suitcases. "I thought that since Grif was in Quebec for the makeup game, you'd stay home, and we could cook and watch a movie."

"We were going to cook and watch the hockey game at his place. Would it be okay if AJ came over to our place instead?" My heart squeezed. I should've thought about her first. I'd figured she'd go off with Kaiko and Jack or want some alone time to decompress.

"Or I can play car service and drop you two off. They have another game tomorrow night we can watch," AJ replied, taking my suitcase for me.

Mercy cocked her head as we walked to the familiar SUV. "I could be up for watching the hockey game if we stayed home, and it involved home-cooked food. Can I help cook?"

"Absolutely. We're going to compare kofta recipes," I told her, as I got into the front seat of the SUV.

"Oooh, a cook-off? I'm in. Especially if you're making grandpa's recipe." Mercy was a great sous chef, and decent in the kitchen herself.

"Oh, I am," I replied. Baba's omega dad had taught me to make it when I was little.

AJ loaded our bags in the back and got in. "We'll place a grocery order when we get to your place–but only if it's okay with you, Mercy. I'm not trying to steal her. If you like, I can drop you two off and go home."

"Eh, I should hang out with you anyway since I know you the least of her guys. Do I get an entry, too? I could make those lamb kebabs Riley makes." Mercy was on her phone in the backseat as AJ drove out of the parking lot.

"Only if you make that sauce to go with it." I looked over my shoulder and grinned. It was mostly garlic and Spencer's recipe.

"That's a given." She grinned back.

Our block looked extremely quiet, even for winter break. AJ pulled into our unit's parking space. It was *icy,* rivulets of water cutting through it.

"Everyone's still gone for break?" AJ asked, looking around at how empty it was.

"Yes, though there's not much break left. The heat's supposed to be back on today." I frowned as I checked my texts from campus housing.

"The *heat's* been out?" AJ got our bags out of the back.

"For most of the block. It's all campus housing. Heat's shitty anyway. We can always order some little heaters. Or electric blankets." Mercy shrugged.

"Good idea. I didn't think of electric blankets. We don't need heat, right? That's what blankets and sweaters are for." I texted the resident director for family and pack housing.

Me

Is the heat back on yet?

Ice glazed the front stairs. Water *leaked* out the front door to the building, which ran down the street.

"Princess, this doesn't look good," AJ said as freezing cold air hit us. Ice and water were everywhere–the floor, the walls, and the stairs.

"Shit." Mercy ran up the stairs to our place.

I took a bunch of pictures and sent them to housing, shivering with cold.

"Ver!" Mercy yelled. "Fucking shit, everything's flooded."

My heart dipped. "Oh no."

"Careful. I think a pipe burst." AJ helped me up the icy stairs, which alone were a safety hazard.

I sloshed into our soggy, icy place and rushed to my plants, most of which had cold damage. My automatic watering system had frozen, too. "My plants."

"Where's your breaker? Kitchen?" AJ asked. "Be careful. Don't turn any lights on."

"Yes." My poor plants. Maybe I could save some of them. I put them on the coffee table, then sent more pictures to the housing office.

"Everything's wet. What do we do?" Mercy came out, crestfall-en.

AJ stood in the dim kitchen, wiping off the counter. "Do you have dorm insurance?"

"Yes. I took a video before we left. I always do." My heart fell as I looked around. Everything in the living room was wrecked, from our big couch and TV to the pictures on the wall as water also dripped from the ceiling.

"Good. Before you do anything else, take another to show the damage. Then let's put everything you're taking with you on the counter. I'll get some garbage bags. We might be able to salvage some of your clothes. We'll toss them in the washer. Electronics and anything paper is probably ruined, but that's what insurance is for. I'm guessing you had most of your important electronics with you anyway," AJ said.

"My console." Mercy crouched by the TV and sniffed. "I have a game buddy I take on the road with me. But *my console.*"

"I know, and I'm sorry. We're going to have to work fast because we're losing light. Be careful. You don't want to slip. I turned off the electricity so no one electrocutes themselves," AJ said. "Do you have a lantern?"

I found our emergency lights and then took the videos. I was freezing, feet and legs soaking wet. The kitchen was the least damaged, mostly due to dishes not being paper or fabric. I took my sourdough starter out of the fridge.

My room was the worst, water dripping from the ceiling. Our important documents were in a little water and fireproof safe in my room, so they were fine. Those went in my backpack, along with my jewelry, especially my grandfather's ring.

A lot of the clothes in my dresser were pretty gross, but I put the important things in the garbage bag. My closet was slightly better, but they'd need some special care. Most of my shoes, purses, and anything on the floor were done for.

My books. My poor books. Sure, I had an e-reader, but I loved my paper books, too.

They were only clothes and things.

Still. *My books.*

Though I gulped a little, because most of my clothes and accessories would be expensive to replace. I'd painstakingly accumulated them from modeling jobs, resale sites, sample sales, and years of buying a few quality pieces instead of cheap ones.

My plants in my room didn't fare any better than the ones in the living room. I moved the few I thought I could save into the kitchen.

"What now?" Mercy sniffed, putting a wet trash bag on the counter as I returned to the kitchen with another bag.

"This second? We put everything in my car. We head to a store or two and get you whatever you need. Then we go to the market and get any snacks and food you like, along with the ingredients for dinner. We'll return to my place, where we'll wash everything, make dinner, and watch the game. You both can stay there. It'll be *fine.*" AJ slung an arm around me.

But this was our place. Mine and Mercy's. Our cute place.

"Okay." Mercy shrugged hopelessly. "Normally I'd suggest getting us a fancy hotel and room service, but I'm so over hotels right now. You have room for us?"

"We do, and I understand that. At first, being on the road was exciting, then I just wanted to go home," AJ told her.

Housing

You're back already? I'll send maintenance over in the morning, but this looks bad.

Do you need me to find an empty dorm for you to crash in?

"I don't want to impose. They can find us a dorm." My heart roared in my ears as I shivered again. So much was gone. Our couch. My comfy mattress.

AJ's forehead pressed against mine. "It's not imposing. Seriously. It might be good for you to spend a few days with us, given you and Grif were talking about moving up your timeline. Like a trial run. Also, you've been away."

"Makes sense to me. I don't want to move in with you if you're gross," Mercy replied. "Also, *dorm?* We don't even have pillows and sheets, and I just roomed with you for like two weeks. I want my own room."

While players got their own rooms, when I traveled with the team, I shared hers.

"I'm going to start carrying everything to the car. Be careful, please?" AJ grabbed the bags. "Verity, if any of your high-end leather items have water damage, especially purses and shoes, bring them anyway. We can take them to the leather spa and try to get them rehabbed."

"Thanks. I didn't think of that." I leaned against the counter, the gravity of everything hitting me.

"Are you okay? We might be able to save some of your plants." Mercy wrapped an arm around me.

"We have insurance. It's just with everything..." I sighed.

"Our place was so fucking cute, too." Her shoulders slumped.

"Will you be okay staying with them?" I asked softly. While I liked the idea of being close to my boys, I worried about her comfort.

Mercy rolled her eyes. "Dibs on the guest room, if they have one."

"They do. And of course. I'll..." My cheeks warmed as I remembered Grif telling me I could share his room.

"Play musical beds." Mercy shot me a smirk.

"It makes sense to stay with them momentarily. Living with people tells you so much about someone." I texted housing.

Me

We can crash at my boyfriends' for now.

"I'll order some noise-canceling earplugs for sleeping." She laughed.

"Mercy." I laughed. My phone buzzed again.

Creed

Are you home safe?

I sent a bunch of pictures.

Me

Our place flooded. We'll stay with the guys for a few days.

Creed

Ugh. Sorry. It's probably a good idea. You have a lot to work through.

Me

True.

I'd been texting him a lot about how to move up the bonding timeline while being a responsible guardian to Mercy.

"This all?" AJ said as he carried some of my plants. His limp was more pronounced than usual.

Mercy held up her console. "I'm going to see if I can save this."

"Go for it. If you think of anything, we can try to come back," he said.

I nodded, as I looked around one last time. "We've got a few days until the storm. If it's bad will you be okay with us there, too?"

"Of course that's okay. You'll feel better if you're snowed in *with* them." AJ grinned as I locked up.

"Oh, yeah. Otherwise, she'd be trying to get to them in the snow to make sure they're okay. She was a hot mess in Hawai'i." Mercy snorted, two bags over her shoulder as we made our way down the stairs, her leading the way.

AJ took my arm. "Let's go to the store. I know this is a lot, but you'll feel better after a home-cooked meal."

"That's the last of it." Mercy set bags on the counter of the guys' kitchen, which was littered with sacks and containers.

As was their glass dining room table. The fancy washer in their laundry room hummed away. We'd dropped off our nicer clothes at AJ's favorite dry cleaners. Both of us had things lying all around the living room and dining room to dry. My plants occupied the hall bathroom and the laundry room. My sourdough starter sat by the stove.

When AJ mentioned heading to a store for essentials, I'd thought we'd just go to Swoop, which was a buy-everything-but-still-discount store. You know, where you could buy everything you needed *in one swoop*.

After that, we'd gone to Hardwick's, an extremely upscale department store. While I loved Hardwicks, especially their gourmet food hall, I hadn't been expecting that. Especially since he paid for everything.

We'd also gone to a very cute Middle Eastern grocery that made me miss my grandfather. Baba's omega dad had always been my favorite. Growing up, I'd endure visits to Baba's family in Bayside solely for him. His death a couple of years back had crushed me. He was one of the few people who saw me for me.

"Great. Mercy, let's see your room first." AJ headed upstairs.

I hadn't been upstairs here, and Mercy had only been to their place once when we'd exchanged Christmas presents.

"I still think you need a coat rack next to the shoe rack." Mercy glanced at the elevator as she grabbed her backpack.

"We have a coat closet." AJ shrugged. "Didn't you have one where you grew up?"

I thought for a moment. "We had pegs and cubbies by the door with everyone's names on them. The hall closet was full of sporting equipment."

"A coat closet is so formal. A coat rack is easy to grab and go. Where will I put my umbrellas?" she prodded.

Did Mercy have an umbrella?

"We have a bin for them in the closet. So, the upstairs is a work in progress. We really only use the gym. Well, Jonas uses the library. Though we do like the terrace when it's not freezing," AJ said as we passed a landing full of boxes.

A library? If I promised to be nice to his books, maybe he'd let me use it.

We stood in a living area with a couple of overstuffed couches and chairs, along with a TV and some lamps. A small bar area was in one of the back corners. The carpeting was soft, and the couches were stuffed with pillows in earth tones. It looked over onto the main living area and was bright and airy. Cute art hung on the walls, including a beautiful painting of a cabin in the woods.

"Dean did this area up in the colors he thinks are your favorites," AJ said to Mercy. "If it's not your style, we can fix this however you like. We just wanted to fix up a space so you can have friends over and play video games. We hardly ever use it anyway."

"Oh." She frowned a little and turned to me, questions in her eyes.

I put my hands up in surrender. "This is all them. All I did was mention to Grif that I'd talk to you."

"If I moved in, I could have friends over?" Mercy looked around. It was a pleasant space.

"I mean, it would be your home, too. All your friends are Maimers, right? If anyone's a dick, we'll tell Rusty on them." AJ laughed. "We want you to feel comfortable."

"AJ." My free arm slid around his waist as gratitude filled my chest. I hadn't expected this.

"Not all my friends in New York are Maimers. Though the couple who aren't I've known forever, and Verity would have no problem calling their moms. But this... you thought about me?" Her face lit up. "These *are* my favorite colors."

"It's mostly Dean. Come see what he did to the guest room. Well, your room. The idea wasn't to exile you upstairs, more to give you some privacy," he added.

"Whoa." Mercy looked over at a glass wall, which showed us a beautiful view of the city, a lattice-covered deck with some patio furniture and a barbeque.

"Firepit's on the roof. Yes, you can put a greenhouse or garden there." AJ grinned at me. "Just be nice to the neighbors, since they have rooftop patios, too. We're not the only penthouse up here."

"No topless sunbathing. Got it." Pity.

We entered a spacious room that was not only done in all her favorite colors but also one of her black and white nature photographs, one that was taken on a family vacation. It took up an entire wall. Several plants hung around it, making it feel almost real. There was another *stunning* view and glass double doors led out to a balcony.

"Oh shit, this is beautiful." Mercy walked up to the wall, enthralled. "Who tinted it?"

"Dean. He's not finished. Sorry the room isn't put together. We weren't expecting you to move in so quickly. It's a good thing we started when we did." AJ nodded to the bare bed that had bags from the home store on it.

Blankets and Beyond. Fancy. I usually went to Home Things because of their coupons. Oh, was *that* what they were doing at the home store when Jonas talked dirty to me?

Baskets and shelves filled the closet. It was small for a walk-in, but larger than what we had at our apartment or in the room we'd shared growing up. The freshly painted bathroom featured a shower with beautiful tiles and double shower heads.

"Someone knows my favorite brands?" Mercy stood in the shower holding a shampoo bottle.

"Dean's been stalking your socials to figure out what you like. Grif thinks it's creepy." AJ laughed.

"In this case, it's sweet." Mercy grinned. "This... this is *all* really sweet. Though a lot of work, considering I'll be eighteen in six months."

"It is," I nodded. Clearly, the guys had paid attention.

AJ shrugged as we left the bathroom and went back into the bedroom. "This would be your *home.* The last thing we'd want is for you to feel like you *have* to move out when you turn eighteen. Especially since your birthday is during the off-season. You'll want to relax and see everyone you haven't seen all season. This way you have a base and don't have to worry about finding a new place right away and can go spend a month or two in London, or Rockland, or wherever."

The thoughtfulness overwhelmed me.

"Oh, I... I could go to London for a month or two, couldn't I?" Her eyes got misty as her plum scent went salty with sadness. She *really* missed Dad.

"You could. I want to go for a week or two, to see Dad and the littles. But you could stay for however long you want. Same with Grace. Or even go back to Research Circle. See Hale. Visit Mom in jail." My voice grew soft. She hadn't seen her since last summer, though they talked on the phone sometimes.

Mercy gulped. "Yeah. Dare's trying to get into a summer music program in London. It would be fun to be there together."

"You should do that," AJ said. "We spend a lot of time at Dean's cabin in the summer. There's hiking, a lake, rivers, waterfalls–and a backhouse that you would love. Not to exile you, but so you have your own space."

"Backhouses are great. We lived in Grace's this summer. I like hiking. Also, water." She nodded as she checked out the closet.

"You can stay even after you're eighteen, if you want to save to buy a little starter place you can use as an income property later, instead of renting," AJ added.

"That sounds like a great and very generous option." It wasn't that I didn't want her to go off and live her own life. I didn't want her to feel like I was pushing her out so I could be with the guys. After all, I'd lived at home until May.

"Right. You know rich people things, like investments and property and hiding money and stuff," Mercy poked around, examining the dresser. "Teach me?"

"I only do legal things," he warned.

"Fair." She nodded. "I like the idea of saving up and then buying something. I'd *love* to get a cute little townhouse, like where we live on campus."

"There's so much you can do with them, too. From making each floor into a unit, like where you live, to buying two or three next to each other to make a nice, big place," he told her, eyes gleaming.

Every word out of his mouth made me more in love with him.

"If this is my room, what does Ver's look like? I'm guessing she's downstairs with you?" Mercy put her bag on the desk.

We walked downstairs, and he gave us a quick tour. I already knew where some things were, like the laundry room and the guest bathroom.

"This is the den where we play video games, or where you can watch something if the living room TV is in use." AJ showed us a cozy, windowless room with a big couch, some beanbags, and a big TV.

"There's Jonas and Dean's rooms, of course." AJ pointed to their doors. Dean's was all the way open, giving me a good view of his art corner.

"Okay, if a door is closed, *knock,* especially if it, um, sounds occupied. If it's cracked open, you still might want to knock because we don't always wear clothes," AJ added. "Though generally, a cracked open door means it's okay to enter."

"I think I'll be fine upstairs." Mercy laughed.

"Game room." He showed us another room with a pool table, bar cart, shelves, and shelves of puzzles and board games, and several arcade games.

"Grif's room." He indicated the door next to Dean's. "My room." He pointed to the door at the very end of the hall, then stopped at the door in between. "When I first moved in here after graduating from business school, it was just me. I picked the best room for myself and used the room next to it as my office because going upstairs felt weird. I hardly ever used it. So, um, I cleared it out..." His eyes met mine. "For you. I, um, hope you like it."

My hand went to my heart. "Thank you."

Aww. It was the little things he did, like making sure I had the right shoes and taking my dress to his family's tailor, which got me. Also, having a room where I didn't have to go up and down the stairs made things so much easier for me.

AJ pushed open the door. As we entered, I exhaled sharply. Cream, peach, pink, and gold dominated the room. Recessed lighting illuminated the textured walls, which featured wood paneling, cream wallpaper, and a plush headboard quilted in giant diamond shapes and accented with gold.

Above the bed hung a *chandelier.*

"Wow," Mercy breathed.

"I know you're more of a seafoam and sky-blue girl, but Dean chose these colors for you," he told me.

"I love it." It was so delicate, yet warm and inviting.

My eyes immediately went to the window seat, which was filled with cushions that looked like flowers and curtains that hung on the *outside* of the seat so you could close yourself off from the room and enjoy the view of the city.

Next to it stood a table, with a little rose plant, and an overstuffed chair, with a lamp and a bookcase behind it. A study nook had a built-in desk.

"This entire room is all Dean, with a little help from Grif. My office didn't look like this," he told me.

"You picked this room for your office because of the chandelier, didn't you?" I teased. A chandelier in a bedroom felt a little weird.

The bed was *round* and up on a dais, which made it look almost couch-like. Unmade, oodles of pillows and bags from the home store covered it.

"This is extraordinary." I eyed the giant bed and all the things I could do in it.

"Dean chose the chandelier. Though it was Grif who thought you needed an enormous bed in case you demanded we all sleep together. We don't have a pack bedroom." His look went guilty. "We've never been a puppy pile sort of pack. Also, we go to the cabin for Dean's heats, because well, this is a high rise and New York City has laws. But we could see that you might want us all together if someone has a bad day or something."

Me, too, and not all those ideas were for sleeping. Oh, no. I'd like us all together for other things, too.

"Oh, there are *laws* about heats in high-rises? I mean, it makes sense. But what if you can't afford a second home?" I ran my hands over the bookcase, my heart breaking for all my ruined books.

"Most upscale hotels have heat suites. There are heat hotels, both full-service and self-catering, many of which take insurance. The Omega Centers also have free heat suites which were supposed to be quite nice, but they book fast," AJ explained.

"The closet is huge." Mercy came out of the closet, eyed the wall with a beautiful landscape painting of a garden, and walked back into the closet.

"That feather comforter and flannel sheets you wanted are on there somewhere. Jonas washed some of the things, too," AJ told me, pointing to the bed. The carpet looked soft and plush, though there were a few patterned rugs that all matched.

Oh. Jonas hadn't gotten them for my place, he'd gotten them for *here.*

"They redid your bathroom completely in the world's fastest remodel." AJ led me inside the giant marble bathroom with a big tub that was partially sunken, a gorgeous double sink and vanity area with lots of lights, good mirrors, tons of storage, and a glass shower with a bench in it.

"This bathroom," I breathed. As I explored, I realized that some of the artful decorations in the tub, toilet, and shower areas were railings and non-slip features and the thoughtfulness hit me. There were lots of non-slip rugs, too.

I came back out to the bedroom and entered the walk-in closet. It was big and beautiful, with two separate clothing areas, a dressing table, a pink chaise, and so many built-in drawers and shelves. Opening a few of them, I found places for shoes, accessories, and even a built-in jewelry box.

"Was the closet already like this?" I asked. It was the perfect closet for me.

"Um, mostly. They freshened it up and added stuff, like the pink couch. I haven't looked in the closet in years until yesterday when I hung up your dress." He nodded to the cloth bag hanging by the ornate full-length mirror. "It's drafty and smells weird."

Mercy fiddled around with the different sections of drawers and shelves, and examined the clothes closet area.

"The dress." I unzipped the dress and beaded fabric spilled out. "Oh, AJ."

"I can't wait to see you in it. Grif can't wait to see it draped across his bedroom chair." His breath was warm on my neck as he came up behind me.

An expensive designer dress like this didn't go on the floor.

"It's exquisite, thank you." Should I turn around and kiss him? The urge to kiss him tugged at me.

There was a click and a whoosh of strange-smelling air.

"Shit, I found the secret room," Mercy squealed.

"What?" AJ stood at her shoulder. One section of shelves had swung open.

Zipping up the dress bag, I joined them. The room was small and dark, lit only by the closet light behind us, until Mercy found a switch on the wall. It smelled odd and a bit musty.

A soft glow illuminated the cream-painted room. Taking up most of the room was a tree that was both sculpted into the wall and painted. A circular reading nook resembled a giant knothole. Inside the nook, there was enough room to put a small mattress. The space was cozy, with more shelves and drawers.

"I had no idea this was even here," AJ breathed. "I never toured it. Literally, I got a key card in a box at my graduation dinner after I finished business school. My parents told me that I was moving back to New York and had two weeks to find a job if I didn't want to work for them. I'd already planned on moving back and had been interviewing, but getting a place of my own as a present was a plus."

A *home* for a graduation was an extraordinary present.

It dawned on me. The window seat, the amazing closet, the hidden room. "This was their omega's room. From whoever had this before."

"That makes sense. All I know is that a pack with young children lived here and moved to the suburbs. And, well..." That guilty look took up his face again. "I'd always sort of wondered if my room was the pack bedroom."

"Look, there's a note." Mercy pulled something off the tree. "Welcome to your new home. Even though I understand if you knock this down and rebuild it, I left it for you. I thought you might need some comfort in your new home, with your new pack. Once, I was in your shoes, moving to a new place, to live with my new mates. As exciting as it was, it was a bit unsettling, and this has brought me a lot of comfort over the years. We tore out the carpet and put in wood flooring and repainted the walls. I hit it with a couple of de-scenting bombs, but it might need a few more. Enjoy. Lots of love, Cecelia."

"Oh." I put my hand over my heart. "That is the sweetest note."

"It is. This is amazing," Mercy said, exploring the small space.

"Maybe Grif should have my room." It needed a fluffy rug and some fairy lights. Maybe some poufs.

"Your room? No. Might he like a secret nest in your closet? Possibly. Given how the closet has two distinct sides, and the bathroom has two sinks, the omega shared this room with someone." AJ got close to me again, making warmth creep through me.

"True." I'd be okay with Grif having a nest in my closet if that was something he wanted. Some gammas had nests.

Mercy prowled the small space, frowning. She got out her phone, used the flashlight, and then pressed it on the wall opposite where we came in.

"But wait, there's more," she exclaimed, as another wall popped open. "It's another closet. A dude closet."

"Oh, Grif's? That would be tidy." The scent that hit me when I entered the closet wasn't Grif's rain.

It was AJ's vetiver.

"I think I'm in AJ's closet. Oh, fuck, your room is big. You could build a little office in here, no problem." Mercy's voice sounded muffled.

"Mercy, you shouldn't go into other people's rooms without permission," I told her.

"Okay. Sorry. I got excited." With a shrug, she came back to the little nest room. Mercy shut off the lights, and we all returned to my closet.

"It connected to *my* closet?" AJ rubbed his chin. "Yeah, I had no idea."

"It's quite clever," I replied. There were so many possibilities.

"I'm going to take my stuff upstairs and shower really quick before we cook. My pants are still wet and I smell gross," Mercy told me.

I should do the same. While we'd changed shoes in AJ's car, we hadn't changed pants.

"Start the rice before you go up." As soon as the words were out of my mouth, I put a hand to my face and laughed. "Sorry, not my house. I don't even know if you have a rice cooker."

AJ grinned. "We do. It's on the counter and very fancy. Jonas needed one that sings."

"The singing ones are the best. Kaiko's aunt has one." Mercy left, and I closed the door to the nest.

"I had no idea that it was there–or it connected the rooms," AJ told me. "I have no issue with offering Grif this. We'll probably have to redo it. As cute as that is, I'm not sure he could fit in it. This was clearly a hideaway, not a place to fuck."

"True." It would be a squeeze for me because of my height. It would be a pity to get rid of it. "I promise not to use the expressway to sneak into your room if the door is closed." I grinned and went back into the bedroom. No, *my* bedroom.

I put my crutch down, and took stuff out of the bags, looking for bed sheets.

"Here, let me help you." He found what had been washed and helped me get the mattress pad on. "I'm not willing to share Grif with you. That's a hard boundary."

"Of course. I respect your boundaries, AJ." Confusion shot through me as I tried not to flinch as I recalled what had happened in the storeroom in the arena.

With the mattress pad on, we started with the flannel sheets. I didn't even know they made *round* flannel sheets.

"Thank you. Of course, that's different from me and Grif sharing *you.* I hope you understand that." He tucked in the sheets on his side. "Like that night at the arena."

"Oh." It made me think of something Jonas had said about parts of us that were just for each other. I found the blanket and the fluffy down comforter. There was also a brocade duvet cover that went with the decor and a soft flannel peach and cream one.

I ran my hands over the soft and cozy fabrics. I stood and turned. But AJ was still there. Right there.

Dropping the blankets, I smashed my lips into his, as my hands entwined in his hair.

He didn't move, and my heart thundered in my ears. My head ducked as my cheeks warmed. "I'm sorry, AJ. I think I misunderstood."

AJ's hand cupped my face. "Princess, it's not that I don't want you. Oh, how I want you. I'm a little disappointed we can no longer have a sexy wager in our cook-off because I planned on watching the game with my cock in your mouth."

It was a near growl as his eyes flashed with something primal. His scent grew fierce with arousal. I could feel his hard-on through his suit, which made me rub my thighs together as I imagined how he might feel inside me.

"What makes you think you wouldn't be wearing my thighs as earrings?" I laughed. A sexy wager? I was all-in.

With a turn of his body, I found myself pushed into the closet and backward onto the pink chaise. He straddled me, hands on each side of my face, caging me in.

"The thing is, *Princess*. I'm not like them. In bed, you're *not* my equal. I'm your *king,* and my rule is absolute." Hard-on digging into me. His face hovered inches from mine, desire in his brown eyes.

He continued, "I'll respect your limits, and I'll absolutely make you come when I give you permission, of course. But understand me when I say that they give you pleasure–I *take* it."

Yes, please. The idea of calling him *my king* made me wet.

"Jonas ties me up and makes me come until I pass out. You tie me up and edge me until I break. Grif fucks me against a wall with my hands pinned above my head until my knees turn to jelly. I ride Dean and tell him he's my good omega. Got it," I breathed, as my pussy ached for a cock to fill it. Sure, I'd taken care of business on our trip, but it wasn't the same.

His eyebrows arched. "That mouth. I wasn't kidding when I told Grif you need to be punished more."

I smirked as I gazed into his brown eyes. "I'm yours to punish, my king. Also, reward. Because I can be a most loyal subject."

"You think I'll reward that mouth by putting my cock in it?" His look dared me as his voice grew growly.

"Put it where you wish, my king." Oh, I liked this game. I honestly didn't care where his dick went as long as I got some. I'd suck him so good he'd reward me with a hard fuck.

Or perhaps some tongue to my pussy.

"Someone wants to be dicked, badly. But do you want mine? Or just *a* cock, and I'll suffice. I'm the richest dick in the pack. Also, I'm Grif's alpha. It would be prudent to be on my good side." A hint of hurt tinged in that growl as he pulled back and met my eyes, still caging me with his body.

I cupped his face with my hand. It had a bit of stubble, besides his usual goatee. My thumb caressed his jaw, trying to wipe away that hurt. "I care more about the fact that I like spending time with you. You're not just a convenient dick. Even if Grif were in his room next door, I'd still ask you to rail me right here on the chaise. Might text him and ask if he wants to watch you wreck me, though."

Kissing him, I continued, "I'm not after anything other than your companionship, though I would *love* your cock. It's as magnificent as you are. I *missed* you, AJ. You. Yes, I missed them, but I also missed *you*."

If AJ needed reassurance, I'd give it to him. Though, I didn't know what else to say to let him know my interest was genuine.

"Thank you. I needed to hear you say that." AJ pinned me with his body as his hand fumbled with his belt.

He leaped to his feet; the chaise moving back with me still on it. Before I could react, he whipped the belt around my wrists, tying me to a closet post.

AJ shot me a smug look as he made sure they were secure. I could get out of it. After all, I had brothers and was pretty good at escaping.

But I wouldn't.

My body burned with need. I wanted to be taken on a chaise like I was in a historical novel. *Seduced by the Alpha Duke.* Yep, I'd read that.

AJ closed the closet door and walked toward me with a predatory, almost menacing look, sending shivers of anticipation through me.

Rail me hard and fast, my king.

I opened my legs and tried to look like a stricken actor in a movie. "I yield, my king. You've conquered me. All my lands are yours."

"Oh, yes, you're mine, Princess. As are all your... lands." He smirked, unbuttoning my pants and yanking them off with enough force to pull them off in a single motion, but not enough to damage them.

Giving the pants a shake, he folded them and set them on a shelf. He hung his suit coat up on a hanger.

When he turned, the predatory gleam had returned to his eyes. His gaze ensnared mine as he slowly peeled off my pale green panties, which he tucked into his shirt pocket.

"How wet is that alpha pussy?" AJ buried his face in my folds, my body bucking. "Don't you dare come until I say," he growled, the vibrations of his voice on my clit sending sparks of pleasure through me.

"Yes, my king," I breathed, body shaking.

"Mmmm, so wet." He licked my length, sucking and teasing.

How was I supposed to not come when his touch, his tongue, felt like *this?*

"You're going to want to be quiet. I'm guessing you're a screamer," he told me. "You'll look so beautiful, gagged and blindfolded in my room."

Desire shook me. I wanted to be this king's spoils of war. "I'm yours to plunder, my king."

His chest shuddered as he chuckled into my pussy. AJ pushed back and my body screamed for more as a whimper escaped my lips at being deprived of his tongue.

"This will be quick, but believe me, there will be more." His look seared into me as he stripped off his pants and briefs, putting them on the shelf with everything else, and rolled up the sleeves of his button-down. A scar marred his left knee and leg, probably from whatever surgeries he needed after his hockey injury.

AJ climbed onto the chaise with me, positioning himself between my legs. "Can I have you bare, Princess? I don't have any condoms and I haven't gotten on birth control yet. You know who my only partner is. Tell me if anything hurts your leg. I'm sure it's not in top form after that long flight."

His beautiful dick was *right there.* Hard, with pre-cum dripping from the tip, knot inflated. My tongue licked my upper lip.

"Perfect. I'm on birth control and, well, you live with my partners. Safe word is *fruity little drink.*" I smirked.

Shut up and dick me.

At the same time, I appreciated it.

"We're playing like that?" Amusement twitched on his lips. "Fine. Remember, *don't come* until I say."

Before I could answer, my legs were over his shoulders, as he plunged right into me with one long, forceful stroke.

Pleasure, desire, and the sheer wanting of not being dicked for well over a week overwhelmed me. It took every ounce of self-control to not come at that singular stroke. I had a feeling his punishments would be a lot rougher than when Jonas spanked me on his bench.

"Eyes on me," he ordered.

I took in the magnificent man before me, wishing he was shirtless–and that I could touch.

One of his hands rubbed my clit, making me squirm as he continued to pound me. The chaise thumped into the pole, my ass slamming against his white button-down.

"Princess, you squeeze me so nice and tight. When I do tell you to come, I want you to lock me," he growled.

"Yes, my king." My voice shook. How much longer could I hold on?

From the gleam in his eyes, he knew. His hand closed around my throat as he thrust into me. "You're so beautiful like this. Helpless and tied up, your legs over my shoulders as I pound into you. If only Grif were here to have his cock down your throat."

This dirty talk didn't help. The image of them touching and kissing me together made my insides quiver.

"Not yet." He smacked my ass as my back arched. "Mmmm, you feel so good. You're mine, Princess." The closet filled with his heady vetiver scent, and alpha pheromones, making me shudder with desire and need.

"Yes, my king. I'm yours."

He was as much mine as the others.

Please let me come, I silently begged. The thrusts were so deep that his inflated knot kept brushing my clit.

"Does that greedy pussy of yours take knots, Princess?"

"I've only taken one in my ass." It was a chore to get the words out, as I struggled to keep from coming while keeping my eyes on him.

"That's something I look forward to doing. Knotting that ass as Grif fucks your mouth. We'll work up to the pussy," he told me.

I could see in his eyes that I was *his.* Not just in this *I'm conquering you* moment. What we had differed from what I had with the others, what he had with Grif. But there was no doubt that we had something.

Oh, I'd warm his cock while we watched TV.

"I'm going to come," he growled, pulling almost all the way out. "You can come, too. More than once if you need to, but make sure you lock me good, Princess. I want to see stars."

AJ slammed into me, and the reply died on my lips as I let go, allowing the orgasm I'd been holding back to consume me. It was as violent as it had been on the plane with Grif.

More.

My pussy locked his dick, which spurted warm cum inside me.

He peeled my legs off his shoulders and laid on top of me with a satisfied look on his face. AJ ground his knot against my clit. Another orgasm racked me.

"That's it. Come for your king. Show me that I make you feel just as good as the others. Better even. Your lock feels fucking divine. Do you strangle Grif's dick like this as he squeezes your throat with his giant hand and calls you his good little cum dumpster?" AJ cupped my face with his hand, still grinding against me.

"Yes, my king." The words barely made it out as my body exploded with *another* orgasm. His dirty talk would be the end of me.

AJ pressed his lips to mine, his tongue plundering my mouth as his gyrations ceased. The fact that he was kissing me and we were now here after everything melted me. Those fervent kisses stole my breath, putting it wherever he'd stashed my heart.

My legs wrapped around him, bringing him close, as I kissed him back, trying to show him with my lips that he mattered as much to me as his packmates.

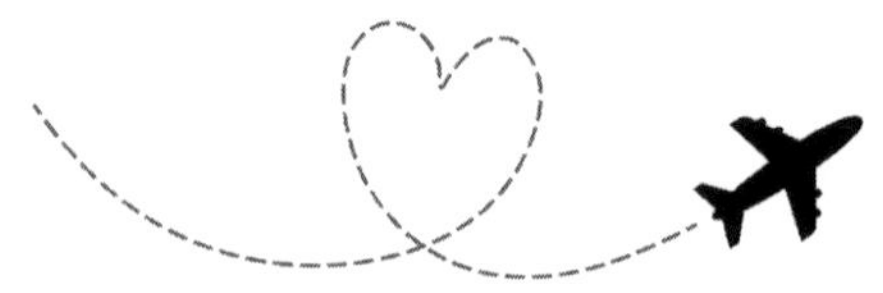

Chapter Eighteen

AJ

Cock buried inside Verity, our lips crashed together. Any doubt I had about our little alpha wanting me for the wrong reasons had dissipated.

It was still a little hard for me to accept that women would want me for anything other than my lineage, name, genetics, and the power and connections my family offered.

While I appreciated the fact that Verity found me attractive, I didn't want that to be the only reason she wanted me. Same with me being convenient.

I yearned to be as important to her as everyone else in the pack. Because I might just be in love with her.

Those words lit me on fire. *I missed you.* I desired her. Not only her beautiful body. No, I craved a place in that giant, kind heart. I ached to see her face light up *for me.* How I wanted to spend nights sitting with her watching sports. I yearned to curl up with her on the couch while waiting for the guys to come home, so I wasn't so lonely when they traveled.

Breaking off the kiss, I fumbled for the belt that restrained her hands, still locked inside her. I'd never been locked by a female alpha before. For a moment, I really had seen stars. My still inflated knot was a little miffed that it wasn't buried inside that warm cunt.

Being locked inside her made me fully understand why alpha females had trouble taking knots. They had to relax in just the right way, while still being able to do what they were made to do.

It made me want to train her to take my knot. Preferably *before* Jonas. No, I wasn't competitive *at all.*

That sweet ass would take my knot later tonight.

My belt fell to the floor, and I rolled us onto our sides, which was difficult on the narrow chaise. I rubbed her hands and wrists, a groan escaping her pouty pink lips.

"That feels good, my king." Her eyes went half-lidded.

She was wearing makeup, though it was a light, natural look. I'd kissed off all her shiny gloss. Did she wear cosmetics because she liked to be made up? Or was it armor much like my own clothing?

A hit of anxiety shot through me as I wondered if she'd still admire me in sweats the way she did when I wore a suit.

"Are you okay, Princess?" I asked. That had been fast and hard.

“Beyond okay. That was amazing,” she breathed as her salt and driftwood scent flared with want.

“Good.” I rubbed her arms and gazed into her eyes. Her lock loosened enough for my cock to slip out, though I was ready to go again.

“We should get dressed and get dinner going.” A sigh escaped her lips. “I don’t want Mercy to wonder where we are.”

“I’m pretty sure she’s not.” Rolling off the chaise, I scooped her up and gave her another kiss on the nose as I moved to the secret door. “We need to shower.”

We should have stopped here and showered first after wading through the water in her apartment instead of going shopping straight away.

“If you want to have a nice soak after the shower to help with any stiffness after the flight, you should do it. Three people cooking at once gets a little crowded, anyway. If you miss the first bit of the game, I won’t tell.” Opening the door with one hand, I flipped on the light of the secret room and opened the door to my closet.

She looked up into my eyes. “That’s a tempting proposition, my king.”

My king. I *adored* hearing those words drip from her swollen lips.

“I’d be alright with you using the passage to my room sometimes,” I told her as we entered my closet. “After all, I have some clothes that you would look *ravishing* in, and I know you’ll care for them.”

"Like me wearing one of your soft custom dress shirts with the monogramming and nothing else?" She gazed around at the contents, which were hard to make out in the darkness.

"Mmmm, yes." Or one of my T-shirts. "I... I'm not trying to shut you out. Honestly, if Grif and I are sleeping, I don't care if you slip in next to us. Especially if you have a bad dream or get a mean text. Just use your ears and nose. I just like to have Grif to myself sometimes."

She looked up at me. "You're allowed to have boundaries, and I'll be cautious. I'm guessing it's like when I was in Jonas' room, and he wouldn't let Dean in. Said he didn't get to see that."

Relief that she understood whooshed over me as we emerged from the closet.

My room was bigger than the others and had a large balcony. Sometimes, when the weather was pleasant, I moved messier art projects out onto it. The room was dark, the curtains open, the city illuminating it. It didn't have a corner view like Dean's room, but it still was nice.

The couch and table I had in the corner weren't for show. I had my own coffee cart and mini-fridge in here. When they were gone, I often had my morning coffee on the balcony. The carpet was plush and soft under my feet, and the walls a soothing pale gray with dark green accents.

"AJ, this is beautiful," Verity breathed, eyes fixed on the skyline. She looked around the room. "I see what Mercy was saying. It would be easy to fit a desk in here."

"True. Mostly, I don't want to work in my sleeping space." Especially since I liked to create in here.

An open bookcase, filled with books, art supplies, souvenirs from my travels, and things from my hockey days, sectioned off my art studio from the sleeping and living areas. She probably couldn't see it in the darkness.

"Fair." She gazed up at me, feeling right in my arms. "Grif might not want me to cross his space to sneak into your room, though."

"That's if he wants it. He might not. Even if we redesigned it, it's a small space, and he's a large guy. That could be *your* hideaway reading nook. You can keep all your books in there," I chuckled.

The look on her face said she wasn't averse to the idea. I should give her access to our shopping accounts so she could order replacement things, especially clothing. It had most likely taken her years to build her wardrobe.

Though if she was anything like Jonas, she'd order books first.

I carried her into my bathroom, the low light coming on automatically. Like my bedroom, it was sleek but comfortable, done in white marble and black wood with bronze fixtures. It had a floating sink and a sunken tub with steps that looked out on the city. A pile of soft dark gray towels sat in a hutch by some large plants.

There was also a spacious shower with several safety bars.

"It's like a luxury spa," she breathed, taking it all in.

"That's the point. I got it redesigned when I moved in." I set her down on the rug in front of my long shower. It was my one big remodel and worth every penny.

I stripped off my shirt and tossed it into the wicker clothes basket. Then I turned on the low shower lights and switched off the others to give us a relaxing glow. At the wall, I programmed the shower. Wisps of lightly scented mist curled into the shower as I warmed it with the steam function.

"I love the bench. Is that a pillow on it? For shower naps?" Verity stood next to me, completely naked. She sniffed the air. "It smells nice in here."

I took in her muscled abs, her toned legs, and golden breasts. "I like to scent the steam with eucalyptus oil."

"Fancy." She grinned.

Picking her up, I opened the glass door and stepped in. Gently, I laid her face down on the long bench, positioned her head on the pillow, then pushed the button on the panel by her head and I got a good look at the little fairy tattoo.

I'd seen the little flower on her inner thigh as I fucked her. The only tattoo I had was our pack tattoo, though Grif and I had talked about getting matching tattoos at some point.

Water cascaded down on her naked back from the six water bars above her. The water would change patterns, intensity, and temperatures as it ran through the sequence.

"It's a horizontal shower, though I like *shower bed* better. There are several programs–for waking up, going to sleep, and when my leg really hurts. I can change the program if you don't like it. Let me know if the temperatures aren't right," I told her as I used a short version of the program I'd custom designed for my leg, since our bum legs were on the same side.

"I love it." Her eyes closed, and the delicious moan that escaped her lips made me want to have her all over again.

Later.

I turned on the overhead rain shower for myself, since it wouldn't bother her experience. As she laid there, I washed myself off. The shower worked through the program, then returned to simply cascading down her back like she was lying under a waterfall. Verity looked like a goddess from my grandmother's stories.

"Did you like it?" I asked as I soaped up my hands and ran them over her curves.

She looked up at me, sleepy and satisfied. "Now that is how you shower, Cow Boy."

"I'm most definitely the winner of our cook-off." Mercy looked over at us from her perch on the ottoman, smug. She wore some sweats from her high school and a tank top, her wet hair in two braids.

I'd never seen her hair not in two Dutch braids.

I surveyed the remains of our dinner–a platter of three varieties of lamb kabobs, grilled vegetables, bowls of sauces, and rice, which were spread out on the coffee table in the living room. The Knights played the Quebec Étoiles on TV.

"Yours were good, Mercy," I admitted. It was possibly the best of the three, with its very Greek flair. Who knew the head of a biotech company would have good recipes?

That sauce. The garlic breath was worth it.

"I'm so full. Everyone did such a good job." Verity curled into me on the couch in some pale blue striped lounge pants and a T-shirt that said *Marquess Fútbol* from her suitcase.

My hand ran down her shoulder. "I have to say your recipe was excellent."

I'd wanted to win. Those two cooked circles around me tonight.

"I liked yours." She looked up at me and smiled.

We watched on the TV as Clark stole the puck, the Étoiles chasing him and getting it away. Someone knocked over Carlos, and Grif pushed him up against the glass and punched him. The person hit him back as a minor scuffle broke out. The Knights were up 2-1.

Mercy grinned. "What do I win? You two not being nauseating for the rest of the night?"

"Driving lessons, as soon as I get my car back from Hale?" Verity replied. "I'm cleared for driving now. I got the email while we were gone."

Mercy snorted. "Hale's not giving you back your car. Though I'm happy to help you steal it back from him. How long is the drive?"

"Much longer than the ultra-bullet. Even if there isn't a direct route. I told him a million times it was to *borrow* until I can drive again. I like my car and I worked hard to buy it myself. He's supposed to drive it out with my flower bulbs." Verity rubbed her temples.

"It's a *nice* car," Mercy agreed. "But you need a convertible. A pink one."

Verity laughed and shook her head. "Please don't buy me a car."

"Oh, but I will because I can." Mercy waved her phone around, both of them giggling.

"I was thinking more like you could choose dessert or not have to wash the dishes," I told them.

"Fair. That means Verity washes up because you grilled. I'm still hungry. I'm going to cut up the pineapple." Mercy popped up with a quickness that made my knee ache. She went to the kitchen, taking some dishes with her.

"Pineapple?" I blinked. We hadn't bought one at the store.

"It's her favorite. She brought it in her suitcase. Not that you would, but don't tease her by taking food off her plate. Years of Hale doing that has made her a little violent when that happens." Verity shrugged as she sat up and grabbed the platter.

"Noted. Grif is like that with his special snacks–though they're all labeled." Siblings could be colossal assholes. There was a reason I didn't talk to most of mine. I was one of seven. Most of them were good children who worked for our dads.

Since the game had gone to a commercial, I joined her, grabbing some more of the dishes.

"Look how much snow has already piled up on the balcony. Good thing we don't have practice tomorrow." Mercy had her face pressed to the glass.

It was freezing when I'd grilled out on the terrace. By the time I'd finished, snow started coming down.

"I have a feeling that the storm might come early," I replied, joining her. "What sort of car does Verity have?"

"A fancy sedan with a moonroof. It has a great stereo so I understand why Hale wants to keep it. Ver worked her ass off to buy it outright, even did a job for them to get a discount. She wanted the little convertible, but the parents needed her to have a car they could fit car seats in, so she could ferry the littles." Mercy showed me a picture on her phone.

There was a slightly younger Verity in a gray suit and a stunning necklace getting into a silver sedan. Her hair, nails, shoes, watch, briefcase, sunglasses, and makeup were not only perfection, but the right choices for that particular luxury car brand. Classic and classy, while still oozing power and elegance. *A car as confident as you,* the copy read.

I'd buy that.

"It would be nice to get her a convertible. Something that fits me, her, and barely my duffle. We joke because Kaiko got her older sister one. But I'm sort of serious. Verity likes cute things. She should have a car that doesn't fit a car seat while she can." Mercy showed me another picture. It was a mid-priced trendy convertible made by Deloitte Automotive.

"I could see her driving that." Maybe I should get my own car and pick something Verity could drive. My parents always had a driver, so I liked being a rebel and using the metro.

"Right? It's so her," Mercy nodded.

"It's sweet of you, though you should save your money. Someone's teaching you to be smart with it, right?" I asked, because I could think of all the things I'd buy at seventeen with a professional athlete's paycheck.

Also, rookies could be dumbasses with their money. Grif was fine in the minors because our pay was shit for the work we put in. Once we'd moved up and started receiving those big paychecks, he'd been tempted to make bad choices. Many of which I'd been able to talk him out of. I'd also set him up with a business manager to help him with his goals. While I was all for him helping his family, he should plan for his future, too.

"Yep, most of it gets put away and the Maimers are making me take an online class. It's pretty good. Again, teach me about investing. Please? One of the parents' biggest arguments against professional sports is that it's a short-lived, unstable career. Which I'm well aware of." Mercy nodded as she chopped up the pineapple with the skill of someone who'd done it before.

She put the pineapple in three bowls. "I want to save as much as possible because I don't know how many years I'll get to do this. After I finish high school, I want to look into one of those university programs for professional athletes and work toward my history degree. When I'm ready to retire, I'll teach at a high school and coach skate smash."

"All very smart things," I told her, looking around. Verity seemed to have disappeared. Mercy had such a practical streak. How much of that was Verity?

"This is the car I want at some point." She showed me another picture on her phone.

"I could see you driving that." It was a sporty green 4x4 buggy. A little much for NYC, but perfect for going up to the mountains where the cabin was. We'd need to upgrade our SUV and 4x4 so that Verity and Mercy would fit.

Verity joined us. "I rebooted the laundry." She glanced at the windows and the storm brewing outside. Her face fell. "Oh, it's snowing. What's the best way to get to campus? They've fixed my greenhouse, so I should go in tomorrow. There was so much I wanted to get done over break and it didn't happen."

Her scent soured, and I put an arm around her.

"It's easy enough, but we should keep an eye on the storm. They'll understand if you don't get everything all fixed before classes start," I told her.

"I know," she sighed. "Still, it wasn't supposed to be like this."

My grip on her tightened. I liked things to go according to plan, too.

"It'll be fine, Ver. I'll even help," Mercy assured, putting the top and rind of the pineapple in the food scrap bin. "Game's back on." She grabbed all three bowls and forks.

"I can do the dishes during intermission? I don't know your house rules," Verity said as I led her back to the couch.

"That's fine. The big one is to clean up after yourself. Leave public spaces as you found them. If you need the dining room table for a project, great, just give us a heads-up. Same if people are coming over. Respect private spaces. Ask before using Grif's piano. Don't fuck up anyone's game progress. Lose puzzle pieces to your own detriment. Don't leave dishes in the sink overnight. If you bring dishes into your room, bring them back out." I couldn't think of anything else, though Jonas probably had some.

Once again, Verity curled into me, and it felt so nice, so natural. I *enjoyed spending* time with her, though part of me wished Grif was here, too.

"Can I eat anything I want?" Mercy asked with her eyes on the TV, the game back on.

"As long as it's not labeled. Also, label anything that's only yours. Anything you finish, put on the grocery list. Don't put empty or practically empty containers back." I took a bowl and had a piece of pineapple. It was perfectly ripe and sweet.

"Fair." Mercy popped a piece of pineapple into her mouth.

We watched the game as the Knights continued to hold on to their lead. Throughout every commercial break, Verity would get up, do a couple of things in the kitchen, and then sit back down.

She must be a bit like Jonas. I kept things neat because I liked to take care of my stuff. Jonas liked everything to be orderly because it distracted him if they weren't.

Between the second and third period when they went to intermission, Verity returned to the kitchen to finish cleaning. Mercy put away the laundry. I caught up on work emails.

"Do you need help?" I asked Verity. The dishwasher was running, and the platter sat in the drying rack next to the sink.

Verity shook her head as she hand-washed the blender and rice cooker pot. "I'm fine."

I walked the balconies, seeing if anything needed to be put in, covering the main furniture, and moving the small table and chair on my balcony into my room.

When I came back out, Verity wasn't there. I walked up the stairs to do the same for the terrace, including moving the grill into the hall and quickly cleaning it.

Right as the game came back on, I took a seat on the couch. Verity wiped down the counters. Mercy plopped down on the ottoman with a box of the cookies we'd bought earlier.

"Verity, game's back on," I told her. "It can wait."

"Almost done," she called from the kitchen.

The third period started off fast and furious, as the Étoiles tried to even the score. Jonas tried to block their forward, but he knocked him down and went for the goal. Dean caught the shot as he slid to the left. I cheered.

"Ver, you're missing the game!" Mercy yelled.

"I can see it from here," Verity said as she *mopped the floor.* "AJ, I love this steam mop. It's incredible."

Why was she mopping the floor? Did we spill something? I'd swept up before we ate.

She finished and *started again.* Meanwhile, Grif plowed through the Étoiles' defenses and scored again, bringing the score to 3-1.

Mercy looked over at her sister and then back to me. "You might want to deal with that."

Verity was moving chairs and steam-mopping *the dining area*, which we hadn't even used.

"Should I throw her over my shoulder and bring her to the couch?" I asked.

"Or let her know you'll still love her if she doesn't mop everything three times after every meal. Or no one will shout at her if she misses a spot. This will become important when she uses the oven. One good thing about living on our own was that no one will critique our cleaning or get mad at us for not doing it perfectly. We're tidy, but we're not perfect." She bit her lower lip like Verity did, anxiety in her eyes.

Her look grew fierce as her plum scent became spicy with anger. "If you're that kind of pack, I'm forcibly removing her, fuck the snow."

My heart wrenched. "I hadn't even thought about that."

This wasn't her place. She was so proud and liked doing everything herself. I'd have to let her know that *nothing* was expected from her. Not cleaning, not anything else.

"You should. Ver will automatically think she needs to do most of the cooking and cleaning since she has the 'least value' job. Because that's how it was at home," Mercy sighed.

"Fucking shit." I shook my head, glad they were away from that. I stood. "Thank you. I don't want either of you to feel you have to do more than anyone else, okay? And no, no one's going to yell at you for not cleaning the counter well enough. Jonas will get grumpy if dishes are left in the sink too long, though."

"Noted. You don't do weird language nights, right? While I'm all for conducting conversations in other languages and watching foreign movies, I'm opting out of mandated *we only speak this lan-*

guage on this day dinners." Mercy made a face. Then she thought for a moment. "Unless they're fake languages. I'd consider learning some fandom language because that could be fun."

"As someone who has a translator for a mother who made us do that growing up, I empathize. The fake language idea is fun. I'm sure there's some space-movie language Jonas would love us all to learn." I looked over at Verity. "The kitchen looks great. Come sit down. Want a beer?"

"I should do it one more time." Verity's brow furrowed.

"It's clean enough, Princess. We will still love you if it's not perfect. You don't need to mop the floor unless you spill something. No one will be mad if things are not spotless. You don't owe us because you're staying here." I went over and put my arms around her.

"But..." Her face crumpled.

"I know." I held her tighter. "We have a cleaner who comes several times a week. The floors are fine. The only reason why we even have the rules we do is because Dean will leave dirty dishes everywhere."

"Okay. Are you sure? This isn't my house." Her brows furrowed.

My heart broke. "It'll be your home soon enough. And no, you don't have to repay us for staying here, not with cleaning, *not with anything else.*"

Her body relaxed, and I took the steam mop from her and put it in the kitchen cupboard where it lived with the broom and dustpan.

I opened the fridge. "Let's have a beer and watch the game. Unless you want some wine? Also, I know where Jonas keeps his good bourbon."

"Why does my bathroom have a wine fridge?" She stood at my shoulder and grabbed a bottle of beer.

"I have no idea." I shrugged and grabbed one of my own. "Now come on, let's see if Grif scores that third goal."

We sat back on the couch just in time to see Nakey block someone from getting near the Knight's goal as Carlos stole the puck and raced to the other side. Someone blocked him, and he passed it to Dimitri, who was having a bad night. He missed, and the Étoiles got it. Grif whizzed by, stole it, and shot it into the net.

His goal music played, and the crowd threw bones onto the ice. Three goals for Grif. Good for him.

"You're okay. I've got you." I wrapped my arms around her. While I'd known that her parents were shitty, I hadn't truly grasped what a place of their own might mean to them.

I should have. There was a reason I'd moved to Bucharest after graduating from NYIT when I hadn't gotten a PHL contract. Why one summer I'd run away to join the rodeo. Sure, I loved my parents–but I couldn't stand living with them.

Mercy got up from her seat and joined us on the couch, putting an arm around her sister.

"You're both safe here," I told them. "In this pack, everyone has a voice, everyone matters. If something's wrong, if you don't like something, are concerned, or are just pissed, tell us any way you like. Face to face, group chat, lipstick on the glass doors."

"Good." Mercy gave me a look like she couldn't wait to write a complaint in makeup.

"You and Mercy made yourself your own little sanctuary. Now it's been destroyed and you're back under someone's roof. You might be stuck with us in a snowstorm, but you *matter.* I promise," I assured them both, giving Verity another squeeze.

We watched the rest of the game, all three of us on the couch. After the game ended, Mercy popped up off the sofa with a cat-like stretch, put away the cookies, and looked at her phone.

"I'm going to bed. Smell you later." Mercy waved.

Verity gave her a hug, whispering something, and then Mercy ran upstairs. The snow was coming down hard now and the windows rattled a bit. Yep, we were in for it.

"Would you like to take a bath and go to bed?" I told her. "If not, we could always watch the post-game or a movie?"

"I missed some big fútbol games. Do you have any we could watch?" Her eyes flickered at the window. "That's a lot of snow. I need to go to the greenhouse tomorrow."

"No one expects you to do anything in a blizzard." It was probably her first.

She frowned. "But do they?"

"They don't. Hey, I have a couple of games we could put on. Do you need a snack?" I suggested. While I was full from dinner, I could eat a crunchy snack. We had a lot of chips now.

She nodded. "Can I make hot cocoa and popcorn? That's what my Mama and I always had. We always watched games together. Dare would often join in. Sometimes, Mumsy or Harry, depending on who was playing. During games, there would be no talk of anything bad. Even if we were mad, the games were always a safe space."

"That sounds amazing. I think we have what we need." I grabbed the remote and pulled up the fútbol games we had as options. Sure, popcorn worked.

Verity's eyes focused on the gas fireplace. "Can we use that?"

"We can even move the couch closer and tilt the TV." Given the weather, that plan sounded nice–hot cocoa and a fútbol game in front of the fire.

Verity went to the kitchen, and I moved the couch and coffee table and repositioned the TV. I got out a few soft blankets and switched off most of the lights in the living room, leaving on that one strand of fairy lights. The air filled with the smell of chocolate and popcorn.

"Now that's cozy." Verity put another mug on the table. "Let me grab the popcorn."

I sat down on the couch and texted Grif that I was proud of him. Verity switched off the kitchen light, then joined me with a bowl of popcorn. I pulled a blanket over us and took a sip of hot chocolate.

"This is delicious," I told her as chocolate exploded over my tongue. Jonas' good bourbon would go well in this.

She beamed and snuggled into me. "Thanks."

This. I wanted so much more of this, and I'd have it too because there would be many nights when the guys were away, and here we were without them–or waiting for them.

"So, which game should we watch?" I asked, grabbing the remote. Not that it mattered. Because I had her.

Chapter Nineteen

Grif

"The Étoiles have a little feast set up. Get changed and join us," Kylee, our PR person, told us when we returned to the visitor's locker room after our win.

The Canadian teams often organized a meal or a night out for the opposing team. It was a nice little tradition with the understanding that everyone would be civil, even if it was a rough game. *What happens on the ice stays on the ice.*

At least in Canada.

Coach Atkins talked to us, then we hit the bikes and ice baths. Being away from AJ ached. I'd sleep with Dean and Jonas tonight.

Which was fine because most everyone assumed the bite on my neck was from Jonas.

Jonas, Dean, and I showered and got dressed. My phone was full of texts. I hadn't had time to see more than Verity and AJ telling me I'd played a great game. *Later.*

As we walked into the room in the arena where the food was set out, we found the team leaving, a few with boxes in hand.

Well, in the corner of the room, Coach yelled at Dimitri for having an off night. Dimitri's broad shoulders sunk as his head bowed in remorse, dark hair falling in his face.

"We're leaving already?" My stomach growled at the smells as I spied a buffet.

"The storm's coming early and *fast*. Toronto wants to postpone tomorrow's game. Storm's already hitting New York hard. If we leave right now, we *might* make it back to New York before they close the airport," Elias told me. "If we wait any longer, we might get stuck. Might get turned away as it is. Grab a box. Food's good."

"Oh, thanks." I'd rather not get snowed in and be kept away from AJ and Verity.

We grabbed our food, thanked our hosts who wished us safe travels, and piled onto the bus. I shoved food in my face, watching the snow come down, finishing my food right as we got to the plane. We rushed onto the plane and took off faster than we ever had, as the pilot apologized for what could be a rough flight.

I texted AJ that we were coming home early as I sat in my usual seat, giving Lucky a pat. Carlos passed out pink under-eye masks.

"Does Lucky want some?" Carlos asked.

I shook my head. "They make his fur sticky."

"Fair." Carlos threw the package to Sarah who was making grabby hands. Catching it, she shared with Nia then passed it back.

Dean cuddled into Jonas in the seats across the aisle. Yeah, I'd like to spend the night in bed with AJ.

A loud fart echoed through the plane.

"Ugh, Lucky," Carlos yelled. "Who fed Lucky cheese?"

Yeah, not me. It wasn't Lucky who farted, either.

Dean scowled at his phone and leaned across the aisle to me as he sat with Jonas. "Verity thanked me for her room, which means AJ showed it to her when she was over. He wasn't supposed to do that."

"I hope she's safe. She's not responding to my texts." I frowned, worry settling in the pit of my belly.

Jonas gave me a pointed look. "Obviously, you didn't read the group chat. She's fine."

Oh, she must have come over to watch the game. Between the stress of the day, the game, and the food, I dozed off on the quick flight and woke up to a very bumpy landing.

Coach Atkins stood to address us. "The streets are fucked. It's probably better to take the metro than driving or calling a car. Please be safe. Obviously, there's no game or practice tomorrow."

Our car wasn't parked here, anyway. The metro it was.

"You okay?" I asked Dimitri as we got off the plane. He was scrolling on his phone and frowning.

Dimitri shook his head. "Family emergency. Sorry, I shouldn't let it affect game play."

"It's fine. It happens. I hope everything's okay," I told him. He was raising his teenage siblings. His sister lived with him and attended a fancy omega academy here in the city. His brother was at an exclusive boarding school on the West Coast.

"Me, too. Here, you left Lucky on the plane." Dimitri pretended to hand me my imaginary cat and walked off in another direction.

We got our things and got on the empty metro. AJ had texted me back, but Verity hadn't. The location app wasn't working.

"I can't get ahold of Verity," I whispered to Jonas, worried. She *had* gotten back from Hawai'i. When we'd called AJ before the game, like always, I'd talked to her.

"She's okay, promise," Jonas replied. "Check the group chat."

"Oh, okay." I'd do that later. Right now, I just wanted to get home before my balls froze off.

The short walk to our place was brutal. Snow soaked my shoes and pants. Shivering, we took the elevator up to our floor. A wall of warmth hit me as we walked in. At least the heat worked. Only the fairy lights were on. A fútbol game played on the TV. The fire flickered in the background, making it feel cozy and inviting. It smelled like chocolate and popcorn.

AJ lay on the couch, his arms around Verity. She slept in his lap, a blanket over them. He looked over at us and waved, a smug look on his face.

"You asshole." I made a face at Jonas as I took off my coat. "You knew she was still here." It made perfect sense with the storm for her to stay over, rather than risk going back to her place.

"You should have read the group chat. Verity and Mercy's place flooded. For the time being, *both* of them are staying with us. That's why AJ showed her the room." Jonas put his shoes on the rack by the door and hung his coat up.

I dropped my bag on the floor and rushed over, my heart bursting at seeing *both* of them. They looked adorable together. An empty bowl of popcorn and two mugs sat on the table.

"She was tired and couldn't stay awake," AJ whispered as he pulled me in for a kiss.

Desire and want pulsed through our bond. Mmmm. Sure, I'd seen him this morning, but I'd missed him even more than usual.

"Princess, they're home. Their game tomorrow is canceled because of the storm." AJ nuzzled her with his nose.

Her eyes blinked open. "Grif."

"Hi, Kitten." The look on her face warmed me right up as she threw her arms around my neck and kissed me until my toes curled. I was taking her to bed tonight. It didn't matter how many blowjobs Dean earned while she was gone.

If AJ climbed in with us at some point...

Though Verity and I needed to have that talk. If not tonight, tomorrow. I had to tell Coach Atkins the truth. Soon. I'd felt a little weird while playing tonight, despite scoring three goals. The last thing I needed was to collapse during a game.

Her hand raked through my wet hair, and she frowned. "You're wet."

"And I'm hard. I got two shutouts while you were gone." Dean pulled her from me, spun her around, and kissed her.

"You're wet, too. Wet and cold." Verity's frown deepened as she cupped his face with her hand. "Why are you all wet?"

"We walked through a snowstorm, Little Alpha." Jonas snapped a kiss.

"You all need to shower and change before you get sick. What if you get sick and we can't get you to the doctor because of the storm?" Verity scolded, putting her hands on her hips.

"Wanna put me in the shower and warm me up?" Dean wrapped his arms around her.

"We'll do that right now. No one's going to get sick. I'll take care of Dean, you take care of Grif," Jonas told her.

She nodded as she climbed off Dean. His face grew stricken, but I wasn't about to relent, and I sent Jonas a silent look of thanks.

"I promise to spend time with you later." She kissed Dean, then came over to me. "I'll make us a bath, Tiger. Thank you, all of you, for the thoughtful rooms for me and my sister. It means everything." Verity kissed me on the cheek and padded off toward the bedrooms.

I sat down on the couch and took off my wet shoes and socks. "What happened?"

AJ motioned for us to come closer, and they sat down and started removing their soaked footwear.

"The heat's been off in their place and the pipes burst. It's flooded. Most of their shit's ruined. We tried to save what we could, which is why there's plants everywhere, mountains of laundry, and a game system in a bowl of rice," AJ replied.

"As you should." Jonas nodded.

"Oh, and don't throw away the weird baggie on the counter. It's apparently special." AJ shrugged. "Starter?"

I nodded. "It's for sourdough bread."

"The rooms aren't finished." Distress wafted off Dean and Jonas put an arm around him.

"Is that why the table is full of junk food?" My eyes flickered over to the table, which was piled high with tempting treats.

While Dr. Arya's nutrition plan made me feel better than the Knight's one, it wasn't any more fun.

AJ nodded. "Mercy's idea of emergency supplies. We're apparently snacking our way through the snowstorm. We're fine supply-wise, even with them. But I wanted them to be comfortable. Be gentle. That was their home. *Theirs.* They made the rules and no one's going to yell at them for not doing something good enough, for not being enough."

"Oh shit. That makes sense. I knew they were proud of their place, but I didn't think about the other implications." I stripped off my wet socks, the warm air putting feeling back into my toes.

"Anyhow, just be conscious of things. We'll need to show them that they're safe with us." He turned to me. "I wonder, if on some subconscious level, Verity wanting to wait also had to do with being wary of being in someone else's house again."

Jonas put his bare feet up by the fire. "Coming from a shitty home, I feel that. Thanks for the heads up."

Shit. She'd lost everything, including her sense of safety. That tugged on that deeply buried part of me that liked to be secure. We'd love her, show her she belonged here, too.

AJ grabbed the empty bowl and cups off the table. "There's leftover food if anyone's hungry."

"I'm good." I kissed him. "Thanks for taking care of them."

"Absolutely. Go spend some time with her. I'll check on you two in a bit?" His hand stroked my damp hair. "Obviously, you can have your privacy, but if you need reinforcements, I'm here."

"Sounds perfect. I'd like that later." I gave Dean a kiss and left to find Verity.

Her door was open. The bed had been made using the stuff Jonas had bought her. Personally, I wouldn't have chosen all the gold accents, but Dean had done a good job.

In the bathroom, Verity filled two wine glasses. "I hope you like white wine. I can't believe Dean put a wine fridge in my bathroom." She giggled. "It's ridiculous, I love it."

"If there's anything you don't love, you *can* change it." Coming behind her, I wrapped my arms around her waist as I buried my face in the crook of her neck, getting a good hit of her alpha scent and drinking it in.

Drinking her in.

"I love the pink and peach color scheme. However, the chandelier above the bed weirds me out. It was sweet of him. You should take your wet clothes off." She set the wine glasses down on the counter and turned to face me, still in my arms.

Verity tugged my pants off, and I stepped out of them, taking off my jacket and tie so I was only wearing a button-down and boxers, which weren't as wet.

I pulled her to me again. The fact that AJ's scent covered her made me hard. "I missed you."

She kissed me and entwined her fingers in my beard. "I missed you so much it hurt. But I'm here now. What do you need?"

You, naked, with my face in your pussy.

"To know you still love me, still want to be with me, even though I hurt you back on the bleachers—and that I've been keeping secrets." I cupped her face with my hand, my insides twisting with worry. As much as I burned for her, I needed to know things were okay between us. That I hadn't fucked things up too much.

"Why am I so nervous? You already said you'd love me if I were one. How did you even guess?" I added.

"This is where you tell me you're a gamma. I'll still love you. It was the way you reacted that morning in the bleachers and something AJ said the night before. However, don't feel like you need to tell me your story," she told me.

Something AJ said? What? He hadn't known I was a gamma, either.

"I need to tell you my story. I had no idea I was a gamma until a couple days ago. You guessed before I knew. I... I thought I was an omega. I awakened my last year at university–after Dean had. It scared the shit out of me. Before you get upset, I'd been planning on telling you soon. But can you understand why I'd hide it? Why the pack wanted to wait before we let you in on our secret?" Anxiousness twisted in my belly.

"I absolutely understand. Could you walk me through this? How did you not know you were a gamma?" Her eyebrows knitted.

She understood. Something settled deep inside me.

As the bath filled, we drank our wine, and I told her everything. Tears fell from her eyes when I told her about overdosing.

"I'm so sorry you went through that." She sniffed. "How scared you must have been. I completely understand not feeling comfortable with your designation."

The bath got full and the water had stopped automatically.

"I know, Kitten." I kissed her forehead. "My whole life I'd been this big guy who's great at scoring goals and hitting people. So many people thought I'd end up an alpha. When I awakened as an omega, it felt like someone yanked my entire existence from me–and when I saw what happened to Dean after that knothead outed him..."

Verity held me tight, soothing me with her touch and pheromones.

"I didn't know it worked. That I'd actually wrecked myself so badly that I came up as a gamma on tests," I added. "I continued taking shit for years to keep everything locked down tight. Then..."

"I woke you up, didn't I?" She flinched as if slapped.

"Maybe. I also live full-time with my omega." I stroked her hair. "According to my doctor, I'm at that point where I'm in danger of a heart attack or kidney failure if I don't stop taking my heavy-duty blockers. Though I should be able to stay on heat suppressants, maybe take a light scent blocker."

Understanding and concern shot through her face because she couldn't take anything now.

"I'm going to have to come out at some point. But I wanted to tell you first," I added, clinging to her like a lifeline.

"It's okay, Grif. I love you. Please, don't harm yourself by continuing to take things they told you not to," she told me.

"It'll be hard, but okay." It scared the shit out of me.

She pulled my head down and kissed my forehead. "It will be hard. But you have us."

"There's a very good chance I'll push back over to being an omega, which happens sometimes. Also, Dean and I were careless." I told her what happened that morning after leaving her on the bleachers.

"I saw his bite and wondered," she whispered.

"I'm sorry for hiding everything. Before you say it, it wasn't you admitting that you like big omegas that made me hide it. If anything, that told me you were the one and when I was ready, you'd accept me, given I'm not very omega-like."

"Oh, Grif. I love you. All of you. In case you haven't noticed, I'm not the alphiest of alphas." She tipped her forehead to mine.

"That's probably why we work so well together." I gave her a kiss.

"I want to be with you. Gamma. Omega. It doesn't matter. I just want to know if this changes anything between us? What parts of you did you hide from me, and will I be enough for them?" Nerves tinged her scent.

"My sweet kitten, you're enough for me." The fact she stood here and said that she still loved me, still wanted to be with me, set me at ease.

She brushed my hair out of my eyes. My arms tightened around her because I knew how much she worried about not being a good alpha.

"I don't foresee anything changing between us. What I get from you and AJ and Dean are all very different and believe me, I need you so much." My voice lowered as I nibbled on her jaw, one of my hands cupping her ass.

Her arousal hit me as a little moan escaped her lips. "Please, Tiger."

I kicked the bathroom door closed, pulling her pajama pants and panties off. Next went her shirt. Oh, I missed those golden breasts. Picking her up, I placed her on the counter. Spreading her legs, I buried my face in her inner heat.

"You're so wet for me, Kitten, just the way I like it," I told her as I knelt on the rug. I licked and sucked her, as her hands tangled in my hair, letting her know how much I missed her, how much I needed her.

Her back arched and her eyes closed as I explored her silken folds, reacquainting myself with her pussy.

"I'm going to come." Verity trembled.

"Show me how much my sweet alpha missed me," I murmured into her pussy as my fingers stroked her.

Her body exploded as she gushed all over my face. I licked it up, consuming every drop like it was precious. Standing, I kissed her so she could taste herself all over my lips, my face, my beard.

I seated myself inside her, wrapping her arms and legs around me, our lips still locked. She squeezed me just right as I pumped inside her. It was difficult not to come immediately. Picking her up off the bathroom counter, I pressed her against the closed door.

"Does my alpha need to be fucked hard against the wall? Do you need me to slam myself over and over into you until I cum inside your pussy?" I started thrusting hard as she gripped me tight.

"Yes, yes, fuck me hard, Tiger," she moaned.

"I love being inside you." Taking her hands, I pinned them above her head with one hand, the way she liked, and I felt her pussy squeeze me in delight.

I kissed her again, so happy she accepted me so readily. Because I needed her. I needed her to love me as I was. All of me.

"I know there's a lot to work through, but we can do this. Together. We can be good. Together." My other hand tightened around her throat as my eyes gazed into her.

"Being gone for so long, not being here for you, tore me up," she gasped, her pussy continuing to squeeze me just right.

"Come for me again, Kitten. Lock me tight so I can fill you up." I ground against her, giving her a few more hard thrusts.

"Grif." Her head tilted back as she called my name. An orgasm rippled through her taut body. Verity's warm cunt squeezed me like a vice, locking me inside her.

Lips trailed along my neck, licking and sucking all the right places that made my groin clench.

"Oh, that's it, Alpha." Letting go of her hands, I wrapped my arms around her, keeping her pressed to the wall, as I came inside her, our bodies trembling. For a long moment, I held her to me, peppering her face, jaw, and neck with little kisses, our bodies still joined.

Finally, her pussy unclenched, releasing me. She leaned against me, head on my shoulder, arms still around me, body trembling.

"That was so good. Just what I needed," she told me.

"Me, too. You're what I need. Always and forever. I'll say it over and over until you understand right here." I put my hand over her heart, my giant, pale hand contrasting with her golden skin. "And here." I kissed her temple.

She looked up into my eyes. "I'll try my best to live up to that."

Verity lit some candles, refilled our wine, and moved the glasses to the ledge of the tub. She turned off the lights. Her hands fumbled with the buttons of my shirt as she took it off me.

We got in and I pulled her onto my lap. She started the tub's jets and curled into me. Her eyes lingered on the bond mark on my neck from AJ.

"You can touch it if you want. Touch, lick, kiss. When you're ready, feel free to add your own bite. You don't even have to ask. You have my permission to mark me whenever you're ready." I wanted it so much, especially now that I had AJ's and Dean's.

"Thank you. I'll have to examine you and see where I'd like to put my mark when it's time." Her fingers trailed along my collarbone.

"This one's AJ's." I took her hand in mine and put it over it. "You can't see Dean's given he's an omega."

Her eyes roamed my body, which wasn't very visible in the deep tub and long enough for me to stretch out comfortably, even with her in it. It might get a little cozy with three, but for the two of us, it was *perfect*.

"Here." I took her hand, pulled it under the water, and wrapped it around my dick. "No, he actually bit me there," I added at her incredulous look. It was surprising she hadn't noticed the night we'd fucked during the Maimers game.

She snorted. "That's very Dean. Where will you mark me?"

"Maybe here?" My hand caressed the underside of her breast. "Or here." My fingers brushed over her inner thigh, near her tattoo.

"Those sound wonderful, and I look forward to it when we're ready," she breathed, lips exploring my neck. "You can choose."

"Good, because I want to feel you right here." I put her hand on my heart. That's what I needed. Then I'd be complete.

Chapter Twenty

Verity

I bit my lower lip. Part of me loved this conversation about bites and bonding, but part of me was afraid it would end like last time. "I liked it when you called me *alpha* while we were fucking."

"You're mine, Kitten." His arms wrapped around me, rain scent comforting.

He was a gamma. One who'd been an omega first, for a couple of years, and could be an omega again soon. I didn't even know that was possible.

That meant that we could actually have some sort of connection. We've just ruined ourselves with drugs because we didn't trust our instincts.

I handed him a glass of wine and sipped on my own. Candles flickered around us. The water was warm and bubbly. Glorious.

Grif explained a little more about the doctor's appointments, the effects of the blockers on him, and what could happen if he didn't stop.

"While I feel bad that this might derail your plan, I worry about your health. I want you around for a long time." I laid my head on his shoulder.

"Mmmm, I like to hear that, Gorgeous." He sipped his wine. "Be patient with me? I have no idea what's waking up. I... I'm a little scared."

Wisps of his burnt sugar fear made my belly tighten, and I rubbed my hand along his beard. "I'm here. We'll figure it all out."

Grif stole a kiss. "That's what I needed to hear, Kitten. I have a confession to make. That whine on the airplane when you flew with us to Glitter City. That was me, not Dean. Freaked me out. I haven't whined in a very long time."

Part of me melted, and I kissed him. "I'm sorry I woke things up. I never meant to endanger you."

Even though it sounded like this would have happened regardless, I still felt guilty.

He shook his head. "Don't be. It could be so many things, too. Developing a resistance to the drugs, my relationship with AJ, not to mention living with Dean. If I push back over to being an omega, will you be okay with that? I know you didn't sign up for two omegas."

"I signed up for *you,* whatever you call yourself," I assured.

Two-omega packs were becoming more common. Especially as the population of male omegas grew and people debunked the old myths that kept packs from having more than one omega–and omegas mating with each other.

I put the wineglass down and kissed him. "I love *you.* All of you. Maybe I need to show you in here like you did out there."

That wall fucking had settled something inside me. I wanted more–and right now my leg felt just fine.

Facing him, I straddled him and slowly slid down on his rock-hard shaft. "I love that you're always ready for me."

"I'm yours to fuck," he sighed as I seated myself on his cock.

Putting one hand on his shoulder to brace myself, I tangled my other in his hair and rode him. "You feel so good."

My hands and lips explored his face and body as I ground against his cock, riding him slowly, both for my own satisfaction and trying not to let water slosh all over the floor.

"Oh, that's it, Kitten, you ride me so good," he groaned. "I love how good you feel."

"You're mine to ride," I growled, grinning, loving this, as I continued to ride him, one of his hands toying with my clit until orgasm rocked me.

"Come for me," I told him, my pussy squeezing his cock as tight as I could as I ran my tongue over the infinity heart tattoo on his chest.

"Yes, Alpha." His eyes gleamed as he held my hips, slamming me onto him so hard water splashed over the sides, and he came inside me.

Locking him, I slumped onto his chest, spent and satisfied. We laid there in the bathtub, talking, until the water cooled, refreshing it and turning the jets back on twice. We talked about all the fear he'd had as he hid his designation. The self-loathing he'd felt at himself, and hatred for whatever DNA threatened to ruin his dreams. How he felt like he *had* to succeed so he could help his family.

I told him the entire story of my omega dad meeting the alpha parents at the chemistry conference, realizing that he and Mumsy were scent matches, and the fallout of their idiocy.

"This was why I was trying to take things slow. Well, that and I do have Mercy and my studies to think of. My parents could have solved so many problems by simply taking time to get to know each other before yanking my dad out of his university mid-term, moving him to the other side of the country, then mating him within a week," I admitted, glad to finally tell him the root of my wariness.

He nodded. "I hear you, and that's valid. He left mid-semester? The idea of trying to work out scholarships and credit transfers makes me nervous for him."

"It gets worse. Dad had a live-in alpha girlfriend. He picked up and left when she wasn't home, sending only a text. The alpha moms kept her from him, called her a stalker when she tried to talk to him, and got campus police involved." I winced because she and Dad were serious and he didn't even speak to her about it before leaving.

Grif's jaw dropped. "That poor girl. She just probably wanted to have a conversation. If she was an alpha, why couldn't she stay with him? Join their pack?"

"Right? That would make sense. While the alpha moms said it was that initial possessiveness, I think a lot of it was that she was a piano major," I said softly. A fantastic one. Creed and I had looked her up after the whole story came out.

"Oh no, not a music major." Grif grimaced. "I'm sorry, but your parents are snobs."

"Absolutely. Dad was an undergrad when they met, but Mumsy, Baba, and Mom were all in a chemistry PhD program together when they met and talking about forming a pack together. I understand them wanting to choose practical careers, but they go overboard in pushing the sciences–and crushing dreams that don't fit their narrow purview of what our lives should be like." I sighed, pushing away thoughts of what I could have had if they hadn't barked me into turning down those offers to play professional fútbol.

Grif kissed my temple. "I'm glad you're helping your siblings with their dreams. And you know, if you get the chance to chase yours, we'd fully support you."

"You would?" I blinked. Wow. My fútbol days were over, but the fact they'd fully support it meant everything.

I leaned in and kissed him. Then I sighed.

"The story gets worse. Dad's girlfriend that he abandoned died–leaving behind a baby. Their baby. Dad nearly left the parents after that. She hadn't been stalking him; she'd wanted to tell him she was pregnant. The alphas knew they fucked up, and it took a lot of work for them to get through that. Dad spent twenty-something years looking for baby Grace." I leaned into him. Because that just hurt my heart.

"Oh fuck. Okay, okay, I could see how that would make you wary of going too fast. I'm so happy that you found your sister." His arms wrapped around me.

"Me, too. Grace was overwhelmed when Creed found her. She thought Dad abandoned her." I winced. "It turns out that Mom *hid* Grace from Dad, thinking it was the right thing. She also helped the records get messed up so he couldn't find her. Now she's in jail for child trafficking. That part fucked with my head, because one mistake, one rash alpha judgment, came back decades later and destroyed *everything.* Not only am I terrified of turning into the parents, but I'm worried that one errant alpha choice that seemed like a good idea at the time would tear down my life and everyone else's years later. What if I do that?" Fear flooded my chest.

"Oh, Kitten." He nuzzled me. "You're not going to do anything remotely like that. Not to mention, you have two alphas in the pack with you that I trust ineffably. Ones that you can go to for a second opinion. Part of the whole reason behind packs is so that alphas have checks and balances. Obviously, the pack you grew up in failed at that. But we won't because you have Jonas and AJ–and they have *you.*"

"Oh." I'd never quite considered that. "The parents failed at a lot of things. That's the main reason we couldn't date. They didn't want us to fuck up like them."

"For fuck's sake. That's why? I'd thought they didn't want you to date because then they'd lose their free labor," he told me.

My head lolled from side to side. "There definitely was some of that after Creed moved out for engineering school."

Grif planted a kiss on my temple. "Thank you. That explains so much. While we didn't have a lot in my family growing up, we had plenty of love. Sure, we got in trouble, certainly us older ones looked after the littles and did chores. No one ever was truly mean."

"The thing is, none of the alpha parents thought they were being mean when they tore us down. They thought it made us tough." I sighed. Telling him all this took a load off my chest.

"We won't be like that." He squeezed me. "I promise."

"Good. After you left me in the bleachers, I started to put things together. It shook me. Fault or not, I made a bad choice, and we were both hurt by it. I love you, and hurting you is the last thing I want to do." Tears streamed down my face.

"I know, Kitten." He kissed away my tears. "That doesn't mean you need to rush. However, I appreciate that you and Mercy have been talking about ways to make it work. It means the world to me. To us. As you can see by your rooms, we have, too."

"Can we make this work?" My fingers trailed down his face. I needed everything to be okay. Somehow.

He took my hand and kissed my fingertips. "We can and will."

Grif poured us more wine. I refreshed the hot water, and we continued to talk more about our fears and dreams and hopes. What life might look like with Mercy and me here with them. Where we fit and what we could do to support each other.

And what things could be like for us long-term–after my PhD and hockey. I loved the picture he painted, about fixing up the house in Boston. Him telling me about different things he wanted to explore with music. How AJ wanted the pack to travel more. The sailing race Dean always wanted to enter. Jonas' dream to go on a cross-country motorcycle trip.

"This is all new for me, too. I'm scared shitless about embracing what I've been fighting against all these years," he told me.

"I'm here. While I love sheer research, maybe I *will* be a professor after all. It would give me more time to spend with you over the summers for adventures. If I work at the same university Jonas coaches at, then I can come watch them during practice and heckle the coach," I laughed.

For all my fútbol dreams, being a professor and my flower research was always my endgame.

Grif snorted. "Be the super-hot coach's wife. I love that."

"Hey, are you two okay? You've been in there a long time," AJ said from the other side of the door, giving it a little knock.

"You can come in, AJ," I called.

AJ came in, a sheepish look on his face. "Sorry, while we talked about you using the passage to my room, we never talked about me using it to yours."

"It's fine. Sorry, I didn't mean to monopolize him." I frowned a little because while we'd needed to talk, it was late.

AJ shook his head as he sat on the raised platform of the tub, looking like a god in the flickering candlelight. He wore only sweatpants, and I saw the pack tattoo on his bicep that matched the other guys.

"That wasn't it, Princess. Monopolize him all you need tonight. I wanted to make sure you were okay. *You.* I can feel that he's fine through the bond, but I can't feel you. Sorry it took so long, I sort of fell asleep, and before that you were..." He smirked. "Occupied."

Heat seared my face. "You're bonded. You can feel that now."

"I knew you'd fuck him. It's not like I can read his mind. Also, I can block it out. So next time we have a cook-off with a sexy wager, he won't miss a goal at an away game because my dick is down your throat as we watch him on TV." He threw a smirk at Grif.

I grinned and shook my head, imagining it. "No, it will be you between my thighs."

"Mmmm, do you want to come for him?" Grif murmured, a hand stroking my leg.

"She did earlier." AJ's eyes blazed. "She looked so pretty tied up with my belt."

My pussy quivered at the thought. "Can I have you both together?"

"You want me to knot that ass of yours while Grif chokes you with his dick so you don't wake the house?" AJ cupped my face with his hand, which then ran down to my throat, encircling it. "I'd love that. Just remember who's in charge–and it's *not* you."

His words made me clench. *Take me, please.*

"I know that you can be a good girl for us." Grif's voice went gravelly as his hand tangled in my hair at the back of my neck.

My hips arched at their dirty talk as my thighs rubbed together. "Oh, yes please, Tiger. I want you both to fill every one of my holes with your cum."

AJ's hand curled tighter around my throat as he tipped my head up. "You're forgetting something, Princess."

"Please, my king. I want to be tied up and conquered by both of you," I begged, the desire to be fucked by them both at once overwhelming.

"Oh, I like that." Grif's eyes blew out with need, as the hand between my thighs toyed with me.

"Good girl, you beg so sweet. How many holes have you gotten, Grif? You did get a boner in tonight's game." AJ's eyes gleamed as his free hand tweaked my nipple, hard, sending shocks of pleasure and pain through me.

"I've had that sweet pussy twice. Maybe I should have this ass. Get it all ready for you," Grif breathed in my ear.

"She'll take it like a good girl. You want it so bad, don't you?" AJ continued to play with my nipples, rolling them between his fingers.

"Please," I breathed as Grif's fingers thrust in and out of me.

AJ's gaze flickered over all the bottles in the pretty rack by the tub. He pulled one out and handed it to Grif.

"Thanks." Grif took it from him. Of course, Dean had put waterproof lube in my bathroom.

"Take his dick and suck my cock. Just like you did that night in the storeroom. Show me how good you take us–because my knot is a reward, not a right." AJ put a towel down on the bathtub step.

"Yes, my king." I shivered as Grif worked my ass, my clit throbbing. I loved what we did that night at the arena.

Grif lubed up his cock, and sat me on it slowly, stretching me as AJ took off his sweats and briefs.

"You feel so good," Grif whispered, moving me up and down his length.

"I love you inside me," I told him. I reached for AJ's hard cock, wanting to lick off the drops of pre-cum beading on the tip, glistening like a jewel in the candlelight.

AJ swatted my hand. "No hands. Touch again and I tie them."

Before I could answer, AJ shoved his cock in my mouth.

"Take it all, Princess. Tap my thigh three times if it's too much. Otherwise, no touching," he growled. His hand wrapped around my throat. The other tangled in my bun, keeping me immobile as he conquered my mouth with his cock.

I took it as deeply as I could, because I didn't have any other choice with the way he was holding me. Being at his mercy like this sent quivers straight to my pussy.

"That's it, come when you need to, Kitten," Grif murmured in my ear, kissing my jaw and my throat as he continued to bounce me on his dick, the other playing with my clit.

AJ's nostrils flared as he growled a little growl that made my pussy shake with pleasure.

Grif smirked. "My hole, my rules."

"As soon as you're in my room, it's my rules," he growled.

The two of them going back and forth was so hot it made me clench. Hard.

"That's it, strangle my cock. I'm going to come soon, and flood your sweet ass with my cum," Grif whispered. "While I like AJ's hand around your neck, I think mine's better. You take us so perfectly." His hand brushed my clit, and I came, struggling with AJ's cock in my mouth.

But I didn't tap out. Instead, I squeezed AJ with my throat so that I could get in a deep breath through my nose.

"Suck me down, Princess," AJ demanded. His hand on my neck loosened, gripping my jaw instead, holding my head tight as hot ropes of cum shot down my throat.

I swallowed him down, trying to meet his eyes, letting him know how hot I found this, my clit throbbing.

"You sucked me so good," AJ praised, his thumb stroking my jawline as he pulled out his dick, the gesture, and his praise making me preen.

Grif took a few more hard strokes, as he lifted me up and pulled me down on him, hard, coming inside my ass as he pushed me to his chest. "That was beautiful, Kitten. This is what I need. You are what I need."

I melted. Because I adored what we had–and I *loved* this.

"You both fucked me so good," I breathed, my eyes closing as I rested my head on his chest, feeling his heartbeat, as AJ stroked my hair.

He yanked my head back so my eyes met his. AJ's grin grew sinister. "We're not done yet, Princess."

I couldn't wait.

"This way," I told Grif as he moved toward the closed door of my room that led to the secret hall, both of us wearing fluffy, soft bathrobes. One of them was seafoam green and had my *name* embroidered on it.

"I thought we were going to AJ's room, but we could make your room work if you'd rather be in here." Grif cast a look around my room, which was lit by only a bedside lamp. "Oh, the bear."

The bear he'd given me at the Maimers game before I left had the place of honor among the pillows mounded on the circular bed.

"He was good company while I was away," I assured him as I took his hand and led him toward the closet.

"We're taking the expressway," AJ replied, striding inside, where a light was on.

My bathroom only had two bathrobes, so AJ only wore a towel, having joined Grif and me in the shower as we'd rinsed off from the bath.

Grif blinked as we walked inside. The closet still smelled of AJ and me–and sex.

"I've lived here for years and never found what Mercy discovered in minutes," AJ added as he pulled open the panel in my closet.

"She's got that sort of mind. Always has. She'd find the hidden rooms and passages whenever we'd go to historical places. It's part of why the parents don't want her to be 'just' a history teacher. She could be a great structural engineer or architect if she had the interest. Which she doesn't." I tugged Grif into the small, dark room.

He sucked in a breath. "There's a passage connecting your *closets?* That's what you were talking about?"

"Oh, it gets better." I switched on the light, revealing the cute tree-shaped nook.

"It's a nest. I didn't know this was here," Grif breathed as I showed him the note.

"Me neither. No pressure, but it's yours if you want it. We can redo it however you'd like," AJ told him, squeezing his shoulder.

"It's adorable. Small, but adorable." Grif looked around. "I'll think about it? But Dean doesn't get a nest in your closet if I pass."

"No, he doesn't." AJ opened the door to his closet.

We walked through AJ's overly organized closet and into his room. Unlike the last time, the light was on. It was lovely and uncluttered, with a little sitting area in one corner, and a large bed, filled with pillows in forest green, black, and gray. Not a pack-sized bed, but one that would easily fit the three of us.

What drew my eye was the large bookshelf that separated the room into another part that I hadn't noticed earlier. "What's over there?"

"Want to see my art, Princess?" AJ took my hand and led me over to what was clearly a little studio.

"You're an artist," I breathed. "I knew Dean drew, but not that you painted."

The floor here was tiled. A paint-covered drop cloth covered one area, with an easel on it. On it sat a half-finished landscape, a reference picture clipped beside it. There were other paintings, along with shelves and drawers of art supplies.

"I mostly do landscapes. I did the one in your room, and the one of the cabin that's upstairs. Lately, I've been doing a lot of commissions—painting the views from people's vacation homes so they can hang it up in their penthouses and offices." AJ shrugged, gesturing to the easel.

"It's beautiful." I examined the nightscape, which was of a skyline I didn't know and just like the reference photo.

"He's good, isn't he? This is the view from the roof of the cabin." Grif held up a landscape of trees–and a waterfall.

"They're all so good." I put an arm around AJ's waist. "I had no idea."

My gaze fell on a slab of marble nearly as large as me, half-carved. I stood a step closer. It looked like a naked man was trying to escape from the rock.

"I occasionally do some carving, mostly in marble," he told me.

AJ let me examine his art for a few more moments, then he pulled me out of the studio area, turning off the lights so only a small light illuminated the bed area.

"Are you sure this is what you want, Princess?" AJ murmured as he peeled the soft robe off my body.

I nodded as it slipped to the floor.

"Words." His hand slapped my ass, the stinging going straight to my clit.

"Yes, my king. Make me the filling in a hot man sandwich." My pussy grew damp at the thought of having both of them at the same time that way, even though I'd already been fucked several times tonight.

"I *really* like this *my king* business," Grif breathed, coming up behind me as he put a hand around my throat. "You're ours tonight, Kitten."

Yes, please.

"I'm in charge. You don't come unless I give you permission. Me, not him. You do what I say–and he does to *you* what I say." AJ's voice was gravelly. "Now get on the bed."

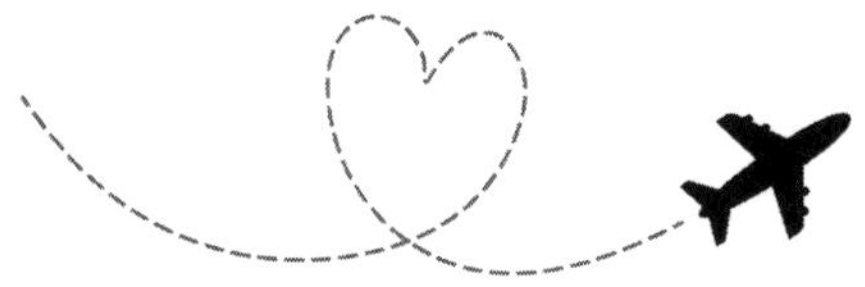

Chapter Twenty-One

AJ

Verity climbed onto my bed, nestling herself among the pillows, driftwood scent syrupy with happiness.

If I painted people, I'd paint her just like that–relaxed, happy, and completely naked.

People weren't my thing, at least with paints. My fingers itched to sculpt her. To chip away at the stone until only a nude, happy Verity remained.

"Suck Grif's cock while I get things ready, so he'll get his three holes from you for tonight. No, you don't get to come until I say–and *no hands*," I told her as I picked up the robes and towels off the floor and hung them up in the bathroom.

When I returned to the dimly lit bedroom, naked, Grif laid on the bed with her. He murmured quietly as he stroked her hair, his cock in her mouth. Their scents entwined, making my room smell like a storm on the beach, laced with the sweetness of desire.

He was too soft on her, but that's what she needed from him.

Opening my drawer, I looked through it since I wanted a toy for her ass. After that day in the greenhouse, where I promised to take care of her at another time, I'd gotten a few things in preparation.

What about a gag? I looked over at her, the cute little noises she made getting me hard. Maybe. The blindfold? Oh, most definitely. The restraints, too. And the nipple clamps.

How had I gone from hating her to buying sparkly pink nipple clamps?

Grif finished fucking her face, and the two of them cuddled on top of the covers of my bed. I loved seeing her submit to him. Verity trusted us. While I didn't know that much about her past, I knew enough to treasure that she gave it to us so wholeheartedly.

"Look, I've got something for you." I crawled on the bed and held the nipple clamps up. "Will you let me decorate your beautiful body, Princess?"

She nodded as I attached the clamps to her pert nipples, watching her face, searching for them being too tight.

By the way she rubbed her thighs together, she liked them. Good.

"Those look so pretty on you." Grif stroked her hair which had come out of its bun.

"I've got this, too, so I can get you ready for me." I showed her the toy, which had a bit of a knot on it. "Be quiet, or I'll gag you. Everyone's home and I don't want to share your cries. Though I love your cute noises," I said as I put the blindfold on her.

Again, her face indicated that she *liked* the idea. Good.

"What's your safe word?" I got her on her knees and lubed up her ass and worked the toy in, Grif playing with her breasts. Everything we'd gotten for her was pink, a stark contrast to the dark colors in my bedroom.

"Fruity little drink." She smirked.

Grif smothered a laugh, and I shrugged. After all, she'd come up with it.

"Good girl. Don't be afraid to use it. Now, don't you dare come. You won't like the punishment, promise," I growled, as I continued to work the toy into her.

Grif teased her blindfolded face with little kisses.

"Look at that, Grif." Toy fully seated in her ass. I sat back on my heels, admiring her for a moment. "All she needs is to be tied up."

"Perfect." Grif kissed her on the lips and turned her so she was on her back.

Taking the rope, I tied her arms to the bed, giving her plenty of slack so we could move her as we pleased. "Too tight?"

She shook her head.

"Words." I moved her hip so I could smack her ass, smelling her desire flare as my hand landed on her bare skin with a crack.

"It's not too tight, my king." Her lips pressed together, as if suppressing a smile.

"She looks beautiful," Grif murmured, running his hand down her arm.

My pretty princess, ready to be conquered.

Grif pushed her thighs open and swiped her with his fingers, then tasted them. "So wet. Taste?"

I licked her off his fingers. "Oh, Princess, you taste delicious. I think I'll have some more."

Burying my face in our greedy girl, Grif teased and taunted the rest of her body. Cute noises and moans escaped her lips as I sucked and kissed that sweet pussy, driving her closer and closer to her peak.

"I… I'm so close. May I please come, my king?" she panted, writhing in her bonds.

Oh, how I loved hearing her call me that. Hmmm, should I let her?

"Not yet." I reached up and tweaked a clamp, making her gasp and drench my face with her juices.

"You'll look so beautiful coming on his face," Grif told her, squeezing her ass cheek.

"Clean up my face," I told her, climbing up her body so she could kiss her juices off my lips as Grif teased her ass and pussy.

That look crossed her lips again, the one that said she wanted to come. "Not yet, Princess. We aren't even inside you yet. Show me how you take Grif's cock."

Grif threw her legs over his shoulders and started fucking her pussy. "That's my girl. You feel so fucking good."

I ran my hand over her smooth ass. Removing the toy, I lubed her back up.

"Are you ready for me, Princess? I'm not going to be gentle. You come when I say, and when you do, I'm going to slam my knot into you and fill your ass up with my cum. You're going to take it like the pretty little cum dumpster you are," I told her, getting cozy next to Grif.

We repositioned her and I worked two of my lubed fingers in her ass, making sure she was good and ready.

"Yes, my king." Her voice went breathy, the air heavy with her arousal and pheromones. She wouldn't last long.

Lubing my hard cock, I worked myself inside her tight hole. A little gasp left her lips as I slid into her up to the base of my knot.

Grif ran his hand over her leg. "You did that so good. Do you feel all nice and full with both of us inside you?"

"So good," she sighed.

"You do feel good, Princess." I pumped in and out of her, getting into a rhythm with Grif. I could feel him through her thin walls, as her muscles squeezed me.

As we fucked her, Grif played with the clips on her tits as I toyed with her clit.

"I'm going to come, Kitten," Grif told her. "Don't come until AJ tells you. Lock me when you do."

I rubbed her faster because as Grif came inside her, I'd come–and I wanted my knot in her. "Come for me, Princess, so I can knot your sweet, tight ass."

Grif quickened his pace, and I *felt* him come through her walls. Shit. I had no idea how good it would be to feel Grif while I took her. She moaned, body trembling.

As soon as he came, I felt her muscles spasm, both in orgasm and as she locked him. Her ass squeezed me like a vise. *Fuuuuck*.

I pulled out and slid back inside her, continuing to play with her clit and hold her tight as I pushed my fully inflated knot through her ring of muscles.

"AJ," she cried, as I filled her ass full of my cum, knotting her tight with Grif locked in her pussy.

"You took us so good, Princess," I praised, stroking her ass. "Everyone okay?"

"So good," she sighed.

"Amazing." Grif leaned over and stole a kiss from me.

When she unlocked him, Grif removed her blindfold and kissed her. Murmuring to her, he undid her wrists and rubbed them.

I laid on top of her, and rolled us so we were on our sides, careful of my knot still locked in her ass. Grif got her back and threw a warm blanket over us as I held them both. Our three bodies entwined. I stroked her back and his hair as the storm raged outside.

As far as I was concerned, it was only this room, only us, and nothing else.

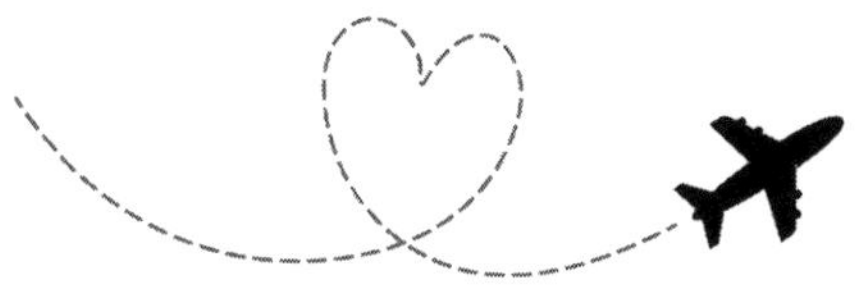

Chapter Twenty-Two

Grif

A body pressed into me. A golden, toned body, with long dark hair. Another toned, golden body with short, dark hair lay on the other side of me. Oh, I was sandwiched between Verity and AJ, in AJ's ridiculously comfortable adjustable bed.

We'd fucked her good last night. After she'd fallen asleep, AJ had taken me in the shower. Then we climbed into bed with her.

For so long, I'd told myself that I didn't need alphas. Didn't deserve alphas. That even AJ, who'd waited for me for so many years, didn't truly want me for me. It was just that biological alpha-omega pull.

But he did. So did she.

Lucky me.

The bond I shared with Dean and AJ felt quiet. At some point, AJ had drawn heavy curtains over the windows, blocking the light. The clock told me that if it were a usual day, it wouldn't be *that* early.

Today wasn't a normal day, it was a snow day. My phone confirmed everything was closed, and the city recommended that non-essential personnel stay home.

With everything I'd been through, it would be nice to have a day or two to be snowed in with everyone—especially the sleeping goddess next to me. The image of her tied up and blindfolded while being knotted by AJ would live in my head forever.

She could probably use a couple of days to relax with us as well.

By the chill in the air, I had a feeling the electricity had gone off. The building had a generator, but it was for the elevators and safety systems. We had one, but it wasn't automatic.

Carefully, I extracted myself from them and went to the bathroom–where the lights didn't turn on. I threw on AJ's bathrobe.

My gaze fell on her when I came back into the bedroom. I'd turn on the heat, have her for breakfast, and then cook for her. After all, I promised her that months ago.

Picking her up, I carried her from AJ's room into mine. She stirred as I tucked her into *my* bed, glad I'd gotten those flannel sheets and heavy blankets.

"Ummmpf?" Her eyes fluttered open.

"Go back to sleep." I gave her a kiss and threw my new thick, down comforter, with its soft dark green plaid cover on top of her. Putting on my slippers, I entered the laundry room where we kept the generator and turned it on, making sure it was properly ventilated.

"Oh, you got it." Jonas stood there, also in a bathrobe and slippers. "I slept through it, sorry. I'd made sure I topped it off the other day, but if we need more fuel, the cupboard is stocked."

"It's fine. I can start the generator." I shrugged.

"Thanks for doing that. The storm's shaping up to be bad. We should be fine," Jonas told me. "Would you like me to make breakfast? I was going to get in a workout before everyone got up."

"I'll make breakfast later. Enjoy your workout." I slipped back into my room, closing the door, and getting under the covers with Verity.

Wrapping my arms around her, I dozed for a bit. When I felt Verity stir, I burrowed under the covers and buried my head between her thighs. Drawing my tongue up her soft folds, I tasted us still on her.

Best breakfast ever.

Cute little noises escaped her lips as I licked her into wakefulness.

The blanket lifted, and her face peaked under the covers. "Hiya, Tiger."

"Good morning, Kitten. I'm a little busy eating breakfast. Can I help you?" I smirked, gazing up at those blue-green eyes.

"Mmmm, you can bury your cock inside me," she hummed, her driftwood scent going sweet with desire and need.

"Can I?" I gave her clit a long and teasing lick, then met her gaze.

"Oh, yes, you can." Her eyes gleamed. "Though that feels delightful."

Shimmying out from under all the covers, I sank my cock deep inside her wet and waiting warmth without any preparation. My arms wrapped around her.

"Like that." She giggled, arching her back and moving her hips to meet my thrusts.

As much as I loved fucking her against the wall with her arms above her head or seeing her tied up and at AJ's mercy, I also loved *this.*

We play wrestled as we fucked, laughing and kissing. Finally, I pinned her to the bed, making her come as I came inside her, then collapsed on her chest, burying my face in her breasts.

"That was a very delicious breakfast," I told her, gazing up at her. "I think I have enough energy to cook for you now."

She laughed, then recognition crossed her face. "Please wake me up like this anytime. Can I help you cook?"

"I'd love that." Cooking beside her sounded fantastic.

"We're in your room?" She looked around.

"Didn't want to wake AJ." I propped my head up on my hand so I could see her better.

Verity took the robe I'd been wearing earlier and disappeared into her room to get dressed. It was still a little on the chilly side, so I threw on sweats and walked out to the kitchen.

I started the coffee, looked to see what we had, then attempted to make her a chai latte according to the instructions of the package I found in the cupboard.

"Bacon, crispy potatoes, fruit salad, and frittata?" I asked as she came out looking delicious in leggings and a sweater. We were not only fully stocked, but it looked like AJ had hit the warehouse store.

She kissed my cheek and ran her hand through my hair. "Perfect."

"I made this for you. Though I have no idea if I did it right." I handed her the steaming chai latte.

Verity took a sip. "This is amazing. Thank you."

We cooked together, chopping and whisking as delicious smells filled the kitchen. Jonas came downstairs, wearing only workout shorts, his tattooed chest glistening with sweat.

"Morning, Little Alpha." Jonas snagged Verity and kissed her.

"Hi, Jonas." She smiled, and it traveled all the way to her eyes like it did when she was truly happy.

We made her happy.

I made her happy.

Jonas left to shower and wake up Dean. There was a thumping down the stairs and Mercy appeared, wearing sweats.

"Bacon." Mercy snagged a mostly cooked piece out of the pan with her bare fingers.

"Set the table?" Verity looked at me. "That okay?"

"Yep. Dishes are in the cupboard by the oven," I told her, as I tossed the fruit salad with a bit of orange juice.

"Hey." AJ appeared, wearing only a pair of flannel pajama pants. He snagged me for a kiss. "Mmmm, coffee."

"I've got some of that for you." I poured him a mug. He drank his black like Jonas and I did. Dean liked his mostly cream when he didn't have a matcha latte.

"Do I get some coffee?" Mercy asked.

"Help yourself." I gestured to the cupboard where the mugs were as I made Dean a matcha latte.

"Morning, Princess." AJ ran a hand down her face and she melted into him.

They looked amazing together–and they were both mine.

"Hi." Dean bounded in and gave me a kiss, then hugged Verity, burying his face in her neck.

Jonas came back in, shirtless, with wet hair. We sat around the glass dining room table and dug in.

"I guess I'm not going to the greenhouse today." Verity looked longingly outside at the snowstorm, which was still raging, as she took a bite of bacon.

"No one's going anywhere if we can help it. Not that anything's open." Jonas took a bite of frittata.

"Movies and board games? We probably can't order burritos, but I think we have everything we need to make them." Dean grabbed more bacon.

"Yes, blanket burrito night sounds fantastic. I want to work out later." I took a gulp of coffee. At some point, I wanted to spend some time at the piano. Verity's song was coming along nicely.

"Me, too. Can someone teach me how to fight now? I know you hesitated before, but there has to be something you can show me," Verity asked as she ate some potatoes.

"Actually, there is," AJ replied. "Back after I was first injured, my physical therapist showed me how I could use my cane as a weapon. I can teach you some moves. I totally forgot about that."

"You should combine it with both trying to get her to bark at you and throw off yours. She's improving a lot." Jonas took a bite of fruit.

Verity's nose wrinkled. "Improving? I still can't bark anyone."

"It'll come, Sweetheart," Jonas assured. "You're so much better at resisting than a few months ago."

Mercy's brown eyes blinked. "You're doing what now?"

"Helping me so that the parents can't bark at me ever again." Verity's look grew pained, and I squeezed her hand in reassurance.

"Do you need help with anything? Fighting, barks?" Jonas offered Mercy.

"Rusty and some others have been teaching me fighting moves. Please, teach me whatever you want. I don't have a bark yet because I'm not awakened. But I'd love lessons on how to not get barked at by the parents, especially if I'm going to spend part of the summer in London." Mercy looked at Verity, eyebrows knitting. "It'll wake up soon, right? Hale was a senior in high school when it happened. I'm the only unawakened alpha on the team. Even Kaiko is a full alpha."

"You're younger than Hale was when he was a senior. It'll come," Verity assured.

"We're here. If you're holding your own as a crusher on a professional skate smash team against adult alphas, it's going to be a little bitch to control your alpha when it wakes up," Jonas told her. "I speak from experience."

"Um, okay." Mercy shrugged and took more bacon.

Her point of reference in alpha awakening was probably Verity, and I had a feeling it wasn't typical.

"Verity, if you need to practice purring, I volunteer." Dean licked his lips.

Mercy's head cocked. "What's wrong with Verity's purr? You know, that's why Mumsy is still salty with you. Hopey likes yours best and bitterly complains that it doesn't work over the tablet."

"Nothing's wrong with it. Dean just wants to snuggle with her," I snorted.

"Oh, is it something you need to keep doing then, like working out, and with no littles she's not getting practice? Curious, since I can't do that yet either." Mercy plopped another slice of frittata on her plate.

"It turns out purrs have settings. I'm only good at the soft purr used for babies." Verity laughed. "Been working on it, though."

"Work on it all you want. I like having my head in your boobies." Dean gave her a big smile.

Mercy snorted. "You're supposed to *hear* alpha purrs? I thought since they were a special thing, the whole point was to not hear it, just feel it."

"You've only ever heard Verity purr," I breathed. We had some work to do.

"I mean, I guess my mom purred for me when I was little, but I don't remember. Dad purrs for me sometimes when I'm upset or sad, and that's not silent, but he's an omega." Mercy shrugged. "I thought the recordings they played in alpha lessons at school were dramatizations."

"Usually you hear them. Except for the baby purr, which is very quiet or silent so you don't startle or wake the baby," Jonas explained and took another bite of food.

Mercy nodded. "Which would be why Verity's the best."

"Would you be interested in going to alpha camp this summer for a few weeks during the off-season? The one I went to was fun. Learned some good shit. Much better than the classes we had in school. Especially since you're missing those last-year alpha classes." AJ took more potatoes.

"Ooh, like the camps where you learn massage and cooking, or the kind where you live in the forest and beat people up? Both are fine, but I'd rather go to the first one." Mercy grinned and shoveled more food into her mouth.

"That sounds like a good idea. I always forget those exist," Verity said softly as she took a sip of her chai latte.

The good camps were exclusive and expensive, training the next generation of young alphas in everything from self-defense to running a household to pampering their omega. Not to mention a good place to network with other young alphas. Dean's dad had a lot of contacts from his days at alpha camp.

"Oh, we should send you to one where you learn sailing," Dean interjected. "We have a sailboat at the lake by our cabin."

Mercy nodded as she snagged more bacon. "I've always wanted to learn to sail."

We finished breakfast and cleaned up.

"So, during a snowstorm, we hang out and watch movies and play games and do inside shit?" Mercy gathered up the plates.

"Yep. Want to pick first?" Dean offered as he put away the food.

"They should absolutely get to pick because everyone here always chooses the same things," AJ teased, rinsing plates and putting them in the dishwasher.

"If you let Verity pick, we're going to be watching something about fairies or unicorns. Can we bake cookies? Then maybe watch one of the Defender League movies?" Mercy asked, putting some silverware in the sink.

"Please tell me you like the Space Explorers movies? I always get outvoted." Jonas' eyes pleaded with them as he wiped off the counters.

"Um, *yeah.*" Mercy nodded. So did Verity.

They liked space movies. We were fucked.

Jonas grabbed Verity and kissed her deeply. "You are amazing."

"We should all learn a fake language, maybe from those movies?" Mercy added. "You know Gwen is fluent in one."

Dean snorted as he put something in the fridge. "So is Carlos. It's probably the same one."

"I would have guessed Clark. Fake language, why not?" I shrugged, gathering up the mugs. "Should we make some cookies first?"

"We got everything for candy cookies." Verity went to the cabinet. "I even bought things to make you a not-chocolate batch, Jonas."

"Candy cookies? Fuck yeah." Honestly, I didn't care what we watched or ate, I just wanted to spend time with everyone.

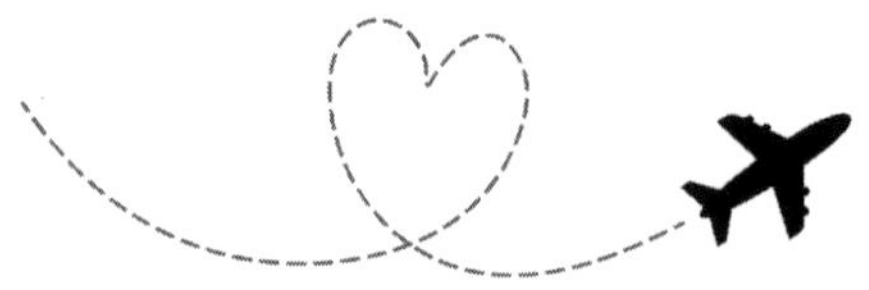

Chapter Twenty-Three

Jonas

"You suck my omega so good, Sweet Girl," I told Verity as she gave Dean head as I fucked him.

Dean gasped and squirmed under us. I smacked his ass so he'd be still.

We were in my room as the storm continued to rage outside on day two of our snow-cation. Mercy and AJ cooked lunch as Grif sat at his piano writing something.

Now, Dean could receive his second shutout blowjob. The first was last night when AJ tugged Grif off after blanket burrito night, and she ended up spending part of the night with us.

Until Grif had slipped into my room in the middle of the night, because someone left the door cracked, and he *stole* her out of bed.

"I love your blowjobs so much, Little Alpha." Dean's perfume and cozy scent flooded the room as he tangled his hand in her ponytail. "I'm close."

"She'll suck you down so good." My hands held Dean's hips as I kept thrusting, my knot and balls smacking against his ass as my own pleasure built. "I'm close too, and I'll fill up this sweet omega ass just like you'll fill up our little alpha's belly so full of your cum that she won't want any lunch."

"I could come just from those words," he moaned.

"And I'm going to knot you," I gasped as I withdrew almost fully, then plunged right into his slick omega ass.

"*Alpha*," he cried, as sheer lust pelted my bond with Dean. My knot slipped past the ring of muscles and locked inside him.

"Are you okay, Love?" I smoothed Dean's hair as his body shuddered.

"So good, Babes." His scent went syrupy with happiness as he stroked Verity's cheekbone with his thumb. "Mmmm, I love shutout blowies."

"Are you okay, Little Alpha?" I asked. She hadn't gotten much attention this morning, and it was almost time for lunch.

She released Dean's cock and wiped her mouth with the back of her hand. "Delicious as always, Hot Stuff." Her gaze turned to me. "I'm so full, Alpha Jonas. You're right, I might be too full to eat. Our good omega gave me all the cum."

Though no orgasms. Hmmm... I owed her a reward.

Maybe after lunch.

Perfect. My hands smoothed the fresh down comforter I'd put on my bed as I'd completely remade it after lunch with our fluffiest feather bed and our softest sheets. Of which I may have gotten after my conversation with Verity while she was in Hawai'i.

I lit a bunch of candles, several of them new since she liked lavender-scented things, and added a relaxing blend of oil with lavender notes to the diffuser. The oil warmer was already plugged in. Going into my closet, I grabbed a couple of my silk ties and put them on my nightstand.

Now, to get Verity. Though I wasn't beyond putting her over my shoulder, carrying her to my room, closing the door, and not letting anyone in.

In the kitchen, Dean, and Grif both had on hockey-themed aprons. Flour dusted *every* surface. Ingredients and kitchen tools littered the counters.

More bread? Verity had made Dean bread last night to see if her sourdough starter was okay.

I pinched the bridge of my nose as I took in the chaos. The floor—I'd steam-mopped it after breakfast. Yeah, this was why I didn't encourage those two to bake.

"We're making cinnamon rolls." Dean grinned, flour in his hair, as he ground something up with a mortar and pestle.

"We'll clean up. Verity and Mercy have never had our recipe. We thought they'd go really well with the beef bulgogi you're making tonight," Grif added as he rummaged through a drawer. "Found it." He held up some sort of weird metal hook.

I took a deep, calming breath. "That sounds like a delicious dessert. Just please make sure the kitchen is clean so I don't have to tidy up and do dishes before I cook. Since that makes it take longer."

Then they complained about being hungry.

Ugh. *This mess.* I couldn't even. Also, I personally thought that was an odd pairing. However, making cinnamon rolls was a *long* process. Which meant they'd be occupied for a while.

AJ sat at the dining room table catching up on work. Sure, we had a snowstorm here, but it was business as usual in many places.

"Where's Mercy and Verity?" I looked around.

"Since the electricity's back on, Mercy's hooked up her game buddy to the upstairs TV since her console is still drying and is swearing at her friends." AJ, in sweats and a holey henley, looked up from his laptop. "I think Verity's in the laundry room, trying to save some of her clothes."

"We should buy them some things after the storm." Grif was attaching the hooks to our fancy stand mixer.

Oh, that's what they're for.

“I’ve already ordered a few things for them and gave her access to the shopping accounts. But feel free to take them.” AJ tried to type with one hand and text with another.

I went over to AJ and lowered my voice, though Dean and Grif were now bickering over what type of cinnamon to use. “Hey, I owe Verity something. Keep an eye on them for me.”

“Only if you owe her a cock in the mouth.” His eyes lit up.

“Oh, yes.” And so much more. “Thanks, AJ.”

“Anytime.” He smirked.

The laundry room reeked of vinegar. Verity had a spray bottle and a baleful look.

“How’s it going?” I put an arm around her waist and snagged her for a kiss.

“I can’t get the mildew out of these things.” She gestured to the clothes soaking in bowls or laid out on every surface.

“How important are they?” I asked as I checked the fuel levels on the generator. It could go out again at any time.

Verity sighed. “Honestly, not really. I think I’ll let them soak. Wash them on hot one last time. And then…”

“That’s for the better. Are you done? Because I think someone is due a reward.” I came up behind her and pressed myself into her. My lips attacked her neck, and the spray bottle in her hand fell to the floor.

“Jonas.” Her driftwood scent flared with sweet desire.

I picked her up and carried her back into my bedroom and shut the door. Balancing her on my hip, I pulled back the comforter and sheets and set her on the bed, watching her expression as she sank into the softness.

Usually, I didn't allow street clothes in the bed, but she'd just put on some leggings and one of Dean's shirts when we had lunch.

Her nostrils flared and her eyes gleamed. "Wait, is this..."

I picked up the ties from the nightstand and flicked out my pierced tongue. "Oh, it is. Is that okay, Sweet Girl?"

"Please." She pulled off her shirt and tossed it on the floor.

There was nothing under that shirt but golden breasts and erect nipples. Grabbing her by the ankles, I pulled her to me and peeled off her fuzzy socks and leggings.

No panties either? *Lucky me.*

I positioned her naked body on the bed and made sure she had enough pillows. Taking the ties, I secured her to my headboard, using the hidden rings meant for that purpose.

Standing back, I admired my work. "Are you comfortable, Sweetheart?"

"I am. Yellow if I'm not, red if I need you to stop." Her gaze smoldered as she spread her toned legs.

Grabbing my phone, I started my relaxation music playlist, and soothing sounds filled the room. I flipped off the lamp, so the room was lit only by the window and candles.

Nice and cozy.

"I'm going to feast on you and make you come over and over." I crawled on the bed, caging her with my arms.

My lips crashed against her, and I kissed her long and hard until she writhed under me. My kisses covered her face. They trailed down her neck and languidly skated over her collarbone where maybe one day I'd mark her. I explored every inch of her body: her shoulders, her elbows, the backs of her knees.

"Jonas." Her voice shook.

I knew what she wanted, but she didn't ask, being patient. Wow, it was nice to have a patient lover in my bed.

My kisses trailed up her leg. I traced the little flower on her inner thigh with my tongue. Pushing her thighs open wide, I buried my face in her softness.

"Yes, *yes*," she cried, back arching.

"Come whenever you want. Though if you cry too loud, we're going to have company." My pierced tongue flickered over her clit.

An orgasm shuttered through her body. I explored her with my tongue and mouth, as two of my fingers entered her, getting her ready to come again.

It didn't take long for her body to explode in pleasure again, her juices bursting all over my face. *Good girl.*

I looked up at her to make sure she was okay. Bliss coated her face.

"I also bought a little treat for your pussy." I took the little pale green toy out of my nightstand. "It's a knot trainer. It inflates and helps to stretch you. If we use it sometimes when we're together, eventually it should make it easier for you to take a knot."

"Perfect. I might still get that piercing that helps lady alphas take knots." That smolder in her eyes intensified.

Mmmm. I'd love to see her pussy pierced. She'd also look beautiful with nipple rings.

I inserted the little toy into her pussy and programmed the remote on the first setting. Then I got back to work getting all the right spots with my tongue.

"There, there, there," she cried, legs wrapped around me.

"Oh, yeah?" I slowed down, as I lazily wrote declarations of love on her clit with my tongue.

Every time she got close, I backed off as the toy continued to pulse inside her. Its purpose was to stretch, not give her pleasure.

I got the lube and squirted her ass with it. My fingers worked it as I attacked her pussy with full force.

What an enjoyable way to spend a snowy afternoon, just the two of us.

She gasped as another orgasm shot through her. I didn't stop, working a third finger in her ass, making her come again and again.

As promised.

"Are you okay, Sweet Girl? Because if you are, I'm going to take your ass and knot you." Should I leave the stretcher toy in her pussy? Yes, I think I would.

Her blue-green eyes met mine, arms still over her head. "I'm feeling so loved and worshiped right now. Please, take me, Sexypants."

"Now how could I deny a request like that?" I cleaned off my hands and got the lube, giving her ass and my cock a good squirt.

Sexypants? I'd take it. Because I had all the pierced sexy in my pants.

Holding her legs, I entered her sweet ass, noting that she felt fuller with the toy in her pussy. I started to thrust, keeping her gaze. "Does my sweet girl need a nice, thick knot?"

"Oh, I do," she sighed, eyes blown out in desire.

Taking my time, I thrust in and out of her tight ass, being mindful of her leg. Verity writhed and moaned.

I glanced at the door as I continued to thrust in and out of her, working myself toward my own release.

No one had knocked asking to come in–or join. I'd have to thank AJ later for keeping them distracted.

"You take me so good, Sweetheart," I praised, rubbing her clit. "Come for me so I can knot your beautiful ass." My knot was fully inflated and ready to seat itself inside our sweet girl.

"Please, Jonas, please," she begged, back arching.

Verity came, her muscles spasming. As she did, I pulled out and thrust back in.

"That's it. That's my good girl," I crooned as I worked my knot past her ring of muscles, seating it fully inside her, and shooting her full of cum.

"Oooh, that feels so good," she sighed.

"Oh, you do." I worked the little toy out of her and cleaned it with a wipe. I'd clean it better later.

Still locked inside her, I pulled on the ties, releasing her from her bonds. Laying on top of her, I rolled us to our sides and took her hands in my wrists, rubbing them and her arms.

"Are you okay?" I asked her.

"Boneless." She kissed me. "That was the best reward."

"You are amazing and wonderful. I'm here to support you in any way you need, especially as you and Grif work things out," I assured.

They had some work to do, but I could see that connection between them.

"Thank you." She kissed me again, then rested her head on my shoulder, cuddling into me.

"I love that you're here with us. You need a rest so bad. After this, we'll have a nice bubble bath, and I'll give you a good rubdown." And I'd put my cock in her mouth if she asked me to.

"I'm feeling so spoiled," Verity sighed.

"I love spoiling you." Already she looked so much happier than she had when we'd come home from our game in Quebec.

Yeah, I didn't see her and Mercy returning to their place after it was fixed. We'd need to finish all our renovations. At least we'd gotten started. Tomorrow I'd see if Mercy wanted to go running so I could get to know her a little better.

Our little snow-cation should be the first of many. We needed more blanket burrito nights. Summer evenings on the porch. Her being in my bed.

I kissed my blissed-out sweet girl.

Yes, there was no doubt that our little alpha belonged with us.

Chapter Twenty-Four

Dean

I looked through my art supplies for my paint brushes. Mostly I preferred to work with pencils or charcoal, but I did paint sometimes–like when I'd added color to the picture in Mercy's room. I'd never done that before and wanted to try that with something else.

First, I needed to figure out where I'd left my brushes. We were on day three of being snowed in. While the power had come back on, another storm was hitting.

And I loved it.

We got to relax and spend time together playing games and watching movies in front of the fire. It was fun learning about Mercy and Verity's favorites–and teaching them about ours.

Though Jonas had downloaded some app to all our phones so we could learn some fake space language together. Whatever. It made him happy.

At least our place was big enough that everyone could spread out and have space.

Like right now. I was drawing. Grif played the piano. Jonas hid upstairs reading. Mercy and Verity had been baking more cookies.

That was something else I liked—all the cookies and treats. Like the cinnamon rolls we made yesterday. Or the coffee cake we had this morning.

Good thing we had a gym in the house.

Music serenaded me as I walked out into the living room. He'd play, write things down, frown, play something else, erase things, then write more things and do it all again.

It was nice seeing Grif compose. I kicked myself for not getting him a piano the moment he'd moved in.

Helping myself to a cookie from the cooling rack on the counter, I went upstairs. I might have left my paint brushes lying around up there.

I peeked in the open door to the gym. Verity, in a sports bra and leggings, smacked one of the punching bags with her crutch.

"Good. Again. Tell him to stop, then hit him if he doesn't," AJ instructed.

"I'm never going to get it." Her head hung.

Putting his hand under her chin, he tipped her face up. "Believe in it. Want it. Claim it. Now do it again."

I let them be. Alpha lessons would be good for her.

Mercy had gotten her game system working and was playing with some of her friends. I waved, and she waved back, then returned to shooting things and swearing over her headset.

My paint brushes weren't in any of the boxes on the landing or lying around.

Jonas sat in the library, curled up in the book nook, reading a thick volume with a spaceship on the cover. "Hey."

I dove in for a cuddle. "Hi. I'm looking for my paint brushes."

"I think they're in the office on top of a box." Jonas planted a kiss on the top of my head.

The office attached to the library was full of AJ's shit. Though we were thinking about making it a guest room so we'd have some place for Jonas' sister to stay when she came to visit. My brushes were right where he told me. I grabbed them and returned to my room.

Getting out my paints, I took the small black and white picture of Verity I'd printed on canvas and highlighted elements with my paints. *A little color here... a dab of glitter there...*

After a while, someone knocked on my open door.

"Can I come in?" Grif wore loose jeans and had the hoodie Verity had given him over his flannel. He looked so snuggly and delicious.

"Please." I looked at the picture and nodded.

"Oh, that's pretty. I especially like the glitter accents." Grif wrapped his arms around me as we gazed at the black and white picture.

"It's time for dinner, isn't it?" I was making pork chops.

"No. I... I just..." Grif turned away.

"What do you need?" I stood and pressed my lips to his forehead, which was a little clammy. He didn't quite smell right.

"I need a hug." He rested his head on my shoulder.

"Always. Want to watch a movie or snuggle or something? Maybe eat some of those cookies?" I wrapped my arms around him. He struggled with the lower dosage of blockers.

"This is silly, but can we build a blanket fort in the den and watch a movie in there?" he offered.

"That sounds good. I was ready for a break, anyway." Blanket forts fixed a lot of things, especially when you didn't have a nest.

Which he didn't. Verity offered him the *secret nest in her closet,* and he wasn't sure he wanted it.

Um, I wanted a nest in Verity's closet.

We gathered blankets, chairs, and pillows from around the house, moved the den couch, and built a massive blanket fort. I found hooks and clips, so we could make it truly epic.

"Think fast." Grif threw a cushion at me.

It hit me in the face. Laughing, I dove at him. "You're in for it, Gumdrop."

We wrestled on the den carpet, like we had when we were kids. All we needed was for my mom to bring us a big plate of treats.

He pinned me to the ground by my arms and kissed me. "Yield."

"I suppose." I kissed him back and rolled into him, enjoying a snuggly moment.

We finished making our fort, and I pulled up the movie and he grabbed some snacks. Getting cozy in the fort in the dark den, with only the movie for light, I felt him relax. His scent changed back to normal.

Snacks eaten, I used him as a pillow. He stroked my hair, both of us covered by fluffy blankets. We didn't do this nearly enough.

His scent was coming through more and more, too. Mmmm. Maybe we should close the door and get a little sexy in our tent. When had we last fucked in a pillow fort?

"Grif, are you in here?" Verity called from the doorway of the den. She smelled like AJ's body wash, as if she had just taken a shower. Alpha lessons must be over.

He paused the movie. "Hi, Kitten. Dean and I are watching a movie."

"Oh, okay." She walked in so we could see her, but she didn't enter the fort. Now she wore leggings and one of Grif's hoodies, hair up in a poofy bun.

"I'll make dinner in a little bit, if that's okay?" I asked her. The movie wasn't over and I was full of cookies. And snacks. Mercy and Verity were now in charge of snack shopping.

"Mercy was talking about pizza. One place we like is having a special before the next storm hits. A few other places are too," she said. "Though we can absolutely have your dinner instead. Or as well. You've seen how much she eats."

"True. Kitten, do you want to watch the movie with us?" Grif asked.

She hesitated at the mouth of the fort. "This is a beautiful blanket fort. I especially like how you used clips and hooks to suspend it from the ceiling. I always used stools when making them for the littles."

My omega preened at her compliments.

I held out my arms, wanting to squish-cuddle her. "Come in."

"If you insist." Verity crawled into our fort and got into my arms as she arranged the blankets around the three of us.

Grif turned the movie back on, as he, Verity, and I nestled together in the fort, watching the movie, drinking our hot chocolate. The tent filled with our scents, making it feel cozy.

Our little alpha in our fort felt *right.*

This snow break was incredible. If Verity stayed, we'd have so many more days like this.

I couldn't wait.

"I'm so full," I announced, and piled on the couch with everyone, except Mercy, who was on the ottoman. Which seemed to be her favorite spot. I sat between Jonas and Grif. Verity curled on AJ's lap, her legs on Grif.

Mercy and Jonas had gone out and returned with *three* pizzas, burritos, beer, and a giant cake.

Verity chose the movie, and it was this bizarre movie about a fairy king and a maze. It would be amazing to watch after a couple of special gummies.

When it finished, we cleaned up. AJ went to take the trash and recycling down to the dumpsters in the parking garage. Verity and Grif whispered all cute-like as they did the dishes. Jonas and I tidied up the living room.

Mercy looked at her phone. "I've got to raid a fort with Gwenifer and Kaiko. Gwenifer never gets to play video games, so I can't miss this. Smell you later."

With a wave, she ran up the stairs.

"Living with a teenager is weird." Jonas put the table back.

"Who's Gwenifer?" Grif asked as he wiped down the counters.

"Gwen. Ladybug. No idea why she calls her that." Verity got the broom and swept the floor.

Grif wrapped his arms around her waist and whispered in her ear. Now he had on a flannel. Her eyes widened, and I could smell her sweet desire and feel his arousal through our bond.

I wanted some of that.

"Alpha Jonas, would you like to watch me, Grif, and Dean? Grif has something fun planned." She put the broom away and looked at me like she wanted to eat me. Her tongue moistened her lower lip.

Now *that* was what I was talking about.

"Thank you for inviting me, but I decline this time. AJ and I are going to watch a boxing match. Have fun." Jonas continued cleaning up.

What? I'd take it.

"Oh, we will." I went over to Jonas and gave him a kiss.

"You don't have to ask anymore, Love," he murmured. "I'll let her know, too."

About time. "Thanks, Babes."

Practically skipping down the hall, I joined them in Grif's room. Grif shut the door and turned the small lamp on, giving it a cozy glow.

Hmm. Maybe I should get him more pillows and blankets.

"Jellybean, I've been wanting to put Verity in the swing and then tell you what to do with her," Grif told me as he took off his flannel shirt. "Let you lick and touch her. If you're good, I'll fuck you into her."

I almost came in my pants. "Oh, yes, please." I gave Verity a smoldering look. "I know how to eat pussy now."

"Oh yes, you do." She waggled her eyebrows.

My clothes came off like they'd evaporated. Grif, only in boxers, picked up a now naked Verity. She squealed a little as he spun her around in his arms, then placed her in the swing gently, like the princess she was.

"Lick her pussy," Grif said as he adjusted the buckles on the swing.

"Gladly." Kneeling between her legs, I feasted on her. She made happy noises as I licked and teased her the way Jonas taught me.

She moaned again as Grif kissed her and played with her breasts. Each of those cute little sounds made me hard.

"Dean," she gasped as she came all over my face.

"Switch. I'm going to fuck her now." Grif patted my bare ass to get me out of the way.

What did I do now? My erect cock dripped with slick and pre-cum.

"Give me that pretty cock, Omega," Verity demanded, batting her eyelashes at me.

"Yes, Alpha." Didn't need to tell me twice.

Verity opened her mouth and let me feed her my cock. Oh, yes. Her throat squeezed me as she sucked me down.

Grif stripped and plunged himself inside her.

"I'm going to come, Little Alpha." I looked at both her and Grif for permission.

"I'm going to fill her pussy with cum," Grif told us.

Verity moaned and shuddered, the room filling with her arousal and alpha pheromones. She sucked me down as I came in her mouth. Grif came in her pussy.

"Mmmm, you're delicious, Hot Stuff." Verity licked her lips. "That felt amazing, Tiger."

I leaned in and kissed her. Grif came over with a wet washcloth and cleaned us up. Though he didn't let Verity out of the swing. I enjoyed pleasing her while she was all tied up like a cute little package. Though at some point, I'd love to be in her place.

Her and Grif sharing me? *Yes, please.*

"You did a great job." Grif put his arms around me, kissing me.

"Do I get a turn now?" My dick slicked at the thought.

Grif's kisses trailed down my neck. "Oh yes, while I fuck you."

Please.

"Come here, Hot Stuff," Verity said from the swing.

Entwining my hands in the straps to control the angle and keep her steady, I entered her.

"Little Alpha, you feel so good," I moaned, relishing the way she felt as her walls squeezed and teased my cock.

"I love being fucked by you," she told me, watching with interest and lust as Grif came behind me and started toying with my ass. "You're such a good omega."

Mmmm, tell me that again.

Grif nuzzled my neck, his lust pelting me through our bond. "Are you ready for me to fuck you into her?"

"Shit, yes." I gazed at Verity, my eyes going half-lidded as desire rose within me, as I thrust in and out of her.

"I like watching you with each other." She licked her lips as Grif put his hands on my hips, stilling me.

A happy noise escaped my lips as Grif entered me, thrusting into me–and pushing me into my little alpha.

"That feels so good," I sighed, as we got into a rhythm.

"Oh, it does." Verity's head lolled back in pleasure.

She squealed and as she did, her pussy fluttered and squeezed, then locked me.

"Oh fuck, I'm going to come." I'd never get enough of how it felt with her milking my dick like that. It differed from being knotted, but still filled my omega heart so much.

"Come for us, Jellybean," Grif urged, picking up the pace as he kissed my shoulder.

I came inside Verity, spent, holding on as Grif continued to thrust inside me, my cock locked in Verity's pussy.

Warmth filled my ass as Grif came inside me.

"Oh, Jellybean, I love fucking you," he sighed, continuing to kiss me.

"You took him so good," Verity praised. "Such a good omega."

My omega preened because he loved being told that. Over and over.

"Cuddle her, I'll be right back," Grif told me with a kiss.

She was still strapped in the swing but had unlocked me, so I knelt at her side and put my head in her boobies. Stroking my hair, her quiet purr vibrated in her chest.

"Now that is a pretty picture," Grif said as he undid her restraints, rubbing her wrists. "Are you okay?"

"I am." She beamed.

Grif scooped her up and put her in his bed. I dove in. These flannel sheets and down comforter made it so much cozier. I nestled in between her and Grif, humming with happiness and contentment.

He stroked my hair, and she purred again as the three of us cuddled together. Yeah, this was perfect.

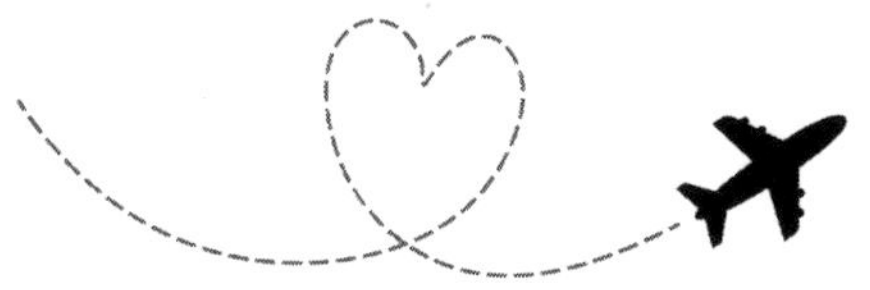

Chapter Twenty-Five

AJ

The living area was dark except for the glow of my computer. I'd had an online meeting in another time zone and continued to work. In a bit, I'd check on Grif and Verity, who'd gone to bed together.

The snowstorm was finally letting up. Though I'd enjoyed this a lot. Even when the power went out. Again.

Should I join them in bed? Or simply deposit Verity in another bed so I could have my way with Grif? Our bond was still new, and I wanted him all the time.

Though I desired her as well. She'd crawled under my skin and stayed there.

We could always fuck her together then have some shower sex after she fell asleep. That was always a good time.

Power was back on in much of the city and the metro was running. While a lot of things were still closed, people started to venture out again. Tomorrow, or rather today, we'd go to Verity and Mercy's place to see if anything else was salvageable.

I'd probably go into the office for a bit, too. More because I needed a little space. Sure, it had been a lot of fun playing board games and watching movies. Verity was conscientious about ensuring I had time with Grif. Mercy was a pretty cool kid. I could see those two living with us working.

Still, nerves frayed a little with us being cooped up together. Like Jonas getting a little obsessive about tidiness given the cleaner hadn't been here since the snow started.

Or Dean trying to keep Verity all to himself today, which caused Grif to get huffy and bang doors.

A little space would be good. Maybe the empanada place was open and I'd bring those back for everyone–and some groceries, if there were any to be had. We were running low on fresh things.

Someone came out of the hall. Probably Jonas. I'd told him I'd make sure everything was locked up before I went to sleep. Unless he was getting up for a snow run in the dark.

Which he might.

The fridge opened, and the slender figure illuminated by the light *wasn't* Jonas. No, it was Verity.

In only a T-shirt.

She got out a pitcher of something she had made earlier. Verity reached up and got a glass from the cupboard.

Oh. *Only* a shirt.

"Nice ass," I chuckled.

That ass waggled at me. "You want some of this?"

With a little laugh, she turned around and took a long drink, lounging against the counter.

Oh, did I.

"Still working?" She finished her drink and rinsed the glass, putting it in the sink, then put the pitcher back in the fridge.

"Just finishing up. Grif's asleep?" I finished my email and sent it off.

"Yes. I was thirsty, and I can't sleep. I need to get into my greenhouse, but we don't have permission yet. But the greenhouse manager, who's been *living there* to make sure no one's plants die, assured me that all my replacements have made it, even ones my sister sent, and are safe." Anxiousness tinged her scent.

"Well, that's good." I closed my laptop. It was dark except for the light above the stove and the small lights by the elevator. And the glow of the city since we'd opened the curtains as we ate the meatloaf and mashed potatoes Grif and Verity made.

"Yes. But I'll feel better when I get everything set up, and Hale brings me the bulbs." Verity moved to the glass doors in the dining room that opened out to the balcony. "Your view is amazing."

"Oh, it is. You can't sleep?" I stood.

"No. Sadly, not even a good fucking from Grif made me pass out." She put her hands on the glass, which made the hem of the shirt rise, giving me a peek of bare ass.

That sounded like a dare. I came up behind her. My bare feet found a couple of beads that hadn't gotten swept up after she and Mercy made bracelets earlier.

I'd known bracelet making was a thing in skate smash, but I hadn't realized the players made their own.

She hummed, still looking out the window. "It's sort of peaceful, enjoying the bustle of the city below but being way up here."

I stripped off my sweats. "So someone needs to sleep?"

Pressing my chest to her back, I cupped her bare ass. We hadn't had any alone time since I'd had her in her closet.

"AJ." Her voice went breathy as my fingers entered her warmth. She moved a bit, and I smacked her ass.

"Don't mind me. Keep enjoying your view. It is breathtaking." I kissed her again, her skin tasting of sweat, sex, and Grif.

What a combination.

She moaned softly, but let me tease and touch her. Her scent bloomed with arousal, and her muscles fluttered around my fingers.

"Hands up, legs apart, Princess. I'll get you ready for bed. Just keep enjoying that view." My other hand freed my cock from my briefs.

"Yes, my king." Her hands went higher on the glass, her legs spread apart.

Putting my hands on her hips, I plunged my cock into her pussy.

"Hmm, that feels spectacular," she murmured, eyes on the city like a good girl.

"Oh, you do. I like this ready access." I kissed her neck as my balls thumped against her ass, my body pressing her into the cold window.

But I'd warm her up after.

"How's the view, Princess?" My hand snaked around and started rubbing her clit, making her gasp.

"So nice," she sighed.

This was going to be quick, especially given I wouldn't be knotting her, much to my knot's chagrin.

"Come for me, Princess," I ordered. The hand on her clit increased its pace, and my other wrapped around her throat. "Make sure you lock me."

"Yes, my king." She moaned, and a few thrusts later, her muscles spasmed and fluttered around me as she orgasmed.

Her pussy locking my dick brought on my release, and I came inside her.

"Is the view still nice?" I kissed her neck again. My hand cracked against her ass as she tried to turn around.

"Perfect." She leaned into me.

Wrapping my arms around her, I enjoyed the view with her until her pussy unlocked me.

"You can put your hands down now." I turned her to face me, and I kissed her lips, which were sweet with sugary tea.

She rested her head on my shoulder. "That was a good way to enjoy the view. We'll have to do that again sometime."

"Oh, we will." I smoothed the hair out of her face. "Would you like to use my shower bed? It has a sleep setting."

She nodded, licking her lower lip. "I'd like that a lot."

After, maybe I'd fuck her again against the window in my room. Then she could enjoy a different view.

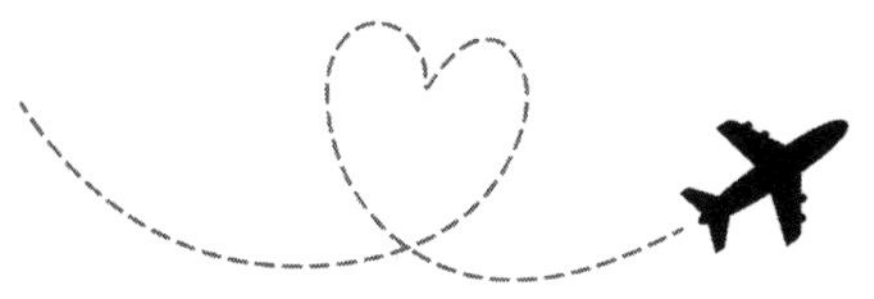

Chapter Twenty-Six

JONAS

"Are you sure you're okay up there? We have a 4x4. I'll come get you if you need me," I told my sister over my headset as we played Go-goKart.

Hana snorted. "We're fine. We have plenty of food, water, and power. It's a boarding school in a remote area. Things on campus are pretty normal. There's just no trips into town."

Be snowed in with hundreds of teenagers? *No, thank you.*

"What about you? Back to practice?" she asked as her blue go-kart raced across the screen, chasing after me.

"Most of the streets are dug out, and the deliveries are getting into the stores. But the training center flooded when their generator failed, so it'll be another day or two before we can get back to practice," I replied, trying to keep my lead over her.

Some of the team had also managed to get themselves snowed in and were trying to make their way back despite things like airport closures and train delays. How the fuck did Dimitri end up on the West Coast? He literally got off the plane in New York with the rest of us.

"This morning, we went to Verity's place to see what else was salvageable," I added. Which was practically nothing. We'd ended up going to Athlete's World since that's where Mercy liked to buy clothes, then visited a couple of boutiques, as well as Blankets and Beyond.

Then came home to a delicious array of takeout that AJ had brought back.

"Tomorrow we're going to the university to get her greenhouse set up before classes start," I added, as my go-kart darted past a patch of sand.

"Oh yes, your lady alpha that you moved in. I can't wait to meet her." She laughed as her go-kart snagged a power-up and shifted into turbo-speed.

"You're going to love Verity–and her teenage sister, who wants to be a history teacher. Though there are beads *everywhere.* It's like living with you and Charlie all over again," I chuckled.

Charlie's mom–my hockey coach–had held on to Hana and me tight after we'd run to her that night I'd hit my alpha mom in self-defense. They'd moved us in, helped us with legal issues, and been a family to us.

Hana's go-kart sped past me. I threw a coconut to stop her.

She swerved and passed the finish line. "I won. Again. Anyway, this has been fun, but I have dance practice to run bright and early. Love you, Jo."

"Love you, Han." I signed off and left the den.

Dean's room sat empty, Grif's door closed. Through the bond it felt like they were sleeping. AJ's door was shut. Verity wasn't in her room. Earlier, she'd been working on lesson plans for the class she was teaching.

Going into the living room, I started to *tuck in the house,* as Dean called it. I put away some wayward pillows, emptied the dishwasher, programmed the coffee pot, swept up some tiny beads that seemed to multiply every time I blinked, and set the alarms.

The lights glowed upstairs. I crept up to see if someone left them on or if Mercy was playing a game. She was itching to get back to practice and hang out with her friends, though she'd gone to the rink with a bunch of them to help clean up.

Singing came from the sitting area. Verity sat there with a tablet.

"I miss you. Dad says Mumsy's not mad. Can you come home now? I don't like this house; I want the old one," a little girl's voice pleaded. "Why aren't you here? I want you."

My heart broke.

"I'm not in New York because anyone's mad at me. I'm here taking care of Mercy and going to university. This summer I'll visit. Promise. I love taking care of you, but you have Dad, Mumsy, *and* Harry," Verity told her.

I kissed the top of Verity's head, not knowing what else to do. She looked up at me and smiled.

"There's a man in your house," the little girl squeaked. It was the little blonde one. Hope.

"Oooh, which one?" another girl's voice said. A light brown face appeared. "It's the blue one. We *like* the blue one, Hopey."

"I'm Jonas, hi." I waved. "They're staying with us."

"Because of the snow," the second one said. Tru, I think?

"If I get a job in New York, can I live with you?" Hope asked.

"If I'm still living in New York when you get a job, we'll talk about it," she assured.

Right, that was what our future held–siblings staying with us for school breaks or the summers. Possibly because they ran away. I didn't mind that one bit.

"I'm going to get my job in Rockland so I can live with Grace," Tru said. "The towels there are *warm*."

One could only imagine the comforts the Thanukos household offered.

"Living with Grace is always a good choice." Verity nodded. Hope didn't look as convinced.

"Blue man, what science are you?" Tru asked, with the innocence of someone who'd grown up assuming everyone had one.

"My degree is in Statistics. I attended BosTec like your brother Dare." But I hadn't gone to BosTec to be a pro hockey player. I'd played hockey for anger management and financial aid purposes, then took the opportunity to go pro when it happened.

She sucked in a breath. "I knew I liked you. Math's my favorite. I'm going to solve Garamoci's Theory of Everything before I finish high school."

"How old are you?" Should it surprise me, though? I was pretty sure everyone in that family was exceptionally gifted.

"I just turned seven." She grinned at me.

Yep, I sure didn't know what a Diophantine equation was when I was seven.

"Want my notes?" I offered. "I tried to solve it for two years when I was at BosTec. The math department has a contest–if you solve it before you graduate, you get all your tuition back. So far, no one has ever done it."

Because it was an *unsolvable* equation.

Tru's look went stricken. "You gave up?"

"Never," I lied, not wanting to discourage her. "I just got so busy with hockey, working, my degree, and dating Dean. Suddenly, I was graduating. Solving it after graduation doesn't get you the prize."

"Stats, I didn't know that." Verity leaned into me.

"I love stats and numbers, especially in regard to sports," I told her. "Numbers are soothing. I sort of thought I'd end up doing stats for a team or something."

"Did you know I can recite pi to a hundred places? I'm going to get to two hundred like Grace," Tru beamed. "When I solve the equation, Spencer's going to hire me. I'd love your notes. I promise to give you credit. Maybe Spencer will hire you, too, and we can work together."

Verity ran her fingers through my hair. "Yes, and build spaceships."

Tru nodded vigorously. I had no idea what the two things had to do with each other. Spencer was in *biotech.*

"I like spaceships." Okay, I enjoyed reading fictional books about space travel and watching space movies. I was so happy Verity liked the same ones I did. Mercy also had suggested we learn a fictional language as a pack and I was *all over* that.

"Do you like unicorns?" Hope's head leaned into her sister.

"I do. My sister loves them. Is that your favorite?" I'd seen that animated unicorn movie she loved a billion times. Verity liked it, too.

Hope nodded. "I'm going to make unicorns when I grow up."

"AJ's sister has a petting zoo. She'd love a unicorn." Science was already breeding miniature tigers and giraffes, so why not unicorns? "Anyway, it was nice talking to you. I'm going to bed." I gave her another kiss on the head.

"My eyes." Mercy stood there in PJs and a large grin, holding a bag of chips.

I snorted, returned downstairs, and got ready for bed. Turning out the lights, I left the door cracked and fell asleep.

"Jonas?" a soft whisper nudged at the edge of my consciousness as I slept.

Without opening my eyes, I lifted the blanket so Dean could crawl in.

The door clicked shut, and a warm body crawled in, settling under the blankets with me. A head lay on my chest, and strong arms wrapped around me. While the body was taut and muscular, it wasn't Dean's body. The sea salt and driftwood wasn't his.

I held her tight, making sure we were covered. She fretted and tossed in my arms like she couldn't get comfortable.

"Do you need to come so you can sleep?" I whispered, my hands already under her panties. We had a long day of labor at the greenhouse tomorrow.

"Please." Her voice grew breathy as my hand slid between her folds.

Oh, yes, I loved it when it was only her and me in bed.

Sleepily, I fingered her until she orgasmed, collapsing on me in a cloud of driftwood. I slipped inside her softness, tenderly fucking her, until we both came.

"That's my girl, now sleep." I pressed a kiss to her forehead as sleep took me.

I awoke with Verity's head in the center of my chest, hair fanned out around me. Her finger traced the tattoos on my chest and arm.

"Hey, Sweet Girl. It's early. Do you want to sleep more?" I whispered. I should get up and go for a run. With all of us cooped up here and no hockey practice, I had to get my ass out of the house every day and run off some steam so I didn't explode.

"I really should go to the greenhouse," she muttered sleepily.

"We're all going to the greenhouse," I assured, stroking her hair.

"I know. I just want to get a head start. Will you tell me what this means?" Her fingers caressed the fairy that was part of the tattooed sleeve on my arm.

"It's a story Pop, my omega father, told us. I only know his English translation. They didn't want him to teach us Korean, even though my dad literally met him while in Korea for work." My controlling alpha mother didn't want us to have a way to communicate that she didn't understand.

"Well, that's shitty. What did your dad do that took you away for years at a time?" Her finger traced the beanstalk.

"Canadian Foreign Service. This story..." I moved the finger back up to the fairy. "It's the story of the Fairy and the Woodcutter. It's basically a cautionary tale of patience and being happy with what you have. Pop told us stories when the alphas were fighting, to distract us."

She nodded. "Mama did that, told us stories in French that her grandmother told her when she was a girl in Dijon. I did that a lot for the littles. Especially in the year between Mom going to jail and the pack breaking up. Though mine tended to be flower mythology stories."

Which would be why the littles were pouting over her being gone all these months later. Who knew what home was like for them without Verity running interference?

"What's this one?" Her fingers moved to the two cranes on my chest.

"Pop and my little brother." If only I'd been able to save them.

I *had* saved Hana and myself. Our alpha mother could get bad sometimes when Pops was alive. Without him to soothe her rages, she was intolerable after his death.

"You have a little brother?" Verity asked.

I shook my head. "Had."

"Oh, Jonas." Her scent became salty as she stroked my hair.

"She's in jail. Hana and I are safe. We told the pack to fuck off–including our older brothers, who got out and never looked back, knowing full well what that meant for the rest of us. They didn't protect us." Or help us when we were living with my coach. Or reach out when we were at university.

No, none of them had anything to say until I went pro.

Oh, I had plenty to say to them then.

"Hana and I chose our own last name because we didn't want to be associated with them. Roughly, *Seong* means *to succeed.* It's our way of telling everyone where to go. Pop would have loved you. Taught you to make Korean pastries. He died right before my sixteenth birthday. Brain tumor." I winced, because without him to soothe the alphas things got intolerable, fast.

She wrapped her arms around me. "You were so young."

"I was old enough that if my old coach hadn't had a lot of interesting friends, I could've been tried for assault after my alpha emerged and I attacked our mom to keep her from hitting us. I was angry for a very long time. Part of me didn't think I deserved Dean. Because how did I know I'd be a good alpha with shit examples?" I laid my soul bare for her so she'd understand.

"You're worth him." She kissed my temple.

"As are you. So, I see you, Sweetheart. I understand why you took alpha blockers out of fear of turning into your parents. My mom actually had been mandated, several times, to take them, but never did." Because of the stigma. And that cost lives.

"Do you ever have contact with your pop's family?" Verity continued to hold on to me.

"A little. They're nice people. Hana knows them well. She even spent some time studying in Korea. One day we should all go there." I snuggled into her, taking all the comfort she'd give me.

"We should. Thank you for sharing that with me," she told me.

"Your turn. What's the story of this little fairy?" My hand caressed her shoulder where the perky little fairy sat on a mushroom.

"I like fairies. I awakened as an alpha at an away game back when I was an undergrad. Our team had no other alphas, and no one knew what to do. I was freaking out. So, they brought me to the club. I danced it out, got hammered, and apparently, we ended up all getting tattoos," she laughed. "None of us recall much of that night other than it was a fuckton of fun and we were lucky our conference didn't enforce a pre-game party ban."

They did what? With anyone other than Verity, that could have been a bloodbath. Newly awakened alphas could be a lot. I could have easily knocked my mother permanently unconscious.

"I love your little tattoo. And the flower?" I was so curious.

"Freddie didn't like the fairy tattoo because it's *basic.* When we broke up, I wanted another. So, I got one there for myself." She gave me a kiss, then rolled out of bed to use the bathroom, in only a shirt.

I got up and stretched. I should go for a run, but I'd love to have a little alone time with her.

She came back out. "Do you want to come with me to the greenhouse? Or do you want to come with the others?"

I'd like to come in you while in your greenhouse, Sweet Girl.

"I'll go with you. Why don't I make breakfast and see who wakes up? Maybe we'll even stop at a bakery I like. They've reopened and I want to give them some business." Yes, I wanted to see what noises she made as she tried fish-shaped waffles filled with delicious things.

"Sounds perfect." She disappeared.

I used the bathroom, then went into the kitchen and started the rice and the coffee. While it cooked, I got dressed. When I returned to the kitchen, I made her a chai latte. AJ had brought home a few fresh things, including milk last night, but not any fresh vegetables. Instead, I sauteed some frozen ones. We had eggs since AJ had bought a ton of them.

Opening the curtains to let in the light, I frowned at the *handprints* on the glass doors leading out to the balcony. Had they been there yesterday? I didn't remember, since other people cooked and we'd been gone most of the day.

Ugh. I got the window wipes out of the cupboard and cleaned them off.

Putting the wipes away, I returned to cooking and fried some eggs. As Verity came out, I put some rice in a bowl, along with the vegetables. Placing a fried egg on top, I drizzled it with some chili oil and added sesame seeds and dried green onions.

"Your breakfast." I put it next to her mug.

"Thank you." She beamed, put her phone on the counter, and began to eat. Verity was wearing those jeans that hugged her ass and a Maimers hoodie, her hair in a bun.

Getting my food, I sat next to her at the breakfast bar.

"I loved you coming into my bed last night." I leaned in and kissed her.

Mercy thundered down the stairs in sweats. "Ooh, breakfast?"

"Help yourself, there's still two eggs in the pan, and coffee in the pot," I told her, figuring she'd smell food and want some. She was a growing young athlete and ate accordingly.

Mercy grabbed some food. Her eyebrows arched at her sister's presence. "Ver is going running with us?"

"We're going to the greenhouse early. You can always run there. We might stop at a bakery so you can have a post run reward." I grinned.

Mercy had become my running buddy. It was fun to go running through the snow with her. I would've thought that with her being from the South, she wouldn't be up for it, but she was.

"That sounds fun. Do we get coffee, too?" She shoved eggs and rice into her mouth.

"I have dining dollars and meal swipes I need to use before the new semester starts. So, coffee for everyone, and lunch is from whatever in the student union is open and taking meal swipes," Verity replied.

Verity's phone rang. She frowned and answered it.

"Saph, is everything okay? Are they delaying our access to the greenhouse again?" Exasperation ran through her voice. She rubbed her temples. "My siblings are where? Okay. I'm on my way. Make sure they stay there. They didn't tell me they were coming today."

Oh shit.

Verity ended the call and downed her latte.

"Tru couldn't wait for me to email the notes, booked herself a flight, and is at your greenhouse because she doesn't know where we live? I guess we'll get her, feed her, and call your parents to see what to do next?" My brow furrowed as I downed my coffee.

She shook her head. "It's actually Hale and Dare with boxes of flower bulbs. These are earlier versions of what I was working on, but a much better specimen than anything I might buy."

Verity came over and kissed me. "It's adorable how you rolled with the prospect of one of the littles showing up. Because it already happened, only she showed up at Grace's because she was pissed about moving to London and missing math camp."

"How do small children fly internationally without their parents?" I asked, finishing my breakfast. Though, I understood being pissed at having to move and miss important things, given I'd been force-moved many times.

Often right in the middle of hockey season.

"They fly private and know how to access their passport. She got online and figured out how to schedule herself on my sister's pack's private plane, then called herself a children's car service both to the airport and to their house when she got to Rockland. We literally woke up to her eating cookies in the living room because she knew the door codes." She snorted. "No one had thought to call Spencer because the flight crew knew who she was and figured we were flying her out for math camp."

"It was wild. Mumsy was pissed. Dad, while not condoning running away, was proud of how clever she was. So was Grace." Mercy took a gulp of coffee.

Oh, we were in for it, weren't we? I'd get my research to her today.

"They're safe, right?" My heart still ached for my little brother. It had been an accident, and I'd been too small to do anything, but it still hurt my heart.

"Yes," she nodded. "Grace is prepared to move them the moment she thinks they're not. I'm more worried about Chance. Having Baba and Mama's full attention isn't nearly as fun as he thought it would be. Though he joined his school fútbol team, so that's helping him make friends."

"We'll keep an eye on him, too," I agreed.

"Thanks. I'm so excited that Hale brought my car. I missed driving." She put her empty mug and bowl in the sink, her shoulders doing a little happy dance.

"Do you really think he did, Ver?" Mercy's eyebrows rose as she ate and texted at the same time.

"Of course he would. It's my car. I wasn't expecting them for a few more days. Wasn't Dare going to stay with Hale until BosTec starts?" Verity rinsed the dishes.

I'd have to see about a parking space for her. AJ was talking about getting a car, too.

"I'm going to get my things and text everyone where we're going so they don't worry," Verity told me as she put the dishes in the dishwasher. "Mercy, are you coming with? I can't wait to visit that bakery."

Oh, I hoped she loved it as much as I did.

"I'll run to campus because I need to work on my stamina. I'll grab the coffees at the student union and bring them to the greenhouse?" Mercy grabbed my bowl and hers and took them to the sink.

"Perfect. If they give you any trouble using my dining dollars, call me." Verity left the kitchen.

"I'm pretty sure Hale didn't bring her car. He's not going to give it back. Even though she told me not to, I should just buy her one, right?" Mercy rinsed the dishes and added them to the dishwasher.

I knew what she wanted to get her, and I shook my head. "Don't give Deloitte Automotive your money. They're fuckers that don't treat their workers right."

They also owned a hockey team. Filled with fuckers.

"She needs something cute and fast, though. If not a convertible, something like in those car racing movies we were watching." She gave the pan a scrub and added that to the dishwasher.

"Yes, she does." I could see it now. Verity had enough taken away from her and she deserved nice things. Yes, if Hale didn't bring back her car, I had the perfect one in mind.

Chapter Twenty-Seven

Verity

"You *what*?" I shrieked at my brother Hale. All the happiness I'd felt from trying fish-shaped waffles with different fillings at the bakery I'd gone to with Jonas evaporated.

My younger brother had done some bizarre shit in his life.

Nothing topped this.

"Your car was old. You live in New York City. You don't need one." Hale shrugged, as he stood there, unrepentant.

My younger brother was my height, but had a more traditional alpha build. Like usual, he wore too-tight jeans and cowboy boots. He had Mom's long, luscious brown locks, tanned skin, and nose, along with Dad's face and blue eyes.

Right now, those eyes blinked at me as if he'd done nothing wrong.

"It's not that old," I fired back, well aware that despite the cold, we weren't the only people in the greenhouse area and attracting stares.

The fact that people watched me didn't temper my anger.

"That was my car. *Mine.* That I bought with my own money and *lent* to you." I threw the lily bulb in my hand at his chest.

"Ow." Hurt crossed his face as saltiness tinged his fruity scent, which always reminded me of pluots and honey.

Dare chuckled, wearing his usual heavy eyeliner and all-black, including his *BosTec Orchestra* hoodie. "Wow. I didn't realize your voice could still reach that pitch."

Picking up another, I threw it at Dare. "You knew and didn't tell me. Hale, you're not supposed to street race anymore. While I can get another car, we can't get another you."

I threw another bulb at Hale for his stupidity. Bulbs he and Dare cheerfully dug up from several of the gardens on the Marquess and Briar campuses, carefully labeled and boxed, and *brought on the train instead of in my car.*

"Verity, it's okay, whatever it is," Mercy said, coming outside with a tray of coffee cups from the shop at the campus center.

"No, it's not," Jonas said from where he mixed potting soil for me.

We worked at the outdoor tables next to my greenhouse–soil, pots, equipment, and plant bulbs *everywhere.* The greenhouse manager had brought in heat lamps, which helped with the chill.

"He *wrecked my car street racing,*" I shrieked, throwing another bulb. "Then, took the insurance money, bought a motorcycle, and wrecked it. All this happened *before Christmas,* and he *didn't tell me.*"

I threw several others in rapid succession, taking care to make sure they were all from the same box, so the strains didn't get mixed up. How did he even get the insurance money? It was *my* car. What was I still even paying insurance on?

"You promised not to wreck it. You promised." I threw another. "Street racing! Last time you did that, you nearly died."

I did one nice thing for Hale, and this was what I got?

Mercy gave him a hard stare that was a dead ringer for Mom's angry look, her plum scent spicy with anger. "You're shitting my dick. You did what now?"

"Ow. You throw hard," he pouted. "Why are you so mad? You just said you could get another car."

"Yeah, not what she said," Jonas replied. "What is your plan to replace it?"

Hale looked like a trapped animal. "Do you know how much a car like that costs? Given the university shut down my side business, I can barely pay my rent, even with my jobs. There's no way I can buy you a car. I bought the motorcycle so I could get to work. I didn't crash it while racing."

"No, just jumping cars," Dare tattled, sorting through the plants my sister had sent from her backyard.

"Dare." Hale looked hurt. He didn't mean to be as reckless as a kappa, but he was. Our little brother Pax was proof the chaos gene didn't come from Mom, but *Dad.*

Dare's dirty hands went up. "I don't want Ver pissed at me."

"You sure as shit don't. She does a fuckton for all of us, and this is what you do?" Mercy put the coffee down on the table where the box of pastries sat.

"Your side business? You aren't supposed to do that anymore. Hale, you could get arrested for that." I pinched the bridge of my nose.

"What's his side business?" Jonas gave him a look.

Dare shrugged. "He's an organic chemist. What do you think it is?"

He'd manufactured a drug that tested like a legal recreational substance but acted like something stronger. Mom had been so proud of the formula that she'd looked the other way with the understanding that if the university–or police–caught him, she wouldn't protect him.

Though after Mom had gone to jail the other parents had asked him to stop–and he'd agreed.

So I'd thought.

Hale rolled his blue eyes. "Technically, it's not illegal because it's too new. But yeah, the university was butthurt."

Mercy punched Hale in the arm. "You ding-dong. I should drink your coffee."

Dare scurried over and got his and took a gulp. "Thank you for getting us coffee, Mercy."

"Verity paid for it." She scowled. "I was going to learn to drive on that car, Hale."

"It's okay." Jonas held me tight. "Mercy, we got you some fish-shaped waffles. They're in the bag on the table. They don't get any."

"I... I didn't mean to. Being an adult is a shit show. I didn't realize how much everyone else did for me until I was alone, and no one was there to do all the things." Hale's voice broke.

"Same," Dare sighed. "There are things I now have to do that I didn't even know needed to be done."

"Why are you upsetti?" Dean barreled in with Grif and AJ.

"Hale wrecked her car." Mercy punched Hale again. "He's also been street racing and dealing drugs."

"Ow, Mercy." Hale sighed and rubbed his arm. "Hey, I never realized how much things like rent and bills cost. Sometimes I give Mom money so she can buy things in jail."

Oh. I didn't know he gave her money. Visiting, but not money. Mercy did, but not much or often. Usually for holidays.

"You could have told me when you saw me at Christmas," I fired back, as Dean took me from Jonas and hugged me tight.

Hale's head hung. "I know. Dare told me to."

"Wait, you deal drugs, jumped a car with your motorcycle, and you street race?" Jonas frowned.

"The jump was sick. Let me show you the video." He got out his phone, then froze. "Um..."

This was my life. Hale came out of the womb causing trouble. Like somehow newborn him caused a power outage in the hospital nursery.

"Want me to have security escort them out?" Saphira asked, in her lab coat, coming out of her greenhouse from checking on her flowers. "Hale, that's some dumb ass shit, even for you. And I was there for all *seven* times you blew up or set fire to the lab at Briar, and when you fell through the roof, and fell off the roof."

"Greenhouse roofs don't count." Hale shrugged.

"Don't wreck my greenhouse. They just fixed it," I growled, so angry and upset my stomach hurt.

"I... I'm sorry, Ver. I dug up all the plants and boxed and labeled them like you asked. It was hard work with the cold ground. I started setting your greenhouse up for you, because I know how you like it," Hale pleaded.

Which he had–and planted ordinary lily bulbs that I'd bought, in their place on campus. All my bulbs on campus had been planted as part of various annual campus beautification projects.

Okay, and a senior prank.

Though he'd dug up the bulbs in the garden behind the house of the university president, which I'd asked him to leave.

I sighed as I kicked the ground. "You can stay. Unless the greenhouse manager kicks you out. How long are you two here for?"

"We'll head out to Boston on one of the late ultra-bullets. It's shitty that someone destroyed your research, and it's shitty your place flooded and ruined all your shit." Dare sipped his coffee.

"Why don't we get some work done?" Mercy directed. "Lunch is courtesy of Verity's expiring dining dollars. But if everyone works hard, I'll take you to Tito's for dinner."

"Ooh, I like that place." Dare nodded.

"Tito's is open?" Jonas asked, drinking his coffee.

She nodded. "Yeah. Gwenifer's working tonight, and I want to tip her massively. She's worried about making rent because she couldn't work during the storm. Her boyfriend was stuck on the West Coast with his university hockey team so he couldn't work either."

"That sounds stressful. I appreciate you bringing me the bulbs. Hale, I won't demand you buy me a car, but I'm *very* disappointed that you couldn't be honest with me," I told them.

Hale ducked his head as his cowboy boots kicked air. "Sorry, Ver."

"Good. Now, let's get to work." I gave everyone jobs, needing to focus before I smacked my brother into the next state.

Jonas snagged my waist. "Are you sure you're okay? AJ brought the SUV. I can dump their asses at the train station."

"It's fine." I rubbed my temple. "The parents told me I'd regret lending him my car."

We set up all the tables and containers. Hooked the systems back up. Figured out which bulbs got replanted. It was hard, dirty work, which the cold didn't help with.

"Lunch." Dare came out of the lab. He and Mercy had gone to get food.

"Thanks." I finished potting my bulb. I went over to one of the outdoor sinks and washed my hands.

"Professor Thorne?" a male voice said.

"Hi, Angel." I turned around and saw my student from last semester.

"Um, can you go easy on Samantha? She's a good person." Angel wore a hoodie, shorts, sunglasses, and flip-flops.

Good people didn't wreck someone's life's work.

I sighed as I dried my hands. "It's not up to me. There was a lot of damage."

"She, um, didn't do it because she hated you. Sure, she sort of talked shit online, but it's her whole social media persona, not who she truly is." He shuffled his feet.

"Please tell me she didn't do it for likes?" Though there hadn't been a video of it.

"Someone offered her money to do it. She took it to help pay her tuition, not realizing how bad it was. Then they ghosted her, and she never got paid. She got caught. They said she wouldn't get caught." Angel frowned.

I paused. "Someone was going to pay her? Do you know who?"

"She doesn't even know who they actually are. Anyhow, she's really sorry." His head bowed. "One poor decision and everything she's worked for..."

That was how bad decisions went.

"I'm so sorry for everything she went through, but like I said, it's university property. However, if she can figure out who it was, that could help," I told him.

"Oh, it could? Thanks, Prof." With a wave, Angel walked off.

I entered the lab and found everyone in the lounge eating an assortment of food.

"Is everything okay?" Grif put his arms around me.

"Someone paid the girl who wrecked my greenhouse. Well, she was supposed to be paid," I said, leaning into him. His scent got sweeter with every day.

"Shit." Grif squeezed me. "Do we know who?"

"No. It could be anyone." I sighed and sat down and grabbed a sandwich. "Thanks again for everyone's help." We were nearly done.

"My money is on Derva. Bitch." Mercy made a face.

"Mine's on Fuckboy Freddie the asshole," Dare added.

"Wait, those two are around? Fuck-a-doodle." Hale made a face and then stuffed half a sandwich in his face.

"And together." Mercy rolled her eyes.

"Fuck, that sounds toxic." Hale downed most of his drink.

Dean looked at his phone. "We're invited to a taco eating contest this afternoon at Taco Hut. Ladybug's bringing her *cat?*"

I looked at the picture of the fluff of orange and white fur. If it had black stripes, I'd think it was a baby tiger. "Are we sure that's a house cat?"

"You can't actually be sure with Ladybug," Dean replied. "She's always bringing stray animals to the rink. That's how Nia got Pupper."

"And there *was* the racoon in a bucket," Jonas added.

"She found Marty in a tree on campus as the storm was hitting. It's been only the two of them throughout the storm. He's so cute. I met him yesterday at the rink when we were cleaning up," Mercy gushed.

"Taco eating contest? I'm down. Like we're eating tacos with the Knights?" Hale perked and reached for another sandwich.

"Yeah, it's something they do sometimes. Usually it's the younger Knights," Dean replied. "Carlos, Dimitri, the rookies..."

"That sounds fun," I agreed. But Carlos and Hale were *not* allowed to be friends. No, I didn't need that catastrophe in my life. Also, I know I'd seen Carlos before, but I didn't know where. Perhaps he'd done some fitness modeling with me–or he had a big sponsor and I'd seen his ads around.

"Great, so we'll get this done, eat tacos, and go to the bar. My sort of afternoon," Hale said as he tipped his chair back, unwrapping the sandwich.

As long as we got everything done. And my actual work, to fix all my research, was only just beginning.

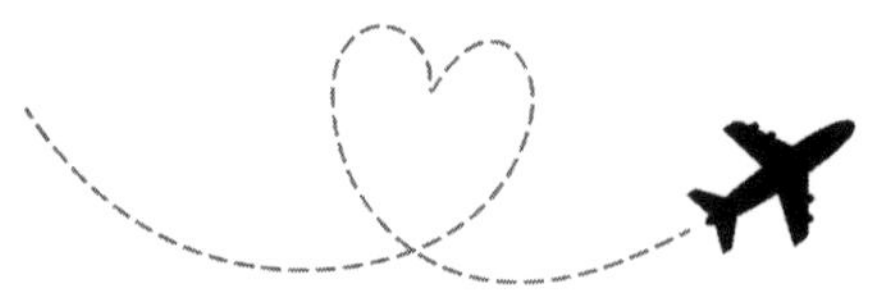

Chapter Twenty-Eight

Grif

"I knew it. Who's going to tell Ladybug that Marty is the zoo's missing baby tiger?" Pauley looked up something on his phone in the locker room after practice. His blond surfer locks were up in a man-bun today.

The training center had been put back together, and we'd had practice to prepare for our game tomorrow against the Royals. Marty, the 'cat' we'd already met at Taco Hut, had come to practice, tucked into Ladybug's hoodie.

"Tiger? It doesn't have black stripes." Clark frowned as he took off his skates, dark hair falling in his brown eyes. His black glasses were on a strap for practice, though he often wore contacts for games.

"It's a mini golden tiger and part of a bunch of animals the Animal Welfare department found in a raid," Pauley added, still scrolling on his phone. "Apparently those fancy genetically engineered mini tigers don't make good pets."

Yeah, that just sounded like a bad idea. Though sometimes I sort of wanted one of those tiny giraffes.

Clark raised his hand like he was in class. "Okay. I'll tell her and take her to the zoo to return him."

"I'll go with you," Dimitri replied. He'd made it back from the West Coast. We still weren't sure why or how he'd ended up stuck there.

"She'll be so sad," Clark added, brow furrowing. "She's had such a good time with Marty."

Dimitri nodded. "And Lucky likes him."

My phone buzzed as I put my gear in my locker.

Sissy

I love you. Our omega says she's taking you to the omega spa next time you visit.

Me

I'm sure she will.

Last night I'd told my big sister everything. She'd helped me figure out which parents to call and what exactly to say. That had gone okay. Also, Dean's mom told me she was proud of me when I'd called her.

Dean was off with the goalie coach and Jonas was meeting with one of the trainers. I went upstairs to find Coach. Nerves bumped around in my belly, but it was time.

"Coach, do you have a moment?" I knocked on his open door.

"Of course, come in." Coach looked up from his laptop. His office was stuffed full of photos and memorabilia, both of the Knights and the teams he'd played for. There were even things for his mates, since his pack was majorly accomplished in winter sports.

I hesitated. It was one thing to tell my family; telling Coach was something I couldn't come back from.

"Did you have a question about strategy from the meeting this morning?" he added, looking a little tired. Was there more gray in his hair?

Shaking my head, I closed the door and took a seat, heart thumping. "It's something else."

"Okay. I never congratulated you on your pack contract. I guess you bonded with Jonas. Good for you." He looked at the picture on his desk of his pack and smiled. "Your Maimer girl is next? Such an exciting time, forming your pack."

His small talk put me at ease, and I couldn't help but grin. "AJ actually. And yeah, Verity's next."

"I heard about the lawsuit with your old agent. It's making a few people in management nervous. Visit legal and let them know you're not mad at us," Coach added, toying with the photo.

"Oh. I didn't even think about that. Of course, it's not the Knights' fault." I'd gotten another bank account and given payroll my new info. Stu smoothed everything over with my sponsors.

The storm had slowed everything down on the legal front. As far as I knew, Chet was still in jail, waiting to see a judge. Though it wouldn't surprise me if his family had gotten him out and he was under house arrest somewhere.

Or had fled the country.

Relief flickered through his face. "I'm so happy to hear that. What did you want to talk about?"

"Um." How did I even say this? "I'm hiding my designation and I'm not sure how much longer I can. I don't know what to do. People have enough trouble with a beta enforcer. I don't want to leave hockey. It's my life. I mean, Dean knows, he was there. My mom didn't even know until last night. Stu knows." It came out fast. "Still, what do I do, Coach? Being outed hurt Dean so much and..."

"Breath, Grif." Coach took a deep breath. "What are you trying to tell me? That you're *also* a hidden omega?"

"Sort of." Everything tumbled out. Well, most of it.

Coach patiently listened, nodding, but not saying anything.

"So there you are." I held my breath, waiting to see what his reaction was, fully expecting anger. Because I'd been dishonest for so long.

"Thank you for coming to me, it means a lot," Coach told me, no anger in his face or voice.

"I don't want my career to be over. We're finally together. Stu says it'll be fine but..." I sucked in a breath, panic overwhelming me. I felt a squeeze of reassurance from AJ and Dean through the bond.

"I know. Could you give me a day or two to think this over? You not being a beta doesn't mean your career's over. You're a valuable player and I'd like to keep you. However, whether you're a gamma or an omega, you as an enforcer could be a hard sell to management. Even if you're the best one out there," he told me. "Unfortunately, stats don't always override designation bias."

"Thanks. I can't guarantee I won't ever get into fights. But I can hand over my enforcer mantle if that helps me stay." I'd thought about it a lot during the storm, and I could compromise.

"I appreciate that attitude. I think coming up with a plan before something happens is the right call. You need to take care of yourself." Compassion filled his face.

"True. I'm feeling good after the snow break." Though Dr. Arya had been leaving messages. Tomorrow wasn't just our game against the Royals, but Dean's birthday. I'd call her after that.

Maybe by then I'd have a plan.

"Thank you for taking this so well. People got so angry with Dean and..." The memories made me shudder.

"I know. Thank you again for trusting me with this. I'll see what I can come up with. You're an asset to the team," he told me.

I stood, feeling like this was a dismissal. "Thanks, Coach."

Leaving his office, I went over to the administrative area and smoothed things over with legal. My stomach rumbled. Chef should be setting out lunch in our dining room.

My phone buzzed.

Jonas

Where are you?

Me

I was talking to Coach. Everything's fine. Lunch?

"Grif Graf. I thought that was you. Can I have a word?" Mr. Longfellow appeared. He was an older man, hair completely white, though he still had a full head. He'd been general manager of the Knights for a long time.

"Of course." I couldn't exactly say *no,* given he was the GM. So, I followed him into his office, not relaxing when he closed the door.

Had someone figured out I was an omega from my locker room encounter with Dean?

I took a seat as Mr. Longfellow sat behind his large wooden desk. Like Coach's office, it was filled with memorabilia from over the years. His suit was very fancy, as was his watch.

"I don't hold the Knights responsible for anything that happened," I blurted. "I already spoke to legal."

That's what this was about, right?

He looked relieved. "Oh, good. What your agent did was quite unsporting. However, this lawsuit against him is making things awkward."

"Awkward for who? The team?" I frowned, trying to think of anyone who might have Chet as an agent.

"Why Mr. Daughtry, of course. He and the Chesterton's are good friends. It might be better to handle things...privately." Mr. Longfellow's look said, *who else?*

"Oh. I..." I bit back that *I'm not dropping the lawsuit.* "I'll speak to my lawyer and see what's best."

What. The. Fuck.

I'd met Mr. Daughtry, the head of the family that owned the team, once. They didn't seem to be very hands-on with the Knights, preferring to work through Mr. Longfellow.

"Good, good." Mr. Longfellow beamed, folding his hands and setting them on his desk. "We're glad you're here with us. Despite that rocky start, you're playing great."

"How was it rocky, if I might ask?" No one had ever met with me about it, other than the Royces talking to me in the locker room.

"You weren't playing your all, but it can be hard switching teams." He shrugged it off, making an empty gesture with his still-folded hands.

"But how? When I looked at my stats between being told I needed to improve and everyone being happy, there was no actual difference. I'm only asking because I want to play the best for you," I added in a feeble attempt to be diplomatic and not frustrated.

Mr. Longfellow's head cocked as he thought for a long moment. "It was here." He tapped his chest. "I'm looking forward to the Knights winning that championship this year. Anyhow, good talk."

"Thank you, Mr. Longfellow." I stood and left, mind reeling.

The GM didn't just ask me to drop the lawsuit against the man who stole from me because the owner was friends with Chet's dad? Did he?

I went down to the Knights' dining room where delicious smells drew me. Someone had laid out an assortment of wraps and healthy sides. I took a shrimp one and loaded up on spinach salad and baked sweet potato fries, and grabbed a recovery drink from the cooler.

Taking a seat at the table by the ping-pong table, I texted Jonas that I was in the dining room. The goalies were still busy.

Jonas, Nia, Pauley, and Nakey came in.

Nakey sighed at the lunch offerings. "It's like they thought we were eating crap during our snow week. Shit, I want a double bacon mushroom burger."

"It's food, Nak. They never make us double bacon mushroom burgers." Pauley grabbed two chicken wraps.

"I still want one." He pouted, taking a chicken wrap.

Pauley put an arm around his mate. "We'll pick up the ingredients on our way home and make them for dinner. The kids will be excited to have an indoor picnic."

"I did eat a lot of crap," Nia laughed, taking a chicken wrap.

"I was snowed in with Verity and her sister. We had fresh bread and cookies every day," I laughed. Okay, Dean and I contributed to the treat fest.

"Team Mom stayed with you?" Nia smirked as she added rice and a bunch of fruit to her plate. She'd redone her hair and it was now in twists.

"Team Mom and her sister are living with us. The pipes in their place burst," Jonas replied as he added two wraps, grilled vegetables, and rice to his plate. "How did everything go?" He sat down next to me.

"With Coach? Great. But something else happened. I'll tell you about it soon?" I stuffed salad into my mouth. *So hungry.*

He glanced over at everyone else. "Sounds good."

Mercy walked in, in short shorts, a tank top over a sports bra, and knee pads.

"Hello young Maimer, are you lost?" Nakey asked, taking a bite of his wrap.

"Nope." She grabbed a smoothie out of the cooler. "Oooh, you have sweet potato fries. Fuck-a-doodle. Shrimp? What?"

We had things like that because Dean was an omega and Chef tried to make sure everyone's nutritional needs were met.

Getting a napkin, she piled fries into, then plopped down at our table, turning the chair backwards first. "Hello, boys."

"Hi, Mercy. We're still on?" Jonas asked, taking another bite of food.

"Yep. I forgot about the choreography workshop, but we'll make it." She stuffed fries in her face, looking around. The room also had an air hockey table, a large TV, and pictures of various retired Knights of note.

"Perfect. One of the rookies wanted me to help him with a few things on the ice anyway," Jonas replied. "He's afraid of being traded."

I knew that feeling well. My eyebrows rose as I looked from Jonas to Mercy and back again. "Exactly what sort of mayhem are you two planning?"

"Alpha stuff." She shoved more fries in her mouth.

Hmm, I wasn't so sure about that.

"Have fun?" I was taking Dean out on a birthday date to see a sailing exhibit at the natural history museum.

Her eyes rested on a photo on the wall. "Why is there a necklace of noodles on the picture?"

"Ask Ladybug. Pretty sure she made it. That picture is of the queen of the goalies. First beta goalie in the PHL," Jonas nodded.

"She's one of Dean's favorites. She publicly defended him when he was outed. EBUGs like her. When Dean was an EBUG, they sacrificed a lasagna to her. Back when I was with the Hurricanes, the EBUGs set a tiramisu on fire and released it into the ocean on a pyre," I replied, taking a sip of my drink.

Mercy snorted. "Weirdos."

Yep.

Her phone beeped. She checked it and rolled her eyes. "I have to get my ass to practice. So long and thanks for the fries."

Stuffing the last of the fries in her mouth, she grabbed her smoothie and left.

Nia laughed and looked over at us. "How is living with a teenager who can bench more than you going?"

Jonas frowned at her. "Why does everyone say that? I can bench more than her."

"Barely," I chuckled. They'd had a contest the other day.

We ate our lunch, then left. "Car?" Jonas glanced at his phone. "Dean's grabbing food with the goalies, then hitting the gym."

Inside the SUV, I told him in greater detail about my conversation with Coach, then told him about the exchange between me and Mr. Longfellow.

Jonas rubbed his chin. "I don't like it. The owner can't ask you to drop a private lawsuit because he's friends with them."

"I know." I leaned into him, seeking comfort, a little shaken.

Jonas wrapped his arms around me. "We'll tell AJ, Stu, and our lawyer."

"What if the charges against Chet don't stick?" I buried my face in his shoulder, wishing AJ or Verity were here. But she was in class and AJ was at work.

He stroked my hair. "We'll get him."

That was more important than recovering the money he stole.

"I don't understand what Mr. Longfellow meant about my playing." A frown tugged at my lips. "I don't need her to play a good game. She even told me as much."

"No, you don't," Jonas agreed. "However, I saw your face when she wished you good luck in the tunnels that one night. Back on the plane, the night you met her, did she wish you a good game?"

"Yeah, she told me I'd smash it and play the best game ever. It's not like she used her bark to make me play well." Which was very illegal in athletics. I made a face, trying to honestly figure out what was going on.

"Grif, dearest?" Jonas tapped his forehead to mine. "She doesn't need a bark. She's yours. You would do anything for her, just like she would for you."

My eyebrows rose. "What does that have to do with hockey?"

"Everything. It makes perfect sense. Something in you knew what she was to you long before you ever knew she was an alpha. She encouraged you. You rose to the occasion. You shine a little more during games when you talk to her beforehand or know she's in the stands." He ran his hand through my hair.

"I do?" I leaned into him.

Wait, it *was* her?

"Obviously, you won for Dean. That chance meeting on the airplane gave some part of you a little extra jolt. You're a lucky man to have found something so rare and special." Jonas continued to stroke my hair.

My eyes closed. I was full of food and nice and cozy with an alpha I trusted. "You're all special."

They were my family. My everything.

"She's your fated mate, you ding-dong," he replied.

I snorted, eyes opening. "You sound like Mercy. Also, *fated mate*? Are you reading romantasy again?"

That usually ended with him chasing Dean through the forest by our cabin.

"There's nothing wrong with romantasy. She's your soulmate, your scent match. It's just taking a while. Something in you knew," he told me.

Scent match? We were well-suited for each other. Neither comfortable with our designations, both broken in our own way.

"I could see that. But I never dreamt of her." Why would someone like me get something so many people never found?

I'll take it.

"Now who's reading romantasy? Most scent matches don't dream of each other," he teased.

Someone pounded on the window. Dean opened the door and slid into the back seat with us.

"Here I thought you were making out. Hi. What are we doing here? Each other?" Dean squished in with both of us.

"Talking about how Verity and Grif are soulmates." Jonas shrugged.

"Aww, I love that for both of you." Dean leaned in and kissed me. "I can't wait for our date." He turned to Jonas. "And my dinner."

AJ and Jonas were making him dinner tonight. I'd left special birthday bread to rise. Mercy and Verity would cook him breakfast tomorrow.

"I want to just be like this for a moment," Dean said, holding us both, happiness coming through our bond.

"It's your birthday eve. You can do what you want," I replied. Something inside me really liked us cuddling each other. There was so much uncertainty.

But Coach took the news okay. Verity still loved me. The people I'd told so far had been accepting.

Maybe, just maybe, everything would be okay.

Chapter Twenty-Nine

Verity

"Are there any questions?" I surveyed my plant mythology class. At Briar, it had been a small upper-division seminar class. Here, it was something that satisfied a cross-discipline requirement, so it was *large.*

Mercy sat in the very back. With *Jonas.* It was something we did in my family–sitting in the back of each other's classes or presentations, waiting for them to notice. I hadn't expected those two. It shouldn't surprise me. They were becoming besties, and it was adorable.

Mercy raised her hand. "Can we do the paper as an interpretive dance?"

"Yes. If anyone would prefer to do a thirty-second interpretive dance in front of the class instead of the final paper, I'll accept that. I'll give exact details closer to the due date." It was hard not to laugh at the request.

I saw a couple of faces light up, like Gwen, the Knights' pink-haired EBUG, who sat by Mercy.

A few students asked actual questions about the syllabus and the brief lecture I'd given. I dismissed them a little early, because that's what the first day of class was for.

"Good luck at your game. I'm working the night shift at Tito's tonight and tomorrow," Gwen told Mercy.

"We'll be there after the game. See you then." Mercy gave her a hug and Gwen left the classroom with a couple of her friends, but not before waving at me.

"You're here." I grinned at her and Jonas.

"I know how much this class means to you. Also, I love the new stories you added to the syllabus. I'm going back to take a quick nap before the game. You kids have fun. Also, that skirt is cute." Mercy waved and left.

The long skirt was something new I'd gotten shopping with the guys.

Jonas gave me a kiss. "You're a fantastic professor."

"Thank you." I linked arms with him and we left the room. "It's an interesting mix of students. While the omega flower arranging club makes sense, I think half the hockey team's here."

"Who are now all off to the strip club," he replied as we walked down the hall toward the labs.

"Strip club?" I waved at Saphira, who was off to teach her class. She looked Jonas up and down and smirked at me.

"Yep, they were going to the *Treasure Room* to check out the *daily offerings?* I'm not sure if they meant the dancers or if they have cheap afternoon food specials like the one I worked at did." He shrugged.

I chuckled as we entered the break room so I could get my stuff out of my locker. "It's not a strip club. The *Treasure Room* is what they call the campus needs pantry since we're the NYIT Kings. Gwen heard they had toothbrushes and cheese sticks, which made everyone very excited."

"Okay, that makes sense," he chuckled. "The pantry at BosTec really helped me out. I send them money every now and again."

"What a great idea. Marquess didn't have a needs pantry. I love that we have one here anyone can use. The fresh stuff goes fast, hence the cheese run." I put my teaching things away and got my backpack.

I put on my coat and slung my backpack over my shoulders. "Ready?"

"Ready."

We walked down the hall, and someone called, "Verity."

I turned and saw Dr. Winters. "Jonas, I'll only be a moment."

"How did it go?" Dr. Winters grinned at me. Today's suspenders and bowtie had plants on them.

"Great. It's going to be an amazing class. Also, I'm working on getting everything back on track." I leaned on my crutch.

"I believe in you. Hey, we might need you to present at the next trustee meeting. Bertie's being annoying. Because no matter what university you're at, there's always that one trustee. Make sure you drop that you're supported by Compass BioTek," he told me.

"I'll do whatever you need. I'd be happy to share my research with the trustees." My heart twisted a little.

At the same time, I knew this was part of academia. One reason Baba got out of it and went private when we'd all moved to Research Circle, was *because* he constantly had to justify things in a way he didn't have to in the private sector.

"I knew I could count on you. Hopefully, it won't come to it, but I wanted to give you notice, because I know how you like to be prepared. See you later." Dr. Winters hustled off.

"Thank you." Well, I knew what I'd be doing in my spare time–putting together a presentation so if this Bertie guy tried to discredit me by calling me in at the last minute, expecting me to be unprepared, I'd be ready with the best presentation ever.

Jonas gave me a concerned look. "Everything okay?"

"Just Dr. Winters letting me know that I might have to defend my research to the trustees." I rubbed my temple. "Normal stuff."

"Okay." He gave me a squeeze.

The two of us left the building and set off for the metro. We were going to the outdoor market so he could buy ingredients. I'd never been to this one, and I was quite excited.

"I'm extremely confused about the interpretive dance option? Though honestly, depending on the topic, I'd much rather do a dance than write a research paper," he told me as we navigated the icy, snowy campus.

"Mmmm, you can dance for me anytime, Sexypants. It's something my dad always offers his students, and usually there's a couple of takers," I replied. Though not as many as you'd think.

We got on the metro, and I sank down into an empty seat, and checked my phone.

Dad

I hope your class went well. So proud of you getting to teach it!

Aww, he was?

Me

Thanks, Dad. It's going to be a great class. Might even have a few dancers.

Dad

I love it. I might have some, too.

Jonas was beside me and leaned in. "Oh, your dad texted. That's nice."

"He did. Creed and Hale texted too, but I'm not speaking to Hale." I scowled. I still couldn't believe he'd crashed my car and didn't tell me.

But I texted Creed back, telling him what I told Dad.

"Hale's a lot," Jonas agreed, texting someone on his phone. "Though I did some street racing and motorcycle recklessness when I was younger, so I understand the appeal. But I wasn't racing a borrowed luxury car or engineering test-proof party drugs."

"I bought that car myself." Right now, I couldn't afford to get another, and I wasn't going to let my sister buy me a car, because she needed to save her money and be responsible.

At least we had great public transportation here.

"I know, Sweet Girl." He hugged me to him. "You're strong and independent and self-sufficient, and I love that about you. But you don't always have to be. You have us now."

I was so happy for that. A picture of Dean and Grif popped up on my phone. "Are those two okay out on their own?"

How much did Grif not being a beta change things?

Jonas kissed my temple. "They're not far. We can get to them if we need to." The metro slowed, and he stood, offering me his hand. "This is our stop."

I took his hand, and we got off the metro, navigating the people and stairs with my crutch as we exited the station. Jonas led me down a few streets until we got to a massive outdoor food market filled with vendors selling everything from meat and produce to clothes and sunglasses.

Delicious smells teased my nose, making my mouth water. It was far beyond the farmer's markets we had back home in Research Circle.

Jonas grinned. "This place is amazing. Let me show you my favorites."

"I have them." Jonas took the bags off my lap as the metro stopped.

We disembarked and walked toward their penthouse. The sky had gone gray. A chill hung in the air, but it wasn't supposed to snow again tonight.

They'd tried so hard to make Mercy and me feel welcome. Last night, she'd been with AJ in the upstairs office as he explained something she was learning in her online finance class. It was sweet. Also, she'd been let in on Grif's secret, but Mercy was epic at keeping secrets.

"Hey, I need to see something in the parking garage, come with me?" Jonas asked, as we got in the elevator, taking it down instead of up, bags of food on his arms.

"Sure." Leaning on my crutch, I tried to calculate in my head if I had enough time to frost Dean's cake the way I wanted before I had to go to the arena with Mercy.

We headed toward the SUV, which was parked next to their 4x4. Next to that was a *hot pink* sports car.

With a *giant* bow on it like we were in a holiday car commercial.

I exhaled sharply as I leaned on my crutch. "You got Dean a car for his birthday?"

Jonas chuckled. "Oh, Sweet Girl. This is for you. The license plate says so."

The plate inside the sparkly frame read *PLNTPROF.*

"Sorry, *Team Mom* was taken–so was *Sweet Girl*," Jonas shrugged.

My knees shook a little as I got a good look at it. It was ultra-fancy and straight out of the car racing movies we'd watched during our snow-cation.

"Jonas, I told you not to buy me a car." It was completely impractical and even smaller than Grif's sports car. I wasn't sure it even had a trunk.

Jonas' lips curved into a smirk. "You told your sister not to buy you a car. Not me."

My breath caught in my chest. It was the little details that got me. Like it wasn't as low to the ground as Grif's, so it would be easier for me to get in and out. The eyelashes on the headlights. Even the little fairy hanging from the rearview mirror.

Not to mention the personalized plates.

"It's beautiful, but it's too much." I ran my hand over the hood. It wasn't a convertible, but she was a beauty.

It was *much* more expensive than what Mercy teased me with. Also, a car like this would draw attention.

They'd also bought Mercy and me *a lot* of things to replace what we lost, even though I'd eventually get the dorm insurance money.

He put the bags down on the hood of the 4x4. Pulling me to him, he pressed his lips to the top of my head. "This is nothing. Don't you realize that I'd do anything for you, Sweet Girl?"

"Thank you, Jonas. No one has ever done anything like this for me before." I pressed my lips to his, hoping to convey everything words couldn't say.

He tasted of the candy we'd tried at the market. The scent of moss wrapped around me, as did his alpha pheromones.

Jonas broke off the kiss. His eyes met mine as he swept my hair out of my face. "I know. And it's a pity. Because you deserve the world, Verity."

"You don't need to buy me expensive things. I would've gotten a new one, eventually." I cupped his face with my hand, my thumb caressing the scar on his jaw.

"In this pack, hard work doesn't go unrewarded, Sweet Girl. Anything worth having is worth taking. We're yours for the taking, Verity. *Take us.*" He kissed me again, hungry and needy.

How did I ever get so lucky to have found this wonderful and beautiful pack? One that got me in a way that no one else ever had.

I let my backpack and crutch slip to the ground and unzipped his jeans.

Take him? *Yes, please.*

"I claim you, you're mine, Jonas Seong," I murmured, lifting my long flowy skirt, hoping one day we could formally bite and claim each other.

His pierced cock sprung out of his boxer briefs as his pierced tongue flickered out. "Mmmm, Sweet Girl, my cock is happy to see you. What are you going to do with it?"

"This." Putting my hand in the center of his chest, I pushed him against the hood of the car, hoping this part of the garage was private to us, or at least the penthouses.

In all honesty, I didn't care.

I speared myself on his cock. "This cock is mine."

Bracing myself against him, I took him fast, like I'd be driving this car on the open road. My pussy was dripping, part with need, part with all his pheromones.

"Oh, that's it, take me," he gasped.

"One day I'm going to bite this throat, right here, Sexypants." I nibbled his neck as I continued to thrust myself on him.

"Yes, please. I can't wait to do the same." His hands grabbed my ass, helping to both steady me and quicken the pace.

"Jonas." Something about the angle of his pierced cock, the way his inflated knot brushed my clit, made me squeal with pleasure.

That friction. Yes please.

"Take me." Scooping my ass with his hand, he got me into an even better position, his arms making me feel safe and secure.

His intoxicating scent combined with me being on top made me feel sexy and powerful as I pounded him against the hood.

"Yes, that's it," I cried, smashing my mouth with his.

"Come all over my cock," he groaned as his teeth grazed my neck.

My hips arched, and I pulled up so I was almost at the tip, delighting in the way his piercing dragged against my inner walls. As my orgasm took me, I dropped down on him, hard, taking his full-length into me.

"You feel so good, Sweetheart." He pushed my hips down, my pussy fluttering hard-on his cock as his swollen knot rubbed against me.

I gasped as gravity and my greedy pussy made his knot dig into me. It slipped into me, stretching and making itself right at home, as bits of pain shot through me.

Oh fuck. I'd just taken Jonas' knot. Sheer desire overwhelmed me as his knot fit into me, my pussy fluttering around it.

Jonas growled with pleasure.

"Fuck yeah, Sweet Girl," he muttered as his hot release shot into me. "Oh fuck me, you feel so fucking good. I love that my knot is buried in your fucking pussy. I knew you could take me, you sweet, perfect little alpha. You're fucking perfect for me, for us."

The pressure of his knot was almost strangling. We'd played with the knot trainer toy a few times, but never was it like this.

Those dirty words made me clench, locking him to keep all that cum inside me, even though his knot nestled firmly into my pussy. Pleasure bolted through me so fiercely that I forgot to breathe. My pussy pulsed around his knot, strangling it, stinging with the stretch, and everything disappeared but sensation.

There was no garage. No car. No Jonas. Just pleasure so fierce it was painful.

"Jonas!" I screamed. "It's too much, it's too much." Panic coursed through me as it felt like his knot–and the pleasure it brought–would split me in half.

Jonas knotted me. Not what I'd planned on doing today. Especially since I'd locked his knot without even trying.

"Relax. I've got you, Sweet Girl. You took me so fucking good. My knot is strangled so tight I can barely see," he whispered, pulling me to his chest and rubbing my back. "I love you so much." His purr filled the garage.

"I love you, too." Aftershock after aftershock took me, as I laid there overwhelmed and full. My body slowly relaxed, accepting the knot, though I could still feel it stretch and pulse.

"That's it." Jonas kissed me. "You feel so good. I have you." He continued to purr, making me feel warm, comfortable, and sleepy.

"I need to frost the cake," I murmured as my lock let go, but his knot still held firm.

"His birthday isn't until tomorrow. If you frost it later, so be it. Just relax, Sweet Girl, you took me so so good." He clutched me tighter.

"I like that idea." I laid there on his chest, hearing his heartbeat, feeling his purr. My phone rang a couple of times, but I couldn't reach it. I was so nice and comfortable lying against him.

Finally, his knot slipped out of me, and cum gushed everywhere. I had to change for the arena, anyway.

My legs wobbled. My pussy was unhappy with me as I pulled up my panties, leaning on the car for support.

Jonas tucked himself in and zipped up his pants. His arms pulled me to him, and his hands ran up and down my back. "That was the best, thank you. Are you okay? I didn't intend for it to happen."

"Me neither. It's fine. I feel a little weird. My poor pussy isn't going to be fucking Dean into oblivion tonight when I get home, but I'm fine." Okay, it ached a lot. Only partially in a good way.

"Dean will live. We can go get you that piercing if you want. Though the healing time could be pretty long." Jonas kissed me deep.

"Um, hey, we have to leave for the arena soon and you've been down here awhile," Mercy's voice said from over by the elevator, interrupting us.

"It's safe. Come see your sister's present. I think you should take it to the arena tonight," Jonas said, still holding me to him.

Mercy came over to us, makeup and hair done, but not in her suit yet. She sucked in a breath. "Fuck-a-doodle, that's a beautiful car, Bub. Even if you stole my thunder."

"Sorry, Squirt. You can find something else to buy her." Jonas tugged on the end of one of her braids.

"I mean, go big or eat a sandwich." Mercy opened the car door. "Ooh, look at that interior. Hale's going to shit a pumpkin."

The white leather interior was striking.

"Probably two. He isn't going anywhere near my car. We can take it to the game. Drive up in it like we're famous or something." I grinned at her, excited to get behind the wheel of such a gorgeous car.

Mercy laughed. "We should. I'll wear my hot pink suit. You wear that light pink one and your nice watch and some dangly earrings. Maybe steal a pair of AJ's oversized sunglasses."

"Sounds perfect." Jonas kissed me again. He handed me my crutch and backpack, then grabbed the groceries. "Let's go upstairs."

"You need a shower," Mercy teased as we got in the elevator.

That I did. I looked at Jonas. “I can’t believe you got me a car.”

Or that I took his knot.

“I told you.” He put an arm around my waist. “I’d do anything for you.”

I’d do anything for them.

Anything worth having is worth taking. Understood.

Chapter Thirty

Dean

Water rained down on me in the shower. I sang loudly, soaping myself up well with de-scenting products like I always did before a game. It was my birthday, and I couldn't wait for tonight's game.

"Hi, Hot Stuff," Verity said from the bathroom doorway, interrupting my song and dance.

"Hi. Going to give me a birthday fuck before my game?" I grinned, turning so I could see her through the clear doors of my slate and granite shower. I'd gotten birthday fucks from Grif and Jonas. All I'd gotten from her was a birthday blowjob.

Not that I was complaining.

But there was no such thing as too many birthday fucks, especially since Jonas had stopped cockblocking us.

"Did Jonas rail you too hard yesterday?" I joked, the water cascading over my naked body.

That shirt of his in the laundry reeked of lust and sex from my two favorite alphas and was now in my nest.

Embarrassment tinged her scent.

"Oh, do tell, Little Alpha. Did you christen the backseat?" That would be why the parking garage smelled of alphas and sex when Grif and I came back from our date.

"The hood. We may have gone a little too hard." She winced, but I got a puff of sweet arousal from her along with her driftwood.

I shut the water off as I got the picture. "Little Alpha, did you take a knot in the pussy for the first time on *the hood of a car*?"

No wonder she didn't want a dick in there. Jonas' knot was huge, and she was an alpha. What was he thinking? It should be special with candles and soft sheets.

And me watching.

I got out of the shower, wrapping a towel around my waist. "I have just the stuff."

Rummaging through the cabinet under the sink, I took a green bath fizzy out of the basket and put it on the counter. "This will ease your sore bits later." I held up a pink tube. "This will make you feel better now, so you're not all squirmy during the game."

I pulled up her skirt. Instead of her usually fancy panties, she wore loose little satin shorts.

"Oh, panties hurt?" I tugged them down and put some of the cream on my fingers.

"They do." She winced again. "You're going to put that on me? I can do it myself."

"Let me take care of you, Little Alpha." I kissed her on the lips as I rubbed the cream tenderly into her.

She leaned into me, her head on my shoulder. "Oh, that feels nice."

"It does, doesn't it? I get it at the Omega Center. It's great after getting dicks for days. Oh, I can't wait for you to be there for my heat." I continued working the cream around her opening and inside her.

"You want me there?" Surprise crept into her voice as she leaned into my fingers.

"Of course. We can coordinate it, so Mercy is in London or Rockland and then you don't have to worry. It would be good for you to be there with us. Especially since if Grif goes off his heat suppressants, too. I might throw him into heat and then it'll be one big fuckfest." And hopefully better for him than last time.

A moan escaped her lips as she rubbed herself against my hand. "I'd like that."

My fingers weren't long enough to get that cream all the way in there. "Let me get it into all the right places."

I pushed her so her back was to the wall. Dropping the towel, I stroked the cream all over my dick.

"It's the opening that's sore, not inside." She grinned but didn't protest.

"Oh, I'll get it in there so good." I squirted more on her opening. Cupping her face with one hand, I guided myself into her with the other. "That doesn't hurt, does it?"

A blissful look crossed her face. "It feels good."

"Just because I'm an omega doesn't mean I can't take care of you, too, Darling," I told her, capturing her lips with mine as I gently fucked her against the wall. Because I loved her. Also, I'd never actually fucked someone against a wall like this. Usually, I was the fuckee.

I liked this. It was more the way she fit against me, nestled between my naked body and the wall. The way her blue-green eyes looked up into mine. My guys were bigger than me. It was nice to be larger than someone else for once.

"You're taking care of me so good," she told me, grabbing the tube off the vanity and rubbing more cream into her entrance. "On your birthday, too."

"Don't worry about locking me. Let me make you feel good while I get all that cream inside you." I started rubbing her clit. The cream made my dick feel all nice and refreshed and wouldn't affect my ability to cum at all.

Maybe someone would suck it before the game.

"Yes, right there," she squeaked, her scent changing in that way it did right before she came.

Another scent tickled my nose, but I kept loving my alpha and rubbing her little nub because I liked the noises she made when I touched her there.

Verity tensed under me but didn't push me away.

"It's my birthday, Jonas," I gasped as I continued to move in and out, getting closer to my release. "Also, it's medicinal."

"Medicinal fucking?" Jonas' voice grew amused. He smelled like body wash and egg custard.

"Yeah. You fucked her too hard, and she's sore. My dick is making sure the cream gets in all the right spots," I replied.

"I… I'm so close. Can I come, Omega, please?" Verity groaned as she squirmed under my ministrations.

Oh? No one had ever asked my permission to come before.

"Always, Darling. Come all over my cock and I'm going to cum inside you and make you all nice and full." That sounded like something one of them would say to her, and I rubbed her a little more.

"Dean," she cried as she orgasmed in my arms.

While she didn't lock me, her pussy fluttered and squeezed deliciously, making me cum. I leaned into her, making sure she felt all nice and snug between me and the wall as I came and came and came.

"You took me so good," I praised, stroking her hair. "I love fucking you."

Her eyes closed, and she leaned her head on my shoulder, her body aftershocking in my arms. "My pussy feels better, thank you."

Jonas leaned on the vanity. He picked up the tube. "Oh."

Yeah, he knew exactly what that was.

"I fucked you too hard, Little Alpha?" Putting down the tube, he pressed his bare chest to my back, wrapping his arms around the both of us.

"A little," she whispered. "It's mostly the after part that hurts, not the act."

"I'm sorry." He leaned around me and kissed her. "It's wonderful that our omega can make you feel better."

"Oh, our omega did the best job, Alpha Jonas." She smirked.

Our omega? Yeah, I liked that. A lot.

Jonas turned to me. "Love, Grif made your smoothie, and there's some steamed eggs if you want them. I picked up the not-as-spicy chili crunch sauce yesterday."

"Thank you." I kissed him. He usually ate this egg custardy stuff before a game, along with some rice. It was pretty tasty, though he liked to put spicy shit all over it. Grif also made killer protein smoothies.

"There's cake. That's why I came in here," Verity added. "I thought we could have birthday cake before you go."

"You made me a cake?" I'd seen the cake, but I wasn't sure if it was for me or if she was making cake pops.

Should I have cake before a game? No.

Would I? Abso-fucking-lutely.

I got my delicious dinner last night. Grif had even made me bread. This morning, I'd opened presents and Mercy and Verity made biscuits and gravy with crispy potatoes for breakfast. Now I got *cake?*

Amazing.

What the nutritionist didn't know didn't hurt anyone.

Verity kissed me. "I did. Put on some pants."

"Aw, no pantsless cake? You know, tonight, I'm going to get a shutout. After the game I want you, Grif, and Jonas all together with me in bed," I told her, imagining how amazing that would be.

Getting a shutout against the Royals while Verity watched would be the cherry on the sundae of my amazing day.

Also, it was my birthday. I had a special surprise for her.

Oh, I couldn't wait.

Something smacked my ass as I did my goalie stretches during our warm-up at the arena before our game. I popped up off the ice and skated after Grif and hit him back. Carlos busily tried to put pucks down people's pants.

The music in the arena shifted to the birthday song. The monitors in the area flashed with a birthday cake and *Happy Birthday Double-D.*

For me? I waved at everyone as I ended up on the monitors.

Everyone sang to me as Nat-the-Knight came down from the ceiling on a swing dressed in goalie gear and a jersey with a one on it–my number. *Awww.*

A couple of kids watching warm-ups held happy birthday signs. One even brought me birthday bread. I made sure they all got pucks before I returned to the locker room.

"Here, Lucky. I can't eat the birthday bread, but you can have it." I pretended to feed it to him, wishing I could have some too instead of having to worry about shit like safety.

While some players stayed dressed, a few took off their jerseys and pads. Nakey took off almost everything, as usual.

"Kiss the bunny. It's my birthday." I went around and got everyone to kiss my stuffed bunny, like always. The one Grif had won me years go.

Carlos had everyone pet Lucky as people finished their pre-game routines.

"You okay, Gumdrop?" I put my arm around Grif, who seemed a little off.

"I shouldn't have had two slices of cake earlier," he confessed, leaning into me.

"It was a delicious cake." I gave him a squeeze, understanding completely.

Coach got us revved up, and we returned to the ice for our intro and the national anthem. Finally, the puck dropped.

Winston smacked the puck around down at the Royals' end. Jonas and Elias were on defense. From my place in the net, I looked over at the family section.

Verity, in Grif's Jersey, sat with AJ, who also wore Grif's jersey. She blew me a kiss. I did a dance and made a heart with my hands. Grif's jersey. Yeah, I'd fix that shortly.

Grif threw someone against the boards after they clocked Clark a little too hard. Gloves dropped and Grif pummeled the guy like always. He didn't seem as enthusiastic as he usually did.

The linesman dragged Grif away. Grif shook his leg like he had a cramp. As he passed the family section, he banged on the glass in front of AJ and Verity and made kissy faces.

The cameras projected them up on the large monitors above the arena. You could clearly see that she wore Grif's twenty-six.

That's my cue.

Throwing down my stick, I took off my mask and skated over in mock-fury.

"It's my birthday. You wear my number," I told her, trying to sound more *angry-alpha* and less *diva-omega.*

I stripped off my shirt, so I was only in my pads. I'd left off the undershirt.

Grif resisted the linesman and eyed the shirt in my hands. "Really?"

"You said I could on my birthday." I leaned in and tapped my head to his helmet.

"Oh, I did, didn't I?" He grinned at me.

Verity laughed as she held out her hands. "Give it to me, Hot Stuff."

The Royce kids were sitting in front of AJ and Verity and waved at me frantically. I waved back.

The crowd cheered and laughed as the screens displayed it for the entire arena. I tossed my jersey over the glass. AJ caught it and handed it to her.

Chuckling, she put my jersey on over Grif's. Oh she looked beautiful wearing number one.

"SHE LOVES ME!" I shouted, putting my hands up in victory.

"I do love you, you goofball," she shouted back.

"Gumdrop, I love you, too." I hugged Grif, mostly to rub my sweaty chest all over his jersey.

Grif laughed. "I love you, Jellybean."

"Grif Graf, go to the box! Donovan, get in the net. I'm only being lenient because it's your birthday. Don't try me," the linesman shouted, making a face like she didn't get paid enough to put up with us.

Waving, I did a bare chested victory lap back to the net after swiping a new jersey from the bench. I'd let Silas know I'd be doing this, so he'd have one ready.

I put my jersey and goalie mask back on. It was silver like a knight's helmet and had a knight charging into battle on it. Both our pack crest–a Celtic knot made of sticks and pucks, and the infinity knot heart Grif and I had as tattoos was worked into the design.

Picking up my stick, I held it up like a sword. The crowd roared. Verity, in my jersey, appeared again on the jumbo screens as she blew kisses at me.

Best birthday ever.

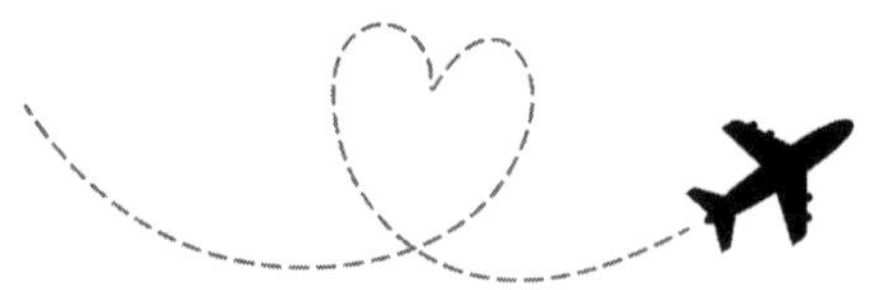

Chapter Thirty-One

Jonas

"Does this mean you're next?" Nakey snorted as we watched Verity put Dean's jersey on from the bench.

"I'll leave the jersey dramatics to them," I laughed as the lineman dragged Grif to the penalty box and Dean pranced around the net with his stick.

The game restarted. Since we were short Grif, the Royals went into a power play.

Carlos teased and taunted the Royals, literally skating circles around them. Stealing the puck, he barreled toward their goal, the Royals on his heels. Right as they were about to steal the puck, he skated backward, taking the puck with him and flinging it to Clark.

Clark raced it behind the net and slapped it in for a goal, the goalie a split-second too late to stop it.

The crowd cheered as Clark's goal song played, which might be from a Defender League movie. Coach changed the lines. Grif drummed on the glass in the penalty box and did a victory dance for Clark.

As did my omega.

"That is what I like to see," Coach praised as Clark and Carlos came in.

Finally, they let Grif out of the box, and he came back to the bench. Pauley climbed over the boards and joined everyone on the ice.

Plopping down on the bench next to me, Grif leaned his head on my shoulder. "Yeah, I ate too much cake."

I had no idea what that had to do with anything, so I just put an arm around him. His rain scent seemed a bit off, but it could be sweat.

Coach sent Elias and me back in. I popped in my mouth guard, grabbed my stick, and skated out toward the net.

The Royals came for us, hungry for a goal now that we were on the scoreboard.

I came around the other side, trying to both cut the forward from the Royals off from trying to sneak in a shot around the corner and not give her anyone to pass to. Elias chased her around the net. Clark stole the puck and got it down the ice.

A forward nabbed the puck and made a run for our goal, only for Carlos to take it away from her. I stood firm at the top of the crease, ready to block anyone and everyone who approached.

Grif chased after her, but faltered, trying to get it away from her, as another forward thumped him. He slammed his elbow into him, knocking him away. Clark stole the puck from her, tripping up someone as he passed it to Carlos, who skated toward the goal.

Dean gasped.

"What's wrong, Love?" I turned to him, dread coursing through my bond with him.

"Babes, something's wrong." Panic surged through his voice. "Something's wrong with Grif. GRIF!" It was half-shout, half-wail.

I turned to see Grif's stick fall from his hand in a clatter as he slumped to the ice.

Chapter Thirty-Two

Grif

I barreled down the ice after that Royals forward. She was determined to score.

Not tonight, Royals. Not tonight.

It would help if I felt on top of it. I'd thought that having a little rest while in the box would do it. But I still felt shitty. Probably from all the cake we'd had for Dean's birthday. I'd been craving sweets even more than usual, so I indulged and ate too much.

Though I'd felt tired and sluggish all day.

Maybe I'd caught a cold?

As I caught up to the forward, I moved to knock her down and steal the puck. I stumbled. An elbow from one of the other

Royals clocked me. I elbowed him back, pushing him away, trying to regain my balance.

And the puck.

Clark got it and passed it to Carlos. I got into position, ready for one of them to pass it to me. I stumbled again.

What was wrong with me? I felt weird… heavy.

Coach should call a line change soon. I'd have a sports drink and a hydrogel. Yeah. That would help me shake off this sluggishness.

Maybe during intermission, I could get some pickles or a banana.

Carlos passed the puck to me, but I no longer had a line to the goal. The strange feeling washed over me again, and my hand shook. Panic flooded me. I shot the puck back to Carlos, who was in a better position to score. My stick fell out of my hand and I slumped to the ice.

I heard a crack and everything went black.

Chapter Thirty-Three

AJ

Wrongness coated me. The arena grew silent. Grif didn't move. A strange sensation coursed through the bond as I watched in horror while my beloved slumped on the ice.

Get up, Boo-Boo. Get up.

That wrongness turned to fear as he didn't move.

Move, damn it.

Players rushed toward him. Dr. Mosser jumped over the boards as the refs blew their whistles.

"Grif." Panic wafted off Verity.

A growl ripped from my lips. Not at her, but at everyone else–warning them to get out of the way as I got to my omega. My love.

My mate.

I shot out of our row and flew down the stairs to the glass. People yelled at me as I backed up, then took it at a run.

The fastest way to get to him was over the glass.

In a way only an alpha trying to help their injured mate could, I leapt up to the top of the glass and jumped down onto the ice. Pain shot through my leg, but I didn't fucking care.

Only Grif mattered as my basest, most primal instinct to protect my mate came out. *Must. Get. To. Grif. Now.*

I tore across the ice. People shouted at me. Ignoring them, I made it to his side and hauled his body into my arms. *Mate.*

"Grif, I'm here, talk to me," I growled, taking off his helmet and touching his face, protecting him with my body.

"You shouldn't be here," someone said.

I growled, keeping him close.

"Wake up, Grif," I demanded. The bond had gone quiet, which made me nervous.

"That's Grif's bonded alpha. AJ, can you put him down so Dr. Mosser can look him over? An ambulance is waiting if we need it." Jonas crouched down next to me.

I snarled at him. Grif was mine.

"Hey, you shouldn't be here either. Where are you all coming from?" one ref grumbled.

"Here you go, Plant Prof, he's right here," an accented voice said. "She's Grif's, too."

"Grif." Sea salt and driftwood surrounded me as Verity crouched down with me.

Verity stroked my arm. "AJ, let's allow them to do their job, okay?"

Mine. I glared at her.

"I know you're worried, but please let the doctor look at him, AJ." Jonas' words were sharp enough to knock me back to reality.

"Oh, sorry." I realized I was holding Grif to me and growling at everyone. Jonas, Verity, and Dean crouched by my side on the ice.

Actually, the entire team was there.

"AJ?" Grif gasped, opening his eyes as I set him down.

"Grif." My heart soared.

That strange sensation coated me again as he started to shake. Emergency personnel swarmed him.

"GRIF," I bellowed as his scent went rotten and anguish filled our bond.

Arms tightened around me.

"Let them work," Jonas growled, keeping me from running over to him. "You can go with him, but let them do their fucking job."

"They'll take care of him," Verity said softly as she held Dean who started sobbing.

"Was he not feeling well?" Dr. Mosser asked us. "Any symptoms?"

"He didn't seem alright on the bench. He told me he ate too much cake." Jonas eased his grip on me.

Grif collapsed. He fucking collapsed.

"He said that to me, too," Dean sobbed.

"They're taking him to Manhattan General," Dr. Mosser told us. "Jonas, Dean, I'm guessing you're going with him."

"I've got this, Double-D. Go," Jean-Paul told Dean, clapping him on the shoulder.

"Go," Coach said. "Don't even think about not."

They loaded Grif onto a stretcher and carried him off the ice.

"Okay, let's go. AJ, ride in the ambulance with Grif. The guys will change, and I'll drive us to the hospital, and meet you there," Verity said, looking no-nonsense, voice full of authority.

I gave her a kiss. "Thank you."

"What's wrong with him?" Dean sobbed as I followed the stretcher off the ice.

But I knew. Guilt coated me. We hadn't done enough for him. I hadn't done enough.

We knew we were on borrowed time.

That time had just run out.

Chapter Thirty-Four

Verity

"We're here, whatever you need. Do you need me to fly out and take care of Mercy?" Creed offered over the phone as I sat in Jonas' SUV in the underground parking garage of the hospital.

"For the moment I have it sorted." Which was why I was still in the car.

The Maimers had an away game but weren't staying over. I'd called Rusty's omega out of desperation, who assured me that Mercy could stay with them tonight. They'd make sure my sister got to practice in the morning.

"Okay. Let me know the moment you need help. I think it might be time to tell Grace," Creed added. He'd been watching the game with his roommates.

"Already did. I needed advice. Anyhow, I need to go. Love you."

"Love you." He ended the call.

My phone buzzed.

AJ

Where are you? They're moving him to room 305.

Me

Getting Mercy sorted. On my way.

Others had texted, but I didn't have the energy to deal with them. I sent Mercy a text updating her about what was happening, so she didn't worry.

Grif. A sob escaped my lips as I leaned on the steering wheel, allowing myself a moment to fall apart.

He'll be okay.

He had to be.

Jonas assured me that his collapse might not be bad. Yet all I could think of was I collapsed due to a stroke and how awful that was.

How it could have been so much worse.

No. Happy thoughts. Grif would be fine. Maybe he did eat too much cake.

Wiping my eyes, I grabbed my crutch and purse, and made my way up to the third floor. *Critical Care.* Tears pricked my eyes. I walked past the nurse's station looking for his room–or the guys.

"Can I help you?" a woman in scrubs said from behind the station. The beta had a pinched face and a permanent sneer.

"Just going to 305." I texted AJ.

"I need you to sign in. Not everyone can enter," she snarked.

"Absolutely. I'm here for 305." I showed her my ID.

She typed on her computer and looked at my ID. Her look twisted into an accusing snigger. "You're not his pack. I can't let you in."

"I'm one of his emergency contacts." We'd added each other as emergency contacts specifically for this sort of situation.

"I see that. His pack's here, so there's no need for you. Go on now, before I call security." She looked me up and down like I was worthless.

"I'm his emergency contact. He's my *boyfriend.*" I made my voice hard. The itch to get to Grif, to hold his hand and make sure he was okay, buried under my skin. This woman was keeping me from him, and I struggled to keep my alpha in check.

"Don't even try to bark me because it's illegal to bark hospital employees. I'm calling security." She picked up her phone.

"Well, don't let little old me stop you from doing your job." I strode past her, holding my head high. I was pretty sure I had a right to be with him and she was making things up.

"You can't go back there," she sputtered.

"Bless your heart." Giving her a sunny smile, I didn't stop. No one was keeping me from him.

AJ met me in the hall. "There you are. Mercy's sorted?"

"Yes. Now I can focus on him. What's wrong?" My heart wrenched, and I kept seeing Grif fall to the ground in my mind.

AJ tugged me into a small waiting area where Jonas was holding Dean. "It's his kidneys. Dean already called his doctor. There's a good chance we can't hide his designation. While I might be able to buy everyone off to keep everything off his record like we did with the overdose, I'm not sure we should."

"Me neither. We need to make sure they're running the right tests. Which they're not because currently they think he's a beta who had too much sex and booze. Grif's family is texting me. I told them I'd update them when I knew what's going on," Dean said quietly, though we were the only ones in the room.

"Let's hold off the parent patrol for as long as we can. Hopefully, it won't be that serious," Jonas agreed.

A bunch of security came into the room.

"That's her. She can't be in here," the woman from the front said.

"Why the fuck not?" AJ snapped.

"She's not listed as pack. Only pack and immediate family can be in Critical Care outside of visiting hours," she snapped. She had major mean girl energy. Ugh.

One of the large security guards paused, eyes focused on Jonas and Dean. "Wait, you're..."

"We are. Grif Graf's in the hospital," Jonas said. "Someone should plan for that. The media might even be here already."

"You can't make her leave," Dean pouted, coming over and pulling me to him.

"You're Team Mom." The guard looked at me, then to the woman in scrubs, and shrugged. "Team Mom's with Grif Graf and Double-D. Everyone knows that."

"I'm on his file as an emergency contact. I'm one of his alphas and I can be here." Authority filled my voice. *Nope, not leaving.*

The guard shrugged. "Sounds reasonable. This is the waiting room. People wait here."

With a jerk of his head, they turned to leave.

"She's not…" She pouted as the guards ignored her.

Jonas put an arm around me so I was between him and Dean as his amber eyes focused on her and narrowed. "Verity can be here."

AJ joined us with a glare that said *don't make me call my lawyer.*

"Fine." She stomped off in a huff.

"Good job standing up for yourself." Jonas planted a kiss on my temple.

I held Dean, stroking his hair, not saying anything because there wasn't anything to say. AJ and Jonas texted and made phone calls.

"Grif is an *omega?* You didn't think to tell me?" Kylee, the Knight's PR person, ran into the waiting room, looking frazzled, heels clacking on the ground. The no-nonsense brunette beta was usually calm and put together.

"Coach told you." Jonas' words were matter of fact as he looked up from his phone.

"Coach Atkins knows?" Her voice rose in pitch. "Fuck. No. It's all over the news."

Dean sat up. "The news? Someone outed him? This is literally his worst nightmare."

"Who'd do that? Barely anyone knows," I replied, still holding Dean tight, my belly in knots.

"We *were* careless in the locker room a couple weeks ago," Dean admitted. "He broke through his blockers when he spiraled; anyone could have figured it out, even with AJ's quick work in trying to de-scent everything."

"Blockers. Is his collapse related to bad blockers or something?" Kylee asked, a frown tugging on her lips.

"More like he's approaching the point of no return. He told Coach because he was getting ready to come out. You were on the list," Dean told her.

She nodded and typed something on her phone. "Got it. Given that Chet Chesterton is holding a press conference from jail, I'm guessing it's him who outed him."

Jonas sucked in a breath. "Chet knows. Fuck."

"That fucking asshole," I muttered, my hands fisting.

AJ gave Jonas a look. "Do you think this is related to Bunty telling Grif he needed to drop the lawsuit against Chet, because Cal and Bertie are buddies and it's making poker night awkward?"

"What?" Kylee pulled over a chair. "I need to know everything, and I needed to know it an hour ago."

"Bertie?" I looked at AJ.

"Bertie Chesterton, Chet's dad. One of my dads sometimes goes to that poker night. Cal Daughtry is awful at poker. Oh. Huh, I wonder how much Cal owes Bertie." AJ texted someone.

I looked up *Bertie Chesterton, trustee, NYIT,* on my phone and showed it to AJ. "Albert Chesterton?"

"Yep." AJ didn't look up from his phone. "Why?"

"The trustee that's giving my department problems about my research is named *Bertie*." My hands shook. That made sense–and I hadn't realized Chet's father was a trustee.

"Bertie's giving you problems about your research?" AJ gave me a look, then returned to texting.

"For all I know, the haters, the threats, the person who got Samantha to destroy my research, were all orchestrated by *Chet*." Considering he knew how important my research was to me, that tracked. My belly churned.

After all these years, Chet still wouldn't let it go.

Though he'd been quiet for some time. It must have been me dating Grif that set him off. Because apparently, I couldn't have nice things.

"Makes sense. Grif wasn't succumbing to his demands," Jonas agreed, giving my hand a squeeze. "So, he took to the internet and stirred shit. When that wasn't working, he got his dad involved."

"That's pretty much how Chet operates. Make trouble, get daddy to bail him out, repeat," AJ replied, eyes on his phone screen.

Kylee gave us a look. "Chet, *what?* Though I remember that Chet wasn't happy Grif was dating Verity."

We filled her in on everything, including my history with Chet.

Her phone rang, and she took it. "He what? He's not allowed to hold press conferences without a written script, a teleprompter, and a chaperone. No, Cal's *not* an appropriate chaperone. Handle it. I don't care if you have to drag him away. I'll be there as soon as I handle things here at the hospital." She ended the call, exuding anger. "Mr. Longfellow is giving a press conference. The game isn't even fucking over."

Jonas turned on the TV. There stood Mr. Bunty Longfellow, the general manager, addressing the press. A man, possibly even older than Mr. Longfellow, hung behind him in a very expensive suit, head bald and gleaming.

"Cal and I are sad to do this. But we're a family, and we don't tolerate dishonesty," Mr. Longfellow told the reporters. "The termination is effective immediately and we'll recommend that he not be permitted to play for any PHL team."

Kylee grimaced, a manicured hand covering her face. "He did not."

"You're buying out his contract?" a reporter replied.

Mr. Longfellow shook his head. "Termination, not buyout."

Dean's cozy scent soured as he scowled at the TV. "They can't fire him. Especially without a test. Suspend him while it's sorted, but not fire. It's the law."

"I'm on this." AJ grabbed his phone and stormed out of the room in a cloud of alpha indignation.

Jonas looked like he'd explode, anger wafting off him in spicy mossy puffs. "Not how this works. I'm texting our union rep."

Kylee got on her phone again, expression livid. "I said get him off the mic right now or so help me, you won't like the consequences."

"Can you even legally fire Grif Graf, given the way contracts are now structured? This isn't the old days," another reporter said on the TV.

"This came down from both the Daughtry family and one of the other owners. Between his lawsuit and that model he's seeing, I don't think Grif's PHL material." He shrugged. "It was a mistake to bring him on."

He did *not* just bring me into it. Reporters clamored for his attention. The other man gave him an unhappy look when he said *other owners.*

"You're going to block him from playing based on his designation? That is illegal. Not to mention there are other omegas in the PHL," another reporter replied.

"Not enforcers." He shrugged. "Look, I'm simply carrying a message from the owners–"

Several people came up around him, including the assistant general manager, who looked ready to murder someone.

"I'm sorry, but this press conference is over," the Knight's assistant manager ordered. "Anyone who doesn't disperse now will be banned from future press conferences."

Mr. Longfellow fought the security. "Don't touch me. I'm allowed to fire someone for dishonesty."

"Other owners? Are the rumors true and Cal Daugherty has been secretly trading away bits of the team to pay off his gambling debts," another reporter asked, chasing after him and the other older man.

"While I know you have questions, this press conference is over," the assistant GM said as everything went black, then cut to two very confused commentators.

"Well, then," one said from behind their desk with the Knights and Royals logos in the background. "I'm not sure that's legal? They could buy him out, trade him, give him away, but I don't think they can outright fire him for simply being another designation. I mean, we don't even have official confirmation."

"The fans won't like that either. I just hope Grif Graf is okay," the other commentator said. "In all my years in this sport, I've never seen anything like this."

Kylee looked like she was about to have a panic attack, scent sour. Her phone rang, and she answered it. "I saw that. Yes, I'm with his pack now. I'll be right there."

AJ came back in and looked at Kylee. "Our lawyers are on it. This is illegal."

"Good. I have to go. Thank you for sharing everything with me." She stood and hurried out of the room, phone ringing again.

"My advocate from the Center is calling." Dean sighed as he held up his phone. "Fuck. Grif was outed. What do we do?"

"Talk to your advocate to see what resources the Center can offer. But right now we confirm nothing publicly." AJ hit the wall with his hand. "Chet needs to be stopped."

"Yes, he does," I agreed. Anger rose up in me. How dare he?

"That part about the team being sold off bit by bit to pay off Mr. Daughtry's gambling debts is weird," Dean said, answering his call and going out into the hall.

AJ sucked in a breath, realization in his eyes. "No, that makes perfect sense. Bertie makes it his business to know everyone else's, then uses that knowledge to his advantage."

"I want to hurt someone for Grif." My hands fisted, my purple painted nails digging into my palms. So much anger coursed through me.

"I know, Little Alpha. I know." Jonas held me to him. For a long moment we just stood there.

Dean came back into the room and the four of us settled down to wait.

A small, older, omega doctor came in. "You're all Griffin McGraff's? Hi, I'm Dr. Arya. I'm his personal physician."

"I'm Dean, his husband. I called you. Please tell me he'll be okay?" Dean rushed over to her. "Does he need a kidney? Because I'd give him *anything.*"

"It's an infection, a bad one, but not kidney failure. The infection is an indicator of problems to come, problems I've been speaking to him about," she told us, consulting her tablet.

AJ nodded, look grim. "We're aware."

"Infection. So you're pumping him full of antibiotics and taking him off blockers?" Dean asked. "We're his family. We all know."

"For now. There's a bigger problem. We're going to have to note his designation in his file to get him the proper care. Especially because he's spiraling. Given he's unconscious, we need to get him out of it if he's to make a full recovery." Dr. Arya's expression went serious.

Full recovery? I liked the sound of that. We'd deal with everything else a little at a time.

"You're moving him to the omega unit so you can better treat him?" Dean leaned into Jonas.

"It's your choice. They can treat him here, but it would be better to move him. Reporters are here and it will be harder to hide his designation from them if he's in the omega ward," she told us. "But it's also more secure."

Jonas looked at AJ and me.

"Do it," AJ told him, squeezing my hand. I nodded.

"Go ahead," Jonas told her. "The media has already outed him."

"Oh. How terrible. We'll move him and get him stable. You can wait in the external waiting room outside the omega unit on the 4th floor and we'll get you." She turned to leave.

"He's going to recover, right? He'll be fine and play hockey and everything?" Dean's voice broke.

"I hope so." With a long look, she left the waiting room.

"We'll figure it out." Jonas hugged Dean. "Call his family. I'll update Kylee and Stu. Why don't you two get some coffee for us and meet us there?"

"Good idea." AJ put his arm around my waist. We went down to the cafeteria and got everyone coffee.

My phone buzzed as we took the elevator up to the fourth floor, as the PR person for the Maimers texted me.

Sonny

I can't believe the Knight's GM came for you. We've got your back.

Also, we stand with Grif Graf.

Me

Thank you.

That meant everything. I showed the text to AJ.

"Shit. They're in for it," AJ agreed.

Mr. Longfellow had no idea what he'd done.

AJ, Jonas, Dean, and I settled into the fourth floor waiting room, which was outside of the locked doors, guarded by deltas, which marked the omega unit.

"There you are. We've been looking for you," Elias Royce said, looking like he'd run off the ice and thrown on whatever was around. The team was with him, most wearing athletic clothing instead of their suits.

"Is the game over already?" I asked. That seemed fast.

"We walked as soon as we heard they fired Grif," Nia replied.

"Don't you worry, even if they won by forfeit, they didn't score a single goal," Jean-Paul assured Dean.

"You forfeited for him? You heard he was fired and left?" AJ asked.

"Of course we did. Firing him in the middle of a game after he collapsed is not okay," Winston replied, coming up beside Elias and putting an arm around him, the garish lights reflecting off his bald head.

"It's not even legal." Pauly made a face, shaggy blonde surfer hair still back for the game.

"It's fucking bullshit," Carlos added. "What a knothead."

"Grif is an omega? But I could absolutely see our omega throwing someone up against the wall when pissed if she was as big as him." Pauley grinned at Nakey.

Nia laughed. "Same. It's not like we've never seen Double-D fight. We know omegas can hold their own when they're protecting something dear to them."

Oh. She was right. Relief that no one seemed angry, they just all took it in stride, filled me with happiness.

"He'll be okay, right?" Clark looked stricken. He wasn't wearing his glasses.

"We hope so," Jonas replied.

The team had *walked.* Forfeiting not only the game for the team, but possibly getting fined. For Grif.

The owner and GM might think Grif was expendable and not worthy of being a Knight, but clearly the team felt otherwise.

Now, we just needed for Grif to be okay.

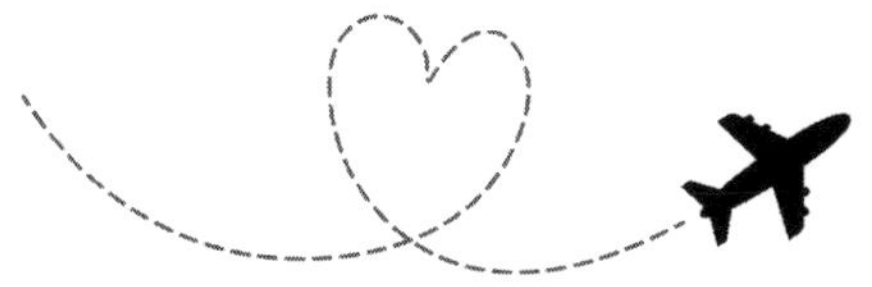

Chapter Thirty-Five

Grif

A groan escaped my lips as I opened my eyes. I felt like shit. Hair covered my face. Not my hair. Long, dark hair that smelled of coconut conditioner. I pulled it away.

"Grif, you're awake. Thank fuck." AJ moved into view.

"Where am I?" I looked around the dark room. This wasn't my room. It didn't smell like our place either. It reeked of antiseptic and unhappiness.

"The hospital. You collapsed during the game." Worry tinged his voice and scent.

Verity and Dean snuggled into me on the hospital bed. Jonas slept on the couch. A chair sat next to my bed. There was a table with some flowers and balloons on it and a couple of containers that might have food.

"I wasn't about to fight them for bed space." AJ stood, closing the distance between us.

"How long have I been out?" I frowned. I remembered collapsing on the ice in the first period, not long after Dean gave Verity his jersey.

AJ reached out and stroked my hair. "It's morning. You spiraled, but once they moved you up here, they pulled you out pretty quickly."

"Shit. How bad is it? Was it my kidneys or my heart? Did I have emergency surgery?" While I felt tired, I didn't hurt. But I was hooked up to all sorts of monitors and an IV.

"You were so fucking lucky. You collapsed because of an infection, which meant they caught it, and could treat it. Fortunately, you woke up before Dean needed to give you a kidney or Verity tried bonding you to save your life." AJ continued to run his hand through my hair.

"I would've been okay with both of those. Did the doctor suggest us bonding?" I looked down at Verity. A soft blanket covered us, but it looked like she was still wearing a jersey.

"That was a Mercy idea." AJ shook his head. "Anyhow, you're on antibiotics right now. You'll be here a couple days, both for the IV drip, and to flush the blockers out of your system so they can run more tests. They're keeping you on suppressants, so you don't go into heat right now."

Which was the last thing I needed.

"Wait, blockers? You had to tell the hospital." Panic sliced through me. If they knew, it would go into my file. If it was in my file, it was public.

If it was public...

"Hey, hey, Gumdrop, it's okay. We needed to get you the best care. Dr. Arya's here, too." Dean purred.

"Everyone's going to know. Coach hasn't helped me come up with a plan yet." The purr wasn't enough to stop me from hyperventilating. My designation was now in my file. But I didn't blame them. Especially AJ.

"It's okay. It's okay." AJ's purr, a rich tenor, added to Dean's.

Another purr hit me right in the chest as Verity purred for me in her sweet, quiet way.

"It's going to be okay. You're alive, and with a couple lifestyle changes can continue to be healthy and live a full life, complete with hockey." Jonas joined us, shoving himself on part of the bed by Dean. His basso rumble joined the purr ensemble.

Their purrs were sweeter than the finest string quartet, and I let them soothe me.

He was saying what I expected.

Still, I wanted to have control.

I wanted to play hockey.

Letting them comfort me, I took a deep breath.

"I didn't mean to ruin your birthday, Jellybean." I nuzzled Dean.

"Don't even think that. I got a birthday miracle. You're okay and that's all that matters. It gets worse, though. You were outed. My money's on Chet," Dean told me quietly.

"Fuck. Everyone knows." That panic swelled up again. *Fucking Chet.* Why couldn't he leave me alone?

"Stu's on it," Jonas assured. "So is our pack lawyer."

"It gets even worse," Dean added, tipping his forehead to mine.

Worse? How could it get *worse?*

"Dean," AJ sighed, holding me tightly. "Let's not overwhelm him. We don't need him to spiral again."

I shook my head, steeling myself. "Lay it on me. I can take it."

"Mr. Longfellow is a moron." Dean proceeded to tell me that I'd been terminated.

"This is literally my nightmare." I clung to Dean and AJ, trying to not be carried away by this shitstorm.

Verity kissed my temple. "I know. Jonas and AJ have been working hard all night, waking everyone up to get this fixed."

I gulped in some of the soothing pheromones everyone was putting out.

"Okay. The team. They know. How are they taking it?" Inwardly I cringed. Did they all hate me for lying? Would they ignore me and do things to my stuff like some of the Aces did to Dean?

"They walked out of the game when they heard you were fired," Jonas told me.

I sucked in a breath. "They did what?"

Dean squeezed my hand. "They support you one hundred percent."

"All the ones with omegas actually thought an omega enforcer makes sense. Omegas protect their families–and that's what you do. You protect your hockey family," Verity added.

"As of four this morning, some of them were still in the lobby. I should go tell the doctor–and them–you're awake. Maybe get some food?" Jonas asked, looking through his phone.

"The Maimers are on your side. Mercy and Kaiko were up late defending you. I already got a text from Queen Twatwaffle who was angry that I let Mercy use *such language* online." Verity scowled.

"Aww, they did?" That warmed me.

Jonas put on his shoes and left, AJ heading out with him. Verity went to the bathroom.

"Jellybean, what if things aren't okay?" My voice broke. I'd been outed and fired while unconscious.

"We sue them. Pretty sure Verity's big sister is ready to fly out here to stab someone with a fork. We haven't said anything other than Stu issuing a statement that you were in the hospital." Dean stayed snuggled into me.

"Okay." I nodded slowly. "What if I can't go on blockers? I mean, the PHL won't let me play without them, and some light ones won't cut it."

Because it could interfere with the game. Like an alpha might be less willing to make a play out of fear of injuring me or some biological shit like that.

"You could always use scent shields. Those, scent blocking briefs, and a shit-ton of de-scenter applied every time you leave the ice might do it. I was researching it for you," Dean admitted.

"Oh. Thank you, Jellybean." I always forgot about scent shields which were silicone stickers you put over your scent glands. I'd worn scent blocking briefs for a long time but stopped wearing them because I felt like I didn't need them anymore.

"There's always your music career. The Boston Symphony and Professor Dublonski have already come out in support of you." Dean showed me the videos on his phone.

Aww.

"Oh, I should text our families." Dean started texting his mom.

"Shit. It's a good thing that I told some of my family before now." I glanced at my phone on the bedside table. But I didn't have the energy to do more than let the parents know I was awake and tell Sissy that she didn't need to come out.

Verity came back and snuggled me. "I'm right here."

"Mmmm, what's this about bonding to save me?" I nuzzled her, though I tried not to breathe in her direction because my breath was nasty.

"I'd do anything for you." She wrapped her arms around me and held me while Dean slipped off to the bathroom.

AJ came back into the room. "Doctor's on the way. Um, Princess? Why did I just get an alert that Spencer Thanukos had a press conference saying that Cal Daughtry doesn't deserve a hockey team and he will hostilely acquire the Knights if he doesn't rehire Grif?"

Verity shrugged. "Spencer figured since the idea of him buying a team scared the crap out of people, him threatening to acquire one might do some good."

"I love that." I leaned in more.

The nurse checked on me and helped me to the bathroom. Dr. Arya came in and basically told me everything my pack had. Though she reassured me that as long as I took good care of myself, I could still play.

Which was half the battle. The other was that I needed a team.

Someone would want me, right?

"Thanks, Dr. Arya. I appreciate all your help," I told her, grateful she'd come to the hospital. I'd probably fared better because she was here.

"I'm so sorry you've been outed. We'll be doing more tests today and tomorrow. Someone from the Center will be here in a bit to talk you through all your options." She glanced at her tablet and left.

Tests, great.

"We need to get the Omega Rights Coalition involved, like they did for me," Dean agreed, looking something up on his phone.

"Whatever helps. Where's Jonas?" I looked around. He'd been gone awhile. But he'd mentioned getting food. I could eat.

A few moments later Jonas came back in, holding a sack and something wrapped in a Knights workout towel.

"I let the team know you're okay. They have quite a spread out there, so I brought some. It's in the bag. Some of the MASO are creating a signup to bring us homemade food. Stu and his agency are doing major work trying to spin this. Also, you've had offers," Jonas added, setting the bag down.

"I have? That's wonderful news. Let me guess, the Mexico City Tigres?" I snorted. They weren't a horrible team, and had a loyal fan base. They were just far.

"Yes. They'll take us all. The Hurricanes will take you back. The Daredevils will take us all. So will the Sasquatches. The Belugas will take you," Jonas read off his phone, then glanced up at me.

"Oh." There were some good offers there.

"The Sasquatches would take us *all*? I'd love to see the budget gymnastics on that," Dean chuckled.

They were the number two team in the PHL and had some very well-paid players. The three of us made decent money.

"Daredevils? Nice. We'll make it work, even if it means you three leave New York." Verity looked at us.

"We will," AJ agreed, squeezing my shoulder.

"That means everything," I told them. Especially Verity, because she couldn't work remotely like AJ.

Jonas' eyes rested on me. "We have options. Though Stu's confident that the Knights will cave. Remember, being fired has nothing to do with you. It's because the owner owes Chet's dad money. Just like you being outed is Chet trying to bully you into dropping the lawsuit."

"Bertie owns part of the team. I've got spies trying to figure out how much and who else in society might have traded Cal's debt for shares," AJ replied.

"We *will* figure this out. Stu said that as of right now, your All-Star spot is still safe. Though you'll need a team by then," Jonas assured, still holding whatever was in the towel.

Shit. That was coming up in a few weeks. "At least they didn't take it away."

"They wouldn't dare." Dean sat up and sniffed. "I smell tomato sauce. Jonas, what are you holding?"

"Oh, right." Jonas pulled the bed tray table over and set down the bundle. He unwrapped it and peeled off the foil to reveal a bubbly, cheesy lasagna. "Ladybug appeared with a piping hot lasagna; she was on her way to class or something."

"Oooh. Wait, is she the one that makes lasagna?" I remembered having some delicious lasagna at some of the pre-season team get-togethers.

Jonas came back with a handful of forks. "It's her grandma's sauce recipe. I think she takes most of the ingredients from the campus dining hall. Which is smart."

"Grocery shopping at the dining hall is the best," I agreed, mouth watering. "Can we dig in, or do we need plates?"

"It's not like we don't all share germs." Dean took a fork and took a bite. Bliss coated his face.

I speared a bite with my plastic fork and ate it, letting the cheesy tomato goodness explode over my tongue.

How did Chet even know I was an omega? At the same time, I didn't feel as panicked as I had when this happened to Dean.

I may not be a Knight right now. But despite the scare, I'd be okay. It could have been so much worse, like I could have had a heart attack or been out for months recovering from a kidney transplant.

Also, I had my pack. An agent fighting for me. My teammates cared about me.

And I had a tray of lasagna.

Yeah, we'd figure this out. Somehow.

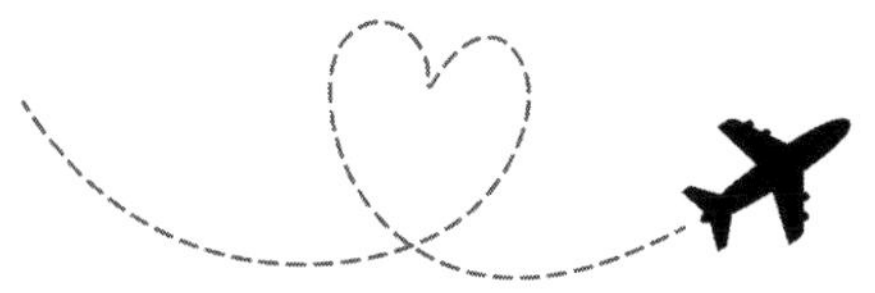

Chapter Thirty-Six

Dean

"You're shitting me?" I gave Coach Atkins the side-eye. He'd come after practice to the hospital to visit Grif and see how we were all doing. Also, he brought some cookies his kids made for us.

Jonas and I had skipped practice, like we did yesterday, and stayed with Grif. It had been a whirlwind of tests and meetings with an advocate, Center lawyers, our lawyer, Stu, and the publicist AJ had hired.

Not to mention fielding phone calls from worried friends and family. Reassuring fans on social media. Following the list from the Center regarding being outed so we didn't miss anything.

As well as dealing with the fact that Mr. Longfellow and Mr. Daughtry were not relenting on firing Grif, despite public outcry. Not even Spencer Thanukos' threat to hostilely acquire the team had worked.

Our lawyer seemed confident that we could fight this, but it would take time. I wanted to deal with this fast because I couldn't play for a team that would disrespect my husband.

"If you and Jonas aren't at the game tonight, the team will fine you." Coach Atkins pinched the bridge of his nose. "We'll be okay without you if you choose to stay here with him. Honestly, if it was my packmate, I would. JP's solid in the net. I'll call up Marlin from the Bantams. We're playing the Gears, so we'll be okay."

The Gears were fucking assholes and played rough to make up for the fact that their starting line was brought to you by nepotism.

Marlin was a decent goalie. He'd been our EBUG before joining our farm team the Buffalo Bantams.

Grif shook his head and looked at me and Jonas. "I'll be okay with Verity and AJ if you want to go play. It's a home game."

"I'm not leaving, especially to play the fucking Gears. I can't believe they'd do this. He's in the *hospital*. We should be allowed to miss without a fine." Jonas squeezed Grif's hand.

"I'm taking the fine. Management can suck it." I scowled. That was a special sort of fucked up right there.

"Understood." Coach turned to Grif. "I one hundred percent support you. A lot of staff and all the players do, too. What Cal and Bunty did was shitty. Anyhow, Dean, Jonas, do what you need to. Just be aware that if you miss too many games against their wishes, you can get in trouble for breach of contract, even with the pack contract."

"We're aware, thanks Coach," Jonas said.

Coach Atkins nodded. "Are you three gone? I can understand wanting to leave the Knights after this. Though, please understand, most of us don't believe in what Bunty and Cal did."

"I know. The support from staff and other players has been amazing. I'm relieved that no one's mad that I lied," Grif told Coach.

"People understand hiding your designation for something you love. As long as you make that clear, most fans will, too. Also, the idea of an omega putting everything on the line for love and hockey? That's the shit my omega reads on the airplane." Coach laughed.

"I'm going to need those book titles, Coach." Verity looked over at him and grinned.

"If Mr. Longfellow and Mr. Daughtry apologize and rehire me, I'd go back," Grif replied. "We want to stay together. Management's not going to let Jonas and Dean go, even if the Tigres have a hard-on for us because they want themselves some giant omegas."

"The Tigres do love their giant players, so I can absolutely see how big omegas that play like you two would be especially attractive. I hope we can fix this so you all stay with us. I'm not saying this just because I'm hoping we go all the way this year," Coach added.

"I just want to play hockey with Dean and Jonas," Grif admitted.

"Take care." Coach Atkins nodded and left.

Jonas stood and held up his phone. "Union rep is on it, too. I'm going to call Stu to see where everything's at."

He left, leaving me, Grif, and Verity alone in the hospital room. AJ had gone to get things from our place and handle some work shit.

Verity looked at her phone. "Dean, you might want to drop in the player group chat that the Brooklyn Blankets are organizing a protest of your game tonight. Omega and gamma athletes in many different sports are upset about this. Several have come out in support. Rusty's paying for food trucks to give anyone with a protest sign free food and hot drinks since it's going to snow tonight."

"Molly's spoken up for you," I told Grif. She was the other public omega goalie in the PHL and played for the Belugas.

"Also..." Verity's head ducked.

"Kitten?" Grif put an arm around her.

"I might have gone on social media last night, after that latest statement from the Knights. I may have said some strongly worded things, like that I was quite disappointed in Knights management and they owed you an apology and a fruit basket. It may have gone viral even before Mercy and Kaiko amplified it." She chewed on her glossy lip.

"That's how we beat them. A combination of the law and public opinion. You're brilliant, Darling." I leaned over and kissed her.

The fact that my social media shy little alpha did all that for Grif warmed me.

"I think our fans need to know that the team is demanding we leave our mate in the hospital to play. We should probably formally address everything. Because they don't want to hear from Stu or a publicist. They want to hear from us," I told Grif, giving his hand a squeeze.

Grif nodded, squeezing my hand back. "That's a good idea. I thought a lot about that, too. After talking to the people from the Center, Dr. Arya, and my sister, I know what I need to do. Let's make some videos."

"Go live with me? Answer questions. Be honest." I was fuming, and we needed to end this bullshit.

The dumb thing was that the Knights had so many ways to legally get rid of Grif, and they chose the illegal one, hoping their wealth and power would shield them from consequences.

So, I was choosing violence.

"Grif, when you're feeling better, the omegas at Creative Collective want to do an interview and photo shoot with you. They want to know if you prefer puppies or alpacas?" Verity looked up from her phone.

Grif rubbed his beard. "Puppies. This is the bathtub of goldfish people? Let's do it. Honestly, let's get that SportsBeat reporter, too. If my career is over, let's burn things down–as long as it doesn't ruin things for Dean and Jonas. Going live sounds great."

I snorted. "I'd rather end my career to make a point than play for a team that blatantly breaks the law and disrespects my mate." My phone lit up from the group chat. "Let's clean up and go live."

"This is going to be comedy. I brought tacos." Carlos came into the hospital room, a bag in his hand, and a Knights cap covering his brown hair.

"I brought beer." Jean-Paul followed, and held up a twelve-pack.

Some of the Knights were here with snacks to watch the game. There were no visitor limits in the omega wing during visiting hours as long as we approved it and everyone signed in. Others were at Nia's for a family-friendly watch party.

The *entire* team refused to play tonight.

Management had brought in *all* of the Buffalo Bantams to play the game instead.

Clark came in, pushing his black frame glasses as they slid down his nose. "I have artichoke dip and chips. Ladybug sent some lasagna. She's refusing to EBUG tonight and is picking up a shift at Tito's instead."

Carlos spread the tacos out on the table. "We'll hit Tito's after the game."

"Ooh, lasagna." Grif's face lit up. "Thank you everyone. This means everything to me."

I sent Gwen a text thanking her. It was sweet that she kept making us lasagna, especially since she was a struggling student. After this, I should buy her some tacos or something.

"*None* of the EBUGs are coming in. Game can't start without an EBUG signing off." JP looked at his phone.

Really, anyone not currently a professional goalie could be an EBUG. Even Coach Kirov could do it. Someone in the Ice Crew was probably a goalie and could do it, too.

My phone buzzed. Ellie, who I'd played with on the Aces before she was traded to the Sasquatches, texted.

Ellie

I got you and Grif Graf. The haters can suck my hairy balls.

I looked up. "Ellie from the Sasquatches sent me a link to a live feed."

While I'd reached out to all the hidden omegas I knew of in the PHL to make sure they were okay, Ellie wasn't one of them.

"Oh, fuck." Jonas grabbed the remote. "Put it on the TV? Because if this is what I think it is..."

Yeah. Ellie said she was a kappa. I was pretty sure she was a gamma.

I put the live feed up on the TV. Ellie got behind a podium in her Sasquatches uniform.

"Hi, I'm Ellie Porter, enforcer for the Sasquatches. First off, I stand with Grif Graf. If you have a problem with that, you can fuck off. Anyone who thinks he isn't a good person for hiding his designation can suck it." Her eyes rolled. "He's the fucking highest scorer in the league right now. Higher even than *me.* So that says a lot for the old *only certain designations can play hockey* bullshit.

Also, people who think omegas and gammas can't play hockey can suck my dick."

Yeah, I knew what was coming. I hadn't asked her to do this.

"Anyhow, I love you all, and I'm fucking tired of hiding. If you pity me, I'll punch you. I don't want your fucking pity. What I want is to play some fucking good hockey. I'm not a kappa, I'm a gamma. I hid my designation for the usual reasons. Apologies to all the little kappas out there. Please don't be mad at me. Instead send your love to the other PHL kappas, like Carlos Rodriguez of the Knights. No apologies to any alpha egos that were hurt by me kicking your ass. I'm not my fucking designation and this changes fucking nada. Gamma power. Love you, Grif. Hey Spencer Thanukos, if I'm fired, put me on your team. Can you imagine the line Grif and I would make? Anyhow, not taking your fucking questions. BTW, asking people how they became a gamma is rude as fuck. Kids, kick names and take ass. Peace." She flashed the peace sign and left the podium.

The signal went black. I turned the TV back to the pre-game broadcast we had on.

"Ellie just came out as a gamma. Fuck." I texted her back, thanking her for the love.

"Ellie Porter gave me a shout out?" Carlos beamed and got on his phone. "I knew I loved her."

A gamma hiding as a kappa was an interesting choice. But Ellie was chaotic as fuck–and had been a drama major at university and did community theatre during the off-season.

The TV commentators kept cutting to the protests outside the arena. There were a lot of people out there, especially considering it was snowing.

The Bantams, in Knights jerseys, came out for warmups. I knew some of them, like Marlin, one of their goalies. Sometimes players from the Bantams played with us, subbing for someone who was sick or injured, or got moved up to the Knights. Carlos had started off as a Bantam.

"This will be an interesting game. Never have we seen an entire minor league team being called up for a game like this. Not even when the workers of Deloitte Automotive struck during a wage dispute and picketed Gears games because the Deloitte's own the Gears," one commentator said.

They cut to a segment that must have been shot earlier with Coach Deloitte. "I don't care who's on the ice tonight. We won't play any differently," he told the reporter.

No, they'd play the same as always–average. The coach was the owner's son and a good chunk of the starting line were his grandkids.

I sucked in a breath. "It's going to be a bloodbath. The Gears are assholes."

You didn't lose to the Gears because they played better. You lost because they injured your players or got their tricks past the refs.

Clark looked thoughtful. "I know some Bantams and they're beasts. It might not be that bad."

"I agree." Carlos took a swig of beer.

The cameras panned over the fans up against the glass for warmups. Many held signs supporting Grif. There was also lots of pink–the color used to support omegas during omega history month and for omega cancer awareness.

"Oh shit, let's cut live from Venice, Italy," one of the reports said.

They cut to Maria Barilla, outspoken queen of the goalies, first beta goalie in the PHL. There was gray in her dark wavy hair and fury on her face.

"If an omega is the best for the job, give them the fucking job. Other countries have omega forwards. My team had *two.* The Knights took a chance on me, they took a chance on Dean Donovan. Why the fuck are they not taking a chance on Grif Graf?" she said as she stood at a podium with the logo for the team she coached in Italy in the background.

"Burn!" Carlos toasted the TV with a taco.

"The queen has spoken." JP raised his beer.

I raised mine and looked at my husband. "See, everyone is on your side. Nice to know we could always move to Italy."

"This is incredible. I can't believe people are rooting for me." Tears pricked Grif's eyes.

I snuggled into him. "I told you they would."

Okay, there was one sports commentator that thought Grif should stay home and make pork chops like a good omega. She'd said the same about me.

I mean, my pork chops were delicious. But I was a better goalie.

On the screen, as both teams warmed up, there was a popping noise. Mounds of purple glitter rained down over the arena and the fans. The monitor filled with animated dancing gumdrops and said *rehire Grif Graf, you ding-dongs.*

Jonas laughed. "How the fuck did the Maimers do that?"

It had to be them.

"The Maimers have their ways," Verity chuckled.

The dancing gumdrops were replaced with a gif of Verity wagging her finger going *Knights Management, Team Mom is disappointed in you. You owe Grif a fruit basket.*

The message was loud and clear. Hopefully, management heard it.

Chapter Thirty-Seven

Grif

"Your Honor, this is a waste of time, and I again ask for the charges to be dismissed. My client has done nothing untoward regarding Mr. McGraff, and if anything, these false charges are an affront to an upstanding businessman who has done nothing but give aspiring athletes a chance," the well-dressed alpha lawyer said from across the table.

I sat in between my lawyer and AJ. I'd been released from the hospital right in time for this private hearing Bertie Chesterton had pushed for, instead of the public one that was supposed to be next week.

Probably in hopes I couldn't attend due to still being hospitalized.

The privileged smugness of all this made me want to gag.

"We have proof that the contracts were forged," my lawyer stated from my side of the table, giving the other lawyer a look as if to say, *what delusion do you live in?*

"But not by my client. Just because they came from his email doesn't mean he did it," Chet's alpha lawyer parried, looking very polished in her suit and fancy accessories.

Mmmm hmm. Sure. She lived in the delusional state of Bertie Chesterton's money.

Chet, in one of his white suits, though this one *with* a shirt, sent me a smug look. He was in between his lawyer and his father. His wife, Winnie, was on the other side of his dad. She was a pleasantly pretty beta brunette, about my age, who kept trying to murder me with her eyes.

"Not only are Mr. McGraff's claims false, but he has caused my client irreparable character damage, along with pain, suffering, and income loss," the lawyer continued. "We'll be counter-suing. Especially since this reeks of designation-bias."

I'd always assumed Chet was a beta who wore too much cologne. He was actually an iota, one of the rare designations that were mutations of the main three. Iotas not only had no scent, but couldn't pick up on scents or pheromones. Barks didn't work on them, which usually made them think highly of themselves. Being an iota could be a little dangerous, since they couldn't pick up on scent cues like everyone else.

They also had a reputation for being a bit smarmy.

Several of Chet's clients had left, and former clients were speaking out against him. I'd like to see him come at me with the proof we had. AJ, Jonas, and Verity had been very busy using their contacts to help build this case.

"This isn't a civil suit for defamation. This is a criminal suit for financial theft and has nothing to do with designation bias and everything to do with *money*." Judge Russo didn't look amused from her position at the head of the table. She was older, no-nonsense and had a track record of disliking privileged assholes or those who took advantage of others.

Judge Russo had been a last-minute replacement for the judge that Bertie had paid off.

"We have ample evidence that not only did Mr. Chesterton forge the contracts, but he manipulated his father's bank to redirect the funds. We submitted proof," my lawyer said.

"Fake proof," Bertie retorted, scrolling through his phone as if this hearing bored him. He looked like a less slimy version of Chet, gray in his hair.

"Don't speak out of turn," the judge scolded.

"If he stole from Mr. McGraff, where's the money? We've submitted his assets, and there's no record of it," Chet's lawyer replied.

Oh, but we found it. Or rather, one of the super hackers in Verity's sister's pack had.

"Again, this is designation bias. Iotas are always shunned. Why would my client even steal money? He has a thriving sports representation business and comes from an esteemed family," Chet's lawyer continued.

"Your client is broke and living off his wife. His agency is in debt. He's been cut off from his trust," my lawyer countered.

She shook her head. "That isn't motivation to steal."

I felt a snort through my bond with AJ. It sort of was. Though Chet hadn't been spending much of the money, he'd stolen. The bit he had was used mostly to pay bills.

No. Those overseas accounts felt like go-funds.

"Grif's salty that I told him not to date his little side piece. You should have listened to me. She's a life ruiner," Chet told me, giving me a snarky look. "Oh, the stories I could tell you about her."

He exchanged a look with Winnie, who clucked and shook her head as if Verity was scandalous.

"So, you chose to ruin both our lives? You harassed her, destroyed her life's work, and tried to mess with her career." Anger boiled inside me. How dare he bring her into it?

His hands flew up in the air. "I did nothing but warn you off her."

That was partially true. We still couldn't pin wrecking Verity's greenhouse on him–even with Samantha's cooperation. All we could prove was him stirring up shit and sending a few mean texts from burners.

Chet's lawyer cleared her throat. "Strike that. None of that is relevant."

"Look, I didn't destroy her greenhouse. Her trying to get my father's position as a trustee revoked is dirty bullshit though." Chet stood and looked like he wanted to throw something. "That girl has other enemies."

"How did you know about it, then?" I pushed, wanting answers for my kitten. We hadn't actually tried to get Bertie's position taken away. Verity just brought up to the head of her department what was going on between me and Chet, as well as her own history with him.

"Mr. Chesterton," his lawyer warned, looking like she wanted to strangle her client.

"Look, drop this ridiculous lawsuit and I won't counter-sue you for defamation." Chet shrugged.

"Mr. Chesterton, this is a criminal case, and due to the large amount in question, it is not for Mr. McGraff to decide if there are charges. It's *my* decision," Judge Russo told him.

Chet looked as if this were a personal affront. "I'm the victim here. Grif lied to me about his designation. Which is why I spoke up as soon as I knew, so no one would think I'd misrepresented him intentionally." He put on a look of mock innocence. "I'm so glad the Knights fired you."

It turned out that he'd known that I was a secret omega for years and had been sitting on it. He'd bought off one of my suppliers back when I was with the Hurricanes.

"Oh, so it's okay for you to hide your designation due to bias, but not him?" my lawyer challenged.

"Again, irrelevant. Please disregard, Your Honor." Chet's lawyer gave him another sharp look.

Chet made a face back, like he was a child, not an adult in the middle of a court hearing.

"Chet, shut up and sit down or you'll be sent outside," Bertie hissed. "Your Honor, these charges are erroneous. We're upstanding members of the community."

Winnie rubbed Chet's arm. He squeezed her hand and sat back down.

Judge Russo didn't look convinced. But then Bertie probably didn't know all her secrets.

"I've taken a look at the proof submitted and there's enough to bring this to trial–and keep Mr. Chesterton in jail until then," she told them.

Chet looked startled. "Dad, you *promised.* I've already been in jail for ages. Do you know what it was like to be in prison during the storm?"

I was honestly surprised that Bertie hadn't somehow sprung him.

"It's a hardship, think of the children," Winnie pleaded. "We have a toddler at home and one on the way. I have a career, too. He's a good man and father, he's well-liked in the community and even assistant coaches a youth fútbol team. This is all a misunderstanding. Please, just send Chet home to us." She patted her belly, which wasn't really showing yet.

It seemed heartfelt, not forced. Perhaps she truly loved him.

"Thank you for that, Mrs. Chesterton. After fully reviewing everything, it has been decided that Chet Chesterton won't be brought to trial by the state of New York," Judge Russo continued, expression not giving anything away.

AJ squeezed my hand. No, he wouldn't stand trial by the state, because someone bigger would hold him accountable.

Though, I felt a little bad because of Winnie and the kids.

Chet shot me a triumphant look. "Take that, you ungrateful fraud. You would've gotten nowhere without me, and this is what I get for it? I made you and your career. Expect my countersuit tomorrow."

Winnie did an excited dance in her seat and reached over to squeeze Chet's hand.

"Mr. Chesterton, *please,*" Chet's lawyer told him, expression bewildered.

"Hard work got me where I am. I made it despite all your attempts to keep me down. Why, Chet, why? You made money when I did? Why derail contracts? Keep me from getting to the Knights?" I craved answers for all the weird little things he did that we still couldn't explain.

"I didn't need you getting uppity and leaving me. Guess it didn't work." Chet stood. "If you'll excuse me."

Well, then.

Winnie got up, looking pleased. She glared at me, then hugged her husband excitedly. He kissed her and whispered in her ear.

The door opened, and the meeting room filled with people in suits and uniforms that said FFCD.

"Chet Chesterton, on behalf of the Federal Financial Crimes Division of the Bureau of Investigation, you're under arrest for bank fraud, wire fraud, contract fraud, tax evasion, tax fraud, and grand financial theft of multiple people," one of the men in suits said.

Winnie looked like someone kicked her puppy. Her hand went to her stomach. "No."

We'd done it. We'd amassed enough proof to escalate this to a federal level. The Feds didn't play, especially for things like manipulating the bank system and hiding untaxed money overseas.

"DAD. You promised! Otherwise, we would've left the country." Chet looked like he was going to shit himself.

Oh, so it *was* go-money.

"Bertie, you can't. The children. You promised. When I married into this family and took on your bullshit, you *promised.*" Tears pricked Winnie's eyes.

"Shut up, I'm sure this is all a mistake," Bertie hissed at both of them. He looked at his phone, most likely trying to figure out who he could exploit.

Winnie flinched as if slapped. Chet wrapped his arms around her and whispered to her.

"Don't feel bad," AJ hissed, squeezing my hand.

We'd done what we could to make this case Bertie-proof. Bertie would regret some of those recent transactions, thinking all of this would get wrapped up nicely. It turns out the Chestertons weren't as rich as they made themselves out to be, and this lawyer was *expensive*.

He made a good salary working for the bank. But his family had been cut off from the main Chesterton fortune *because* of Chet and all the payoffs, antics, and other indiscretions.

Winnie owned her house and had a modest income from her job in marketing, but she didn't seem *rich.* Though we hadn't done any digging on her.

The lawyer looked over at Bertie, terrified. "Everything's in order. We have to let them take him. I'm sorry, Chet, but you're being remanded to a federal prison until you can be tried in federal court."

With a wave of the suited man's hand, two uniformed officers handcuffed Chet.

"No, please no." Winnie clung to him and cried.

"You can't do this. Don't you know who I am? Who my family is?" Chet spat, though he didn't fight them. "Winnie, love, you have to let me go." He gave her a kiss.

"No. Please don't take him from me." She let go, but continued to cry. Bertie gave her a look of disgust and made no move to reassure her.

I felt bad that she and the kids would pay for what Chet did. Hopefully, she had a nice family or good friends to help her out.

"This isn't going to stick," Bertie told the man in the suit.

"Albert Chesterton, you're under arrest for willfully allowing the exploitation of a federally insured banking system." The man in the suit looked bored, as if he did this all day long.

He might.

Bertie looked startled. "I would never. Chesterton Financial is an old and elite institution."

Yeah, he hadn't seen that coming. But then he knew that his son was using the family bank to exploit clients and how he was doing it. His bank wasn't tamper-proof if you were a Chesterton.

"Handle it," Bertie snapped at his lawyer as he was taken into cuffs.

"We'll be in touch," the man in the suit said to us as he left with Chet, Bertie, and everyone else who came.

Winnie was full-on hysterical sobbing as the lawyer tried to reassure her.

I couldn't help but wave at Chet, both joyful and relieved that he'd be punished for not just what he did to me, but the others he stole from.

"Case dismissed." The judge stood and left.

The lawyer led Winnie out of the office, and she shot me a withering look.

"Don't," AJ warned.

Our lawyer looked at us, triumphant. "Well done. It worked. Good thing I don't have any money in Chesterton Financial."

"Thank you." I hugged AJ, because so much of this was him.

"Chet's an asshole. I feel bad about the wife and kids, but that's not our problem. Chet is a menace and has harmed more than you. There are so many people rooting for him to rot in jail." AJ hugged me back. He took my hand. "Let's go have a celebratory beer and tell the pack?"

It felt like a load lifted off my shoulders. "Let's."

Chet would pay for his crimes. Now to get my job back.

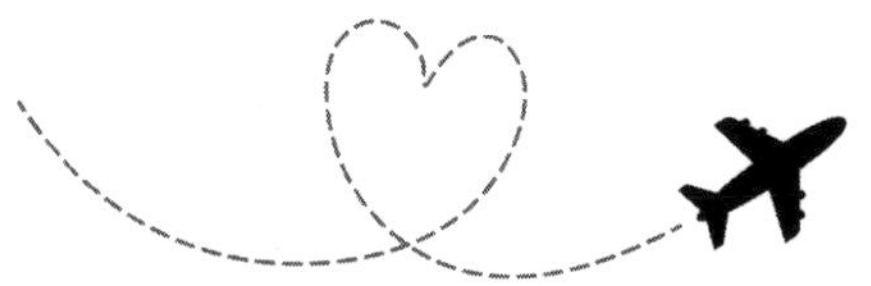

Chapter Thirty-Eight

Jonas

"Great practice everyone, see you tomorrow," Coach Dodd told us. The older alpha was all bundled up against the February chill.

Unlike some of my teammates, I loved practicing outside.

While the team had been boycotting practices and games for a week, we hadn't wanted to let our skills get rusty. It started off as a group of us playing around at the outdoor rink at the Roganfort Center. We'd practice a little, then play against whoever wanted to.

Now the entire team showed up for practice. So did Coach Dodd, one of the assistant coaches. Coach Atkins had been here earlier.

We were prepared to do this as long as we had to, and our union supported us. Sure, at some point the Knights could come after us for breach of contract, but would they fire the entire team?

Lots of people were watching us, including some people with sticks, ready to join us. How often did you get to play a pro team?

"Looking good, Knights." A middle-aged man in a suit came over to us, walking on the ice in his loafers in a way that only came with practice.

We all eyed him warily.

"Can I help you?" Elias asked, stepping forward to speak for the team.

"I hope so. I'm Louis Daughtry, Cal Daughtry's son. My family owns the Knights. While we love it, it's also a business. It's hard for the Knights to operate when our players are on strike and management is subject to countless pranks and glitter bombs. I'm here, without my dad's knowledge, to fix things. What do we need to do to end this walkout?" His look was both frustrated and earnest, and his posture seemed sincere.

There it was. The Bantams were trying hard, but we were playing some tough teams soon. Every loss affected our chances of going to the playoffs.

Game attendance was still down. Not because of the Bantams, we'd been encouraging everyone to support them, but because fans didn't agree with what management was doing. Or they didn't want to deal with the protesters.

Or the glitter.

Many people were calling for Mr. Longfellow to retire and for Cal Daughtry to step down. Our assistant GM and Kylee looked ready to quit at any moment.

Dean leaned into me. "Is the son coming good or bad?"

"Good, I hope?" I whispered back. Hopefully it meant they were scared.

Elias crossed his arms over his check and gave him a measured look. "You know why we walked and what you need to do. All of this happened without proof or even talking to him, less than an hour after he collapsed and was carried off the ice. We won't stand for this."

"Not to mention even though numerous organizations, including the PHL, have informed Mr. Daugherty and Mr. Longfellow that their actions are illegal, and given them instructions on how to rectify the situation, they've ignored them," Winston added.

Though so far they hadn't been arrested or anything. Probably money and privilege at work. The Knights had been fined, though.

"To be clear, we want Grif hired back, not bought out or traded or given away," I added, arms crossed over my chest. We were already pursuing them legally. Though that could take a while. The quicker we got Grif back on the ice, the better it would be for his mental health.

Louis nodded. "I see. You'd play with an omega enforcer?"

"We have this whole time. It's not a problem," Elias told him.

"I don't see what the issue is, other than the father of Grif's old agent is friends with your father," I snapped.

"Yes. Bertie and the whole Chet thing." Louis grimaced as if the thought gave him a headache. "I'm sorry for all this. Our parents and Bunty have always been very closed about the way they handle things and we've always been content to let them handle it. Now, my sister and I are taking a closer look at things and becoming more involved."

As they should. I was curious who else might own little bits of the Knights besides the bit Bertie owned. Not that he owned it any longer.

Elias gave him a look. "We told you what we want."

"Does Grif even want to come back? Also, can he?" Louis frowned and rubbed his chin.

"Yes and yes," I replied. Okay, he needed a few more days to recover, but that was it. He'd been meeting with some awakening specialist from the center that worked with athletes and she had lots of good ideas.

"Besides being reinstated, he needs an apology from Mr. Longfellow and a fruit basket." Dean joined us, hanging on my shoulder.

Louis blinked and nodded. "A fruit basket. Okay."

Clearly, he didn't see the meme–or Verity's video.

"The pranks are all the Maimers and that's because Mr. Longfellow went after Verity in his press conference. Don't you own the Maimers?" Dean asked.

Louis raked his hand through his hair. "My children and niblings own the Maimers, not us or my father. He brought it up, given the glitter is becoming excessive. They shrugged and said

FAFO, Grandpa, FAFO." His look grew exasperated. "I don't even know what that means."

That was funny, because that's exactly what happened. Mr. Daughtry and Mr. Longfellow fucked around and found out.

Louis looked at the rest of us balefully. "If we rehire Grif back, you'll all come back?"

Elias looked around at all of us. "Yes?"

"Yes," the team agreed.

"Okay, good. Also, Compass BioTek won't really try to buy us, right?" Louis' brow furrowed.

Spencer had set a countdown timer. How he planned on implementing a hostile takeover of the team I wasn't sure, but whatever worked.

"I don't think it's that bad an idea," Carlos shrugged. A few others nodded.

Louis sighed. "I'll see what I can do then. I'd love to see the Knights go all the way this year. While I adore the Bantams, we're not going to do that with them."

Elias extended a hand. "I appreciate you taking the time to talk to us."

Because Mr. Longfellow and Cal Daughtry hadn't. Louis shook his hand and left.

Coach Dodd was still there. "Huh. I hope they fix this. The Daughtry family and Mr. Longfellow have always done right by the Knights. I hope everyone's... okay."

The idea that one or both of them might be showing early signs of dementia had been floated by the press.

"Me, too." Elias nodded.

"I do like playing outside, though," Jean Paul added. "Reminds me of home."

"Me, too." It was a pleasant change of pace. I missed playing outside on ponds.

Still, it would be nice to get back to normal. Hopefully, with Bertie in jail, management would stop being stubborn and do what's right.

While I was ready to sit out as long as I needed, I'd sort of like to have a chance at winning the championships, too. With Grif by our side.

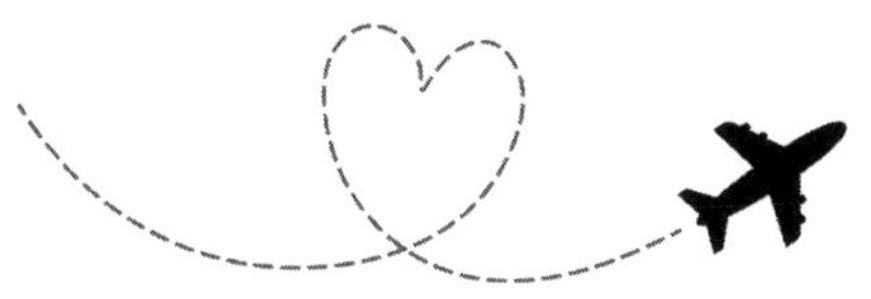

Chapter Thirty-Nine

Grif

Pleasure coursed through me as AJ pumped into me hard, fast, and unrelenting. The sheets of his bed tangled around us as he groaned.

"Oh, yes. Please, Pepperjack," I moaned. Being off the blockers was making me want sex all the time.

AJ was happy to oblige. "Come for me, and I'll knot you so good, Boo-Boo."

I came all over his hand, and he thrust into me, fast and hard, his knot pushing past my ring of muscles.

"AJ." I gasped as his knot seated itself inside me, locking into me as he came.

His arms wrapped around me and he pulled us on to our sides, throwing the blanket over us. AJ's purr surrounded me, making me feel cozy and safe. Something else that I'd been craving since they detoxed me of blockers.

It was a little weird, that part of me so close to the surface. At the same time, I didn't feel like fighting it.

Maybe because I was tired of fighting.

Or maybe it was because I had my pack, my mates. Ones who were absolutely willing to fuck me and snuggle me.

The one thing I didn't like was the loss of control. I disliked how biological imperatives sometimes overrode my rational thinking.

I liked to be in control. I needed to be in control. Of my body. My life.

At least I was still on heat suppressants. There'd been some fear that with everything I was going through emotionally, I'd have a breakthrough heat–which could happen in times of stress. That hadn't happened, thank goodness, since I had enough to deal with.

Still...

No. I took a deep breath.

Baby steps. That's what my advocate at the Omega Center told me. I'd never learned to be an omega, never gave myself a chance to be one. It would take time to figure everything out. What blockers I could use. Other methods that worked in conjunction. Lifestyle changes that made things easier for me.

Not to mention, every gamma was a little different–and I was still registering as a gamma on the tests.

I'd had an interview with the reporter from SportsBeat yesterday. I was supposed to go into Creative Collective for a photoshoot in a few days.

Last night the Bantams had lost, badly, to a team we would have beaten easily.

What if Knights management didn't cave? Eventually, the team would have to go back. While I appreciated it, I didn't want them to be in breach of contract.

A couple of teams had made me some decent offers. If I didn't accept one of them now, would it mean I didn't have one? That I was either done or had to wait for the lawsuit?

What if–

"Grif. Boo-Boo. Stop, please?" AJ ran his hands over me in a soothing way. "I'm knot-deep in you and your mind is going a million miles an hour. I know all this is a lot but relax. We're here. And I don't mean it as in *alphas make everything better* but more as *I love you, I hear you, what do you need?*"

"I… I don't like not being in control." It came out raw.

"I know. Me, too. It'll take time. We're here. It should hopefully mellow out a little. You're getting years of shit all at once." AJ continued to rub my back.

"I know." I sighed. "What if I'm missing out by not accepting one of those offers and waiting for the Knights?"

AJ pressed his lips to my forehead. "The Knights are going to crack. Soon. The other owners of the PHL are pushing for Cal to step down and Bunty to be fired. Not to mention the union is pissed and the team is getting fined like crazy. Someone might even be arrested if they don't stop that soon."

"I don't know if I'd go that far. They love the Knights. They just had Bertie in their ear. I don't want anyone to lose their jobs. All I want is mine back." I leaned into AJ.

AJ held me, stroking my hair, pumping reassurance through the bond as he purred. This was nice. Dean had been trying to monopolize me since I'd gotten out of the hospital. Verity attempted to counter it by having all five of us sleep together in her bed–which was lovely if the plan was actually sleeping.

There was a rustle from the closet. "Dinner's ready," Verity called.

"Okay, Princess, we'll be out soon," AJ told her. He sighed. "Why she used the closet and not the door, I don't know?"

"She's probably stealing your clothes." There was something about Verity in *only* AJ's button-downs and socks that made me want to do some office role-play.

It was early for us to eat, but Mercy has a home game tonight, so we were going to watch her. Given the Maimers had been huge supporters of me, I should support them back.

We came out and saw a feast on the table of fried chicken, mashed potatoes, corn, creamed spinach, and homemade biscuits with honey butter.

I loved it when it was Verity's turn to cook. I gave her a kiss. "Thank you."

"Bread." Dean stuffed a biscuit in his mouth.

Halfway through dinner, the intercom buzzed.

"Were we expecting any deliveries?" Jonas frowned, dabbing his mouth with a napkin.

I shook my head. "Not that I know of."

"This is Bunty Longfellow. I need to speak to McGraff. Is he here?" a voice said when Jonas answered it.

Jonas looked at me. "I told you."

"I don't want to get my hopes up." Especially because he could only be here to tell me that my ass was traded. Probably to the furthest team imaginable, which would probably be Hawai'i.

Or they were giving me to the Dinosaurs. No. They might not win much, but were really nice and had the sweetest fans. It would be a team of assholes who'd see me as a threat.

Like the fucking Motor City Gears.

"My sources say the PHL was convening an emergency owners meeting today. Louis Daughtry genuinely seemed to want to fix things. It'll be good news," Jonas replied.

Hopefully. But honestly, I'd sort of wanted to see Spencer at least try to buy the team. For funsies.

Jonas buzzed him up. A few moments later, the elevator doors opened to reveal a very frazzled Bunty Longfellow, glitter clinging to his suit, holding a fancy gourmet fruit basket.

"Hi, Mr. Longfellow. We're in the middle of dinner. What do you need?" Jonas stood, placing himself between Mr. Longfellow and me.

His shoulders rounded. "McGraff, I'm sorry for the misunderstanding. Your contract's been reinstated. I apologize for any anguish and hardship that was caused. I'm glad you're feeling better and want to remain a Knight."

"Yeah, not a misunderstanding," Dean muttered, glaring at the GM.

"Thank you. I accept your apology and I'll happily return to the Knights. I like being a Knight, Mr. Longfellow." Standing, I walked over to Jonas.

Hope shot through me, and I got happiness from both Dean and AJ in the bonds.

"Very good. Please see Dr. Mosser so we can determine your re-start date. Just to make sure you're not coming back too early. Your health is important. Though I hope you'll come to the gala in a couple of days." Mr. Longfellow looked sincere.

"I'll call him tomorrow. I should be fit to play soon," I replied. "We'll be there."

Even with the walkout, the team planned on attending the Squire Foundation gala. The youth programs shouldn't suffer for management's idiocy.

Mr. Longfellow held out the fruit basket. "Oh, this is for you."

"Thank you." I took the basket from him. It had all sorts of fruit in it, including a pineapple–which would make Mercy happy.

Verity's face buried in Dean's shoulder, trying to not laugh.

Mr. Longfellow looked at Jonas and Dean. "Now that Grif is reinstated, I trust that this walkout is over and we'll see everyone tomorrow?"

"As long as our agent gives us the go-ahead." Jonas nodded.

"Excellent. Again, I apologize for the misunderstanding and a statement has already been made. I hope you'll make one as well." His look was a cross between hopeful and expectant.

"We'll speak with our lawyer, publicist, union rep, and agent. Thank you," Jonas said.

"See you tomorrow. Let's win that game." Mr. Longfellow left.

I started laughing as I put the basket on the counter. "He brought me a fruit basket. Well, I guess I'm a Knight again."

Fucking shit. I'd been reinstated. I danced in excitement.

"As you should be. This whole thing was stupid." Jonas gave me a huge hug.

"I knew it would work out." Dean kissed me.

"Me, too." AJ wrapped his arms around me. "Chet's in jail. Bertie no longer owns a share of the Knights. You're now a Knight again. Life is good, Boo-Boo."

Verity came over to me and kissed me.

I looked at all of them. "Life *is* good. I'm grateful to have all of you standing with me. I couldn't ask for anything more."

Chapter Forty

Verity

I entered the training center which bustled with skating lessons and youth hockey practice.

Taking the elevator, I went up to the second floor. The Maimers had already finished practice. Mercy and Kaiko were doing schoolwork together in the breakroom since I'd had class.

An older man in a suit came down the hallway.

"I don't know you." Mr. Longfellow frowned at me.

"Oh, it doesn't surprise me, Mr. Longfellow. I'm just *that model.*" I gave him my sweetest smile. I'd seen him around but hadn't interacted with him.

He blinked, obviously not getting it. Poor guy. It was probably time for him to retire. Despite the requests for him and Cal Daughtry to step down, that hadn't happened.

At least Grif was reinstated – and Chet was in jail.

"Oh. Are you new? What do you do here?" He eyed my backpack and my outfit, which was seafoam green pants and a matching polka dot blouse. They flickered to my credentials. "Chaperone?"

"I'm the chaperone for the Maimers' underage rookie," I told him.

"Oh. Right. They did that. I don't know what those kids were thinking. This is why you don't give children a sports team. Next thing you know, they'll be hiring omega skate smashers." He shook his head in disbelief.

I hoped they did. Rusty had an eye on one she'd seen in Hawai'i.

Also, *kids*? The Daughtry 'kids' that owned the Maimers were all older than me. They weren't given it, either. They pooled their money and brought a franchise to New York. They were around more than the hockey Daughtrys and I'd met them all a few times.

Mr. Longfellow's phone rang. He looked at it, sighed, and turned down the hall as he answered it without another glance at me.

Well then.

"I'm here to pick up the package," I told Rusty as I entered their dining room.

Rusty laughed as she played air hockey with Liv. "Are you sure about that?"

Mercy gave us the side-eye as she closed her laptop. "You two will never get bored with all that, will you?"

"Never." I grinned. "How's the schoolwork going?"

"Essays are stupid and math can die. I don't need this to skate fast." Kaiko dramatically slumped over her own sticker-covered laptop.

"Stay in school, kids," Liv joked as she hit the plastic puck across the table. Rusty leaned over the table and hit back.

"Thanks again for your support," I told them.

"Anytime. No one messes with one of ours. It's nice that Grif is back, though no one would have blamed him if he went elsewhere," Rusty told me as she smacked the plastic puck into Liv's goal.

"I'm glad he's back, too," I told her. Things were hard enough for him right now as they were.

Mercy got her stuff, and we left the training center. None of the hockey players were around because there was a home game tonight. Grif wasn't cleared to play yet, though Jonas, Dean, and all the Knights would be there and the Bantams could resume their regular schedule.

Grif, AJ, Mercy, and I would catch the game in the family section.

But first manicures.

As we took the metro, Mercy told me all about her day and the new dance battle choreography she was learning.

"This place is adorable. I can see why you like it," Mercy told me as we walked inside Margarita Mani's. "We'll have to get some pictures."

We were escorted into the main room. It was cute and pastel. We weren't the only ones here for late afternoon pampering. I'd limit myself to *one* drink this time.

"Are you all caught up with your research?" Mercy asked as her feet soaked in pink bubbly water.

"Sadly, no." I tried to keep the disappointment out of my voice. I shouldn't be mad at myself for not recreating years of research in a few days.

But I was.

"Boo. How can I help?" She took a sip of her mocktail, which had gummy snakes in it.

"So, I might need to go to Greece during spring break." I took a drink of mine, which had a cloud of cotton candy on it. I'd made a very remarkable breakthrough with my other research.

The alpha subduing properties of omega lilies were much easier to access on specific Grecian strains. I should've seen it earlier. Myths often had roots in reality. Fortunately, I was now officially funded by Compass BioTek, so I could afford such a trip.

"Go for it. Though, I'm jelly. Season won't be over yet." She fake pouted. "I want to go to Greece with you."

"We'll do a fun sister trip over the off-season. Are you doing okay with our living situation? I ask mostly because student housing emailed me asking if we wanted to be moved because repairs are going to take a long time." I took a picture of me with my drink and sent it to Dean.

"They're decent guys. Jonas and AJ make time for me, which is nice. Having my own space upstairs helps. If we end up staying there, I think I'll be okay." There was hesitation in her voice.

"I sense a *but.* We can move out," I assured her. As much as I enjoyed living with the guys, her comfort was important.

"Can we get an air filter for the living room? I got a little one for upstairs and it's helping. Sometimes you all are a lot. There's also no door in the hall like back home to help block off your bedrooms from the living areas." Her expression went pained.

Two women came in and started working on our feet. We weren't getting a pedicure as fancy as what I'd gotten with Dean, but we were getting manicures, too, so we'd be ready for the Squire Foundation Gala tomorrow.

It took me a moment. "Oh." Embarrassment coated me. "I didn't even consider that. That's a good idea."

"Scents are becoming a lot," she admitted. "Not only there, but everywhere. Hale says it's normal. How am I supposed to function?"

"It's a lot. Do you need a class or a tutor?" I asked, understanding what was happening. It was usually a sign of an alpha getting close to awakening.

I never had a young alpha stage to start getting used to the strength, senses, and feelings. One day my body went, *whoops, we should be an alpha by now* and jumped right into it with no warning. It was part of why I was overwhelmed by my alpha. Especially since the parents didn't want me to take alpha classes–even the ones everyone had to take in high school.

Mercy thought for a moment. "I don't know."

"We can stop at the drugstore after this," I added. "There's this cream you can put in your nostrils to make scents less. I never use it because it gives me nose zits, but it might work for you."

"Gross." Mercy made a face. "But yeah, I'll try it. Everything's getting to be a lot. Today I broke the punching bag."

"I've done that a few times." I tried not to laugh as the pedicurist rubbed my feet because it tickled.

"Um, I apologize in advance if I'm accidentally mean. The mood swings are a bitch. I made Gwenifer cry. I didn't mean to. Kaiko said my privilege was showing and that I have no idea how the world works." She looked away.

Salty sadness wafted off Mercy, her look full of regret.

"Did you say you're sorry?" I asked.

Mercy sighed. "I apologized. But I still feel bad."

"There's a big world out there. As much as the parents bitched about money, we've led a pretty privileged life compared to a lot of people. I made a lot of mistakes when I was at university, especially when I tried to be funny," I admitted as the pedicurist set my feet on the footrest and dried them off.

I continued, "Please ask me whatever you want. There's so much I never knew about being an alpha. Like no one told me when a lady alpha lives with a male omega, her period gets worse because her uterus chooses violence given she's living with a walking baby maker and hasn't gotten knocked up yet."

"Oh, my fuck." Mercy laughed. "I was wondering what was up because you ate more chocolate than usual."

"Do you have any other concerns about the guys?" I asked tentatively. "If you're okay with living there, I'd like to not wait until the off-season to bite Grif."

While I'd already been seriously considering it, Grif being in the hospital had pushed me over the edge.

Mercy gave me a look. "Bite one, bite them all. I don't actually care. They make you happy and I know you won't let them be mean to me. If I get tired of you kissing all the time, I'll move out when I turn eighteen."

"You're okay with it. Good. I won't have the wedding until summer. I like Grace's idea of having it on an island in Greece in a field of flowers and certainly with my schedule it would be nice to have planning help." Relief coated me.

"When you go during spring break to Greece, you can do wedding recon. Look at places, taste food. Maybe Grace will go with you," she told me. Her nail tech painted her toes dark green.

"Good idea. Look at these pin boards she keeps sending me. It's like she knows me or something." I sent them to Mercy.

Mercy scrolled through them. "This is amazing. So, did you propose? Do alphas propose? I remember when Dad proposed to Harry."

"Baba proposed to Mama. Though she's beta, so they had to get married for their relationship to be legal–like Dad and Harry. I think it's mostly, *hey, we registered our mating, do you want a party?*

Oh, you want a wedding too? Okay, darling, anything for you." I adopted a thick, indulgent accent.

Mercy laughed. "I love that accent. Propose with that."

"I'm going to use my grandfather's ring," I admitted as my toes were painted a sparkly blush. A lot of people had been angry when he'd left it to me with the instructions to give it to the omega of my dreams.

"Aww. Not sure that's going to fit on Grif's giant hand. He could always wear it like a necklace," she replied. "Go for it. Are you going to propose tonight? You could do something silly at the game?"

Oh. I hadn't considered that. Though he wasn't playing.

"I… I ordered the cake we had on our first date for us to have tonight and I'll put the ring on it. I'd make it, but it's one of those labor-intensive cakes." I wasn't having a *let's bake a five-hour cake* sort of day, anyway.

"Love it. After the drug store, we should get him a big ass bouquet like he did for you on your first date." She wiggled her toes, which were now painted with little separators in them.

I grinned as I recalled how chaotic it was. "That sounds perfect."

"Who wants some cake?" I asked as the six of us piled out of the elevator and into the living room. The Knights had won their game, and we'd gone to Tito's as usual.

"Cake? Please tell me that's a euphemism?" Dean grabbed me and kissed me. He hadn't gotten a shutout, but it was a good game and would go far in getting the Knights back on track.

"No. It's an actual cake." I put my shoes on the rack and leaned my crutch by the coat closet. Flipping on the kitchen light, I got the bouquet and cake out of the fridge. Shaking, I took the bouquet over to Grif.

Mercy shrugged off her coat and tried to hang it up on air, then caught it. She turned to Jonas. "We need a coat rack by the door."

"We have a coat closet," Jonas told her, again, as he gathered up everyone's coats.

"Kitten, these are beautiful. What's the occasion?" Grif sniffed the flowers. "I do love eucalyptus."

We'd both worn Dean's jersey tonight–AJ had worn Jonas'. Mercy had gone out with her friends and joined us at Tito's.

Dean eyed the flowers. "Those look a lot like the ones I picked out for your first date with Verity."

"Do they?" With a coy look, I returned to the kitchen and opened the bakery box, positioning the ring in one of the frosting rosettes. Taking the cake, I carefully set it on the dining room table. "Who wants cake?"

"Cake. Did I miss your birth–" Grif sucked in a breath as he took in the writing on the pink marzipan fairy cake decorated with little rosettes–and the ring. *Grif, will you marry me?*

"This is the kind of cake we had on our first date. I didn't make it but–" Before I could finish, Grif's mouth pressed to mine. His beard tickled my face as his arms wrapped around me so hard my feet lifted off the floor.

His hungry mouth possessed mine, tongue exploring as his hardness pressed through his jeans into me. Grif's breezy scent, which now had omega-y tones, surrounded me as I got a hit of his arousal. Finally, Grif set me down on the ground as he removed his lips from mine, leaving me breathless.

"Is that a *yes*?" My heart hitched in my chest. I put myself out there, taking what I wanted. What if I wasn't what *he* wanted?

"A thousand times, yes." Grif pulled me to him and kissed me again.

"Wow, you're pornographic," Mercy snorted. "This is why we need giant air purifiers."

"Noted, Squirt," Jonas told her, tugging on one of her braids.

"And a coat rack by the elevator." She grinned.

"Can we cut the cake? There's a *ring* on the cake?" Dean asked. "Is this fairy cake? Fuck me. This shit is tasty."

"I know the ring is way too small. It's more for significance than anything. It belonged to my omega grandfather on Baba's side. He told me to give it to the omega who stole my heart. You stole it on the airplane. Well, Lucky did." I gazed into Grif's eyes, remembering how he'd made my shitty day so much better.

"Damn Lucky." He kissed my temple. "Your grandfather's ring? That means everything."

AJ looked at Jonas. "I told you she wasn't going to do anything at a game."

"And I told you it would be tonight or tomorrow," Jonas laughed as he got plates.

"What?" I gave them an incredulous look. Because I didn't know I wanted to do it today until I ordered the cake this morning.

"Princess, we know when you're plotting." AJ smirked.

I took the ring off the cake and tried to slide it on Grif's finger. It fit the tip of his pinky and we laughed.

"Little Alpha, I'm ecstatic that you're marrying my husband." Dean kissed me, pulling Grif to me so I was between the two of them. He held me there as he kissed Grif. "Happy for you, Gumdrop."

"I'm happy for both of you." Jonas gave me a big hug. "Welcome to the family, Sweetheart. You, too, Squirt."

Mercy rolled her eyes as she stood against the counter. "You know, for a bunch of smelly dudes, you're okay."

"You're staying? Good." AJ stole me from Jonas, his vetiver scent swirling around me as he pressed me to him.

Mercy cut the cake, and we all had some.

"Hey, if we tell my moms that Grif and Verity are getting married and having a fancy wedding, do you think I can get them to cancel the dinner for Grif and me?" AJ asked. "They're inviting *everyone,* which was not the deal."

Jonas laughed. "You can try. Though she's going to want everyone at that wedding."

"But then it won't be my problem and I can hide." AJ shot me a grin.

I could imagine him ducking into a hedge maze or a closet trying to avoid his parents.

"Dibs on being flour boy so I can hand out bread. This is fantastic cake," Dean told me, stuffing a giant bite in his mouth.

"Delicious." Grif's eyes stayed on me as his tongue darted out and licked his lips suggestively.

My core grew molten as I took a bite and moaned. "Mmmm."

"That's my cue. Smell you later. Literally. Happy for you two." Mercy put another slice of cake on her plate, grabbed two sodas from the fridge, and went upstairs.

We finished our cake and did the dishes.

"Now, if you excuse me." Grif threw me over his shoulder.

"Um, I think I'm the person who's supposed to do that," I play-objected as he gave Dean and AJ kisses.

"I'd like to see you carry him down the hall, Princess." AJ smacked me on the ass.

Grif took me into my room and shut the door, turning on the small recessed lights that made the room glow. The room smelled a bit like all of us because we'd all been sleeping in it together a lot. Well, we'd start off sleeping here and throughout the night people would pair off and go to other rooms. Or I'd get carried off.

Still, it was nice for us all to be together after everything with Grif.

My big, yummy guy pushed me up against the door and kissed me. Oooh, I could use some of that.

As his fiery kisses overrode my senses, he undressed me, my jersey and pants dropping to the floor. He kicked off his shoes and slid off his pants and boxers, leaving him only in Dean's jersey.

"My alpha proposed to me, so I'm going to fuck her so good." His eyes, smoldering with desire, burned into me with the heat of the sun.

"Mmmm, Tiger, give it to me." I kissed him back. A hint of sweet omega perfume curled around me with his rain, making me gush. My throbbing alpha pussy was ready for anything he wanted to give me.

His body pinned mine to the door, and his large hand encircled my neck. Grif took his hard cock glistening with pre-cum and a hint of slick into his hand and guided it into me, eyes on me.

Pressing his mouth to mine, swallowing my moans, one hand still around my throat, he fucked me hard and fast into the door. Every thrust said *mine* while every hungry kiss said *I'm yours.* My ass bumped against the door as bliss filled me.

"Lock me," he whispered in my ear. He continued to kiss me, but those kisses trailed down my throat as he sucked on the chords on my neck.

Pleasure burst over me as I came, locking him tight inside me. *Mine.*

"Kitten," he groaned, as he came, flooding me with his cum. "You were perfect, Alpha." Grif kissed me, caressing my face, and he cuddled me against his chest, us still standing.

Alpha. That made me a bit tingly.

I put my head on his shoulder, clutching him like a rosebush on a trellis. His rain scent was strong and sweet with arousal. The pheromones he put out made my head fuzzy.

Finally, my pussy unlocked him. He scooped me up and brought me to the bed, his cum trickling down my thigh.

"How's your leg feeling?" Grif peppered my face with kisses, hands stroking me.

"It's feeling good. Does someone need to be ridden?" I rolled us so his back was on the bed, and I was on top.

His eyes gleamed in the low light. "Mmmm, please ride me."

"My pleasure, Tiger." My hand wrapped around his cock, stroking its hard and weeping length. Keeping my eyes on his, I slowly lowered myself onto him. "I'm going to take this dick and make it mine."

"I'm yours, Kitten. My cock. My lips. My heart. Every last inch of me belongs to you." He intertwined his fingers in mine as I moved up and down, savoring the way his cock felt as my pussy fluttered around it.

"Dean might have something to say about that," I teased, as I leaned in to steal a kiss, gyrating my hips. "So would AJ."

"Okay, I belong to you, Dean, and AJ. But there's enough of me to go around. And tonight? Tonight I'm all yours." He grinned and leaned in to steal another kiss.

"I can deal with that. Mmmm. Come whenever you're ready, Tiger." I pinned his hands over his head and touched my forehead to his as I continued to ride him. Canting my hips so I got him at the right angle, my clit rubbed against him.

"Oh, yes. You already know you can bite me at any time. Dig your teeth into any place on my body and make me yours forever," he breathed, stealing a kiss.

Need and lust came off him as I brought the two of us closer to our peaks.

I rocked against him, our bodies becoming extensions of each other. Tonight? Why not? Life was fleeting, and I was certain about him. Jonas could take Mercy to the rink in the morning. I didn't have class until later. Grif still had a couple more days of medical leave, then some home games...

"Don't overthink, just do it. Take me now and we'll have our big wedding in the off-season," he added. It was part dare, part keen.

"You want all of me, Tiger?" A little growl rumbled through my chest as I leaned forward, kissing him.

"I do." His fingers let go of mine as his hands went to my hips, helping to move me up and down.

His words made my teeth ache, as my inner alpha yearned to do exactly that. Mark up that pretty throat so everyone knew he had *two* alphas that he meant everything to.

One of my hands tangled in his hair. My kisses trailed down his neck and I sucked hard on the juncture of his neck and shoulder, right over AJ's mark. He gasped, hips bucking against me as I nipped and sucked at it, getting both of us closer to our peak.

"Please, Kitten, Alpha," he moaned, as one hand left my hip and rubbed my clit.

My back arched as pleasure took me, shooting through my body. I spasmed around his cock, locking him hard. He gasped, our eyes meeting as he came inside me.

"Mine," I growled as I moved over to the unmarked side of his throat. I kissed and sucked it hard as my body shuddered and fluttered around him.

"Yes, yes," he groaned, arms tightening around me.

This man is mine. The ache became almost unbearable, and I clamped down on the tender skin hard.

It was more than a love bite. This was a full-on claiming mark as my teeth sunk into him, the metallic tang of blood filling my mouth.

"I love you, Grif." I licked his blood off my lips, then tended to his wound, lapping at it tenderly.

Warmth sizzled through my body, lighting up every vein, every nerve, every synapses, filling it with awareness. Love.

This sensation settled in my chest, like a weight, as something hooked it to another warm awareness, linking us.

I inhaled sharply as I felt *him.* "Grif."

Just like that, I was his.

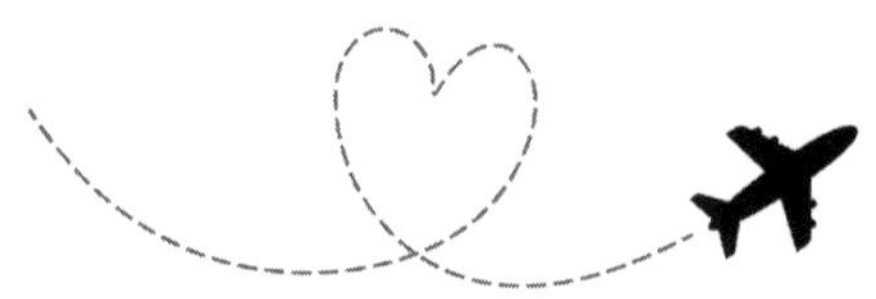

Chapter Forty-One

Grif

She'd bonded with me.

After everything we'd been through, including me hiding my designation from her, she still loved me enough to bond me.

How did I get to be so lucky?

My heart pulsed with happiness as Verity joined the bond, nestling right there with Dean and AJ. I got a hint of smugness from Dean through our bond.

"Mine," I told her. Even though we were still locked together, I flipped us so that my body pinned her to the bed. Kissing her lips, my mouth trailed down her throat and collarbone.

Lazily, I lavished attention on one of her breasts. Toying with her nipples with my tongue, I nipped and sucked, enjoying the sweet mews of my sweet kitten until she unlocked me.

My alpha.

She gasped as I bit down gently with my teeth and her eyes widened in anticipation. I gave it a kiss, then turned to the other breast so as not to neglect it.

No. Not there. Dean probably would. He adored her breasts.

I kissed her abs and licked her belly button. Pushing her legs open, I feasted on her sweet pussy. Taking my tongue, I wrote *I love you so much* on her clit, relishing every wiggle, every moan. Her eyes grew half-lidded as her back arched.

"You like that, don't you?" I said into her pussy as I rolled her bud between my fingers.

"So much." Her chest shuddered.

"Come all over my face, Kitten." I inserted a couple of fingers inside her quivering folds, as I went back to playing her pussy like a piano. Her alpha desire and need grew overwhelming. Part of me was having trouble being patient.

The other part of me loved making her a wanting mess over and over.

Soon.

I kept kissing her, though I moved my kisses to her inner thigh. Tracing her tiny tattoo with my lips, I memorized it because I loved that tiny flower.

Her muscles spasmed around my fingers.

My lips brushed her inner thigh, looking for the perfect place to bite, right by her little tattoo. There. I clamped down at a nice meaty juncture, sinking my teeth into her flesh deep enough to draw blood. Our bond tingled as that second part lit up between us.

"Grif." Her back arched as I got an onslaught of pleasure from her.

Oh, yes. That was it.

I gently licked the wound.

She laughed. "Your beard tickles."

"Does it? What about this?" I buried my face in her pussy, more to tickle her with my beard than anything else.

"Grif," she squealed.

I laughed, then got in bed next to her, pulling the covers over us and resting my head on her breasts.

She stroked my hair and a purr rumbled in her chest, audible, but soft, as we cuddled.

Finally, she kissed my forehead. "I need to use the bathroom. How about if we take a bath?"

"I'd like that. Is there any more wine in the fridge?" That sounded nice. A candlelit bubble bath. Some wine.

More fucking.

"Pretty sure there is. I got some new candles, too." She disappeared into the bathroom.

The too-small ring was still on my finger, miraculously. I set it on the nightstand so it didn't get lost. Maybe Dean had a chain so I could wear it around my neck.

Getting out of bed, I opened her closet so I could look in the mirror. There, opposite AJ's and almost perfectly symmetrical, was her bite.

"Hi." Verity slipped into the closet and wrapped her arms around me, and we looked at ourselves naked in the mirror.

Her unbound hair was a mess. Mine wasn't neat either. But we looked happy.

I was happy.

She leaned in and gave me a kiss. "I love you."

"I love you, too, Kitten." I leaned into her.

Wow. I had bonded with all three of my loves–and they'd bonded me back. Everything was now right with the world.

Chapter Forty-Two

Dean

Looking in the bathroom mirror, I ran my hand through my damp hair, which had gotten a little long. I straightened my silver tie.

"Hey, Jellybean, can you tie my tie?" Grif came in, holding a cream-colored tie, which matched his bead-covered, filmy, cream vest.

All these years and the man still couldn't tie his own tie. If I wasn't around, AJ would pre-knot ties for him—or Grif used clip-ons.

"Come here." I pulled my husband close, inhaling his rainy scent, which was now tinged with bits of all three of his mates.

His beard was nice and trimmed. A fresh bite mark peaked out from the collar of his white tux shirt.

She'd bonded with him. I felt it last night.

Oh, fuck me, I'd felt it–along with them fucking all night long.

This morning, when Jonas had dragged me to practice, they'd stayed home and fucked until Verity had class.

"Will you be okay with a tie? If you want to go tieless and open a few buttons, no one's going to say anything. You might be more comfortable that way. This is a nice vest. Is it new?" I unbuttoned his shirt a little to let his neck breathe.

"AJ got it made so I'd match Verity? Is that even a thing? Most everyone's wearing black and silver." He eyed my tie.

I fixed the buttons on his vest. It was so pretty with all the tiny little beads. "My dad always matches my mom for these sorts of things."

"Okay." He looked at himself in the mirror and loosened another shirt button. "Maybe that? It... it chafes a little."

It would.

Grif held up his hand, the ring from Verity on the tip of his finger. "Do you have a chain I can use? I want to wear it, but I don't have anything."

"Of course I do." I pulled him into my room, and opened my top dresser drawer, then pulled out the cigar box I kept my jewelry in. Grif had carefully covered it with pictures of all my favorite things and given it to me for my birthday back when we were kids.

Sorting through everything, I found one. Taking the ring off his pinky, I slid it on the chain. Leaning in, I put it on him, kissing his neck. "Does that bother you?"

"No." His hand covered mine and squeezed it, love coming through the bond. "Thank you."

I kissed his cheek, his beard soft on my face. "That's what husbands are for."

"It's sweet she gave it to me." He held the ring in his giant hand.

"It is. Hey, um, can I walk you down the aisle when you two have your fancy wedding? Unless you're going to have one of your parents do it?" My head ducked a little. If he did, I didn't want to take it away from him. My dad had walked me down the aisle to Grif.

But if he was going to walk solo or ask AJ, for some silly reason, I wanted to be the one to do it instead.

His face lit up. "I... I love that idea."

I couldn't wait to escort him down the aisle to some classical song while Verity waited for him under a flower arch, looking radiant in some stunning gown.

Grif leaned over and kissed me. He tasted of toothpaste. Wrapping my arms around him, I kissed him back.

"You know, she bonded me. It's your turn." Grif's eyes glimmered.

I sucked in a breath. "You think? Sign me up. I'm fine with you being there. I can be the filling in a love sandwich while she bites me."

Oh, I could see that now. Mmmm.

"I'd love that. Maybe you can be in the swing this time." He nibbled on my neck.

"That sounds delightful." I wrapped my arms around Grif again, though this time I hit something hard in his jacket. "Is your pocket happy to see me?"

"It's her necklace. Is it dumb? According to AJ, I didn't understand the assignment when he told me to get her one to wear tonight." He took out a distinctive blue box as anxiousness wafted off him.

Could you actually go wrong with anything from that store, though?

Inside was a large heart-shaped diamond, surrounded by more tiny diamonds, on a gold cable chain–with matching, smaller earrings. They sparkled in the light, winking at me.

"What are you talking about? It's *beautiful.* Not to mention the symbolism." Aww, he wasn't just giving her his heart, but trusting her with mine and AJ's. Adorable. AJ didn't know what he was talking about.

He brightened. "You think so? I thought it was pretty. With all the fuss about the dress, I didn't want anything that would overwhelm it."

"Good call. You know what would go perfect with it?" I dug around until I found a small velvet box in my drawer.

I held it out to him. "Do you remember this? We could give it to her now."

It had belonged to my Great Granny Donovan. Verity seemed like a ring girly.

"Oh. I forgot about this." He opened it and looked at the gold Claddagh ring with a giant heart emerald in it.

"It might even fit her without being sized," I added.

"It's perfect. Great idea." He gave me a kiss. "Hey, if I say I'm not feeling good and get Verity to take me home, don't worry. I'm fine. I knew I'd feel her once we bonded. But I didn't know I could feel her not feeling good." Grif rubbed his chest.

Ah, it was a ruse to get her home.

"Understood. Did you fuck her too hard and now her leg hurts?" I smirked. Who knew what they got up to without me?

"I think most of her hurts today, and she's pretending she's fine. I don't know if we went too hard or if it's just one of those days. We might need a nice hot bubble bath all together," he told me.

"That sounds good to me." Then I'd make her feel better. I still had a couple of muscle-relaxing bath bombs. Maybe Jonas would rub her legs with his warm oil after.

"Are you two ready?" Jonas lounged in the doorway in an all-black collarless tux that made him look like liquid sex.

Mmmm. If the event was boring, maybe we could find a corner.

"Ready for *you*." I attacked him with a big kiss, ramming him into the doorway.

"Come on, Love." Jonas chuckled and put an arm around me.

I reached for Grif's hand, and the three of us went out into the living room.

AJ was there in a tux that almost matched Grif's. His vest and tie were black, though. As usual, sunglasses sat on top of his head.

"Hi." Verity appeared. Her hair was all the way up, with a few little tendrils escaping. She sparkled as if sprinkled with fairy dust. Her glossy lips made me want to kiss her.

The champagne-colored dress was even more breathtaking than in the bathtub pictures. Especially with the thousands of teeny tiny beads that had been sewn to the filmy overskirt. She looked like a dream.

Grif sucked in a breath. "Kitten. You look radiant. I have a present for you."

"You do?" Verity took the box with the necklace and earrings. Opening it she looked up and *glowed*. "Grif, this is the most beautiful thing I've ever owned."

"Here, let me." Grif put the necklace on her, then the earrings, his lips grazing her neck.

"Sweet baby cheeses, you guys." Mercy came down the stairs in a flowy red dress with a sparkly bodice that made her look like a grown-ass person instead of a gangly alpha teenager. Well, except for her hair still being in Dutch braids, though the scrunchies were red and sparkly.

Grif grinned at Mercy and then dipped Verity deep, kissing her like they were in a spy movie.

"My turn." I gave my little alpha a kiss, Her lipstick tasted like roses. "You look amazing, Darling. Grif and I have something for you."

Verity smiled. Her eye makeup made her look like an ethereal creature. With it she wore this long beaded sheer scarf that looked a bit like wings as it trailed down her back.

Her eyebrows waggled suggestively. "Do you?"

Oh, I had that, too. My cock hardened thinking about whether or not she had panties on under that dress. If she did, it had to be a thong. I loved it when she wore a thong.

Leaning in, my lips brushed her ear. "Later."

In the bath. In the swing. On the bed. It didn't matter.

I gave her the box. "This was my Great Granny Donovan's and we want you to have it."

"Dean." She took the ring out of the box, her hand on her heart. "It's so beautiful. Thank you."

I turned it so the heart faced inward. "You're taken, so it goes like this."

Slipping it on her finger, I kissed her again. Her driftwood scent took on a hint of lust.

I was hers tonight. Even if she didn't bond with me.

"We belong to you." Grif kissed her again.

"That is stunning." AJ came over to admire it. "Princess, you look amazing. I can't believe Vecci hasn't asked you to be in one of their shows."

"I did wear it in a bathtub. However, Dubois asked me to be part of their *bridal showcase* at the Paris Fashion Festival," she breathed. "I got the call from my agent while I was at the lab. They saw the pictures Mercy posted of me on the motorcycles and loved the energy."

"That's amazing." AJ kissed her. "Dubois. Wow. Fuck Vecci."

Even I knew that no one topped the House of Dubois. My mom loved their dresses, and still had the pink Dubois she wore for her graduation from her omega academy.

"The photos were fire. We're going to Paris this summer? Amazing. I want to sit in the front row of the fashion show with Riley while wearing something ridiculous. Maybe a model will fall in my lap." Mercy flashed a grin.

Verity on a runway in a wedding dress? I was so there.

"Are we ready? Dibs on riding with Verity in the pink doll mobile." Mercy linked arms with her sister. "You know there's a doll with your car, well, the convertible version. It's remote control. We should buy it and race it around the training facility."

"You could chase Lucky with it? Or give Lucky rides?" I offered.

"I like the way you think," Mercy replied.

Jonas checked his phone. "We're going all together. I traded in the SUV for a larger one, so all six of us fit comfortably."

"Aww. Thanks, Bub." Mercy slugged him.

Jonas picked her up and held her upside down. "Escape."

In a couple of moves, Mercy was back down on the ground in a pouf of dress.

"Told you." Mercy stuck out her tongue.

Well, that was amusing. Grif snorted and Verity giggled.

Verity grabbed her crutch. We took the elevator down to the parking garage and got in the car. Jonas drove. Mercy sat up front with him. Verity and I sat in the middle, Grif, and AJ in the back. The new SUV was luxurious and spacious enough.

"Quick housekeeping," Jonas said as we drove. "Verity, did you register your bond with Grif yet?"

"Yes, AJ helped me take care of it," she replied, leaning into me.

"I got ours registered, too, since Grif's out now," AJ added.

"Perfect. Have you told those who might want to know personally? I don't want to be stabbed with a fork if word gets out at the gala and it hits the sports news." Jonas chuckled as he navigated the traffic to the fancy hotel it was being held at.

"I have," Verity assured.

"What parents did you tell?" Mercy asked as she took a selfie. "Any?"

"Dad and Mama. They seem happy?" Verity chewed on her lower lip.

I squeezed her. Anyone that wasn't happy about it was someone we didn't need in our lives.

Mercy nodded. "Those two would be."

"Since you're registered, we'll start the process of adding you to the pack. Mercy, I know you're technically emancipated, but according to our lawyer, it would be better to add you to the pack charter as our dependent. It protects you legally, so if something happens to you, we can have a say and it doesn't default to a parent you don't like or something. Are you okay with that?" Jonas asked.

"Makes sense. Especially since our parents' pack doesn't exist anymore. Thanks, Bub. You're so fucking considerate." Mercy grinned.

"Anytime, Squirt." His look grew fond.

We drove up to the hotel. Reporters lined the red carpet. I sent reassurance to Grif through our bond. This was Grif's first public appearance since he collapsed at the game on my birthday. He was all set to go back to practice tomorrow. Also, he didn't like things like this anyway.

"Great, my parents are coming to the gala." AJ put his phone in his pocket and pinched the bridge of his nose.

"Did you think they wouldn't? My parents would be here if they didn't have a conflicting gala my mom was on the planning committee for," I replied. She'd texted asking for pictures.

"Introduce them to Verity and it'll be fine. Come on, let's show some pack solidarity," Jonas told everyone as the valet scanned his phone.

"Yeppers." Mercy popped her gum and got out of the car.

Jonas came around to my side to help me out and took my arm. AJ helped Verity out and Grif handed her her crutch.

Grif walked between Verity and AJ. Both of them tried to shield Grif with their bodies. Mercy took up the rear, waving at people and throwing beaded bracelets.

This was my pack. I had my alpha. My husband.

Hopefully tonight, if she felt up to it, I'd have myself a little alpha as well.

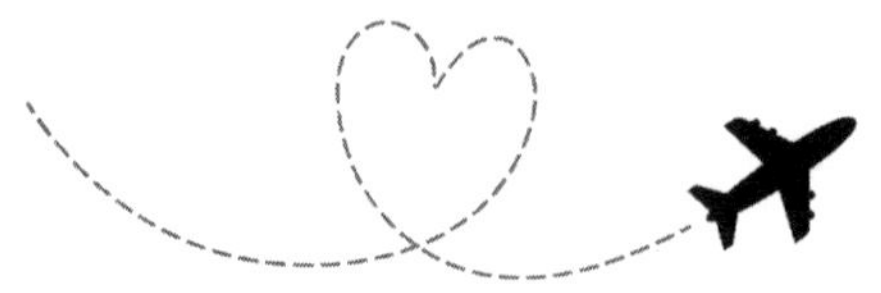

Chapter Forty-Three

Verity

"Freddie's here. Why? Why would he even be here?" I turned to Grif, a champagne flute in hand as the star forward of Southern United sauntered past. Derva hung on his arm in a dress that was a fashion malfunction waiting to happen.

"Image rehab maybe with Chet now in jail? I think he's trying to get himself traded," Grif replied, letting me hide behind his enormous frame.

Black and silver balloons and banners with pictures of kids participating in the Squire Foundation's youth hockey programs adorned the ballroom's atrium. There was an open bar, passed hors d'oeuvres and a table full of things to bid on. Later there'd be dinner, speeches, cute kids, and dancing.

While all the Knights were here, there were some Maimers, and a lot of New York's elite. Mercy and Kaiko hunched over the silent auction table. Some auction items were things like signed Knights memorabilia and experiences, such as a goalie lesson with Dean or the chance to be the mascot for a game. There was also everything from baskets of designer purses to strange handmade things to vacations.

Who knew what they were up to?

Hopefully dinner would be soon because my whole body hurt, and my head pounded.

Maybe I should take another look at the purses up for auction? While the purse hospital had saved some of them, one of my favorites was beyond hope.

Sure, the guys had been amazing at replacing things for us. But they shouldn't have to feed my love of high-end purses.

"Grif, you're here. This is my Ma. Ma, this is Grif and Team Mom." Clark bounded over to us, wearing a Defender League tie. There was an older woman with him. He had a black eye from the fight he'd gotten into in their last game.

Aww, the rookie brought his mom. "Hi, it's so nice to meet you. I'm Verity."

"Hey, Clark. Clark's mom." Grif waved, keeping me close. "I'm here and I can't wait to get back on the ice."

"We miss you. There are so many fancy dresses. Even my senior dance at high school wasn't like this." Clark took a sip of his beer, eyes riveting in another direction. "Oooh. Ladybug looks like Aquatica."

Clark's eyes focused on Gwen, who wore a sparkling blue puffy dress that looked like something you'd wear for your excellent eighteenth party. Her normally pink hair was light blue and down in soft waves, making her look like the underwater superhero in the Defender League movies.

On Gwen's arm was a muscular guy about her age, wearing a light blue suit, his hair dark blue. That must be her boyfriend.

"Right? Gwenifer looks amazing," Mercy agreed, appearing at my elbow. "Auction mission accomplished. I'm going to go bug her." She set off.

"Oh, there's Dimitri." Clark took off, mom in tow, after Dimitri, who looked like a Russian mob boss.

Dimitri's teen sister accompanied him. Her long dark hair, pale skin, black, and silver dress, and red lips made her look like she'd stepped out of a fairytale.

Kylee appeared in a striking black dress and red lipstick I needed in my life. "Verity, sweets, can I steal your honey? I will give him back, promise."

"Only if you tell me what lipstick you're wearing. Grif, go schmooze with some donors. I'll go find AJ," I assured. This seemed a lot like the university and science fundraisers I'd gone to all my life where the parents had to make nice with important people so they'd have jobs and funding.

I spied AJ cornered by two women, one small and delicate, in a black and silver dress, neck bejeweled with diamonds. She had golden skin and long, black hair. The other was much taller, her dark brown hair short, and she wore a sleek pants suit, but just as much jewelry, including a wrist full of bangles.

AJ caught my eye and shook his head, looking frantic. Was he warning me away or did he need saving? These might be his moms.

I strode over the best I could with my crutch, trying to be the epitome of elegance and grace.

"Hi." I slid my arm around his waist.

"Hi." His scent was bitter, but he leaned into me.

"Verity Thorne. It's such a pleasure to meet you." I flashed them my best Southern girl smile.

"Ah, Grif, and Dean's girl." The smaller one, who was clearly an omega, looked me up and down. "I'm so curious about you. Oh, is that dress a Vecci?"

"Oh, it is." I gave her a look as if to say, *what else could it be?*

"These are my mothers. This is Verity. She's in a PhD program at NYIT." His eyes flickered as if looking for the exit.

"Oh. What do you study?" The taller one, who might be an alpha, but I wasn't sure, gave me a look, eyes narrowing.

"My research is in plant genetics. I work with omega lilies," I replied, arm still around AJ.

"Oh. How interesting. What do you do with that?" Her voice and look filled with judgment.

I hated that question. That look.

"My research is proprietary, but I assure you, Compass BioTek has uses for it." I wiggled my hand with the ring Grif and Dean had given me, making sure they got a good look. I turned to AJ. "Kylee took Grif. Should we go find him?"

"We should. With you two being freshly bonded, you should stay close. Mama, Mum, I'll see you later." He took my arm.

"See you later, Iksander," the shorter mom said.

"Thank you." Relief coated him as we left.

"You're quite welcome." I squeezed his hand. "Iksander?"

"What did you think the A in AJ was for?" he chuckled. "Only they call me that. I feel more like an AJ or Alex, anyway."

Iksander *was* a form of Alexander. That seemed just like him, many names for the many parts of him—and keeping everyone guessing as to which was the real him.

"What's the J?" I asked.

"Jameson. Family name on one of the dads' sides. What's your middle name?" he asked as we walked through the throng.

"Noémi Fayrouz. I have two because Mama and Baba gave me the names they'd always wanted for daughters. *Verity* was something they decided on together to fit the whole virtue name theme Dad wanted for all us kids," I explained. Both hoped I'd go by one of those middle names instead, but I liked being Verity.

We found Grif posing for pictures and talking to a bunch of kids who were probably all in the Squire program. We found a seat near and watched, content to not chat with strangers.

"He's going to make such a great dad," I whispered as we watched Grif sign some autographs.

AJ nodded and squeezed my hand. "He will. Dean, however, will be the overindulgent dad that never says *no*."

"I was thinking it would be Jonas." I grinned.

He thought for a moment. "I can see that. We're fucked."

I laughed. All four of them would make great dads one day.

The doors opened for dinner. Already, I was ready to go home instead of making small talk with people I didn't know. AJ would *gladly* go back with me if I asked, but I should at least eat so I didn't appear rude.

"I'm going to run to the restroom," I told him. Giving him a little kiss, only partially because one of his mothers, and a large man that was probably one of his dads, watched us. I left to find the restroom.

When I came out, the crowd in the atrium had thinned as people made their way into the ballroom for dinner.

"Ver, can we talk?" Freddie leaned against the wall, alone, like he'd been waiting for me.

"I guess?" If it came to it, I'd hit him with my crutch the way AJ taught me.

"Not here." Freddie led me to a patio off the atrium that was used for smoking. Given the cold, no one was out here, even with the heat lamp.

There was only one way in and out from the atrium. The patio had a low fence around it with a little gate and looked out onto what could be a small garden, but was hard to see in the darkness. A couple of bistro tables and chairs occupied it.

"What do you want, Freddie?" I leaned on my crutch, not having the energy for this.

He sighed and for a moment, he looked like the weight of the world was on his shoulders. "I wanted to apologize for being so awful to you when you became an alpha."

"Oh. Thank you. You made it seem like I was hiding things from you. I'd always been forthright about my designation." It was cold out here and I wasn't wearing a wrap or long gloves, only my thin scarf, which was more for decoration. I moved closer to the heater.

"I know. With you basically being a beta, we were on even footing. When you awakened as an alpha, the power shifted, and it wasn't something I wanted in a permanent relationship. But I could have handled things better," he told me.

Permanent? It was hard not to snort. There was never any understanding of it being long-term. He was fun, but not someone I'd spend forever with.

"It would especially have been nice if you hadn't tried to wreck my reputation. Or encouraged people to be mean to me. I didn't try to get Coach fired. Just like not going pro wasn't my choice." So much hurt and emotion flowed through my voice.

Freddie nodded slowly. "Yeah. But you were so good. It seemed a waste. I sort of figured your parents didn't let you."

I stared at him. "If you did, then why were you so mean?"

"A lot of it was Chet. He was hurt. Not only that you'd waste your talent like that, but how you treated your coach. Keeping Chet happy meant that he'd get me a good contract, and Southern United isn't bad." He shrugged, leaning against the wall of the hotel, braced by one leg, hands in his pockets, dark hair in his eyes.

"Which is why you want to be traded now?" I gave him a look.

"It's a business, Ver. Chet fucked with my career, and now I have to get it back on track. You know Derva and I go way back. You fucking with your coach like that hurt her. It was like you were doing it to be mean to her," he added.

"Um, I did it because his actions were inappropriate and creepy, not because I have a vendetta against her. Which I don't. Though as I said, I didn't try to get him fired. It just... happened." My brain went fuzzy. What was he talking about? I didn't enjoy working with Derva, but I didn't hate her.

While I vaguely recalled Freddie knowing Derva, I had no idea what she had to do with my collegiate fútbol coach. While I was getting a degree, playing fútbol, and taking modeling gigs for funsies, she was living in New York, modeling her ass off.

"Also, you can't seriously be with those hockey players. This is a rebellion thing, right? You can finally date, so you're with the absolute antithesis of everything your parents stand for?" His eyes gleamed with jealousy.

"No, *you* were the antithesis of everything my parents wanted for me, which was part of why I dated you." It might be a bit mean, but it was the honest truth. He was a beta literature major who played fútbol and wanted to go pro then write adventure novels. Blasphemy in my family.

Though I hadn't dated him because of that. I'd dated him because he was hot. Fit. Knew a million ways to fuck. Was super fun as long as everything went his way.

Grif's rain scent tickled my nose as his arm snaked around my waist. "Antithesis is big word for a fútboler. Hey, Kitten. We should go to dinner."

"That sounds good. It's cold out here." I leaned into him as if I could absorb his warmth.

"Who's in charge of this weird-ass relationship, anyway?" Derva leaned in the doorway to the atrium, the neckline of her dress so plunging I'm sure she had to tape her tits in.

"Oh, Derva." I shook my head.

"Save your patronizing bullshit, you fucking life ruiner. It wasn't good enough that you had to ruin my dad's life because you can't take a joke. But no, you have to ruin my sister's, too." Absolute vitriol laced her voice as the spicy scent of anger rolled off her.

I sucked in a breath. "Are you related to Coach?"

It was the only thing that made sense. Coach's kids weren't around much. They were off living their lives.

"Are you that dumb? Of course, I am. Freddie and I met because my dad used to coach him at summer camp. Then my dad moved us to Research Circle so he could be a head coach in fucking humid, giant bug, sweet tea land." She shuddered. "I was lucky I could live with my sister so I could keep modeling. Did you think when you'd run into me in Research Circle I was there to torment you?"

"I never thought that. Everything that happened with Coach had nothing to do with you personally." Oh shit. My old coach was her dad. How had I not known that? But then while we knew

Mrs. Coach, and that he had grown kids, he didn't talk a lot about his personal life.

She snorted. "Um, yeah. Just like you think you're better than all of us because of your fancy fucking education. You play with *flowers*, for fucks sake. That doesn't make you special."

"Well, of course not." I frowned. Did some of the models I worked with think I thought I was better than them because I was getting a PhD? Hopefully it was just Derva.

Grif gave her a look and pulled me closer. "Yeah, we should go inside."

"Wait, what do you mean about your sister? Isn't your sister older? I remember how she used to go to modeling jobs with you before you were eighteen. How did I ruin her life?" I was so confused.

"Oh, wait." She focused on Grif, eyes narrowing. "That's *you*. You ruined her life. You had her husband put in *jail*. It's leaving her career in tatters."

"Your sister's married to Chet. *That's* how Coach knew him." The pieces fell together. Huh. Small world. Grif had mentioned Chet's pregnant wife being in tears at the hearing.

"Oh fuck," Grif muttered.

"Their marriage was happy. Sure, Chet made a few bad choices, but he didn't deserve to go to jail. She and my nephews shouldn't have to suffer." Anger continued to roll off Derva. "But no, you had to ruin it." Derva lunged at Grif.

Grif put his hands up, not wanting to hurt her, and she knocked him off-balance. He stumbled back into one of the tables, knocking over a chair. A burst of surprise came through the bond from him.

She pulled back her hand.

"Derva, stop this right now," I snapped, not about to let her hurt my Grif.

"Make me." She smirked. Derva threw a punch and Grif caught her wrist before she landed it.

"Derva, I'm sorry your sister is in a bad spot. I feel for her and the kids, but what Chet did was wrong," Grif told her.

"Get off!" She flailed, jerking her hand back.

Derva stumbled backwards. I side-stepped to avoid her. She tripped over my crutch and sprawled on the ground, something ripping.

"Are you okay?" Freddie helped her up.

"You smug, stuck-up, life-ruining bitch." Derva launched herself at me, pushing me back into the heat lamp, knocking it over as she grabbed the filmy scarf around my neck.

Ow. Fabric tore as I tripped. The heat lamp made a crashing sound, me nearly avoiding it. My leg throbbed.

Shit. I wasn't expecting to get into a girl fight with Derva today.

Grif grabbed my arm to balance me. I smacked Derva with my crutch as she tried to throw a punch. I didn't want to hurt her, but I needed her to not try to hurt us.

Frustration and anger at her *trying to hurt my mate* bubbled up inside me. "Derva, *stop trying to attack us.*"

The air sizzled with alpha command and her movements froze mid gesture.

"Oh fuuuck," Freddie murmured, standing back and watching.

I did it. I'd actually barked someone. Grif squeezed my shoulder.

"How dare you? You're not better than me." Derva's face contorted in surprise as her hand flopped to her side.

"Don't. Hurt. My. Mate." I growled. "It's shitty and I'm sorry everything has impacted your family, but neither your dad nor Chet were innocent."

"Wow, you got them both out here. Good for you, Derv. You can have her. Though you already destroyed her stupid research," a voice said just beyond the fence separating the ballroom patio from the hotel gardens.

I couldn't see who it was. But I could guess. Chet's wife. Derva's big sister, Winnie. Wow, I'd never made the connection.

Winnie had moved to New York to work for a big marketing firm and often used her connections to get Derva modeling work. She probably met Chet at a party. I remembered Coach talking about his daughter's wedding.

Wait, *Derva* had gotten Samantha to destroy my research? That made sense. Not only did she hate me, but she could destroy something of mine the way I ruined her dad's career.

"She fucking deserved that for what she did to our Dad. That fucking bitch barked me! You didn't tell me she was a real alpha." Derva slugged Freddie. She turned to me, lips curving into a sneer. "I wish you would've stayed in obscurity where a washed-up, basic bitch like you belongs. But no. You had to date famous people, didn't you? You're such an attention whore."

"No, she's not," Grif snapped.

"Winnie's here? Why did you attack them, Derv? I know you're still mad about your dad. But, um, *laws.*" Freddie looked exasperated in the dim light.

"Honestly, I was never that broken up about Dad going to jail. Because he *did* get creepy with my friends. That's why I moved out." Winnie moved closer to the fence.

Still, all I could see was someone in a hoodie, about Derva's height but curvier.

"But Chet. I love Chet. They won't even tell me where he is. You ruined my life, Griffin McGraff. We have *children.*" Her voice hit an epic pitch. The fear, apprehension, and hatred wafted off her in a spicy, acrid cocktail.

"Grif, I think it's time to go." I tugged on his sleeve, getting a hint of his concern through the bond. Derva blocked the door to the ballroom atrium with her body.

I'd knock her over if I had to. Sure, she was a beta, but I needed to protect my omega.

"I don't think so." Winnie's hands raised. Something glinted on the other side of the fence and I caught a whiff of her fear, her anger... her desperation.

I pivoted in front of Grif as I pushed him in the opposite direction, shielding him with my body. A shot rang out and something pierced my shoulder. Pain exploded through me and I lost my balance.

"No," someone else yelled. "You're ruining everything, you dumb bitch."

"VERITY!" a voice bellowed as I slipped to the ground.

We always protect them at all costs.

Chapter Forty-Four

Grif

Verity moved in front of me. As she pushed me, I spied the outline of a gun. My kitten's scream pierced the air as the crack of a gunshot echoed through the patio.

Intense pain shuddered through our bond, stunning me. Did she just take a bullet for me?

"No," Derva yelled. "You're ruining everything, you dumb bitch."

"VERITY!" I shouted as she stumbled and fell to the ground. Hard.

"What is fucking happening?" AJ burst onto the balcony.

"Was that a gunshot?" Dimitri appeared behind AJ, eyes critically searching the scene.

Derva's sister made a strangled sound, then took off into the darkness.

"She's getting away." My voice broke as I took Verity's limp hand into mine. *Please be okay. Please. Please. Please.*

"Understood." The Russian defensemen *leapt* over the fence and took off running.

Derva froze, looking out into the garden as her sister disappeared, like she was too panicked to do anything.

"Winnie Chesterton shot Verity." Pain burst through my skull. Not my pain. Verity's.

"Oh fuck," AJ breathed as he crouched next to me.

"Wake up, *Please.*" I shook her gently.

Verity didn't respond. Probably because she hit her head so hard. Shit.

"It'll be okay." AJ got on his phone, putting an arm around me. "I'd like to report a shooting."

"What's wrong?" Jonas and Dean appeared.

"Don't let them leave." AJ indicated Derva and Freddie with his chin as he gave the dispatcher the hotel address over the phone and added, "We need an ambulance."

Jonas took up residence in the doorway that led to the ballroom atrium, giving Verity a somber look.

"Verity." Dean ran over to us. Taking off his jacket, he used it to staunch the bullet wound in her upper shoulder, blood all over her scarf and dress.

"What did you do to my sister, you fucking fuck-boy?" Mercy yelled, barreling into the patio in a flurry of red sparkles, Kaiko at her side.

"Is that why you wanted me to come? Not so I could network, but to lure Verity out so Winnie could hurt her?" Freddie roared at Derva.

"I didn't know Winnie was going to shoot them. I didn't even know she owned a gun. Shit, I thought she was going to yell at him, maybe throw a punch." Derva shrugged, not nearly as worried as she should be considering her sister just *shot* someone.

"You bitch." Mercy lunged at her in a cloud of alpha anger.

Jonas caught her. "Not today, Squirt."

Tears ran down Mercy's face. "Let me at her, Bub. Or him. I need to hit someone."

"I know." Jonas held Mercy tighter. "I know. But we can't. Not today."

"I'm on it," Kaiko said as she got out her phone, glaring at Derva.

All I could do was clutch Verity's hand as everyone else moved and spoke around me. She looked so still. Almost like...

My chest got tight.

"Get Grif back from her so I can look. Good job applying pressure, Dean," a male voice said.

"Breathe, Grif. Just breathe. It's going to be okay, Boo-Boo. Dr. Mosser was at the party and he's looking at Verity. The ambulance has been called." Arms wrapped around me.

I pressed my face into AJ's shoulder and inhaled his vetiver scent, trying to get comfort from it. From him.

"She took a bullet for me. I didn't even see the gun until after Verity screamed." My voice came out muffled and ragged, my heart in my throat.

Verity.

"Alphas can be like that, especially when protecting their mates. It'll be okay. We'll take care of her," AJ soothed, rubbing my back.

What if she wasn't okay?

"Is that Dimitri?" Jonas looked out into the darkness.

Peeking up from AJ's shoulder, I saw a large figure come toward us on the other side of the fence.

"Let me go. Let me go!" a woman shrieked.

"Police. There was a shooting?" a voice said from the doorway to the atrium.

"I caught her." Dimitri let himself in through the small gate in the fence. The woman who shot Verity kicked and shouted, slung over his shoulder.

"She didn't mean to. Winnie got upset with Grif Graf because he put her husband in jail. She's pregnant and has a toddler. It's a lot," Derva blubbered, trying to seek comfort from Freddie.

Freddie pushed her away. "I'm tired of hurting Verity to make other people happy. While she can be an insufferable perfectionist, she's not awful."

"Don't talk about her like that. I love her," I snapped. I shivered a little in AJ's arms. It was cold out here.

Dean put an arm around me, sandwiching me between him and AJ, love coursing through our bonds.

The paramedics rushed onto the scene, and I sat there, frozen and terrified, clutching AJ as they put her still body on a stretcher. Blood marred the beautiful dress she and AJ spent so much effort fixing.

I ran after them. "That's my alpha. I'm going with her."

The thought of leaving her side made bile rise in my throat.

"Go. We'll follow," AJ told me, patting my shoulder.

"Go for it," the paramedic told me, then turned to AJ. "We're going to Manhattan General."

I held her hand as we got into the back of the ambulance. At least she was breathing.

But I couldn't feel her in our bond. Her driftwood scent went rotten, choking me. I felt hot, almost stiflingly so. I shrugged off my jacket and covered her with it so she'd have my scent with her.

She looked so still.

Fuck. Chet's *wife* tried to shoot me.

Verity took a bullet for me. My love. My alpha.

My mate.

If she didn't live, I didn't know what I'd do.

Chapter Forty-Five

Jonas

Once again, I paced a tiny hospital waiting room as one of my packmates fought for their life.

And once again, I was powerless to do anything to make it better.

I felt like a shitty alpha.

Not that there was anything I could've done. I hadn't even known Verity had gone to talk with Freddie. Grif went looking for her when she hadn't come back from the bathroom.

While I knew Chet had a wife, I hadn't even considered that she'd come after Grif.

The fact I hadn't planned for that made my stomach churn.

Then again, I didn't know that Verity's old coach, her ex the fútboler, and that beta model, were wrapped up in this.

Fuck.

Grif sat in AJ's lap, beside himself. Rightfully so, considering he and Verity only bonded yesterday. He'd probably felt the whole fucking thing.

Verity had protected Grif with her body. Faced a nemesis.

And *barked*.

While I was worried sick about my little alpha and needed her to be okay, I was proud of her. Because we were alphas. We protected them. When she needed to, she had.

I just wished she hadn't *gotten shot*.

The media was all over this, given how fresh Grif was in the press. Kylee and our pack publicist were on it. Dimitri and a few others were here at the hospital trying to keep us from being swarmed.

Dean looked at me with tear-stained eyes. "I...I was thinking of asking her to bite me tonight."

"She'll be okay, Love." I pulled him to me. His cozy scent went salty with worry and sadness as I ran my fingers through his hair, trying to calm him down.

Inside I was a bundle of anxiety, and it took everything to keep that tamped down so Dean didn't get it through our bond. *Please let her be okay.*

"We're going to take a little walk. We'll be back." AJ had his arm around Grif as they left the waiting room, in a trail of sour rain.

Mercy was on her phone, expression worried. Verity's crutch lay next to her. It had been forgotten when Grif and Verity left with the ambulance.

She looked over at me, eyes teary, makeup smeared. "Who do I tell? Should I tell a parent? I feel like I should tell a parent."

"Start with Creed or Grace? If you need to tell a parent, they'll help you figure out which one," I assured. I hoped we didn't. Though I wasn't sure any of the parents would give enough fucks about Verity to actually show up.

Grace could come ready to stab us with a fork, though.

"Okay. I already texted Creed. I also told my coach what happened. I'm not leaving my sister." Her expression grew fierce. "I texted Verity's friend Saphira because I don't know how to get a hold of Dr. Winters."

Good. Someone from her university should know what happened.

A doctor walked into the room. "Grif McGraff?"

"I'm Jonas, I'm head alpha. Is she okay?" My heart skipped a beat.

He peered at his tablet. "She's not listed as being in a pack. But I have a mate in her record. A Griffin McGraff." The doctor looked around.

"I'm Grif's head alpha." It was hard not to rush him and shake the answers out of him. Was she okay? I'd be gutted if she wasn't.

"I'm her sister, you can tell us." Mercy joined me, look no-nonsense. "Mercy Thorne."

"Please tell us." Dean put his arms around my waist, voice a near-whine.

The doctor's look softened as he checked his tablet. "Mercy Thorne, sister, and one of her emergency contacts. As long as it's okay for me to talk about your sister with them present."

Mercy nodded. "Please do."

"She was lucky. So lucky. The small bullet went clear through her shoulder, so there's not nearly as much damage as there could have been," he told us. "We stitched her up. She'll want some rehab."

Verity was still going to PT for her stroke, so a little more wouldn't hurt. Thank goodness it wasn't more serious.

"We're going to run a few tests because it seems like she hit her head pretty hard when she fell. Then we'll admit her for observation. She's a young and healthy alpha, so I'm sure she's hardy and will heal fast," the doctor told us.

A day or two of observation? We could deal with that.

"Is she conscious?" I asked.

"She's asking for Grif," he told us, looking around as if it would make him magically appear.

"You know she had a stroke, right?" Mercy gave him a look. "Also, the medicines she can't have?"

The doctor gave her an indulgent look. "It's all in her file. She'll be fine and you'll see her soon."

"I think I'm going to be sick." Grif trembled against AJ as we sat in the pack-sized room in critical care.

Well, we sat. Dean snuggled against Verity in the hospital bed. There was food on the table that some of the Knights had brought.

The monitors beeped, as Verity lay in a deep medicated sleep, after having a bad reaction to something they gave her. One moment she'd been with Grif after finishing some tests, the next moment she hadn't been okay.

Life was so fragile.

"She'll be fine. They stabilized her, she'll sleep it off, and be okay," I reassured Grif. "Her scans all look great, just a little concussion. She'll be okay."

I kept telling them that, willing it to be true.

Grif was taking this hard, and I was afraid he'd spiral because of it.

"Dude, I can't believe Verity took a bullet for someone." Hale, looking like trouble in cowboy boots, sauntered in like he had no cares, holding a box of pizza and a bundle of balloons.

"She took it for her mate, you moron." Mercy ran at her brother and hugged him, causing him to nearly drop the box.

He looked over at Verity. "She'll be okay, right? Did they catch the asshole?"

"Yeah. One of the hockey players literally chased after her and brought her to the police over his shoulder, kicking and screaming. Oooh, pizza? Thanks." Mercy took the box. "Cute balloons, wow."

"Oh, it wasn't us." Dare joined him. His pants looked like they'd fall off his ass and I'd never heard of the band on his shirt.

Hale opened the box and took a slice. "It was your friends in the lobby."

"Well, that was nice. It smells good." Dean crawled off the bed and got a piece.

"Where's Grace?" I looked around, fully expecting her to storm in and ask me why I let her sister get hurt.

"At a conference in France. I sort of haven't told her yet because I'm not feeling a Grace tornado right now. I'll tell her in the morning. Creed offered to come, but I told him to stay in Rockland and send these fuckers instead." Mercy shrugged, tying the balloons to a vase of flowers someone had already brought.

Dare looked over at her. "She'll be okay?"

"She's heavily sedated, but she'll be okay," I assured. "Thank you for coming out."

"Absolutely. The shooting hit the news. Mama's beside herself," Dare told Mercy. "I'll keep them at arm's length, okay? But you should text her."

"I will. Please keep them away. The only parent I want right now is Dad–only if he left Mumsy in London." Mercy hugged her brother tightly. "I don't even want Grace or Creed. Just you two assholes."

We sat around, talking. Grif got up and crawled into the bed with Verity, holding Dean's hand over her body.

"Creed got us a hotel. Mercy, want to crash with us for a few hours? Get a little sleep? Take a shower? Change out of your ballgown? Aren't you fancy? You wear that shit like every night, right?" Dare asked.

Mercy scratched her nose with her middle finger. "We were at a charity fundraiser, you ding-dong. You can leave. I got my hugs. I'm fine now."

"You can go with them if you want, Squirt. You can also go home. There's nothing wrong with getting a little sleep. We can trade off. Someone should get some things for Verity, anyway," I told her. We should eventually change, since we were still in our gala finery.

"Squirt?" Hale snorted.

"Only Jonas can call me that." Mercy made a face. "I'll get Verity's things. You'll pack her thongs. She doesn't like wearing thongs in hospitals."

Dean tried not to laugh. "I'm so grateful for that information."

Mercy left with her brothers in a cloud of plum-scented worry.

"I'd like to take Grif home," AJ whispered. "I'm worried about him spiraling. He needs to be tucked into bed and taken care of. We'll come back in the morning and then you and Dean can go home for a bit?"

"That sounds like a good plan if he's willing to leave her side." Because Grif didn't look too good and his scent was still sour.

"Boo-Boo, would you like to go home and shower? Get Verity's things?" AJ got up and went to Grif.

"I… I don't know. I want to stay with her, but I don't feel good." He looked stricken, wrapping his arms around AJ.

"You know this isn't your fault, right?" I told Grif. "Not only didn't you have any idea that Chet's wife would come after you, Verity's job as an alpha is literally to protect you. A job I've reminded her of. She won't blame you, so don't blame yourself."

I needed him to understand that. He took things too hard, too personal.

Grif sat up. "I… I know. It's just…"

Dean squeezed his hand. "I know. Go home, Gumdrop. Curl up with AJ and sleep for a couple of hours. Bring me some clothes? I think I need some hospital thongs."

"I'll bring all the thongs." Grif snorted. He gave her a long look, then turned back to his husband. "You'll watch over her for me?"

"Of course. I'll make sure she gets all the cuddles and knows we're here. After all, I was supposed to spend the night with her." Dean's look grew wistful. "I love you, Gumdrop." He leaned over and gave Grif a kiss.

"We'll be back in the morning," AJ told me. He planted a kiss on Grif's temple. "Come on, Boo-Boo."

Grif kissed Verity on the cheek. "I'm going to leave you with Dean for a few hours. But I'll be back with some clothes for you. We'll take your dress to the cleaners and see if they can get the blood out of it. I love you, Kitten."

"Go rest. I'll call you if she wakes up and wants you?" I offered.

"Thanks." Grif nodded and left with AJ.

"His scent is off. He's sort of clammy. I... I really don't want him to spiral." Dean looked stricken.

"Me neither. That's why AJ's taking him home for a bit." I put the uneaten food in the mini-fridge and checked my messages to make sure no one needed anything. Also, I texted the Knights group chat, letting everyone know that if they were still here, they should go home.

"Will you lay down with us, Babes?" Dean took off his shirt and threw it at the couch, then did the same for his pants.

While it was critical care, she was in a pack suite. The bed was large enough for exactly that–a mate or two cuddling the patient, letting them know they were loved. It sometimes made all the difference in recovery.

"I'd like that." I took off my shoes, belt, and shirt. My jacket had been discarded long ago.

Putting my phone on the bedside table, I crawled on the other side of her and turned off the light.

I kissed our little alpha on the temple. "Good night, Sweet Girl." I reached over her and squeezed Dean's hand. "Good night, my love."

While I closed my eyes, I didn't sleep. Also, I kept getting texts. Texts from Kylee. Texts from the hockey group chat. Texts from Charlie and my sister.

AJ

Grif has a fever, I think he might be sick.

Me

If you need to, take him to the Center Clinic.

I could see Grif making himself sick over this.

AJ

If we don't make it back in the morning I'll have Mercy bring your things.

Me

Don't worry about it. You watch over him.

We could always have Mercy sit with Verity while we ducked home for a few hours. Hopefully Verity would get discharged in a day or two, anyway. Especially since the scans showed there wasn't any brain injury.

Finally, I closed my eyes. Verity would be okay. Grif would be okay.

Everyone would be fucking okay.

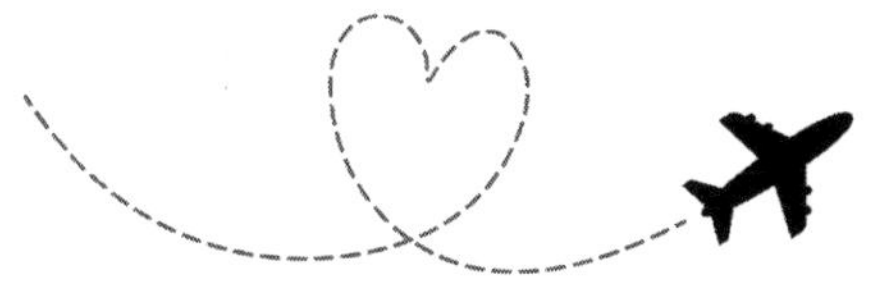

Chapter Forty-Six

AJ

Grif was sicker than even when we'd caught a nasty flu one winter when we were still with the Tsunamis. His sickly sour-sweet scent filled the room.

As much as I worried about Verity, we weren't making it back to the hospital this morning. Dean, Jonas, and Mercy would have to deal with it while I took care of Grif.

Exhaustion pressed down on me. I'd been up all night with him.

I needed to get his fever down. Nothing was working. Medicine. A bath. Fluids.

Fucking.

Right now, he slept fitfully, tossing and turning, getting tangled in my sheets.

With a sigh, I called the nurse advice line offered by the Omega Center.

"Nurse advice. How may I help you?" the man said.

"My omega has a fever, and I don't know what to do." I told the nurse about Grif's symptoms. Grif kept fretting in the bed beside me. I stroked his hair, trying to soothe him.

"Is his heat close? Are you sure it's not a spike?" the nurse asked.

"He's on suppressants." Oh, I hadn't thought about that. But he didn't smell like he was going into heat.

Sure, he'd wanted a lot of physical reassurance, but Verity had taken a bullet for him. It made sense.

"Sometimes suppressants aren't always effective. Has he been on them for a long time? Also, certain recreational substances can lessen the effectiveness of suppressants and birth control," the nurse told me.

I thought for a moment. "His doctor recently changed the dosage."

"That can do it. Also, sometimes breakthrough heats happen during times of intense emotional duress," he added.

Oh. "I thought that caused spirals."

"Oh, absolutely. But depending on where an omega is in their cycle, it can cause a breakthrough heat instead," he told me.

Huh. I'd consider watching your newly bonded mate take a bullet for you as *emotional duress.*

"He doesn't smell like he's going into heat. He smells sick. Before the fever hit, I was afraid he'd spiral." Shit. I wasn't prepared for him to go into heat.

Could we even get to the cabin this time of year? Though we had a 4x4.

"Monitor him, try to get the fever down, and start preparing in case he goes into heat. A breakthrough heat because of emotional duress can be a lot more intense than a normal one." He listed a bunch of things to look for and ways to help him.

Ending the call, I leaned over and gave Grif a good sniff. He still smelled sick, not in heat. Still, it wouldn't hurt to be ready.

I looked up how to prepare for a heat. While I'd been at the cabin sometimes for Dean's heats, I'd never been in charge of organizing anything other than the food. I packed a bag for us, checked for road closures, and then started a grocery order that could be delivered to the cabin in the time it would take us to drive there.

But I highly doubted that's what it was. Mostly because in my experience, Grif had a spiral, not a breakthrough heat.

Still, it gave me something to do.

"Kitten?" Grif whined. It hit me straight to my heart.

"I'm here, Boo-Boo." I put the bag by the bedroom door and came over to him.

"Pepperjack." He calmed under my touch.

Grif still didn't smell like he was in heat. He smelled of sweat and sickness. Yeah, he'd literally made himself sick over what happened last night.

Honestly, I understood. While I, too, would put myself between Grif and a bullet, worry for Verity burrowed inside me.

"I'm right here." Curling next to him in my bed, hoping maybe my body would draw the fever from him, I fell asleep.

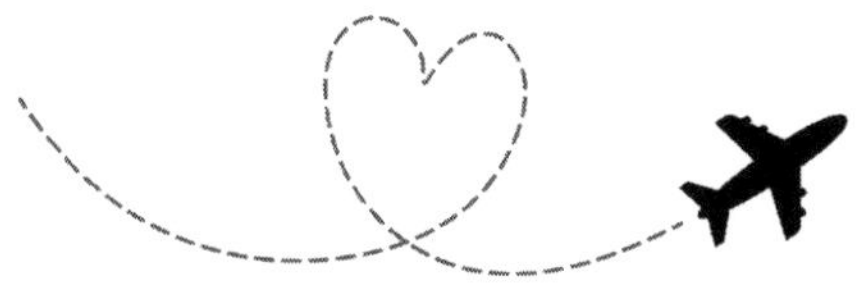

Chapter Forty-Seven

DEAN

Holding my little alpha, I sat on the hospital bed. She was sleeping normally now. The heavy-duty pain meds made her sleep a lot. Though at least she'd be just fine.

I fanned myself with my shirt. It was hot in here. I felt itchy in my own skin, and a little sick to my stomach. It would be nice to go home.

The doctor said we couldn't take her home until tomorrow when they changed her meds to something that wouldn't keep her mostly asleep.

Wiggling again, I took off my shirt, flinging it onto the couch in the hospital room. Maybe I was coming down with whatever

Grif had. He'd had a fever, and all day had been at home sleeping, fucking AJ, or asking for Verity.

At least he hadn't spiraled.

Yet.

Not that him having a fever wasn't worrisome.

A jolt of lust came through my bond as he fucked AJ *again.* Not that I blamed him. When Jonas and I had gone home earlier, I'd gotten myself some *attention.* This entire ordeal unsettled me. My omega wanted to be cuddled, reassured, and fucked until I passed out.

Then fed candy and told I was a good omega.

Jonas was on his phone, frowning hard, texting away.

"Can we just take her *now*?" I asked Jonas. Sure, she was still hooked up to monitors and a vitamin IV, but she was breathing on her own. Really, she was fine, other than having stitches.

When she woke up, she'd want a bubble bath and a chai latte.

Jonas could tuck us all in her bed and bring us some tea. Maybe make us some eggs and rice in the morning.

By then, hopefully, Grif would be feeling better and could join us. Yes, we'd all make her feel so much better.

"Shouldn't you listen to the doctor?" Dare appeared, looking like he was ready to go clubbing in a mesh shirt, tight pants, and chains.

"Eh." Jonas shrugged.

"She'd probably like her own bed," Mercy replied. "Her room is *wild.* Though the chandelier creeps me out."

"What? That's my favorite part. It's like we're in a palace in Golden France," I protested. I'd chosen it special from a fancy lighting shop.

"You do know how that all ended, right?" Mercy snorted.

Okay, so there was a beta revolution because they were sick of the alphas hoarding all the wealth and resources. But visually, the era was stunningly opulent.

Hale appeared, holding something. "Hey, Carlos dropped off enchiladas that his mom made. They smell good."

"That sounds amazing because we finished Ladybug's lasagna." Jonas found some plates.

Mercy made a face. "You didn't save me any? I thought we were friends?"

"It was a small lasagna, Squirt." Jonas put the plates and forks on the table, left over from things people brought us.

Okay, it wasn't that small. When Ladybug brought it, we were starving, and it was hot from the oven and all cheesy and bubbly.

There was a home game tonight, but Grif, Jonas, and I decided to sit out. Coach was good with it. I think they feared glitter bombs from the Maimers if he wasn't. The Maimers had been stopping by and leaving snacks and flowers. So had the Knights.

Hale helped himself to some food, his jeans so tight I thought they'd split as he bent over the table. "Can I get the keys to Verity's car? It'll make things easier."

Jonas gave Hale a sharp alpha stare. "No."

"Oh, come now." Hale tried to ooze Southern charm.

"I told you." Dare rolled his over-made-up eyes. "Can I drive it?"

Jonas shook his head. "No one is driving her car."

"You have such good taste in cars," Hale wheedled.

"I know." Jonas crossed his arms over his chest.

I got up and got some enchiladas. I squirmed again. Something felt wrong.

"Are you okay, Love?" Concern flashed in Jonas' eyes.

"I'm worried about Grif, Babes." I leaned into him and rubbed the spot on my chest where the bond lived.

"You feel warm." Jonas frowned and caressed my forehead.

We sat and ate Mrs. Rodriguez's delicious enchiladas.

Jonas' phone rang. He answered it with a frown. "Is everything okay, AJ?"

From his sour scent, expression, and concern through the bond, things weren't.

"No, that's exactly what you should do. It's fine. We have chains." Jonas paced the hospital room.

Shit. That didn't sound good.

Heat seared me. Could everyone leave so I could get naked and Jonas could take care of me? Maybe us fucking would wake Verity up so we could go home.

Then he could fuck us both in my bed.

"Okay." Jonas' eyes flickered to Verity, then to me. He ended the call.

"What's wrong? Is AJ taking Grif to the clinic?" I took a drink of water. *So hot.*

How much could I take off and still be company appropriate?

"He's taking Grif to the cabin." Jonas looked at Mercy. "Who can take you back and forth to practices and games besides Verity and us? Can Rusty actually, or does everyone just look the other way when she does it?"

Oh. There was only one reason why AJ would take Grif to the cabin. No wonder I felt hot and horny. Grif wasn't sick.

He was going into heat.

"For like how long? If someone gets me the fancy ultra-bullet pass so I can get to class and shit, I can do it," Dare volunteered from his spot at the table. "I'm on the list and I don't have any tests or concerts in the next week or two. But if I miss rehearsals, my professor will have my ass. Not sure how long Creed will buy us a hotel, though."

"We don't have a guest room set up, but the couch in the upstairs sitting area is pretty comfortable. So is the one downstairs. You're welcome to that. We'll be a few days. Maybe a week? Hopefully less," Jonas told them.

"Sounds good." Dare got on his phone.

Hale scolded his phone and nodded. "I have to go back to Research Circle tomorrow because I have work and tests and shit. But yeah, if I can get an ultra-bullet ticket, I'll come for the weekend. Unless you want to call Creed or Grace and have them stay with you? I think they're on the list, too."

Mercy shook her head. "I don't need to be babysat. This plan is fine."

I wasn't sure how responsible Dare was. Hale wasn't responsible at all. But Mercy took no shit and Rusty would help out.

Yeah, when our little alpha woke up, we'd wrap her in a blanket, make a bed for her in the back of the SUV, and bring her to the cabin with us. I wanted to be there for Grif, and we wouldn't leave her behind.

Given how long it'd been since Grif had a heat, it could be intense. Even if she wasn't up to participating, her being close would help.

I texted Rusty to ask for help with Mercy. She'd been asking about Verity, anyway.

"It's hot in here." It was almost a whine as I looked for the thermostat.

Jonas pressed the call button for the nurse, then turned to Mercy. "You have access to the grocery account, buy whatever food you need. No parties. No one takes Verity's car. Call Rusty if you need anything."

"I know how to take care of myself, Bub. Don't worry, no parties. Just me, Kaiko, pizza, and a shit-ton of beads. Kaiko got a giant bucket of new ones. We might bake some cookies. That cake I got during the snowstorm was good. Maybe we'll get one of those, too." She grinned at Jonas.

I never understood exactly where the cake came from, but it was delicious. The cool air hit me as I stood in front of the air vent as it switched from hot to cold. *That's the stuff.*

"I agree with that plan. I like cookies. Also, my girlfriend loved the bracelets you made her," Dare replied.

"We should have *all* your skate smash friends over for cookies," Hale leered.

Mercy's eyes narrowed. "Hale, my friends would eat you for breakfast. But we can get tacos."

The nurse came in. "Is everything okay?"

"No. We need to discharge Verity now." Jonas threw things in the bag we'd brought today.

She frowned. "We can't do that."

"You said she's just sleeping. You said she'll be fine. Unless there's a good reason for her to stay, I'm taking her." Jonas' voice went hard as his alphaness flooded the room.

"I'll get the doctor." She left, looking flustered.

"You're taking her with you?" Dare shook his head. "We'll stay until she gets discharged and bring her back to your place. We'll keep an eye on her. She'll be fine."

"I'm not leaving her behind," Jonas replied. "Dean, put your shirt and shoes on. We're leaving."

"We're going now? Okay. Do I *have* to put my shirt on?" The idea of putting it on made me feel ill. I flopped onto the couch and shoved on my shoes.

"Dean, it's February. Shirt and coat." Jonas unhooked her from the monitors, and one of them beeped angrily.

I groaned and put my shirt on, even though the fabric felt like sandpaper. Yeah, let's go home so I could get naked in my nest. Maybe I'd take my little alpha in there with me. It might be good for her. Make her feel better.

"Can you just take her? Why *are* you leaving for a week? You have games and shit." Dare looked confused.

"Um, because it's illegal to have heats in high-rises in New York." Mercy gathered up the food people had brought us, putting it in a sack. "That's what's happening, right? Grif is going into heat as a trauma response, so AJ's taking him to the cabin. You're joining them because Dean is Grif's husband, and he'll be going into heat in like five minutes, because bonded omegas are like that. Verity's coming with, because it would sort of be mean not to because they're mates."

"You figured it out. Good job, Squirt," Jonas praised, putting on his coat and pocketing his phone.

Was I going into heat, too? Or simply feeling Grif's? Either way, if Verity was fine, I was ready to leave.

"Bub, I've learned more from my alpha teammates in a few months than all the classes I've ever had in school. Also, Dean smells weird. I'll take this stuff and the food back to our place." Mercy gathered up the flowers, balloons, and things people sent.

I smelled weird?

"In case it hasn't hit the sibling group chat, Grif and Verity mated. If she doesn't feel up to participating, it's fine. Given the doctor says she'll be okay, she needs to be near him. She should have a choice." Jonas disengaged the last monitor and wrapped her in a blanket I'd brought from her room.

"Oh, okay. Since she'll be fine, she should totally be with her mate. I just didn't know you could take people out of the hospital," Dare replied.

The doctor ran in. "You can't take her. You're not legally her pack, so you can't consent for her to discharge her."

"Little Alpha?" Jonas shook her gently.

"Five more minutes. I'm so tired," she mumbled.

"I know, Sweetheart. We need to get to Grif. Are you okay with that?" He gathered her into his arms, blanket and all.

"Grif. Something's wrong with Grif. I feel it. Ugh." She rolled into Jonas. "Dean, can you check on Grif for me? I... I'll get up in a moment. I..."

I joined them, running my hands through her hair. She was talking, and that settled my heart. "We'll get him together."

"Okay. Let's go. Ugh, I feel awful." Her eyes closed.

I'm sure she did.

"Her mate needs us and since she's fine, we're not leaving her behind. Dean, grab the bag," Jonas directed, moving toward the door.

"Oh, is he on the fourth floor? We can move her to him," the doctor nodded, concerned.

"It's not that sort of emergency." Jonas shook his head.

I put our phones in my pocket and grabbed the bag, eager to leave as I got another jolt of lust from Grif. "We'll be back, Mercy."

Hale draped an arm around her. "We'll be fine. Have a pleasant trip to Pound Town."

"I can't believe you said that." Mercy grimaced and slugged him. "Bub, I'll call you if I need you, and not expect a prompt response. If it's an emergency Rusty can't handle, we'll call Creed or Grace. Also, I'll take care of Lucky."

"You should call Grace in about an hour, anyway. Let her know that Verity's been released, and we're taking her to the cabin. Don't want to get stabbed with a fork." Jonas looked at the doctor. "Thanks for everything."

I followed Jonas out of the hospital room, as the doctor didn't stop us.

Yeah, let's go to the cabin. Maybe somewhere along the way, we could stop for a quick fuck.

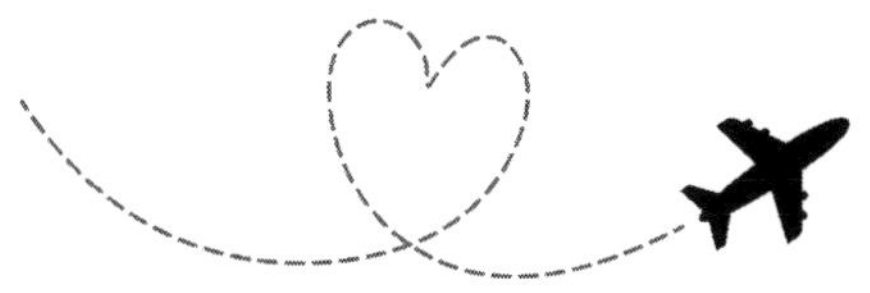

Chapter Forty-Eight

Verity

My mouth tasted nasty, and every muscle ached. Even ones I didn't know I had.

Also, I felt horny. *Very* horny.

My eyes pried themselves open. It took a moment for everything to come into focus. I wasn't in my room–or any room at the guys' place.

No, I seemed to be in lumberjack paradise with a gigantic bed hewn of logs, along with the rest of the furniture in the room, and wood-paneled walls. A fireplace roared in the background.

It smelled like *Jonas*.

Where was I? My phone sat plugged in on the nightstand along with a water bottle, a sandwich, a thermal coffee cup, two pills, and a little tablet.

As well as a text from Jonas.

Jonas

We're at the cabin. Drink your water. Have your tea. Eat your sandwich. Take your meds and a shower. Find us when you're ready. No rush. I love you.

Yes, Mercy is okay and with your brothers.

What? The last thing I recalled was being at the gala and Freddie wanted to talk...

My hand flew to my shoulder. A big bandage covered both sides. Memories smacked me in the face. Some bitch tried to shoot Grif.

How did I get to their cabin? Also, I was *naked.*

I took the medicine, gulping the water. The tumbler had a still-warm chai latte in it. Huh.

The sibling group chat was full of sex jokes. I didn't have the headspace for that, though I checked in with Mercy. Grace's text caught my eye.

Grace

Glad they took you away to recuperate. Call me if you need me.

Made sense. But I still didn't recall going to the hospital, being discharged, or coming here.

Groaning, I made my way slowly to the bathroom. It was done in wood paneling and granite tiles, with a trough sink and recessed lighting.

Oh, that giant tub. It occupied one corner and looked out into a window. All I saw was darkness. The rest of the wall was a slate and granite rain shower with glass doors.

As much as I wanted to find someone and figure out what had happened, they were all probably sleeping. The bond I had with Grif felt quiet.

I'd take a hot bath and be careful not to get the bandage too wet. Then I'd track everyone down and figure out what happened.

Or at least find someone to snuggle with.

Or I could stay in the tub until someone found me. With how deep the tub was, I wasn't sure if I could get myself back out.

Not necessarily a bad thing.

While the bath filled, I munched on the sandwich. Someone had packed me a bag of clothes, which sat on the chair by the fireplace. It was mostly panties and their T-shirts. Sadly, no vibrator because I'd like the unicorn horn one right now.

No. The tentacle one. Definitely the tentacle.

I lit the candles in the bathroom and carefully got into the giant tub. As I lounged in the bubbles, I finished my latte. Oh, yeah, this was it.

Closing my eyes, I touched myself, bringing myself close to my peak.

"Sweet girl."

My eyes opened, though I didn't stop touching myself. "Hi."

Jonas leaned in the doorway, *completely naked.* Smirking, he came into the bathroom, then climbed in behind me, careful of my shoulder.

He reeked of sweat, sex, and omega perfume. Mmmm.

"Let me help you with that." His hand went between my legs.

"Yes please, Alpha Jonas." Sighing in pleasure, I leaned into him as he finished the job, making me gasp and moan.

"Am I in your room?" I leaned my head on his shoulder, satisfied. "I don't remember much past meeting Freddie on the patio at the gala."

"Short version, you got shot at the gala trying to protect Grif from Chet's wife. Now Grif *and* Dean are in heat. You don't remember me taking you from the hospital? Or having a whole lot of sleepy car sex with Dean in the back of the SUV on the way here?" Jonas continued playing with my pussy as he nuzzled my neck.

"I'm sorry I missed it. Both of them are in heat? Aren't they on suppressants?" Worry shot through me. Though I vaguely recalled being in a bed of blankets in the SUV, kissing Dean, and Jonas carrying me.

"Breakthrough heat. Dean's sleeping, so I thought I'd check on you. AJ and Grif got here first and took over the nest and won't let us in. Which is making Dean pouty. We're in his room for now." One hand worked my clit, while three fingers entered me and I moaned.

I moved my hips to get his hands in just the right... *ooh, right there.*

"Jonas." My chest shuddered as I came all over his hand.

Jonas kissed my temple. "That's my Sweet Girl."

"They're in heat? I... I don't know what to do." They were *both* in heat. While I'd seen some heat porn, it was always with female omegas. I had no idea what to expect.

Especially with *two* male omegas.

He chuckled. "You do *them*, Sweetheart. Lock them a lot, and it'll be fine. Start with Grif. He's your mate. When you need a break–if you can leave him–come in here. There's food and drinks in the mini-fridge. I have more pain pills for you, too. They won't make you as sleepy as what they gave you in the hospital."

This was a lot to take in. I'd been *shot.* I was in the hospital. Now Dean and Grif were in heat.

Desire and need shot through me. I grabbed Jonas' hard cock. He gasped. My leg felt okay, so turning to face him, I speared myself on it. Water splashing over the edge of the tub as I snagged his lips. Coming on his hand wasn't enough.

"You need my cock, Sweet Girl? You have no idea how much you're about to get. It'll be their dicks, but we'll make sure you get some alpha cum so you can heal faster. It's nice to have a moment with you." Jonas' eyes closed as his hands circled my waist as he helped me move up and down on his cock.

I sighed as it eased that ache I felt. Like alpha cum making you feel better, I didn't realize the healing properties worked on alpha females. *Good to know.*

Pleasure overwhelmed me as his moss scent intensified, wrapping around me like a sudden summer thunderstorm. The surrounding air grew heavy with our passion and electricity, as if lightning could sizzle through the bathroom at any time.

I explored his mouth, kissing him, feeling his tongue ring. My kisses traced his prickly jaw.

Leaning into his body, I tried to take him deeper, working up to another release. One hand cupped my ass as the other trailed up and down my back. His neck tasted of sweat as I nibbled his throat. Oh, that throat. Mmmm, that juncture at his neck and throat was so satisfying to taste.

A moan escaped my lips, even though I had a mouth full of his salty skin. My hands toyed with his nipples as I ground against him. My teeth ached. Want burst inside me. His moss scent flared with need.

Right there.

"You can bite me if you want, Sweet Girl." His husky voice broke through my reverie.

I looked at his neck, full of my bites, none of which actually broke the surface, but some were close. Shame shot through me, and I stilled on his cock.

I'd almost bit him without asking.

"Jonas, I... I'm so sorry." My head ducked in mortification, cheeks blazing.

Jonas cupped my face with his hands, tipping it back up. His eyes were full of love, not anger, as his thumb stroked my jaw. "Nothing to be sorry about. I'd love your bite. Also, Dean's going to demand it, I'm sure. He wanted to ask you to mark him the night of the gala."

"Oh. I..." I was so close to coming. Need overrode everything rational in my brain.

I want.

Leaning in, he kissed me, long and deep. "Claim us, Verity. Take us. Make us all yours. None of this changes your pretty island wedding with Grif. All the rest of us need is a place in your heart."

Take him.

Something primal rose in me. My inner alpha wanted to sink her teeth into the beautiful tattooed alpha under her, claiming him, making him *hers.*

"Mine." The word ripped from my lips, urgent and feral. My orgasm ripped through me and I locked his cock tight, squeezing it.

Mine.

My aching teeth sunk into his flesh, the metallic tang of blood filling my mouth.

Pain shot through my shoulder. Not the one that was bandaged, but the other. The warm, sweet pain made my pussy throb and pulse around the cock locked inside me as Jonas pulled my hair.

I licked the bite, my teeth marks red against his skin.

Pretty mark.

Oh, yes, my Jonas would look so lovely with my bite on his neck.

"There you are, Sweet Girl. Right there where you belong." Jonas licked the bite on my shoulder.

My chest felt heavy in a good way, like a magnetic force drew me to him. Something sparked in my heart, right next to Grif.

Love, pleasure, and devotion sluiced over me.

Jonas cuddled me to him. "I love you. We were so fucking scared when you got shot. You'll be okay. I'm fucking proud of you for barking at Derva, standing up for yourself, and protecting those you love. We all love you so fucking much."

"I love you, too." I laid my head on his shoulder. We stayed that way as the water cooled, the bubbles fading, curled together, just us.

Mine.

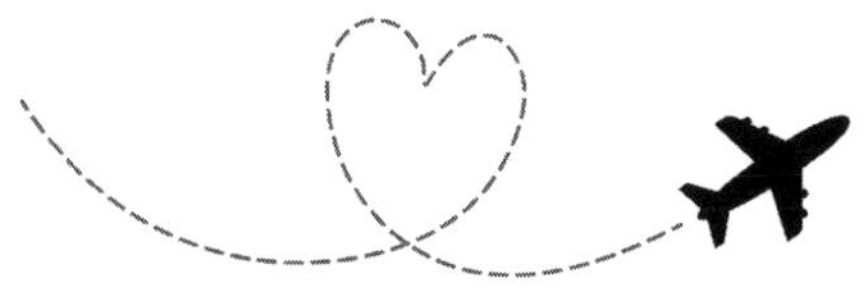

Chapter Forty-Nine

AJ

"More. More, Alpha, please. I need your knot so badly." Grif's whine cut through me.

"I'm going to knot you and fill you up," I crooned, sinking my knot into his slick and needy ass. One hand stroked his hard cock, with the other wrapped around his throat.

He always looked so beautiful wearing my hand as a necklace as he begged for my knot.

"Come for me." I took him hard and fast from behind, his hands and knees sinking into the pillows and blankets that littered the mostly enclosed nest.

Grif hadn't stopped begging for my knot–and Verity–since he'd awoken. I had no idea what time it was or how long had passed.

Or where I'd put my phone.

"Alpha." He came all over my hand as my cum filled his ass.

"I'm right here. You take me so good." I'd never seen him like this. At least this felt like what a normal heat should be. Not the awkward, shitty heats he'd been unfortunate enough to have in the past.

Locked into him, I turned our sweaty bodies onto our sides. I snuggled him into me. Under the sweat, he still seemed feverish. His scent tinged with need, his perfume, and *fuck me, alpha* pheromones filling the room.

If I had less self-control, I'd be in a rut by now. But Grif only had me, and someone had to keep their head.

"Have some water. That's it." I tried my best to get him to sip while not spilling it, then took a deep drink myself.

The sheets of the small nest were sweaty and tangled. The pack size mattress sat on an enclosed platform built into the wall of a room in the attic. Three walls surrounded it, only one of which had a window.

The sloped ceiling held a skylight. Outside the sky was still dark but starting to lighten. A waterfall of tiny lights separated us from the rest of the cozy attic room, which had a soft rug, a giant couch, an ottoman, a fireplace, mini-fridge, and a bathroom.

"Where's Dean?" he whined into one of the many pillows that littered the space. "I want Dean. Where's Verity? I want Verity." Grif's hand flew out, searching for her.

"They're probably sleeping." I couldn't believe Jonas just *took* her from the hospital like that.

Not that I expected him to leave her. That would be cruel. I'd hoped they'd stay in New York for at least a few days. I hadn't expected Dean to go into heat, too.

"I need her." Grif's keen cut right through me.

"You have me. You're okay," I soothed, stroking his sweaty hair.

A new scent entered the nest. A growl ripped from my throat at the threat.

He's mine.

"It's just me," Verity whispered.

"Kitten. Kitten." Grif struggled against my knot. He stilled, realizing we were locked and it would hurt to wriggle out of it.

"Boundaries, Verity," I grumbled. Shit. I must have forgotten to re-lock the door.

Her face appeared through the curtain of lights, as she partially intruded. "Grif, Tiger, may I please enter your nest?"

"Kitten. I need you so much." Grif reached out, making grabby hands.

Verity awkwardly climbed in. She was completely naked, hair up in a bun on top of her head, and she had a bag in her arms.

"I brought some stuff." She set a couple of things on the small shelf which had our water bottles, wipes, toys, and some snacks.

Then she dumped things *on the bed.* Items that smelled of the others in the pack.

Nesting materials.

I hadn't brought any of those. It had been enough to grab what I'd packed and order some food to be delivered to the cabin when I realized that the advice nurse had been right. We'd barely made it to the cabin.

Nothing like driving curvy back roads in the dark with an in-heat omega crying for your cock.

At least it hadn't been snowing.

There hadn't been time to wash sheets or anything, and I was glad we'd left everything clean with a sheet over the nest to keep out the dust.

"Verity," I growled. "We talked about this."

"Not about if he has a heat. It's different. You... you can be in charge. What happens here stays here. I'll never mention any of it. Please, *please,* don't keep me from him. I... I can feel him." Her voice broke as she turned and gave me a baleful look.

Aw, shit. Unlike the previous times Grif had gone into heat, he now was bonded–not just to me, but Dean and Verity.

I'd sort of forgotten that.

No wonder Dean got pissed when I wouldn't let him in the nest.

"Kitten. I'm right here." Grif's hands stroked her as she lay down facing him.

A big bandage covered her shoulder.

And a fucking *bite mark* marred her neck.

"Who bit you?" I snarled, jealousy overwhelming me.

Verity gave me a coy smile as she stroked Grif's sweaty hair. "Jealous?"

I growled again. This one deep and possessive, rumbling through the enclosed nest. Her driftwood scent took on the sweetness of arousal as her blue-green eyes blew out with desire.

"Oh, that's it," Grif groaned. Verity crawled down and took his cock in her mouth.

"You didn't answer me, Princess," I growled, yanking on her poofy bun like it was a joystick.

Her eyes met mine, but all she did was bob up and down on Grif's dick, her scent flaring with desire and need.

I didn't have the patience for this. If I wasn't still locked in Grif's ass, I'd knot the brat right out of her.

"Oh, Kitten, that feels so good," Grif finally sighed as she sucked him down like the good little cum dumpster she was.

She took his cock out of her mouth and kissed him, snuggling in to us. His contentment flowed through the bond.

Verity *was* his scent match. I suppose I could make an exception.

"Fine," I sighed. "You can stay. You're right, we never talked about his heat and it's different. If he wants you here, you can stay." I couldn't fight this. It might make things a little easier if there were two of us anyway.

"Stay, Kitten." Grif kissed her, then kissed me.

"It was Jonas who bit me. I lost control and tried to bond with him first. So I apologize in advance if I do anything awful. I... I..." She buried her face in Grif's neck instead of looking at me.

"Bonding us isn't awful, Princess. We know you love us. I hope you know that we love you right back." I cupped her face with my hand, trying to reassure her.

It's not that I didn't want her here. I just was wary of her seeing that side of him. The side usually only I saw, especially without having talked to him about it first when he could fully consent.

Not that I doubted he would.

"You love me, Cow Boy?" Her look was so earnest it twisted my heart.

"I do, Princess." I kissed her. "Also, I could very well take a bite of you before this is over. But I don't apologize if I end up knotting you." Preferably more than once.

My knot had loosened enough that it slid out of Grif's ass and it twitched at the thought of having her. Taking a wipe, I cleaned us up as Grif and Verity made out.

"Alpha, I need your lock." Grif pushed her onto her back and crawled on top of her.

"Careful of her shoulder," I warned as she winced.

"Take me, Tiger," she begged, spreading her legs.

I shoved a pillow under her, trying to keep the pressure off her shoulder.

As he fucked her, I slipped out to use the bathroom and re-lock the door. I'd let Dean in later, when I needed to grab some food.

When I returned to the nest, he was pounding her, joy on both their faces and in my bond with him.

"Alpha, knot me, please?" Grif begged.

"Do you need to be knotted *and* locked?" I growled into his neck. His ass was slick with need.

Getting on my knees, I straddled his legs and wrapped my arms around him, taking him with my cock, fast and hard. As I thrust in him, fucking him into her, I sucked on the bond mark I'd put on him.

"Alphas," Grif moaned as he took both of us. "Yes. Alphas."

"Grif," she screamed, body trembling.

"I need your knot, Alpha, please," Grif begged.

"Since you asked so nicely, my heart." I pulled out all the way, then thrust into him, pushing my knot past his muscles until I was fully inside him. My cum shot out, filling him.

He leaned his head back so he could look at me and sighed contentedly. "Alpha."

"I'm right here," I soothed. My arms tightened around him as I planted a kiss on his sweaty forehead.

Verity watched us, licking her lips suggestively.

"Like what you see, Princess?" I taunted. Always the center of our attention, she'd never seen us fuck each other.

"So much," she breathed.

Grif and I collapsed on top of her. I rolled us, careful of her shoulder. She snuggled into his chest. Her fingers caught mine and squeezed.

The three of us cuddled, my knot still locked in Grif. Verity alternated making out with Grif and licking the bond mark she'd left on him and hadn't been able to properly tend. I'd been tending to it for her.

It was only a matter of time before he begged for us again.

Her look grew coy as she kissed his other bond mark, the one I'd made on him, sending jolts of pleasure through me, her eyes never leaving mine.

"Princess," I warned.

Verity didn't stop, her pink tongue tracing it.

Grif sighed in pleasure. "Kitten, that feels so good. I want to fuck you again. I really like being between the two of you."

I twisted a little, my knot giving enough to withdraw from Grif.

"Princess, sit that ass on his cock now," I growled.

My dick dripped with my cum and Grif's slick. I grabbed the wipes and a bottle of lube.

Putting a bunch on my hand, I rubbed it all over that little ass that I itched to spank. *Later.* In this moment, I needed to knot her cunt, sink my teeth into her, and show her she was mine so I could go back to knotting Grif.

"Oh, come here, Kitten. I want to feel our alpha through you." Grif's hard cock dripped with slick and pre-cum. He turned and put some pillows behind his back, so he sat up against the wall of the nest.

I pressed the button on the ledge by the bed that closed the shade for the window, and then the one for the skylight, leaving us in darkness except for the fucking fairy lights and the gas fire.

"Take me, I'm yours." She slid herself on his cock, her back to his chest, his arms wrapping around her.

Those blue-green eyes stayed on me.

"You bet your ass you are," I growled, squirting lube on my cock and her pussy. My alpha rumbled to the surface.

I let out a growl. "Mine."

Both of them were mine.

"Mmmm, I like that." Grif nuzzled her neck as his hands toyed with her tits.

"I surrender, my king." Her voice went breathy as she squirmed on Grif's cock. She bared her neck to me, submitting, thighs spread to reveal her wet and glistening pussy.

"Good girl." Without warning, I plunged my cock into her. Her pussy fluttered around me deliciously, and I could feel Grif's cock through her walls.

Mine.

Another growl ripped from my throat as I conquered her mouth, punishing her with my kisses for letting someone besides Grif bite her before me.

I was her king. She was mine. I'd do anything for her.

"Oh, Kitten." Grif trembled, kissing her neck and playing with her breasts.

As I fucked her, I caressed the not-yet-healed bond mark on her inner thigh. It looked angry, but Grif hadn't tended it. I'd have him go down on her while I fucked him and give it some attention, so it healed.

Grif and I moved her between us as single-mindedness overtook me. I'd knot her and claim her.

She didn't fight me. No, she moaned and writhed in pleasure, neck still bared to me, eyes closed. Not that I'd mark her throat. My claim wasn't for the public to see.

Three of my fingers worked her pussy along with my dick to get her ready for my inflated knot.

The one time she'd taken a knot had been uncomfortable. Hopefully, this time would be better, especially with all the pheromones flying around.

"Grif," she cried, body shuddering with pleasure, as her walls fluttered around my cock again.

"Don't you dare lock me yet," I snarled, removing my fingers from her. Thrusting, I pushed my knot all the way inside her while I rubbed her clit. "MINE," I growled as she came again, my knot squeezing inside her as her pussy continued to milk me.

"Alpha," Grif groaned. "I feel that. Fuck." It was a half whine.

"Soon, Boo-Boo." My hand wrapped around her throat. "Who do you belong to, Princess?"

"Yours, I'm yours, my king," she moaned, as another orgasm wrecked her.

"Good. Now you can lock me," I told her, not just enjoying this, but getting Grif's pleasure through the bond.

"Alpha." Her eyes were completely blown out with desire, scent full of need. If she wasn't in rut yet, she would be soon.

Had she ever called me *Alpha* before?

I liked it. *A lot.*

Those muscles clamped around me and the breath whooshed out of me. I'd never been locked while I'd knotted someone before. Pleasure overloaded me.

"Alpha, Alpha, oh fuck." Grif trembled behind her, probably cuming in her ass.

Roaring in pleasure, my hand tightened around her throat as I took her breast in my mouth and clamped down on it hard.

Mine. My princess. To love, cherish, and pleasure for always.

My other hand wrapped around Grif's throat, my thumb caressing my bite mark on his throat.

Mine.

Both of them were fucking mine. They were part of me. I needed them like a fire needed oxygen.

Her blood filled my mouth. The bond between us ignited in my heart like gasoline on a flame. My princess lay right there in my soul, where she'd stay forever.

I'd absolutely make a life and some babies with her. Get that dog. Though I still wasn't walking it.

"Mine." I met her eyes with mine, as my grip on Grif's throat loosened, but not hers.

"Alpha. Fuck. I feel all of that." Grif's voice was rough and needy.

A cute little growl ripped from Verity's lips. "Mine."

Leaning forward, she pushed us backward to the bed, me still inside her, my hand around her throat.

Her teeth sank into my pec, marking me back.

"Yes, take me, Princess. Show everyone that I'm yours," I praised. My hand released her throat and wrapped around her bun, keeping her face in my pec. She needed to wear her hair like this more when we fucked.

"Alphas. That was intense." Grif sighed, covering the both of us with his body.

Verity rested her head on my chest. "I love you both so much."

“I love you, Boo-Boo.” Kissing his lips, I ran my thumb down his cheekbone. “You, too, Princess.” I kissed her, giving her bun a tweak.

They were both mine.

As their pleasure, their love, coursed through our bonds, I knew I was also theirs. Utterly. Totally. Completely.

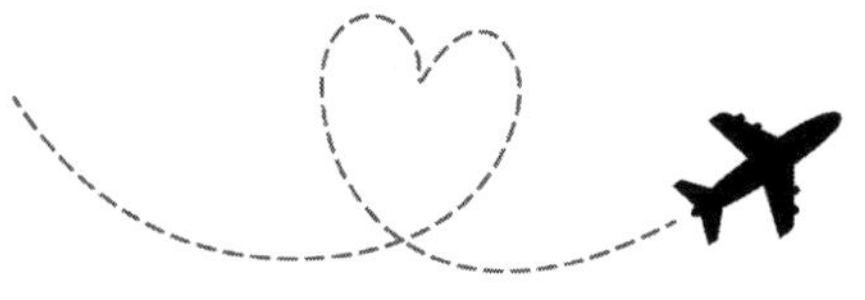

Chapter Fifty

Jonas

"I ... I want Grif," Dean whined again as I took him against the wall of the shower, warm water raining down on us.

"I know, soon, Love, soon," I soothed as I kissed him.

He'd been asking for Grif since the drive here–and had been nearly inconsolable when AJ wouldn't let us in the nest.

Ridiculous.

AJ had a hangup about not wanting anyone to see him with Grif. But Dean and Grif had never gone into heat at the same time before. They'd bonded, so it was to be expected. Also, Dean was used to Grif being with us the entirety of his heat.

"Knot, I need your knot. It hurts." Dean keened like I hadn't given him a half dozen knots since he'd woken up.

"I know, Love. Let me make it better." I thrust my knot all the way into his feverish body, and he sighed contentedly as I came inside him. Hopefully, this quelled the cramps for now.

Locked together, I soaped him down, body and hair, then did the best I could for myself. My knot deflated enough to slip out, and I rinsed us off. Helping him out of the shower, I wrapped a towel around him, peppering him with kisses.

"You're such a good omega," I told him, as we left the bathroom.

"I want my nest." He pouted at the bed in the center of the room.

I'd tried my best to drape sheets over the large, wooden four poster to help make it as cozy as I could with what we had.

Like the other rooms in the cabin Dean had inherited, it was simple, with wood floors, wood walls, a gas fireplace, and wooden furniture. It was cozy. Comfortable. Rustic.

But it wasn't the nest.

"I know. Drink this and try to eat your sandwich, then we'll find Verity." I shoved a sandwich from the mini-fridge in his hand, then stuffed one in my mouth.

"She's awake? Okay." Dean ate the sandwich in record time and drank most of the sports drink.

Verity had been fucking Grif and AJ for a while. I'd felt AJ bite her through our bond. The alarm on my phone went off.

Time's up.

I downed a sports drink, then grabbed a bag that had some sports drinks, hydrogels, and protein bars, along with the first aid kit.

"Do you want anything from here? Pillows? Blankets?" I shut off the fireplace and grabbed the other bag of nesting materials. I'd sent the first with Verity.

Dean grabbed a soft blanket from home and wrapped it around himself–then got three pillows. "Let's get Verity and bring her to my nest."

"She's in the nest with Grif, waiting for you." I opened the door, the cold air of the hallway greeting us. The cabin didn't have central heating. Since we were hardly ever here in winter, it had never mattered before.

The three bedrooms were on this floor. Grif and Dean usually shared this one. Below us was the kitchen, dining room, and living room. Above us, in the attic, was a small bunk room we never used–and the nest.

We marched up the stairs, and the door to the nest was closed–and locked. The key sat in the lock, just as I'd instructed Verity.

The warm air greeting me as I opened the door reeked of omega need, pheromones, and sex, making me rock-hard.

AJ growled. He and his control issues needed to get over it. This heat would be easier if we stayed together.

Darkness cloaked the room except for the fairy lights and gas fireplace.

"Grif, Verity." Dean ran to the nest, elations bursting through our bond.

On the otherside of the fairy light curtain, Grif ate Verity's pussy while AJ fucked him. Good times.

"I locked the door," AJ snarled as I approached the nest.

"There's a key. I gave you space. Time's up." If I really wanted to get in, the bunk room shared the nest bathroom.

Dean fed Verity his cock as Grif's hand tangled in his hair. Their moans filled the room.

"Dean and Grif are bonded. You can't keep them apart. Not having the nest is affecting Dean. Look how happy they are," I replied, still on the outside of the nest.

"Fine." AJ sighed, slipping out of Grif. "I'm done knotting him anyway, though he'll be asking again soon enough."

Well *yeah.* That's what omegas did during their heat.

"Grif, take this." I shoved a small dissolving tablet into his lips.

AJ frowned at me. "What's that?"

"He just got over a kidney infection. Don't need him to get another. Do you want one?" I'd taken one and given them to both Dean and Verity. Nothing was worse than a post-heat UTI.

"Thank you." He took one.

I put the package in the first aid kit and left that and the bag of nesting materials on the ottoman, but brought in the snacks and drinks, stashing them in the small cabinet for that purpose.

"Look, I get it," I told AJ. "I know you're protective of him, but there's no way we can do this without being all together."

AJ sighed again. "I know."

Grif sat on top of Verity and Dean looked upset.

"I want her pussy." Dean's lower lip quivered.

"Have you and Grif had her together? Sweet Girl, do you want both of them inside your pussy at the same time?" I grabbed the lube.

Verity's hair had half come out of her bun as she lay on the bed. "Yes, *please.* Come here, Hot Stuff. We haven't tried this yet."

"Oooh." Dean crowded Grif.

I squirted some lube on our little alpha and helped Dean get situated with minimal shoving and quite a bit of kissing.

AJ left the nest as Grif and Dean got into a rhythm, the two of them sharing her pussy. I stroked my cock, taking it all in.

"That feels so good," Verity moaned. "You two make me feel so full, and I'm going to lock you both because you're so amazing and perfect."

"Take my cock, Sweet Girl. Get me all nice and hard for when your omega needs to be fucked." I lowered it into her mouth, and she sucked on it. "Anyone can come whenever they want, as much as they need to, when we're here in the nest. No need to ask."

Just in case anyone needed that reassurance.

"Alpha, I want your knot," Dean whined as he fucked Verity.

"I'm right here." I planted a kiss on Verity's cheek as I withdrew my cock from her sweet lips. "Thank you for warming me up."

As I got behind Dean, I kissed his spine. "I'm going to knot you so good while you have our girl."

I reached out and squeezed Verity's hand as I entered Dean. Pleasure overwhelmed the bond. Putting my hands on his hips, I took my sweet omega, kissing our bond mark. He was my love. My heart.

And her…

She filled a part of me I didn't even know was missing.

"Alpha, Alpha, I want your knot," Grif called.

AJ came running. "I'm right here, Boo-Boo."

"Alpha, oh, fuck, fuck, fuck, fuck," Dean cried.

"Kitten," Grif gasped as he leaned over and kissed Dean, AJ seating himself in him.

I felt that. Well, I guess she *could* lock two cocks at once.

"Knot me, Alpha." Dean broke off his kiss with Grif, then kissed me like he was going to swallow my soul.

"Always." Kissing him back with the same intensity, I gave him my knot.

His scent intensified, taking on a tone that was almost cloying. Yep, that's what he needed to fully go into heat. His nest, Verity, and Grif.

What we'd seen had been nothing. It was a good thing we were now all together.

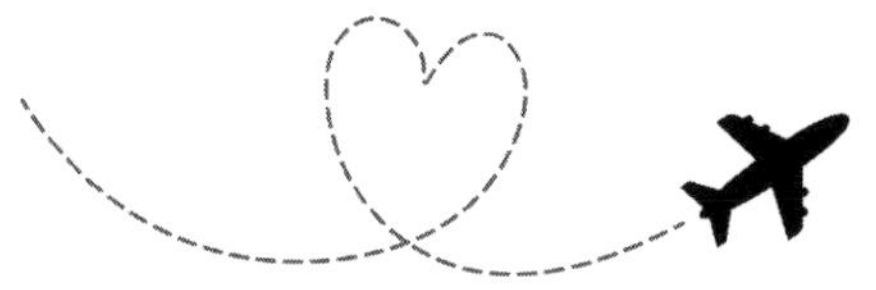

Chapter Fifty-One

Dean

"It's still not right." I frowned at my nest as I repositioned a blanket. While I was in the shower with Grif and Jonas, *someone* had changed the sheets.

Now everything was wrong.

Wrong, I tell you.

Next to me, Grif repositioned a few things, looking proud of himself, as he sat back on his heels, completely naked. "Much better."

"Yes. But it still needs something." Closing my eyes, I sniffed. Did it at least smell right?

No, it didn't.

Grif put an arm around me. "What about the other bag?"

"Other bag?" I opened my eyes and looked around the nest. Pillows. Waters. Lube. Snacks.

"It's over here, Hot Stuff, by the ottoman," Verity said from outside the nest. "Ow."

Ow? Who hurt my little alpha?

I climbed out of the nest. A bag of things sat by the giant ottoman. Things that smelled like pack. Like love.

"Ow." She whimpered again. Verity laid on the couch as Jonas did something to her shoulder.

"Sorry, Sweet Girl. You tore your stitches and I have to clean it and seal it up." Jonas dabbed her shoulder with something–the first aid kit at his side.

I came over and kissed her.

"Hi, Dean." She smiled at me and it warmed my heart.

Bag in hand, I returned to the nest. Dumping the bag out, we got the nest sorted, getting everything perfect.

Almost.

Something beeped. Again. It kept going off and was fucking annoying. I snarled and got out of the nest, looking for the offending beep.

Jonas picked up his phone, and the awful noise stopped. He helped Verity sit up as he handed her a water bottle and some pills.

"That was rough. Why don't I carry you down to my bedroom so you can rest for a bit?" He stroked her hair as she swallowed the pills.

"Stay." My cock twitched. I had something she could swallow. Oh, I did like her lips around my cock. The only problem was that she couldn't tell me what a good omega I was when her mouth was full.

"I'll stay." Her hand reached out. I took it and she squeezed it.

Going back to the nest, I rearranged things again. My little alpha needed a nice place to rest and I piled up pillows for her comfort.

Grif gave me the side-eye at my remodeling. "I just finished that."

I nodded toward the couch as I re-positioned another pillow. "It's for her, so she can be comfortable."

"Oh, okay." He slipped out of the nest.

Closing my eyes, I took a deep sniff. Almost right. Then the scent of driftwood and love, mixed with Grif's rainy scent, tickled my nose.

When I opened my eyes, I saw Grif tucking her into the nest. Yes. That's exactly what we needed. I helped him get her all nice and cozy.

"How's that?" Grif beamed.

"Perfect." She pulled him to her for a kiss. "You, too." Verity grabbed my head and kissed me. "Thank you both for tucking me into your beautiful nest."

Mmmm, this was nice. I snuggled into her, grabbing Grif's hand so he was close. Closing my eyes, I drifted off, safe, warm, and satisfied.

Cramps shot through me, waking me. A whine slipped from my lips. *So hot.*

"What do you need, Hot Stuff?" Verity whispered, stroking my hair. "You're all feverish. Want to ride me?"

Fuck yeah.

Throwing off the blankets, I straddled my little alpha. I sighed happily as I sank into her softness, my hands cupping her lovely boobies.

Mine. My alpha was mine. Her boobies were mine.

My lips smashed to hers. Her lips were mine.

I rode her, moving up and down on her, pleasure filling me. Mine. Mine. All mine.

"Such a good omega. So, so good." Her mouth roamed my body as she moaned.

Ooh, right there. I liked it when she nibbled on me, leaving beautiful marks, showing everyone that I was hers.

Another mouth trailed over my skin as want flared inside me. Grif's hands cupped my hips as he drove himself inside me.

Yes.

"Gumdrop," I groaned as he squashed me between him and Verity as he thrust into me. Yes, I felt so loved and treasured when they made me into a Dean sandwich.

"Oh, yes, fuck him into me," Verity sighed, her scent smothering me with alpha goodness. "Mine."

She kissed him over my shoulder as I matched Grif's rhythm.

Something was missing. I whined.

"Need me, Love?" Jonas kissed my face, his hand stroking me. "Mmmm, my good omega needs more cock? He's in between his little alpha and his husband, but it's not enough, is it?"

"Alpha, please," I keened. I needed it all. My body burned for it.

Jonas fed me his pierced cock, and I hummed around it, sucking contentedly as Grif continued to pound me into Verity. All their scents swirled around me, AJ's scent joined us, and Grif moaned.

Mmmm, all of us together. My omega heart danced with happiness as pleasure pulsed through me.

"I'm going to come, suck it all down, like the perfect omega you are," Jonas told me, his hands in my hair.

Greedily, I drank his hot cum.

"You two look so beautiful, taking us so good," AJ crooned.

"So pretty," Verity agreed as she continued to suck my neck hard.

There, right there. Her intense alpha scent melted me.

"Alpha, more," I whined. I wanted her to consume me fully.

Jonas cupped my face. "Do you want me again?"

Yes. But that wasn't what I sought. My head felt muzzy, and it got difficult to vocalize what I desired.

"Need." I leaned into Verity's lips as she and Grif brought me closer and closer to my release. "Bite. Alpha. Please."

"Mine," Verity growled, and her teeth sunk into me as her lock clamped down on my cock.

"Harder, mark him up good," Jonas told her, his hands still in my hair.

Pleasure ricocheted through me as she punctured my flesh, overwhelming me. My head lolled back as I practically blacked out in sheer sensation. "ALPHA."

My heart warmed, and my soul grew bigger, making space for my little alpha, right next to my alpha and my husband.

Warmth spurted all over my ass, and a body slumped over me, pressing me even more into my sweet little alpha. Verity lapped at my neck, making sheer bliss shoot through me.

I was hers.

Now I needed to make her mine. My body pressed to hers, sandwiched between her and Grif. But her boobie was right there.

No, not the one someone else bit. The other one.

Wiggling into position, I clamped my mouth around it and took a big bite, sinking my teeth into it. *My boobie.* I felt the bond grow and strengthen as love and pleasure pelted me.

Verity hummed as she stroked my face. "I feel you."

Giving me a kiss, those breasts rumbled with her purr, coating me in a warmth that no blanket could ever give.

"Knot," I hummed. That's what I needed to finish the circle of pleasure.

"Well, if that's what you want, Grif's going to have to move a little," Jonas chuckled, pulling me by the leg a bit.

Verity stopped purring and snarled. "Mine."

"Not taking him, just moving him." Jonas gave her a kiss. "You marked him so good." His hands caressed my ass. "Now I'm going to knot this good omega."

"Please," I whined, feeling so cozy and trapped between him, Grif, and Verity. She had me locked tight as her purr curled around me.

"Good omega," she whispered. "Both of you are so good."

Grif nuzzled into me, kissing my back.

Jonas sunk into me and started to thrust. Yes, that was it. I hummed in pleasure, feeling all three of them.

Now, I was complete.

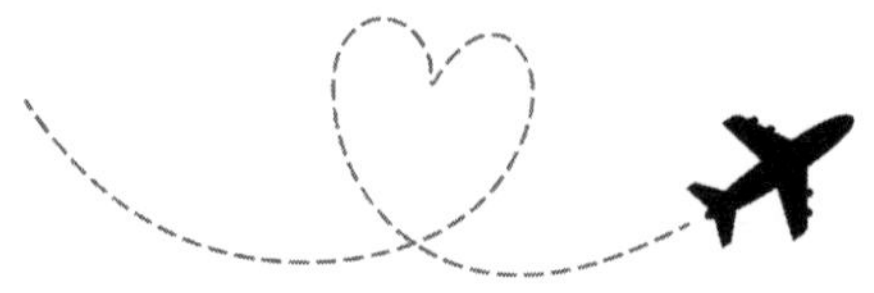

Chapter Fifty-Two

GRIF

"That feels good, Tiger," Verity moaned as I teased her pussy with my tongue. Pulling her thighs apart further, I attempted to see how many ways I could make her squeak.

"*Grif,*" AJ's voice firmed.

I ignored him. Eating Verity out was much nicer than whatever else he wanted me to swallow.

"Grif." AJ grabbed my chin and tried to push a packet of something to my lips. "One hydrogel, then you can have all the pussy you want."

Snarling, I took a taste. Nope. Not as good as pussy.

"All of it," he grumbled.

Taking the packet, I squeezed some of it on her pussy.

"What?" Verity tried to sit up.

Putting my hand on her chest, I pushed her back down into the nest and took a lick. Not bad. I lapped up all the sweet blue gel, then squeezed the rest of it onto her.

"Oooh, I want to play," Dean grabbed different colors and poured them on Verity's naked chest, then swirled them so she looked like a finger painting.

Pretty. I focused on licking up all the gel–and the inside of her thigh where my bite mark was.

"Oh, don't stop. Please, don't stop," Verity moaned.

"I've got you, Princess." AJ joined me as he started playing with her pussy, as I licked the bite mark again.

"Oooh, that's it," she sighed.

Dean's motions caught my eye as he licked the gel off her, adding other colors to make her into edible art.

How fun. Moving to the other side of her legs, I leaned over and swirled the gel around her nipple with my tongue and took it into my mouth and sucked hard.

Verity gasped. "Don't stop, don't stop."

"Huh. I should have thought of this sooner. Mmmm, how does this green taste on you?" Jonas squirted a packet of green on her belly and licked it. "Delicious."

I took a long lick of the green on her belly. Eh, I preferred the swirl of red and purple on her breasts. Returning to them, Verity continued to moan and make cute squeaks.

"Hand me one?" AJ held out his hand.

Out of the corner of my eye, I saw Jonas pass him a packet.

"AJ!" Verity shrieked, her scent going sweet and heavy as she trembled under my touch.

Languidly, I continued to lick and suck all the pretty colors off one breast, as Dean did the same to the other. Jonas trailed his pierced tongue across her stomach. Mmmm, refreshing.

"Look at you. You licked her clean. Great job. Boo-Boo, why don't you have Verity?" AJ told me as he gathered up all the empty hydrogel packets.

Dean pouted. "What about me?"

I grabbed a hydrogel packet and squeezed it onto his dick. "I'm still thirsty."

Lowering myself into Verity's pussy, I pulled Dean toward me. As I thrust into Verity, I took my sweet husband into my mouth, feeling them through the bonds as I pleasured them both.

"That feels so good, Gumdrop," Dean moaned, running one hand down Verity's body, the other in my hair.

"Mmm, Grif you suck our omega's cock so good," Verity hummed, stroking my back as I fucked her.

"Oh, you do," AJ murmured, kissing my neck. His kisses trailed down my side

Jonas leaned in and teased Verity's breast with his tongue, one hand on Dean. "So beautiful."

"Alpha," I gasped, needing to feel complete.

"Right here, Boo-Boo. I'll knot you and Verity will lock you so good," AJ said, snagging a kiss from Verity as he got the lube.

"Mmmm, I want more." Verity grabbed AJ's hair and pulled him in for a rough kiss.

Jonas moved so he could tongue her clit as I contined to fuck her and I stroked his back.

"That's fucking sexy," Dean sighed, tracing designs on Verity's breast with his finger around the mark he'd left.

AJ moved behind me and squirted lube on my ass, even though I could feel it slicking.

"Yes, I need you, Alpha," I sighed, going back to sucking Dean's cock.

Dean whined. "I'm going to come."

"Me, too," Verity gasped, as Jonas' tongue ring grazed her clit again.

"Come, both of you," Jonas said, giving Verity's slit a long lick.

AJ's hard length slid into my slick ass as Dean's hot cum shot into my mouth. I sucked his sweetness down as Verity's pussy fluttered around my cock.

Verity moaned as those flutters became strangles.

"Lock me, good, Kitten," I gasped as her muscles clamped down on me, making me cum. AJ's hands were on my hips as he thrust in and out of me and I groaned.

Dean leaned over and kissed Verity, as Jonas got behind him and speared his ass.

"Knot me, Alpha," I cried, needing to be knotted and locked at the same time.

"Always." AJ thrust his knot inside me.

Sighing with relief and rightness I collapsed on top of Verity. Her arms tighten around AJ and me, as he laid with us.

"Feel better?" AJ asked me.

"So much." Sleep pressed down on me.

"That's my good omega," Jonas whispered to Dean as they curled up next to us.

Verity kissed my temple and stroked my hair.

Cozy with my pack, safe between my alphas, I dozed off, spent.

When my eyes opened, Dean and Jonas were fucking while Verity watched, one hand on her pussy, the other on her breast. AJ slept in the corner in an awkward position.

Mmmm, I could stand to fuck my little alpha right now.

"Hi." I crawled over and nuzzled her. "I want you, Alpha."

She kissed me, pouncing, attempting to get me on my back, nearly kicking Dean in the process. Her hands grabbed my wrists and our noses touched as she grinned and gave a cute growl. "Mine."

"Mine." Rocking my body, I turned us over so she was now on her back, careful of her shoulder.

She tried to escape from under me, wriggling that cute ass. Verity slid out of the nest, giggling.

"I'm going to catch you, Kitten." I rolled out of the nest and grabbed her by the waist before she'd even made it a step.

Smacking her ass, I picked her up and pinned her to the ottoman in front of the fireplace so that she lay on her stomach. "You're mine."

I peppered that beautiful back with kisses as I played with her pussy, keeping her pinned.

AJ crawled out of the nest and kissed me. "You feel cooler. This might be the last round." He kissed Verity. "You need a shower."

"Mine." I'd caught her fair and square. Spreading her legs, I thrust into her, one hand around her throat, claiming her in front of AJ, daring him to try to take me from her.

"Most definitely," Verity sighed happily, her driftwood filling the room.

"Open wide." AJ stood in front of her, his back to the fire, and fed her his erect dick.

She took it greedily. Verity squirmed and I smacked her ass again.

This felt nice, but I wanted more. But I didn't want to be knotted. No, I wanted to feel AJ in a different way.

"Alpha." I held out my hand to AJ.

"You do that so good, Princess." AJ withdrew his dick from her mouth and gave her a kiss. "You need my cock, Boo-Boo?"

I shook my head and pulled him to me. "Fuck her with me."

"Gladly, though, I don't think I can knot her with you in there, too. We know she can lock two of us. So yes, let's have our girl. We don't want her to feel like she hasn't gotten enough cock." AJ stroked her back. "We do love you, Princess. We love you so fucking much and you're doing so so good."

No. I didn't want her to feel like that at all.

I slowed my thrusts. She mewed in protest.

"Patience." I smacked her ass again.

AJ got beside me. One arm wrapped around my waist as he slid his hard cock into her, right next to mine.

His fully inflated knot pushed against me delightfully.

Oh yes, that's it. I'd been wondering what this would feel like with AJ since I'd shared her pussy with Dean. Perfection.

"Oh, I feel so full," Verity mumbled.

"What about now?" AJ worked her ass with his fingers as we fucked her.

"Yes, yes, *yes*," she cried as her body shuddered under us.

The friction of his cock against mine, his knot brushing against me, drove me to the brink.

"AJ, Kitten," I gasped.

"I want some." Dean joined us, crowding us, as he worked his dick into her ass.

"I...I..." Verity shrieked in pleasure and her body bucked under us as Dean filled her ass.

"Fuck," I shouted. Her pussy squeezed and milked me as she grew even tighter, with Dean's cock inside her.

"Jonas, if Dean doesn't need your cock, give it to Verity," AJ directed as we continued to pound her pussy. "Lock us when you're ready, Princess."

"Look how pretty you are with the three of them fucking you. Are you up for my cock, Sweet Girl?" Jonas cupped her face, drawing his thumb down her cheekbone.

She nodded, and he lowered it into her mouth, wrapping his hands in her hair.

Jonas looked over at us. "Be careful of her shoulder."

"I'm going to come." Dean pulled out of her ass, then thrust back into her hard.

Verity cried out, locking us tight, squeezing my cock so hard it might be crushed. *What a way to go.*

"That's it," I moaned as I came inside her.

"Fucking shit." AJ gasped. "Fuuuck."

"Mmmm, I love being inside you," Dean sighed as he stroked her back.

"Swallow me down, Little Alpha." Jonas caressed her hair. "Are you doing okay?"

"Yes," she mumbled, mouth full of Jonas' pierced cock.

Locked into her with AJ, I slumped over her, using her back as a pillow and wrapping an arm around her. AJ did the same.

"Ahh, that was just what I needed," I muttered.

Dean curled up behind me, putting his sweaty face on *my* back. "Mmmm, I liked that."

"Me, too," I told him. Yes, I liked us all together like this.

"That was intense." AJ looked at me, and stroked my cheek. "Are you okay, Boo-Boo?"

"I'm great." Even though I was kneeling on the fluffy rug on the floor, flopped over Verity on the ottoman, I was comfortable–and happy. So happy.

Jonas withdrew his cock from Verity's mouth and gave her a kiss. "Are you alright, Sweet Girl?"

"Mmm, that was delightful," she sighed.

"Dean, do you want to go back to the nest?" Jonas held out his hand.

"I'm okay right here." Dean made a happy noise.

Yes, I felt so cozy here with my pack. *My pack. My mates.* That happiness bubbled up inside me, rumbling through my chest.

"Gumdrop, are you purring?" Dean breathed, kissing my back.

What? I didn't purr. I never had. But that contentment continued to pour out of me.

"Yes, yes, he is." AJ kissed me.

"That makes me happy." Dean purred as he kissed my neck.

"Me, too." Verity's back vibrated. Jonas and AJ joined in, and everyone's purrs blended together in a glorious symphony. My eyes grew heavy from the warmth and being satiated, and I allowed my happiness, my contentment, to lull me to sleep right there on the ottoman by the fire.

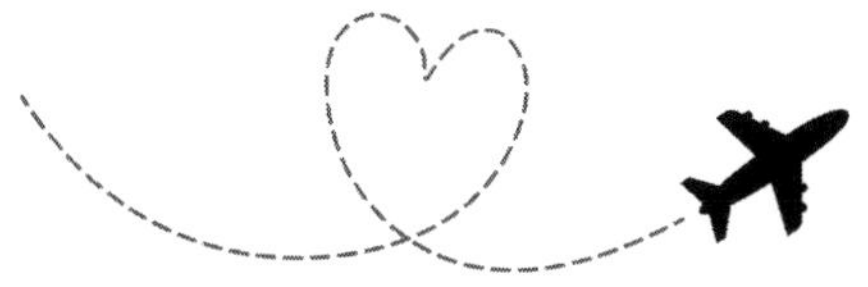

Chapter Fifty-Three

Verity

In the dim nest, the air had grown stuffy and warm, almost oppressively so, reeking of sex. My skin itched, and every bit of me hurt from scalp to toes. I tried to roll out from under the arm over me so I could use the bathroom before my bladder exploded.

As soon as I moved, the arm tightened around me. Ugh. I rolled another way. It tightened again. Ugh.

Reaching for a pillow, I stuffed it under the arm so I could escape. The idea of actually leaving the nest and making it all the way to the bathroom seemed daunting.

The need to pee was greater.

Like it was an obstacle course, I scooted past the bodies, untangled myself from the blankets, and rolled over the pillows.

The lights separating the nest from the room were in sight, and I tried to slip off the edge of the platform. My legs buckled, and I landed on the floor with a soft thump.

A head appeared through the curtain of fairy lights along with a hand.

"Up?" Dean asked, concern on his face.

"I'm trying to get to the bathroom." I shook my head. While part of me wanted to be embarrassed, I was just too tired. All of me hurt.

"Okay." He crawled out of the nest, scooped me up, and carried me to the bathroom, nose wrinkling a bit.

My skin was crusty and I reeked.

Before I could protest that I could use the bathroom by myself, Dean turned the shower on and carefully deposited me under the warm spray, giving me a kiss.

He disappeared further into the bathroom.

It was gray outside, not giving much light. I wasn't sure if it was early in the morning or if the sun was hiding. The only other light was a string of lights that went all the way around the bathroom ceiling.

The shower was large enough that we could all fit in it, and granite, with built-in seating. Water flowed from six wall jets, two overhead ones, and a handheld sprayer. Several bottles lined the small ledge.

The idea of getting out was too much. Welp, it wouldn't be the first time I'd peed in the shower.

Standing was a chore, and the bench didn't get enough spray. So after, I slumped down onto the floor, right under the overhead rain shower, letting the warm water soothe my itchy skin and tired muscles.

Ahh, that's the stuff. It might be a problem for my bandaged shoulder but that was for future me to deal with.

Getting up *off* the shower floor was also a problem for future me.

Dean reappeared and offered me a toothbrush with toothpaste. I wasn't sure whose it was. Did it matter, given how many dicks I'd had in my mouth the past few days?

"Thanks." I gratefully took the toothbrush as he disappeared again. Yes, I was on the way to feeling *much* better.

He reappeared and took the toothbrush from me, and left.

I should soap myself down. I stretched a bit. *Ow.* Yeah, standing to get the soap was a no-go.

Having sex for days after being taken from the hospital after being shot would probably do that.

Though I appreciated that they'd brought me and not left me alone in the hospital.

Everything was a hazy mess of lips and limbs, of moans and kisses. But I remembered being dicked down repeatedly, mostly by Dean and Grif.

Maybe it was over now? I could use a nap.

Not to mention I should make sure Mercy was okay. See how many days had passed. Hopefully, someone had covered my classes.

One thing I recalled about our hazy fuck-fest was that I'd bonded with Dean, Jonas, and AJ. The entire pack was now mine. I hummed happily as I felt them right there in my heart.

Dean came back in, handed me two over-the-counter pain relievers, and left again. I swallowed them, using the water from the shower.

A moment later, he climbed into the shower with me, hanging up a towel on a hook. He took a bottle off the shelf and sat down with me under the spray.

He wrapped his arms around me and pulled me close. Something about that simple act, that caring touch, made me melt, and I let him hold me under the warm water.

"Oh. Whoops." Dean gingerly peeled the bandages off my shoulder.

Jonas had tended to it several times. He'd set his phone alarm to remind him to give me pain medicine. Though I couldn't remember when that last was. Honestly, even though I ached and parts of me throbbed, it wasn't that bad, all things considered.

Gently, Dean washed me, cleaning my shoulder and the rest of me with the three-in-one man wash–including my hair. Taking the handheld sprayer, he rinsed me off and kissed me.

"If you sit in front of me, I'll wash you," I offered.

Dean scrambled over me and sat between my legs. He hummed with pleasure as I worked the soap over his body and tried to get the cum out of his hair. Using the sprayer, I rinsed him off.

"Much better." I kissed his jaw, which was full of stubble. My kisses moved down his neck and I licked the bite mark I'd left, tending to it. He made a happy noise.

Dean stood and got out, drying himself off with the towel, then putting it on the floor like a rug. He turned off the shower and scooped me up.

He carried me to the giant bathtub, which was nearly full, and put me in. The water was hot, blue-green, and deliciously scented with mint and lavender. He turned off the tap, then pressed a button, starting the water jets, then got in behind me.

"Thank you, this is nice." I leaned into him, using his chest as a pillow.

"If I hurt, you absolutely ache." He looked worn out.

"I don't remember much," I confessed, savoring the closeness of Dean and the warmth of the bath.

"Me neither. It felt more intense than usual." His arms wrapped around me.

"I bonded with you. I hope that's okay." Anxiety twisted in my belly.

He snagged my lips with his and I got love through the bond. "Beyond okay. Is the water too hot?"

"It's perfect. I love the way it smells." I nuzzled into him. His chest made a nice pillow.

"I put multiple bath bombs in. I brought the cream. Maybe later I can make sure it gets in all the right places?" he offered.

"Mmmm, that sounds wonderful." Okay, I didn't want *anything* in my pussy or ass for a bit, but I loved the idea of that soothing cream being rubbed all over me.

Grif walked in and used the toilet, not noticing us. He washed his hands and brushed his teeth, possibly with the same toothbrush I'd used.

"Hey, Tiger." I gave him a little wave.

"Kitten. Jellybean." Grif gave us each a kiss. He went to join us in the tub.

Dean put a hand on his chest, stopping him, nose wrinkling. "Please rinse off."

"Okay." Grif disappeared into the shower and turned the water on.

A moment later, the water turned off. He got out and climbed into the tub with us.

"Ooh, that's hot," he hissed, seating himself behind Dean, water sloshing over the side of the tub.

"Is everyone okay?" I asked. Grif's arms wrapped around Dean and me as we laid there snugly in the tub.

"I'm wiped out. But I don't remember it being horrible like last time, thank fuck. It seemed like a big orgy," Grif admitted.

Dean chuckled. "Gumdrop, heats are a big orgy. I liked that we were all together."

"That was nice. Thanks for sharing your nest with me." Grif leaned in and kissed Dean.

"Always." Dean kissed him back.

Jonas came in. "Hey, you three."

"Hey, sexy no-pants." I gazed up at him. He looked exhausted.

"Anyone up for food?" he offered, giving Dean and me each a kiss on the forehead.

"Please," Dean sighed. "I need a matcha latte."

"Coffee and bacon," Grif added.

"How many days have passed? Are we going back today?" The idea daunted me, given how tired I was, but we all had responsibilities.

"We've been here five days." Jonas reached out and stroked Dean's hair.

"Shit, my heats never last that long." Dean leaned into his touch.

"It snowed a lot. Some roads are fucked, and won't be dug out until at least tomorrow," Jonas told us. "That's not a bad thing. We need to make sure your heats are actually over. While we can't stay too much longer, we could all use a rest after that."

"I... I think I'm done?" Grif shrugged. "But yeah, Dean usually spikes right when we think it's over."

Dean kissed me. "Firstsies."

My pussy protested, but if he had a spike, it wasn't like I could deny him.

"I...I can't believe I went into heat." Grif twisted a little. "I'm so sorry. I'll go back on the other suppressants."

"It's not the suppressants. It's you watching your mate get shot. This is all perfectly normal, Grif." Jonas shrugged, reaching out to stroke Grif's hair.

"Yeah, but..." Grif grimaced, and anxiety shot through the bond. I squeezed his hand.

"I didn't tell anyone you went into heat. All I said was that you had a fever, Dean got whatever you did, and I'd taken everyone, including Verity, to our cabin to recuperate," Jonas reassured.

Relief coated Grif's face. "Thank you."

"Oh, I told Rusty so she could help watch after Mercy. Sorry," Dean admitted.

"It's okay. If anyone cares, we'll tell them the fever turned out to be heat. Which is not a lie." Jonas turned to Grif. "You still should go to the doctor or the Center clinic or something and get checked out. Verity, you're going to need a follow-up. I had to fix your stitches twice. It's probably going to scar."

"I don't really care. Thanks for that." If one of my modeling clients did, well, that's what makeup was for.

"Anytime, but don't get shot again." He said with a stern look on his face. "I'm going to hop in the shower downstairs. Then I'll make food. Come down when you're ready. Take your time. Maybe we should fill up the hot tub on the porch tonight. Light the fire pit and roast marshmallows." Jonas gave us each a kiss and left.

"Hot tub? Fire pit? It's snowing." I made a face. Though if we were in the hot tub and roasting marshmallows, that could be nice?

Grif kissed me. "Your Southern is showing. Also, Jonas is Canadian."

"I should get out and make sure Mercy is okay." I didn't want to. It was so nice and cozy here with them.

"She can wait a little longer, relax with us," Grif insisted.

"Okay." I rested my head back on Dean's chest and enjoyed the moment with the two of them. Everything was fine.

Chapter Fifty-Four

Verity

Sitting on Jonas' bed, I scrolled through my phone. My belly sank. Everything was not fine. At least, I didn't think so, judging from all of the *don't worry,* and *I have things under control* texts I'd gotten from Hale and Dare.

Mercy wasn't picking up because her location showed that she was at practice.

"What's wrong?" AJ came barreling in and launched himself on the bed, wrapping his arms around me.

"I think something happened." I winced as I re-read the texts. "Shit. I'm such a terrible sister."

"No, you're the best sister. I'm sure everything is fine," AJ assured, giving me a squeeze.

"Who knows? Mercy was left in the care of Dare and Hale. I'll have to wait until after practice, I guess." I winced. Dare could be quite responsible and punctual.

Hale, on the other hand...

"If she's at practice, she didn't break anything too vital," he told me. "Odds are they wrecked something."

"If he smashed my car, I won't be happy," I grumbled, imagining what chaos could ensue with Hale in charge.

"Jonas will wreck *him* if he does that." He tweaked my bun. "I love it when you wear your hair like this."

"My hair needs to be properly washed and deep conditioned," I replied. Three-in-one man wash didn't cut it on my hair, but it was sweet of Dean to clean me. "I... I'm sorry I burst into the nest. I could feel him so much, and my instincts got the better of me–"

AJ kissed me. "It's okay, Princess. Heats are different circumstances. I didn't consider that you and Dean would feel him. And, well, the soulmate thing. Thank you for literally protecting Grif with your body. I'm sorry I left your side at the hospital, but Jonas and Dean had it, and Grif needed me."

"That's what you should've done." I rested my head on his shoulder. "I don't remember much. Everything happened so fast. At least Winnie will pay for it." Though the police still wanted to talk to me.

I felt bad for Chet and Winnie's kids, though. Maybe they could go live with Mrs. Coach? I remembered her being nice.

How had I missed that Derva was my old coach's daughter? Or that Chet was married to Derva's sister?

Also, Derva was in trouble for ruining my research. It was *Derva.* Shit. I could sort of understand where her hate came from. Still, it was a shitty thing to do even if she was trying to ruin my career the way I'd ruined her dad's.

Freddie was, of course, somehow innocent of everything, and using the publicity to leverage his way to a new team and agent. Even though he should be implicated in luring me out on the patio.

Whatever. As long as he left me alone.

"I'll make food soon. Jonas has the hot tub firing up so we can all enjoy it outside in February. But he put a giant bucket of muscle soak in there, so it should feel pretty good," he told me. "Also, Dean was feeling a little frisky, so he's with Grif and Jonas."

"Mmmm hmm, I can feel that." I had zero interest in that at this moment. Though I had let Dean fuck me medicinally earlier.

AJ kissed my temple. "Do you need anything?"

"Cuddles? Maybe we can put on a game for a bit?" I offered, just wanting to exist with someone for a moment. I could feel the bond pulse between us, between all of us.

"That sounds good. I think we have popcorn and hot chocolate." He stood and offered me a hand.

We went down the wooden staircase, every step making me ache, and I leaned on the banister because I had no idea where my crutch was.

"So that's where my shirt went." AJ looked me up and down. I was wearing one of his button-downs, some leggings, and fuzzy socks.

"Someone packed it for me." I shrugged as we entered the living room.

Though I'd stolen it a while ago.

The cabin was cute and rustic, if a little dusty, like something out of a *snowed-in* romance novel. The furnishings were simple—giant sectional, with a TV and coffee table. A farm-style table. A farm kitchen with wood cabinets, granite countertops, and a hanging pot rack over the stove. Adorable. The gas fire flickered in the living room, providing heat.

AJ got down the popcorn. "Um, I hope it's okay that you bonded with me."

"I'm happy about it. Though your moms are going to want an even bigger dinner now. Probably invite my family, too." I grimaced at the thought as I got out the makings for hot chocolate. Though I'd invite them to the wedding, of course.

"Queen Twatwaffle versus my parents." AJ shuddered as he put the popcorn in the microwave. "Though I know I should fear your match-making grandma."

"Oh, yes. Though, since I told her I was courting a pack and she needed to stop trying to set me up, she informed me there was an omega gift set aside for me. Look. Dean and Grif will be so pretty." Taking my phone, I showed AJ the pictures of the ornate heirloom jewelry sets.

"I love how they assume you'll have a female omega." AJ laughed. "They're very nice."

"Well, someone has to cook for me. Honestly, I might not accept it." I was still surprised since it had been made clear that I wouldn't receive the same things my alpha male cousins got.

"Accept them. In fact, see if she'll send them to you now before she changes her mind. Even if Dean and Grif aren't interested, they're still assets and can be listed as what you bring to the pack when you get added. Might as well take advantage," he told me as he got down a bowl. "If not, no worries. It was worth a shot. But I'm guessing you worry about that."

"Oh, that makes sense. Sure." I shot off a text to my grandma.

Yes, they were adding me to the pack. A pack I brought very little to, asset-wise. Though my investments were doing better thanks to AJ's help. If we were all students or just getting started, it would be one thing, but they were established, and I worried about disparity.

"I've been putting off visiting my parents to pick an heirloom gift out for Grif out of the safe. Because my mothers will want to talk about things. I did order a custom watch for him, though." He leaned against the counter.

"Go when they're not there. Take something, leave a note, and go? I should get something new for them as a mating gift, too. But I have no idea what." I thought for a moment. "Maybe a chain for Grif to wear the ring on since he's using one of Dean's?"

"Great idea. We can go to my family's jeweler together. Maybe a sail boat charm or tie tack for Dean? We'll look together." He opened the bag of chocolate chips and popped some in his mouth.

I squeezed his hand. "I like that. Ooh, maybe an engraved compass?"

Did I get AJ and Jonas bonding gifts? I wasn't sure. Hmmm, maybe I could have one of the heirloom necklaces made into something for the four of them. That could be special.

"Fantastic idea. That or one of those spy glasses so he can pretend to be a pirate when we go sailing?" AJ suggested. "Um, back to us bonding? We should get a mate agreement drawn up for the two of us, since it's always a good idea to have one. While I'll marry you if you'd like, *please* don't make me have a wedding. Unless we're eloping, and it's only our pack."

His words warmed me, and my shoulders wiggled in happiness as I heated the milk in the saucepan.

"As soon as we get back to the city, we'll get your bond with Dean registered, and that agreement drawn up, too. You and Jonas can sort yourselves out on your own." He grinned and took more chocolate chips out of the bag.

I measured the chocolate. Someone had gotten the good kind. "Who ordered all this?"

"Me, I figured you'd all come up eventually, and we love your hot chocolate. I even got marshmallows." Taking out a bag, he threw it at me. "Well, everyone except for Mr. I-Don't-Like-Chocolate."

Laughing, I caught it. "I make a very good hot vanilla, but it's hot pink, and I put sprinkles on it and call it unicorn vomit. One of the littles doesn't like chocolate either."

AJ guffawed as he poured kernels into a special bowl and put it in the microwave. "I'll buy all the ingredients just to see his face when you serve it to him."

"He might like it. It's pretty tasty when spiked with bourbon." I stirred the pot, making sure the heat was low, so it didn't burn.

"Jonas also brought groceries when you all came down. Mostly prepared stuff. He took the old snowmobile to the store earlier to get a few fresh things." He sniffed the air. "That smells so good."

My phone buzzed, and I checked it. "Huh. Grandma already mailed everything. Baba apparently told her to?"

How bizarre.

"The press release." AJ nodded as he got out the salt and butter. "He must have seen it. That went out while you were in the hospital."

I scrolled through my texts. "Mama told him. Baba is apparently very excited that I actually listened to him and found a man in finance. Mama wants to meet all of you."

Hmm, I wasn't sure what I thought of that. If I let them back into my life, it could be hard to enforce boundaries.

"Hey, since we're adding you and Mercy to the pack, and Grif is now out, we're going to change his designation in the charter. Grif's insistent that he doesn't need an asset, but legally we need one. Want to help me pick?" he offered as the popcorn popped.

I got busy stirring the pot, anxiety in my belly. Right, Grif's omega asset. "Um, I… I can't afford an island."

"Who's giving their omega an *island*? Never mind, your sister got one, didn't she?" He laughed as he put some butter in a tiny bowl.

"They wanted to get her a beach house and they let Spencer choose it. So, he picked one that came with its own island. She thought it was ridiculous, but from the pictures, it looks lovely," I replied, as I kept whisking.

"I was thinking of this." He showed me a picture of a beautiful piano with elaborate inlaid wood geometric designs on it. "We could put it in the Boston house. It's an iconic antique and I've been watching for it to go for sale for years. Don't worry about contributing. It's from the pack, not you and me. There's a difference." He kissed my neck, soothing thoughts coming through the bond.

"It's beautiful." I examined the photo. Grif would adore it.

He took the bowl out of the microwave, now full of fluffy kernels. Then he poured butter over it and salted it.

"I… I could buy a fancy seat cushion. Perhaps with embroidered griffins on it?" I had a friend from university that could make him something exquisite.

"Absolutely. I'll set the popcorn on the table and put in an offer." Taking the bowl, he put it on the coffee table and got on his phone.

I added some vanilla and a dash of cinnamon to the hot chocolate and took it off the heat, pouring it into the waiting cups, then adding marshmallows. One at a time, I brought the mugs into the living room and put them on the table with the popcorn.

My phone rang with a video call. Mercy.

"Hi, are you okay?" My heart raced as I sank into the soft couch, which was full of slightly dusty pillows and blankets.

What had happened? How terrible of a sister was I?

"Are *you* okay? That was quite the trip to Drillville you had there. Is the poon palace nice?" Mercy laughed. She looked okay and seemed to be sitting in the Maimers' dining room at the training center.

"Let's not call the cabin the *poon palace.* It's more like the *penetration station*. I... I'm okay. I ache, but I'll be fine. Yes, I already scheduled a checkup." I popped a kernel in my mouth.

"Good. I'm taking care of business here. I haven't even let Hale take your car." She looked proud of herself.

"Thanks for that. What happened? I have a bunch of texts from Hale and Dare." I braced for the worst as I took a sip of very hot chocolate.

She snorted. "Those weirdos. I've been fine while you've been at the boom boom room. Okay, so Dare had to go back to Boston for some orchestra thing he forgot about. Hale was supposed to come for the weekend and stay with me, but he got delayed because of work. And I awakened as an alpha with both of them gone and now they feel like jerks. But I'm *fine.* Honestly, it was better that they weren't there."

"Oh, I'm so sorry I wasn't around–and that they weren't around either. Were you at practice, at least, where there were other alphas?" I remembered how freaked out I was.

"It was Gwennifer. Unlike your teammates back at Marquess, she knew exactly what to do. Because she plays hockey and has been through it a billion times. Anyhow, she was there for me," Mercy told me. "Don't you dare feel bad about it. You can take me out for a fancy dinner or something to celebrate."

Oh, it happened? And I wasn't there?

At least someone was.

"We will absolutely do that. Any place you want. It can be just us, or we can invite whoever," I told her as AJ came back to the couch and held up the remote. I nodded as he turned it on and browsed the recorded games.

"Hmmm, I like it being us and the guys. Maybe Hale and Dare? I don't know. I'll think about it. Probably I'd rather have a big, blowout, excellent eighteenth party. Maybe with a tattoo artist," she replied, tapping her chin with a sparkly painted finger.

I blinked. "Um, sure? I mean, I got a tattoo when I awakened."

"Yeah, that's where I got the idea. Gwen and I got tattoos like you did. Her artist is amazing. She showed me the flash sheet she was making for a wedding, and now I want her for my party. It'll be better than a blowjob from a dinosaur." Mercy sounded very excited.

"You got a tattoo?" My eyebrows rose.

AJ turned and gave me a look. Then he nodded to the screen with the game he brought up. I nodded back. *Good choice.*

"A little one, like you did. It's what alpha females do, right? Well, the cool ones. Pretty much every lady alpha on my team got one when they awakened. I got skate smash skates on my ankle. I got

Gwen a little ladybug on her foot. The artist is part of the Brooklyn Blankets and did a smash-up job," she gushed as she moved the phone and took off her sock, showing off the little design.

"It's cute," I told her. "It might be a day or two before we get back because of the snow. You're okay? Do we need Grace or Creed?"

"No. They've been sending us food deliveries, though. Also, I have two sets of MASOs who keep bringing food. We're *fine.* So. Much. Food. We haven't messed up the place. Carlos has been taking Lucky clubbing and posting it on his socials, which is hysterical. Anyway, between Dare, Hale, and Rusty, I'm not in breach of contract." Her voice lowered. "I'm a little tired of my brothers, though. I love them, but they can go home and leave me alone now."

"I get that." While she and Hale were close, he knew just how to annoy her. "I'm happy you're okay. And I'm glad it happened because I know you were getting anxious about it. I'm so proud of you. You're going to make a great alpha."

I wasn't sure if those were the words you said, but they're the words I wish the parents had told me.

"Aww, that means everything, coming from you. Um, in celebration, Hale, and Dare got me drunk in the living room, and it was bad. I think that's what Hale was actually apologizing for. I'll never drink tequila again, but I'm okay. One of Dean's pillows may not live." She grimaced, nose scrunching.

They what? I knew it would happen eventually. But I'd figured it would be Kaiko and Jack.

"Hangovers are a bitch. We'll get Dean a new throw pillow." Texting my brother and being mad was tempting, but honestly, I'd gotten super drunk, too.

"Oh, I went to my first university house party. It was Gwen's birthday party at her apartment. I took Dare. I had one beer. Valya, Dimitri's sister, invited me to one of Dimitri's parties. But Dimitri said I couldn't come without your permission because he doesn't want to get beat up. Next time." She shrugged.

AJ shook his head. I concurred. A tattoo, getting drunk for the first time, and a university party were enough adult adventures for now. I could practically hear Mumsy yelling.

"Oh. I missed Gwen's birthday. Do you think I should make her some cake pops?" I had a ladybug one on my recipe board. Maybe I should do something else for her, too.

Mercy nodded. "She'd love that. Anyhow, I need to go because we have a promo thing. Rusty wants to know if you survived your first trip to the bone zone. Oh, sorry, I mean the bone*yard.*" She turned as someone said something I didn't catch. "No, Liv, I'm not saying that to my sister."

I stifled a laugh. "Please thank her for me. I'll make her a pie when we get back. Have fun. I love you, and I'll let you know when we're coming home."

"Love you, too." She ended the call.

AJ plopped down next to me. "It happened. You did think it was close."

"Yep. Complete with tattoos and getting drunk. I never should've told her that story." I laughed. It was really nice that

Gwen was there for her. I guess hockey *would* have more teammates awakening as alpha than fútbol.

"Your alpha relatives getting you drunk is pretty normal. At least they did it at the house. They could have taken her to a strip club. Wait, never mind, she's only seventeen. How did she get a tattoo?" AJ took a sip of hot chocolate. "This is amazing."

"Technically, she's emancipated." I grabbed the bowl of popcorn and got comfy.

"She'll be okay. She has us." AJ gave me a squeeze and threw a blanket over us. "I put a bid on the piano. Let's watch the game before they come down and want our attention."

"Perfect." I snuggled into him on the couch as we enjoyed our snacks and the game.

Halfway through the match, the guys thundered down the stairs.

"I'm hungry. When's food?" Grif came over and gave us each a kiss.

"What's food?" Dean slipped onto my lap and gave the empty popcorn bowl a pitiful look. He wore a sweater as snuggly as he smelled.

"Why's food?" Jonas stole a kiss. "Everything's okay?"

"I vote for renaming the cabin the *poon palace*." AJ grinned at me.

I gave AJ a little shove and stopped the game. We'd watch the rest later. "Let's not. Mercy awakened. Gwen took her to get a tattoo, and Hale and Dare got her drunk on tequila."

"I like *poon palace.* Do you want me to talk to Ladybug? That's an overstep on her part?" Dean offered.

"No. It's nice that Gwen was there for her. Slightly concerned about the party at Gwen's that Mercy attended. But Dare said it was just a bunch of students drinking beer, eating pizza, and dancing to warehouse music." I shrugged. It sounded pretty tame.

"As long as it wasn't one of Dimitri's parties. She's *not* ready for those," Jonas replied. "I'm going to check on the hot tub." He gave me another kiss and then opened the door that led to the patio.

"Put on a jacket and shoes," I yelled.

Jonas smirked as he closed the patio door behind him.

"I'll start cooking. You cuddle those two." AJ kissed me, then went to the kitchen.

"It's movie time." Dean's look grew giddy as he took the remote.

I threw the blanket over the three of us and got comfortable. I had a feeling that we were about to watch some childhood movie of theirs that they always watched at the cabin.

But that was okay. Because I was with them.

"See, I told you this would be fun." Jonas took the marshmallow off the stick and popped it into his mouth.

After dinner, we put together a puzzle, which AJ and Grif turned into a drinking game. Then, we'd pulled the portable fire pit over to the hot tub, and here we were, roasting marshmallows in the hot tub, outside, in February.

"It is nice." I turned my stick so I could get the marshmallow an even golden color. "Not excited about getting out."

"I'll keep you warm, Sweet Girl." Jonas gave me a lusty wink from his place in the hot tub next to Dean, amber eyes gleaming.

I sat between Dean and Grif. AJ was on the other side of Grif.

Dean looked up at the sky. The snow had stopped, and it was full of twinkling stars. "That's so beautiful."

"Mercy would love to photograph it. Stars are apparently hard to take pictures of, but she's working on it." I took off the hot marshmallow and ate it. Delicious. I might want another. Even though I was full of the spectacular dinner AJ had made of spiced lamb and rice.

Grif kissed me, licking the marshmallow off my lips.

"If they plow the roads in the morning as promised, I need to head back to the office in the afternoon," AJ told us. "We have two cars, so if you need another day, feel free."

"Coach is very much ready for us all to come back." Grif sighed and leaned his head on my shoulder. "We have a big game in two days, and he needs us. Not to mention the All-Star break is soon."

I didn't want to think about all the things I needed to do. Especially if I still wanted to go with them to see Grif play in Boston for the All-Stars. However, Saphira had been taking care of my plants, and Dr. Winters subbed my class, which was probably fun for my students.

"Let's think about all that later and enjoy each other now," Dean told us. "Then later, we can *enjoy* each other." He winked at me.

"Mmmm, that sounds good." Grif snagged a kiss. "Yeah, I want to make a Verity sandwich."

"I think Verity might want to go to bed all by herself after putting up with us for five days." AJ leaned over Grif and gave me a kiss. Grif smacked his ass, sending water splashing.

"Can we all sleep in a big pile?" I wanted everyone close, though I didn't want anything more than cuddles right now.

Grif nodded and pulled me close. "I like that idea."

"Whatever you two want," Jonas assured. He gave Dean a kiss. "We're yours."

"And I'm yours." Dean gave him a kiss, then snagged my lips and kissed me deeply, his lips tasting of gooey marshmallows.

"Same." Grif kissed AJ, then me.

They were mine. The realization hit as Jonas put another marshmallow on his roasting stick.

I never thought I'd have one omega, and now I had Dean *and* Grif.

I had a soulmate.

And a pack.

A pack who loved all of me just the way I was.

I'd stood up for them. Took them.

Now they were mine.

Happiness and gratitude welled up in me. After all the crap I'd gotten from my family, everything I'd been through, I had my fairytale.

Who would have thought?

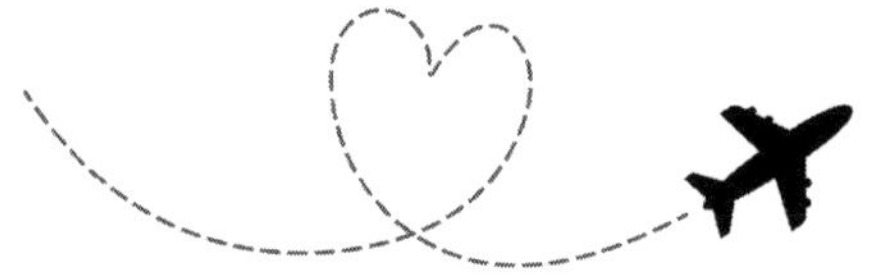

Chapter Fifty-Five

Grif

Stealing the puck from one of the Jersey Titans forwards, I hurried across the ice. Elation burst through me as I evaded the defense, and barreled toward their goal.

Fuck, I'd missed this.

Carlos skated circles around the forward after me, distracting her so I could pass it to Clark. Chased by their defense, he skated around the back of the net, and I went the other way.

The goalie moved, anticipating me. We had a friendly but fierce rivalry.

Clark moved like he was passing to me. Defense got on my ass.

No, we weren't losing tonight.

The arena was a sea of pink, both in the stands and on the ice. February was omega history month and today was our *omega night* game. The Knights wore black and pink jerseys which would be auctioned off to raise money for the Omega Center. Pink hats and Double-D bobble toys had been given out to fans, and there was a special menu of pink drinks and treats.

I knocked down the defender as Clark passed it to Carlos. The defender turned and pushed me, then froze.

"Fuck," he muttered.

"Do it. I won't break." I made the *come at me* gesture. For now, Dimitri was technically our enforcer. But I never shied away from a fight.

I took off my gloves and threw them down. He had no choice now.

His gloves dropped. "Fine."

I threw the first punch. He hit me back.

"You can do better," I taunted, aware that everyone was watching. It was early in the game, and I hadn't gotten into a fight yet. I hit him again.

Come on, fight me.

Getting people to treat me as always was the key to being accepted in the PHL.

"Fine, but if I get shit for hitting you, I'm going to tell them you told me to." He hit me again. Harder this time. Though not his worst.

Shoving him against the boards, I hit him several times. "The only shit you're going to get is for getting beat up by me. Though I haven't changed, I'm still me. Fight me."

This time, he fought back. The people behind the glass cheered.

"You get him, Grif Graf," a woman shouted.

I savored the way it felt to punch someone during a game. Yeah, I'd missed this.

The ref finally blew his whistle and tried to tear us apart. I fought against them, continuing to throw punches.

"I think you've made your point." Elias pulled me off him.

"I guess." I let him rip us apart.

A penalty was called, and the lineman dragged me toward the box. I stopped and thumped on the glass when we skated past the family section.

"Hey, Tiger. You show 'em!" Verity cheered, wearing my jersey.

"Good fight, Boo-Boo." AJ has his arm around her, matching her.

I was so happy those two had bonded. Actually, I was happy she'd mated with everyone. Though Dean wouldn't fucking shut up about it.

Verity made a heart with her hands. I blew them kisses.

"You call that a fight?" Mercy rolled her eyes, one of which was black. She'd gotten in a huge brawl and fractured her wrist and sprained her ankle, so she was out for tonight's away game, though she'd be back for the next.

Also, she wore *Jonas'* jersey.

"Love you, too, Mercy." I flashed her a heart with my fingers.

"Come *on,* Grif Graf. I hate that this is becoming normal. I might have to eject you next time." The lineman tugged on me.

I got into the box where I belonged. A fan hit on the penalty box as the game started back up again. Turning, I braced to be heckled.

"That was amazing. Welcome back," some giant, slightly drunk dude wearing a Knights shirt said. "Nice to see you on the ice again. Glad you're okay."

"Yeah, you show them we're not helpless. Can't wait to watch you at the All-Stars." A slight woman wearing a pink Knights hat leaned into him and grinned at me.

I gave a little bow. "It's good to be back."

It was nice to be allowed to return. To be a Knight again and to have come to an agreement with management. Especially since, in my post-heat checkup, I'd slipped back over to being an omega.

Dean dropped into a butterfly on the ice, stopping the puck, as the crowd cheered.

I glanced over at the family section. Verity was cheering for him, one of the Royce kids on her lap.

This was everything I ever wanted. Playing hockey with my pack, my other mates cheering us on. Sitting in the penalty box after a satisfying fight. Winning a game. Getting to play in the upcoming All-Star game after years of hoping to be chosen.

Hopefully, I'd bring the Knights all the way to the championships and get myself another ring. Despite the challenges we've had this season, it was still a strong possibility.

Verity caught my eye and waved. I waved back, heart full.

Maybe one day, just maybe, it would be our kids on Verity's lap.

"Welcome back, Grif Graf. How does it feel?" The reporter from SportsBeat shoved a microphone in my face as I left the ice after the game.

"Do you think management will be pleased with your performance tonight? After all, you only scored two goals," another reporter asked.

"I'm confident my performance tonight was well in line with how I usually play." My hands itched to punch him. *Only* two goals?

Sure, I hadn't gotten a boner. Dean hadn't recorded a shutout. But we'd won. I'd still have my sweet kitten mewling for me after the game.

"Well, I'm happy to be back," I added, answering her. "Certainly, I'm looking forward to the All-Star weekend coming up."

While I knew a lot of reporters were bursting with personal questions, both about my designation and Verity taking a bullet for me, I wasn't feeling up to it. Waving, I continued on toward the locker room.

"Good job, Grif Graf, Welcome back." Coach Atkins slapped me on the back.

"I'm glad you're pleased with me." It was in earnest because Coach had fought hard for me, and I wanted him to be happy with his choice to back me.

"Feeling okay?" Jonas slung an arm around me. While I'd gotten the go-ahead from both Dr. Arya and Dr. Mosser, I knew Jonas worried.

"Feeling good." Like I needed to fuck one of my mates.

The coaches went over a few things and assigned press duty to people who were not me or my pack. I stripped off my clothes, including the rumble vest, which was one of the compromises so I could continue to play.

Sure, Dean didn't wear one, but he didn't get in as many fights as I did.

Another was scent blockers and shields, but I'd use those, anyway.

I hit the ice baths and showers, and got dressed.

"Who's going to Tito's?" Nia called as she shimmed into her suit, a pretty scarf over her brown twists.

"Lucky and I are." Carlos smacked Clark's ass with a towel.

Clark threw a pickle at him and missed.

"Don't throw pickles at Lucky. He's a good cat," Dimitri scolded.

Dean, hair wet, put an arm around me. "Will you dance with me?"

"Always." I leaned into him.

"Good. We missed you," Nia told me.

I was so glad everyone on the team was fully accepting of me.

Jonas, Dean, and I left the locker room and went to the family room. Verity was talking with some MASOs.

"Grif." She beamed and flung her arms around me. "That was so good. I'm proud of you."

"What about me?" Dean fake pouted.

She kissed him. "I'm proud of you." Verity then kissed Jonas. "You, too."

"Gross." Mercy made a face. "Let's go to Tito's. Gwenifer's on tonight."

We left for the parking garage and got into the SUV. I did like this new, larger vehicle Jonas picked out.

"That was a great game, Boo-Boo." AJ squeezed my hand.

Tito's was busy, full of happy teammates and rowdy fans, as the music blared and the beer flowed.

"Good job, Grif Graf," yet another random fan told me. "Glad you're back."

"Thanks." I was so grateful that the Knights' fans were behind me, too.

Ladybug brought another round of beers to our table. Well, Mercy got a soda and Verity got one of her fruity little drinks. Tonight's was peachy. AJ, Dean, Verity, and I sat at a high top, Verity's crutch leaning against it. Jonas talked to Elias and Winston. Mercy was having a good time with Dimitri's little sister and a few others.

"Team Mom, I *loved* my cake pop bouquet. My boyfriend and I already shared one. They're so cute," Gwen told her. Her hair was still light blue.

"Happy Birthday." Verity gave her a big smile.

"Dance with me." Dean tugged my hand as his favorite song played.

I took his hand in mine and twirled him around. "Hey, can I have Verity to myself for at least the start of the night?"

Since we'd come back from the cabin, it had been mostly puppy piles in Verity's bed or Dean hogging her. Not only did I want some alone time with her, but I think she was getting overwhelmed trying to balance all four of us.

Dean's head lolled as he thought for a moment. "I suppose."

Jonas joined us and we finished our beers.

"Ready to go home?" Jonas asked.

"Yep." I handed Verity her crutch. "Let's go home, Gorgeous."

In the car, Mercy had some sort of weird teenage music playing.

"Mercy, I know you enjoy being a big tipper, but that was pretty massive. Is Ladybug still behind on rent or something?" Jonas asked as he drove.

"She got caught up. But her boyfriend has no parents, so she's taking extra shifts to pay for his graduation fees and graduating player hockey shit. It's a lot for her." Mercy shrugged as she texted someone. "Excellent service should be rewarded."

Fair. I remember working extra shifts to cover things so there was less to ask my parents for. Graduating got expensive.

"Hey, I know what restaurant I want you to take me to," she looked up from her phone. "Can we go to Wilderness Cafe?"

AJ looked puzzled, sunglasses nestled in his hair as always. "I don't know what that is."

It was a chain of family restaurants done up to look like you were eating outdoors in the woods. There'd be servers dressed like park rangers and bear sounds and shit. Not AJ's family's style, though he'd like it.

"Great idea, I haven't been there in years." I told her. A juicy burger sounded amazing right now.

"Love it. Our hockey team in high school always had their end-of-season banquets there," Dean added, giving me a fond look. "Their onion rings are the best."

Those were always fun times.

"Ooh, they are. And that cheese dip they have for the fries," Verity agreed, licking her glossy lips.

AJ looked up from his phone. "Are you sure that's where you want to go?"

"If it's too expensive, that cafe you recommended to Verity and I, the retro one, is fine," Mercy added.

"More like feel free to choose something fancier? I expected a nice steak house. Though it's your choice and I'm always up for trying new places," AJ assured.

"That sounds great, Squirt," Jonas told her. "That's the place where you can roast marshmallows on the table, right?"

"Yep." She grinned.

Yeah, I wanted to see AJ's reaction to singing park rangers and animatronic bears.

"You know, once the updates are finished to the pack charter, we could all dress up and go out for a nice steak dinner together?"

Jonas suggested, giving us a look in the rearview mirror as we drove through the dark streets.

"I'd like that. Um, are you going to tell me what you're getting me?" While I didn't need anything, I understood getting an asset was a legal issue, and I was very curious.

Especially since AJ had given me a nice watch and Verity had gotten me a beautiful chain to wear with her grandfather's ring and a bracelet engraved with the coordinates of where we met.

A smug look crossed AJ's face. "Nope. You waived your right to choose, so you're going to have to wait and find out."

"You'll love it." Verity squeezed my hand.

Okay, if she was involved, it probably wouldn't be ridiculous. That's what I feared, it being some crazy extravagance.

"Question. What if you're a poor pack and can't afford to buy your omega a house or an island?" Mercy turned around in the front seat to look at us.

"It just has to be some kind of asset that belongs to the omega alone. It can even be money in an account in their name only. The center has a calculator to help you figure out what's fair based on income, but there isn't a threshold," Jonas explained.

We pulled into our space, right next to Verity's car, still safe and sound. We took the elevator up. Mercy took off her coat and hung it on the beautiful hand-carved coat rack–with an umbrella bin. It appeared while we were at the cabin. She'd won it in the silent auction at the gala, along with a basket of purses for Verity.

Jonas shook his head and hung up his coat. "I don't understand it, but it is pretty."

AJ took mine and Verity's coats and hung them up in the coat closet with his.

"I do see the appeal of the umbrella bin," AJ admitted, taking Verity's crutch and putting it in said bin.

"Does anyone want a late-night snack?" Dean half-threw his coat on the rack and went into the kitchen.

Jonas repositioned it so that it hung nicely.

"I'm taking mine to go." I picked Verity up and threw her over my shoulder, careful of her injury, which was healing nicely despite her being kidnapped from the hospital by Jonas so she could fuck for days.

"Grif." She kicked her feet.

"Well, this has been nice. Good night." I gave Dean a kiss, then AJ.

"You have fun. I'll check on you later," AJ told us with a smirk.

Mercy gave us an amused look as she rifled through the fridge and took out a tub of dip and a lime soda. "That's my cue to take my snack to go as well. Good game."

Adding a bag of chips, she ran upstairs. I carried Verity down the hall and set her down in my room, closing the door with my foot.

"Oooh, I get you all to myself tonight? So luxurious." Verity leaned in and gave me a slow and smoldering kiss, her hands going up and down my back.

"Mmmm, that you do." I peeled my jersey off her. Today's bra was black.

She took off her shoes as we continued to kiss. I took off her pants to see that she wore a black thong.

"Is your shoulder doing okay?" I threw my suit-jacket and button-down on the floor with her clothes. I didn't feel much pain through the bond, but I wanted to verbally check in.

Verity grabbed my belt buckle and pulled me to her. "Yes. My leg, too. It's a good body day. Also, I made another research breakthrough. I'm catching up on everything and feeling good."

"Oh, I'm so happy to hear that, Kitten." I whipped off my belt in between fervent kisses and kicked off my pants and briefs.

My rock-hard dick was ready to nestle itself deep in my sweet alpha. My *mate.*

"You want me to throw you against the wall and pound into you, don't you?" I wrapped a hand around her golden throat.

And got a whiff of her sweet desire and felt her lust through the bond.

Good little kitten. Being able to tend to my mate's deepest desires and needs satiated me on the most primal of levels.

"Make me scream, Tiger. I've been ready since you got in that fist fight first period. AJ had to put me in a corner and take care of me." Her eyes met mine as she took my hand and guided it between her legs so I could feel that her pussy was dripping.

"Oh, did he now? Did you become so needy that our alpha had to fuck you *at the game*?" A playful snarl ripped from my lips as I pushed her against the wall.

"Yes, he did." She hummed in pleasure as my hand curled around her golden throat. "Fuck me," she begged.

My dick twitched at her words as pre-cum and slick beaded on it. "Far be it to make my alpha wait."

Lining myself up with her needy, wanting pussy, I plunged in. Her warm softness surrounded me as that *rightness* I felt when I was inside her settled over me. Warmth and love flowed through our bond.

A happy noise escaped my lips as I withdrew and pushed in again, feeling her flutter around me. "I love how I fit so perfectly in your perfect pussy."

"I love it when you rail me like this." Bliss coated her face as her ass thumped against the wall as I continued thrusting.

My free hand toyed with her breasts, and I ran my fingers over AJ's bond mark. She raked her nails through my hair and down my back and moaned my name over and over.

"Come when you're ready and lock me," I told her, my free hand continuing to toy with her breasts.

My lips pressed to hers, then trailed down her throat. Dean's bite mark had almost disappeared, but like AJ's, Jonas' was healing nicely, the scabs falling off to reveal the telltale silvery color of an alpha bond.

Verity gasped. Letting go of her throat, my arms wrapped tightly around my love, my alpha, as her body trembled, pleasure coursing through the bond.

Her pussy shuddered, choking and milking my cock. The lock clamped down, making me gasp as I came, my hot cum flooding her.

"Mmmm, I love how you squeeze my dick. You're such a good little cum dumpster," I murmured, nuzzling her.

She kissed the bond mark she'd left on my neck. "I love it when you call me that."

Pulling her legs around me, I lifted her from the wall and brought us to my bed, still joined together.

I pulled the down comforter over our sweaty, naked bodies. The covers smelled of me and Dean, given we'd had a pre-game fuck.

"Mmmm, Tiger, we fit perfectly." She put her head on my chest.

"That we do, Kitten." I pressed a kiss to her soft lips.

The warmth of her soft alpha purr surrounded us as I stroked her hair until she unlocked me. Getting up from the bed, she went to the bathroom. A moment later, she came back with a wet cloth and cleaned me up.

Pushing me on to my back, she straddled me, facing my feet. Her hands seized one of my calves and kneaded them.

"Kitten," I groaned. "Oh, yeah, a calf massage is exactly what I need." Given I'd had so much time off, the exertion of the game made them a little sore.

"Thought so. I love you." Her fingers dug into the muscles, relieving the stress and soreness. After that leg, she did the other.

Oh yeah. This was it.

A game win. A fuck. Some purrs. A calf massage.

Later, either Dean or AJ would want to join us, I was sure.

I turned so I could see that beautiful back of hers as she continued to rub my calf. We'd have to get her a pack tattoo. Maybe we could get something matching as well.

She finished the massage and climbed back beside me, snuggling into me. "How was that?"

"Perfect. I'm so lucky." I stroked her hair as her head laid on my chest.

"You're my Tiger, not Lucky. Who hopefully is playing video games with Mercy and not hiding in a corner watching us," she giggled.

"He might still be at the bar with Carlos," I laughed.

Her eyes met mine as she ran her fingers through my beard. "I'm the lucky one. I never would have thought that a kind stranger on the airplane would bring me so much happiness."

"Me, too. I love you." I hummed as her love and contentment flooded the bond. Yeah, I'd be eternally grateful to whatever force placed us together on the plane–and brought us both to New York. "Even if you thought I played fútbol."

Laughing, I rolled over, pinning her back to the bed as I put her hands over her head and kissed her, straddling her.

"You're my favorite forward. I know we're mated, but I can't wait to have our wedding and see Dean walk you down the aisle." Her blue-green eyes bored into mine, full of love and hope. "Thank you for finding me. I love you, too."

"Always." The universe had given me and my pack a great gift.

For that, I'd be forever grateful.

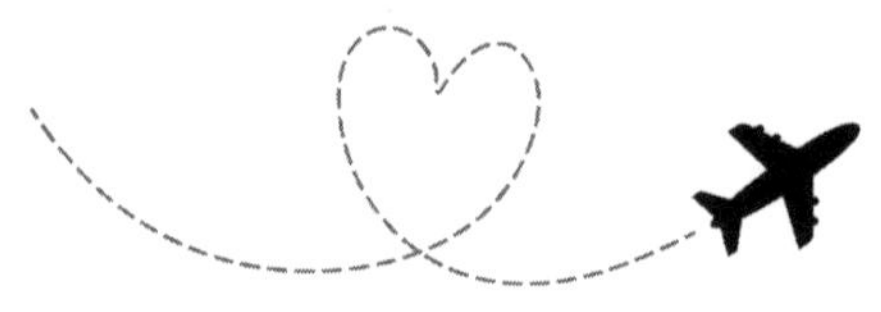

Epilogue

Verity

Four months later

Looking at my reflection in the ornately carved full-length standing mirror, I smoothed the delicate pale gold lace overlay of my voluminous wedding gown. The sweetheart neckline, accented with waterfalls of tiny golden beads, showed off the swell of my breasts and Jonas' bond mark.

My pack tattoo and Jonas' bond mark peaked out of the off-the-shoulder sleeves, my arms bare except for the tiny airplane-with-a-heart tattoo on my wrist that matched Grif. The dress pooled to the ground all around me in delicate pleats, with a trailing train.

"It's too much, isn't it? I mean, Grif and I have been bonded for months now. It's silly enough to have a big wedding like this. Now, to wear this dress?" Oh, how I loved this dress. It was fit for an omega princess trapped in a tower about to be married off to an alpha king who turned into a dragon.

"*Sweetheart*," Jonas warned as he leaned around me to give me a kiss.

AJ was with Grif. Grace and Mercy had gone off to get something. Creed was running interference with the parents. Dean was helping my little siblings pass out bread to our waiting guests.

"First off, you've always dreamt of a big, fancy wedding in a garden. If anyone is stomping on your dreams, fuck them. Also, how long had your sister been bonded before her giant wedding?" Jonas continued lacing up the back of my dress.

"More than a year," I admitted. Of course, Grace's mates had bought a wedding venue with a garden and done it up, and that took time, especially since she wanted the rose garden to be in bloom.

Jonas finished lacing me up and touched my face. My hair hung down in waves.

"You love this dress. You look perfect in this dress. Every single one of us can't wait to strip it off you." Jonas kissed my neck, careful of my makeup, which was perfect and smokey, with a hint of shimmer.

My core tightened, going molten. "You're such a tease."

He looked *so good* in his white tux, an omega lily pinned to his tux jacket.

"I do love this dress," I admitted, swishing the skirt back and forth. Plenty of alpha females wore gold wedding dresses, though they were usually sleeker, sexier. Still, there was no good reason not to wear the gold poofy princess dress of my dreams, other than my own anxiety.

Okay, and Mumsy making an offhand comment.

"You look like a princess–and there's been plenty of alpha princesses in history." Jonas fluffed up the skirt. "If you need me to appeal to your practical side, I'm pretty sure the fancy fashion shop didn't give you the dress purely out of kindness. They're hoping the internet will be flooded with photos."

"True." My lips twitched.

Things had been busy. The Knights won the PHL championship finals against the Sasquatches. The Maimers had gone far but not all the way, so their season wrapped about the same time.

After, we'd made a trip to the *poon palace* so Dean and Grif could have their heats.

Then we'd traveled to London to visit Dad and the littles. After that, I had *four* runway shows during the Paris Fashion Festival, which included one of Vecci's, and the bridal showcase for the renowned House of Dubois. Where Mercy and Riley sat in the front row, and no one fell in their laps.

The House of Dubois *had* let me keep the dress I'd worn. This beautiful, ethereal, *expensive* wedding dress–with a coordinating crutch.

"You're right, it would be a shame not to wear it." My hand flew to my necklace, which was the diamond heart with the matching earrings that Grif had given me.

We'd then had Mercy's excellent eighteenth party, where she'd rented out a club, had a DJ, hired a tattoo artist, and brought in a ton of food.

Now, here we were. In the freaking *castle* Grace had found for me, *on the island I'd been to as a child.* The one where I'd first heard the stories behind omega lilies as we picnicked in a field.

Giddiness shot through me. I was about to have my wedding.

My giant wedding. Everyone was assembling in the garden. Knights, Maimers, friends, all my siblings, all the parents but Mom. Grif's, AJ's, and Dean's entire family, Jonas' sister, Hana, and best friend, Charlie also came.

While I wasn't sure I wanted all the parents there, I'd wanted my younger siblings to attend, which had been the tradeoff.

The castle had an elaborate garden full of omega lilies and other fragrant flowers–the perfect place for a summer wedding. I'd fallen in love with it when I'd visited over spring break when I'd come on my flower-buying expedition for my research. Research that was going scarily well.

"Knock knock," Grace's voice went sing-song, as the door opened. "Oh, Verity. You look radiant."

"Thank you for making my dream wedding happen." I kissed her on the cheek. We'd paid for some, but she'd covered part, so that I didn't feel like I had to accept any money from the parents.

"You deserve the wedding of *your* dreams, not what anyone deems appropriate." Grace wore a long baby pink designer dress. Her blonde hair had grown out and brushed her shoulders.

"You look fantastic." Mercy checked the laces on the back of my dress. "Wow, Jonas, you laced it up right."

My little sister wore a seafoam green one. The dress code was pastels. Her brown hair was down in waves with the top braided.

Jonas bowed. "I aim to please."

"Here. You need something blue. Wear this for the wedding." Grace put a delicate gold cuff bracelet with very pale blue stones around my wrist.

"It's exquisite. Thank you."

"I'm coming in. I want to see," a French-accented voice said as Mama walked in. She was tall for a beta, almost five-foot-ten, and wore baby blue, which brought out her blue-green eyes. Her light brown hair hung down her back.

"Mama." I gave her a hug.

Things were pretty good between us. She'd been a tremendous help to Grace, Mercy, and me in the wedding planning processes and hadn't said a single word against all the fanciful plans.

If anything, she kept suggesting things. I was glad she'd made it out from Bayside.

"Trés belle." She air-kissed my cheek. Her makeup brought out her delicate but striking features. "Grace, everything is superb. Bravo."

"Thank you." Grace beamed. Their relationship had gotten better, too.

"Verity." Baba stood in a black tux but with a baby blue tie and vest. He was a very tall alpha, as tall as Grif, though not quite as broad. Still, he was formidable. His golden skin was darker than mine, but I had his dark hair and many of his features.

"Baba." My stomach twisted a little. Our relationship was still strained.

He gave my mother a fond look, then tilted his toward the door.

Mama laughed. "Come, the alphas need to talk."

Grace squeezed my hand. "See you out there."

"I'm an alpha. I'm eighteen now, and I'm staying," Mercy said as Dare came into the room. She shot Baba a challenging look.

For a moment I wasn't sure if Baba would allow it, but he just shrugged. Jonas helped me sit in a chair by the window because this might take a moment.

Baba launched into the traditional speech, making sure I fully understood my duties as an alpha taking an omega. Some of them were rather *specific*. Jonas kept smirking.

Ugh. I didn't need my father telling me how often I needed to bone my omega. But I kept silent and tried not to giggle. The fact that he'd even offered to do this meant *everything*.

Toward the end of the speech, I realized he clutched a large, carved wooden box.

"Do you understand, Cupcake? Will you remember this and be a good alpha to your chosen omega? Having an omega is an esteemed privilege, not a right," he asked me when he finished.

"I understand, Baba, and I'll remember this and be a good alpha," I replied.

Oh. He hadn't called me *Cupcake* in a very long time.

"Your grandmother sent this for you to wear today." Baba held out the box.

"She did?" I wasn't expecting that. Grandma turned down my invitation, citing another commitment. But I also understood that not everyone could or wanted to travel to Greece.

He opened the box. "It is very special that she's allowing you to wear this. Your favorite grandfather gave it to her when she joined their pack. It has been in his family for a very long time."

I eyed the delicate gold tiara. "It's beautiful."

The fact she'd chosen something he'd given her meant *everything.*

"Wow. Can I wear it when I get a mate?" Dare grinned.

Baba shot him an unamused look as he took it and set it on my head. He stepped back and snapped a photo.

"I won't tell her you had one of the necklaces made into cufflinks and tie tacks." Baba grimaced.

"They're guys. I thought maybe they'd like to actually wear their gifts sometimes." I shrugged. AJ's family's jeweler had done an amazing job, too.

They all wore them today. It was nice to give them something special.

While I was making progress engineering a rose for Grif, it wasn't ready yet.

Baba's look softened in a way I hadn't seen in a long time as his sandy scent surrounded me. He straightened the crown. "You have grown up so fast–and into an amazing alpha. Look at you.

Joining a successful pack. Having *two* omegas. You're working on your PhD at a prestigious university. You're an alpha to be proud of."

"She is," Jonas told him, squeezing my hand.

The tears started to flow. I'd wanted to hear that for so long. I sniffed. "Thank you, Baba."

"Don't cry, you'll ruin your makeup." Mercy got a tissue and dabbed my tears.

"Can I have a moment?" Baba asked Jonas, Mercy, and Dare.

All three of them gave me looks. I nodded, and they slipped out. Jonas sent a shot of love and reassurance through the bond.

"I'm sorry for being a shitty father, Cupcake. I love you. I should've been different, and I understand if you never forgive me. It wasn't you." He cupped my chin with his large, golden hand as his brown eyes met mine. "You are enough. It was *never* you."

Before I could ask for clarification, he kissed me on the forehead and left the room without a backward glance.

For a moment I couldn't breathe. What had just happened?

You are enough. It was never you. A tear rolled down my face. Those words healed a little part of me right there. Even if I didn't know exactly what he meant.

Jonas rushed in and wiped away the tear on my cheek. "Are you okay? What did he say?"

"What I've needed to hear for a long time." That was unexpected. Both him telling me he was proud of me and *apologizing*.

I'd take it.

"Baba is different since the pack broke up," Dare said quietly, joining us, Mercy behind him.

"It... it seems that way," I agreed. Mama had said he was now more like the man she fell in love with–and not the alpha he became.

But I hadn't believed it until now. Huh.

"That was a *very* educational speech," Mercy told me with a snort.

Jonas grinned at me. "It was. I think I should make sure Grif knows his coital rights."

Mercy grimaced. "I'm positive he's making active use of those. Also, I fully expect you to give that to me when I find an omega, Ver."

"I'm not sure I ever want to hear that again, and if I'd realized what we were doing I would have declined," Dare laughed.

"Is my makeup okay?" I sniffed again, turning to look at myself in the mirror.

"It's good. Ooh, I need some photos. This is incredible with you in the chair and the window, the castle wall, and the mirror." Mercy held up her good camera.

She moved a few things around and snapped some photos, positioning me here and there, and having me turn this way and look that way.

"Fuck, this is good." She showed me a few of them.

They looked like the coronation paintings that hung in museums.

"You look like a queen. An alpha queen about to marry her love." Jonas squeezed my hand.

"Is all the important alpha business done?" Dad popped his head in through the door.

"Dad." I got up and gave my omega dad a big hug. He wore a baby blue suit, with suspenders and a bow tie, and I wouldn't have it any other way.

He beamed. "You look *amazing.*" Dad turned to Mercy. "You look so grown up."

Dare grinned. "What about me?"

He *wasn't* wearing pastels. His black brocade waistcoat, black ruffled shirt, and pocket watch made him look like the antihero in a historical romance. Dare had let his hair grow, and it was pulled back in a tail. As usual, his eye makeup was better than mine.

"You look like you should be on a book cover with a title like *Falling for the Alpha Rake.*" Dad grinned and hugged him, too. "Jonas, you look dashing."

"Thank you, Nate." Jonas tipped his head. His hair had been freshly dyed blue, and his eyebrow and tongue rings were sparkly for the occasion.

As was his armored cock.

And my bedazzled vag. A while back, I'd gotten the piercings that helped me take knots. It was well worth the recovery time.

"Nearly everyone is seated, and the littles are about done handing out bread under Dean and Harry's supervision. Ready?" Dad offered me his arm.

He wanted to accompany me out to where we were having the ceremony, and I didn't see any reason to say *no*.

"Ready." I stood and turned and checked myself in the mirror. The tiara was stunning. "Thank you for being such an understanding and supportive little sister."

I hugged Mercy tightly. Her support was everything.

My sister hugged me back. "Don't make me cry. Kaiko worked hard-on my makeup." She handed me my gold crutch.

"Thanks."

Mercy looked at Jonas. "Let's do this, Bub."

"Oh good, you're still here." Creed appeared and gave me a huge hug. "Wow, Verity. It's like you're a model or something. Congratulations."

I laughed as I tried not to get makeup on his suit. He'd been there for me a lot as I navigated being an alpha, being part of a pack, and my two omegas.

"Verity, are you ready?" the wedding coordinator asked from the other side of the door.

I gave myself one last look. "I am."

Mercy got the train of my dress as I took Dad's arm. We walked down the hall of the castle.

"Um, Ver." Freddie stood there, in a light green suit.

"I don't want to talk to you. It's bad enough you're here." Somehow he'd convinced a mutual friend to bring him as their plus-one.

Dad frowned. "You should probably take a seat."

"Go away, Fuckboy." Mercy glared, still holding my train. "You were Derva's character witness. I don't think you fully understand how awful her having Verity's research destroyed was."

No, he didn't. Even the judge didn't. Derva had only gotten community service and had to pay the university for damages. Not that I expected more. Though Derva's sentencing had kept the student who did her dirty work from being expelled, though she, too, faced community service.

"Someone has to help with Winnie's kids. Mrs. Coach can't do it all herself when the baby's born," Freddie shrugged.

It made sense, but I still felt like Derva got off easy considering I still was making up for what she destroyed, research-wise.

Winnie was in jail for shooting me. Her jail time wasn't as long as Chet's, but her jail wasn't as nice as his. Yeah, Chet and Bertie were at the country club of prisons for their financial crimes, while his pregnant wife was at a pretty tough one.

"Why are you here, Freddie? You have a new team, a new girlfriend, and a new sponsor." I leaned on my crutch. He always did land jelly-side up.

"I wanted to say I'm sorry." Freddie shrugged.

"That's how you got her onto the patio in the first place. You know, before she got *shot.*" Jonas glared at him then looked at me. "We can have him thrown out."

"My pleasure." Dare cracked his knuckles.

"We should call security," Dad told them.

Freddie shook his head. "I'm not here to cause trouble. All I wanted to say was that I'm sorry for being a dick, and everything with Derva and Winnie and their dad. I'm sorry I harassed you. I'm sorry I let Derva and Chet drag me into things."

Derva and Freddie were no longer together.

"Um, thank you?" It still seemed weird.

Jonas gave him a hard look. "You could say that literally any other time than at her wedding."

"You look beautiful. I'll go sit now." Freddie went down the hall but in a different direction than the gardens.

"Fucker." Mercy made a face.

"Pretty sure he's here to network. He was really working the room last night," Creed told me as we headed out to the lush gardens.

"Yeah, he tried to corner Stu earlier," Jonas replied. "He has a new team and a new agent, what else could he want?"

"Everything. Freddie always wants more," I shrugged. "As long as he doesn't cause trouble or makes people uncomfortable he can stay."

We left the castle and entered the lush gardens. Roses and omega lilies decorated the gazebo. Our guests sat in white chairs, and there were more lilies and roses everywhere, besides all the flowers in the garden. I could see the giant tent where the reception would be later.

The late June air was warm, but the late afternoon breeze kept it from being stifling. Classical music played softly.

Dad escorted me to the gazebo and gave me a kiss on the cheek. "Congratulations."

He, Creed, and Dare went to take their seats. Dad sat next to Mumsy, who wore a lilac dress and a matching hat. Harry wrangled the littles. Mama, Baba, Chance, and Hale were there with them. Grace and her pack sat right behind them. Riley waved at Mercy.

Jonas and Mercy stood behind me in the gazebo. The crowd was a sea of pastels with many epic wedding hats. Saphira waved at me, and so did Dr. Winters, whose bow tie and suit were green. So many people had come out to Greece, which I hadn't been expecting. Though we had helped a number of people make it out, like Grif's family.

Grif's older sister, Sissy, took her place under the gazebo, wearing a floral dress. He'd wanted her to officiate. Her dark red hair was up. She was as pale as Grif but had many more freckles. One of her alphas held her little girl on his lap.

AJ, wearing a tux that matched Jonas' and an omega lily boutonniere, took his place on the opposite side of the gazebo, but not before kissing me.

"You look breathtaking," he whispered.

The wedding coordinator came up to us with her tablet and headset. "Everyone's in place. Are you ready?"

My belly fluttered as I looked down at the empty aisle. Here I was. At my wedding. In a moment, Grif would walk down the aisle.

Love and reassurance flowed through the pack bond.

I glanced at Jonas and AJ, then nodded. "I'm ready."

"Perfect." The wedding coordinator nodded and left the gazebo.

A moment later, the string quartet played a song that Grif had selected. The littles walked down the aisle, throwing white rose petals from baskets. Hope wore a little gold dress, Tru and Pax had on little gold suits. Well, Pax spun around in circles, then dumped the rest of his basket on Hale. When they got to the gazebo, they waved at me. Harry motioned for them to join him. Pax took his seat. Tru ran over to Grace. Hope climbed on Dad's lap.

I exhaled sharply as Grif, in his white tux, with his gold vest and tie, took his place, holding onto Dean's arm. The music changed to Grif's favorite classical song and everyone stood.

"Fuck, that's sexy," I muttered. My pussy gushed at the sight. His red beard, which had gotten bushy during playoffs, was now neatly trimmed, as was his hair.

"That's my brother there," Sissy laughed. "But yeah, he and Dean clean up well."

Oh, I couldn't wait to take that tux off him.

Did I have to wait until after the reception? Maybe we could sneak away for a moment after taking photos.

Grif's eyes fell on me. Love and lust flowed through the bond from both him and Dean.

Sheer giddiness coated me as Dean walked Grif down the aisle. When they got to the gazebo, Dean gave him a kiss, then took his place next to AJ.

"Hi," Grif mouthed as he gazed into my eyes.

"Hi," I mouthed back, my shoulders wiggling in happiness.

The music stopped. His sister gestured for everyone to sit down.

"Welcome, family and friends, we are gathered here today, in this beautiful garden on this gorgeous island because my little brother found a woman of extraordinary taste," Sissy joked.

She gave a short officiant speech, but I didn't hear much of it. All I could see was Grif. My mate. My love.

Okay, I snuck looks at my other guys. The lust I kept getting from Dean didn't help.

Finally, it was time for the vows.

Everyone chuckled as a little doll-sized pink sports car that looked a lot like mine, only it was a convertible, came down the aisle, stopping next to the gazebo. Dare grinned at me, a remote control in his hand.

Mercy walked over to the car and took out two boxes. "Why thank you, Lucky."

The Maimers and Knights present started laughing. Pax picked up the car and ran back to his seat.

"Over here, Lucky. That's a good cat," Carlos called.

My sister returned to her spot, giving AJ one of the boxes.

I took Grif's hands and gazed into his green eyes.

"I, Verity Thorne, take you as my omega. To care for and cherish, to love and hold, in good times and bad, for as long as we live. When we met on the airplane, I was drawn to you. The moment you climbed into a tub of ice in *October* because you didn't want me to panic, I knew you were mine."

Mercy came forward and gave me the ring I had for him, a gold band with our names and the date inscribed in it.

I sent him all my love through the bond as I put the ring on his finger on the hand opposite his tattooed ring. It was a pretty common practice to wear your rings on whatever fingers were available if you had multiple mates. AJ had given him a pinky ring he wore on his left hand, his pack ring on his right pinky.

"I, Griffin McGraff, take you as my alpha. To care for and cherish, to love and hold, in good times and bad, for as long as we live. When I first saw you on the airplane, all I wanted to do was hold you and make it all better. I promise to do that always." He squeezed my hands.

Dean offered a ring, and Grif slid the pretty band onto my finger, which had been made to fit perfectly with the emerald one he and Dean had given me. My pack ring was on my right pinky.

Sissy turned to Jonas. "As head alpha, do you confirm this union?"

"Yes, as head alpha, I confirm this union and welcome Verity to the pack," Jonas said.

She looked at Dean and AJ. "Do you confirm this union and welcome Verity to the pack?"

"Oh, you bet I do." Dean waggled his eyebrows, and everyone laughed, including his parents, who were sitting with Grif's family.

"Yes, I do," AJ agreed.

"Yeah, I allow these dudes in my life. They're okay." Mercy smirked.

Sissy chuckled, then looked at the both of us. "I now pronounce this union confirmed. Alpha, you may now kiss your omega."

I leaned in and kissed him long and sweet. "You're mine."

Grif sent me a smoldering look that set me on fire. "I am."

Here was to our happily ever after.

THE END

Glossary of Select Terms

Designations

Alpha: Larger, faster, and with better senses, they make up about a quarter of the population. Their barks and pheromones can influence people. Male alphas have knots, female alphas have locks. Their scent has a distinctive note that marks them as alpha. Female alphas can carry children.

Beta: They make up over half of the population and are your average ordinary people. Like the other designations, they can have kids, join or form packs, and an alpha can mate with them.

Delta: They have a lot of alpha characteristics–especially in regard to size, speed, and senses. They tend to make excellent soldiers and security, especially because they are bark-proof. They're rarer than the 'big three' designations (alpha/beta/omega.)

Gamma: Essentially, Gammas are 'failed' omegas. While sometimes a genetic switch is thrown, halting development, most of the time it is environmental. Something is so dangerous in their environment that the body declares it unsafe to become an omega and halts a genetic process. Gammas can have many omega traits, but it varies from person to person. Gammas rarely respond to barks, pheromones, or danger the way omegas do. Common causes of gammas are war, famine, extreme poverty, and asshole parents, and are very rare.

Kappa: The life of the party, they're usually adrenaline junkies with poor decision-making skills. They're an extremely rare designation.

Iota: A rare designation, Iotas don't have scents, they also can't smell other scents and don't respond to barks or pheromones. This can be dangerous because they can't catch the scent-cues other designations can. Because they can't be barked or influenced, some iotas think they're better than other designations.

Omega: Omegas are usually smaller than the other designations and tend to be nurturers and caregivers. They're the most physically compatible with alphas, so they're often sought after as mates, even though they make up less than ten percent of the population. They can and do partner with other designations. Omegas have the same rights as everyone else. Omega males are *very* good at making kids. Omegas have an extra element to their scent that marks them as such. They also produce slick and perfume when aroused.

Sports

Boner: When one hockey player scores three goals in a single game. Fans toss bones onto the ice in celebration.

Bullet: The skate smash player who scores points for their team by making laps around the ice. One bullet is in play in each succession.

Crusher: The skate smash player who tries to stop the other team's bullet from scoring points while protecting their own. Three crushers are in play in each succession.

Discovery League: Skate smash's team-sponsored junior league where teams choose high school and university players who show potential and give them special training and opportunities to prepare them for the draft.

EBUG: Emergency Backup Goalie. Amateur goalies who play during a hockey game if both of a team's goalies can no longer play. The home team is responsible for providing an EBUG who can then step in for either team. A lot of EBUGs are goalies for their collegiate teams and are part of goalie development programs offered by many PHL teams.

Fútbol: Soccer/football. A sport popular worldwide, especially among betas.

IATS: The International Association of Team Sports is the world-wide governing body overseeing team sports such as fútbol, ice hockey, and rugby.

ICIS: International Coalition of Ice Sports is the worldwide governing body for sports such as figure skating, speed skating, skate smash, and curling.

MASO: Mates and Significant Others. A term that encompasses the mates, packmates, spouses, girlfriend, boyfriends, partners, and significant others of professional athletes in team sports.

PHL: The Professional Hockey League. It governs four conferences and eight divisions, totaling thirty-two ice hockey teams spanning four countries.

PSSL: The Professional Skate Smash League. It governs four conferences and eight divisions, totaling thirty-two skate smash teams spanning four countries.

Skate Smash: A contact ice sport where five players from each team skate around the ice trying to gain points. Ten two-minute successions comprised each period, with a thirty-second rest between each succession. They also have dance battles where they perform synchronized routines as a team.

Swing: A skate smash player who plays crusher but can be tagged by their team's bullet to act as such. One swing is in play in each succession.

Other Terms

Alpha-Blockers: A type of medication that dulls alpha senses and instincts. It's most commonly prescribed to violent alphas, young alphas who aren't in full control, and criminals. There's a huge stigma on them, so many who should take them don't.

Defender League: A popular superhero franchise with movies and comics.

Game Buddy: A personal video game device that can also be hooked up to your TV.

Go-goKart: A popular car racing video game, often played on a Game Buddy.

Heat Suppressants: A type of medication omegas take so that they don't go into heat. Typically, female omegas have three or four heats a year, often lasting up to a week. Male omegas have two to three heats a year, usually lasting a few days. Heat suppressants are completely legal, though prolonged use can have side effects.

Location Finder: A location sharing app.

Musify: A social music streaming app where users can both listen to music, and create and share their own playlists.

Scent-Blockers: A type of medication omegas take to blend in/function in society. These range from light scent-blockers that simply dull an omega's distinctive scent to heavy duty ones that lock down both omega scent and instincts, enabling them to hide as a beta. All are completely legal but can be hard for hidden omegas to get. Prolonged use, especially of the heavy-duty blockers, can lose their effectiveness and/or cause health issues.

Scent-Match: Soulmate. That perfect match between two people–usually an alpha and omega. They usually know it by smell. Scent-matches are rare and plenty of people have happy and long relationships without being scent-matches. Sometimes scent-matches dream of each other, but that's mostly in books and movies.

Spiral: Dangerous drop in omega hormones which can result in unconsciousness, irrational behavior, and/or hospitalization. Often a trauma response.

Ultra-bullet: Super fast train that can turn an hours-long drive into moments.

The Thorne Family

The Parents

Adriana Thorne (Alpha, *Mom)*—Former Chemistry Professor; Formerly mated to Nate, mother of Hale and Mercy, presently incarcerated.

Pippa Thorne (Alpha, *Mumsy*)—Research Chemist; Mated to Nate, mother of Creed, lives in London.

Zain Thorne (Alpha, *Baba*)—Research Chemist; Married to Esme, father of Verity, Dare, and Chance, lives in Bayside.

Esme Thorne (Beta, *Mama*)—Translator; Married to Zain, mother of Verity, Dare, and Chance, lives in Bayside.

Harry Thorne (Beta, *Harry/Daddy*)—Restaurateur; Married to Nate, father of Pax, Tru, and Hope, lives in London.

Nate Thorne (Omega, *Dad*)—Organic Chemistry Professor; Mated to Pippa, married to Harry, formerly mated to Adriana, father of Grace, Creed, Hale, Mercy, Pax, Tru, and Hope, lives in London.

The Kids

Grace Thanukos (Gamma)—Theoretical Mathematician at Compass BioTek; Mated to the Thanukos Pack, lives in Rockland.

Creed (Alpha)—Engineer at Compass BioTek, live in Rockland.

Verity (Alpha)—PhD student in plant genetics at New York Institute of Technology (NYIT), lives in New York City with Mercy.

Hale (Alpha)—Undergraduate student in organic chemistry at Briar University, lives in Research Circle.

Dare (Alpha)—Undergraduate student in cello performance at Boston Institute of Technology (BosTec), lives in Boston.

Mercy (Alpha)—Skate smash crusher for the Manhattan Maimers, lives in New York City with Verity.

Chance (Beta)—Middle schooler, lives in Bayside.

Pax (designation still unknown)—Elementary schooler, lives in London.

Tru (designation still unknown)—Elementary schooler, lives in London.

Hope (designation still unknown)—Preschooler, lives in London.

The New York Knights

Forwards

Winston Royce (co-captain) #10

Nia Watkins #23

Pauley Diaz #14

Griffin 'Grif Graf' McGraff #26

Clark 'Wonder Boy' Edwards #55 (rookie)

Carlos Rodriguez #17

LeeAnn Tinsley #15

Vaino Virtanen #12

Anders Larsson #37 (rookie)

Jasper Michaels #73

Sarah Shaw #9

Ela Patel #36

Defense

Elias Royce (co-captain) #2

Jonas Seong #42

Dimitri Belikov #7

Roberto 'Nakey' Diaz #82

Miko Virtanen #13

Mathieu Decker #88

Kimo Nakamura #3

Misha Petrov #6 (rookie)

Goalies

Dean 'Double-D' Donovan #1

Jean-Paul 'JP' Trembley #31

EBUGs

Gwen 'Ladybug' Di Rossi

Marcos Juarez

Tyler Yamato

Management & Coaching Staff

Steve Atkins, Head Coach

Cal Daughtry, Owner

Ben Dodd, Assistant Coach

Svetlana Kirov, Goalie Coach

Beauregard 'Bunty' Longfellow, General Manager

Lars Janssen, Assistant Coach

Oscar Simons, Assistant General Manager

The Manhattan Maimers

Crushers

Jo-Jo Banks—Terror Byte
Rusty Bartlet (captain)—Rusty Nails
Aisha Chapman—Cham-pain
Grayson Cooper—Sabotage
Onyx Harper—Miss Ann Thrope
Mallory Hill—Maullory
Scarlet Lane—Scream Puff
Greer Monroe—Slamazon
Liv Riviera (co-captain)—Cap'n Crush
Martina Riviera—Jalapeno Business
Jack Rogers—T-Wrex
Mercy Thorne—Have No Mercy

Carmen Torres—Carmen Monoxide

Swings

Cleo Archer—Sugar & Spikes

Lindsay Chapman—Lindsanity

Kaiko Hayashi—KaikoLicious

Ash Van Der Waals—Grievous Bodily Charm

Bullets

Lee Chen—Black & Blueberry Pie

Iris Harper—Miss Conduct

Nadia Pugh—Muffin Chop

Roshi Singh—Chicken Dinner

Management & Coaching Staff

Fabiola Marchetti—General Manager

Lisa Meriton—Head Coach

Rhonda Wojak—Assistant Coach

Bryce Hawthorne—Skating Coach

About the Author

A hopeless romantic, Jane Handler grew up reading romance and often got them taken away by her teachers for reading during class. Now she writes why choose, omegaverse, and hockey romance. Keep up with Jane on Instagram at @janehandlerauthor, Tiktok at @janehandlerbooks and Facebook at https://www.facebook.c om/janehandlerauthor

Loving Ladybug

Part One

They call me *Ladybug.*

I'm the only female EBUG for the New York Knights. I'm starting goalie for my university team. I'm also *just* a beta. At least according to my knothead ex. Ugh.

But I'll show him. I'm going to focus and find what used to make me special as a goalie so I can get signed after graduation. Even if putting myself out there is a risk.

At least I have friends who will help me. Like Tenzin, the Knight's new alpha defender, who like me is getting over a broken heart. And Clark, the alpha forward I befriended last season who is a skating ray of sunshine.

Maybe, just maybe, I'd like to be more than friends with Tenzin and Clark. There's something there, something that could lead to a happily ever after–even if with my past I probably don't deserve one.

My feelings for them grow by the day, but will they still care for me once they know what I've done?

Loving Ladybug, Part One, is a why choose omegaverse friends to lovers hockey romance and is the first book in a *duet.* It's ultimately m/m/f. Part one of this duet ends on a cliffhanger with an HEA in part two. This duet is part of the HockeyVerse but you don't need to have read the Finding the Forward to enjoy it.

Printed in Great Britain
by Amazon